THE FORBIDDEN TEARS SERIES

THE
PENDANT & THE
PROPHECY

SAM WITHROW &
AMELIA PINKIS

FRESH INK
PRESS
LLC

FRESH INK PRESS
Cape Coral, Florida

Hardback ISBN: 979-8-9908112-5-6
Paperback ISBN: 979-8-9908112-3-2
eBook ISBN: 979-8-9908112-4-9

Revised Edition, Fresh Ink Press, August 6, 2024
http://www.ForbiddenTears.net

Cover Art: David Leahey
Editors: Natalie West and Fatima Alaeddine
A special thank you to the Guinea Heritage Association.
guineaheritage@gmail.com

CONTENTS

ACKNOWLEDGMENTS

First and foremost, I would like to extend my deepest gratitude to the fans for eagerly yet patiently awaiting the release of Book Two in this series. Your support is the driving force behind our efforts, and I am profoundly grateful. You make my work both meaningful and enjoyable.

At the outset of this adventure, I had no idea what an immense undertaking lay ahead. However, with my co-author, also my soul sister, we persevered and completed this challenging yet exhilarating book.

No author undertakes such a journey alone. I am immensely grateful to the many generous individuals who have accompanied me on this adventure, including my daughter Loryn, my husband Jim, and numerous family and friends — you know who you are. Your unwavering love and support have kept me grounded and taught me the true meaning of generosity and selflessness.

I also owe an apology to my critters — bees, chickens, and doves — for my prolonged absence during the extensive writing and editing process. Extra goodies are on the way. Please forgive me.

Always remember to keep your light within your heart. If you do, darkness will never invade your soul.

Sam

This book has been a challenge, a journey, and a joy.

All my thanks forever to our fans — sharing this with you is a delight.

Sam, you are a visionary, and it's the privilege of my creative life to write with you. Thank you for participating in this ongoing mental breakdown with me and putting up with the innumerable interruptions from the cats and the polar bear.

For Aria, our number one fan. You're my whole heart.
For Sharona, a beacon of light, with all my love, always. Happy very belated birthday.
For Natalie, my soul-twin, without whom nothing is possible. You'll always be my light.
For Maysa, grace and strength incarnate, with all my gratitude.
For Alan, who has cheered this on from the beginning.
Mom, I love you. Thank you for everything.
Dave, I love you, too.
Dad, I love you.

And for my husband and kids — Alex, Adeline, Arianne, Auden, and Anakin — you're my reason for everything. Thank you forever for supporting me. I love you to the moon and back.

Amelia

The
Pendant & the
Prophecy

PROLOGUE

"They've promised that dreams can come true,
but forgot to mention that nightmares are dreams, too."
Oscar Wilde

The screaming was growing tiresome.

Blistering Judean sun glinted off the speartips of the Roman centurions. Three wooden crosses atop the highest hill cast long shadows across the eastern valley. Soldiers picked at scabs and fidgeted in their armor. Wails of women filled the air. The center crucifix's silhouette reached toward the mouth of the cave like an outstretched finger.

Inside the cave, a creature, in appearance like a man, yet not a man, extended his hand forward to touch the shadow cast by the cross. He was too beautiful to be human; it was as if starlight had been braided into the very core of his being. He looked ancient yet still young, frozen for eons in the perfect blush of youth. His hair fell long and white to his waist and shimmered even in the dark, as did the rest of his perfect form. His ice-blue eyes stared at the cross' silhouette with a kind of hunger. He stretched his fingers toward it, to the line of daylight dividing the cave from the sun.

Another piercing cry tore through the air. Behind him, a woman with black-tipped silver horns and a mutilated face broke

XII SAM WITHROW & AMELIA PINKIS

into a series of pathetic sobs and whimpers. She was attended by three gorgeous, waif-like creatures. Two of them held her down while the third dabbed a foul-smelling potion on her wounds. Her face sizzled with each touch.

The man sighed in irritation, retracting his hand and turning back to the shadows.

"Asmodeus, can't you do something about that?"

The three lovely creatures nodded in eerie unison. One passed its hand over the woman's mouth, which sealed shut with skin. Her eyes still screamed and streamed with tears, but the cave was blissfully silent.

Another man stormed up to the cave's entrance, this one black-haired wearing full armor and a scowl that seemed permanently etched into his imperious features. "Why must we always meet here?" he growled, glowering at the white-haired man. "Every angel in the host must be crawling all over this moment."

"That's why this is the last place they'd ever think to look," he replied.

The black-haired man pulled a gruesome-looking knife from his belt and twirled it at dizzying speed. A vein stood out in his forehead, and he clenched his jaw. "I still don't like it. What if Michael—?"

"Shh, listen." The white-haired being held up his hand. The two turned their faces across the ravine to the crosses on Golgotha, listening to the distant conversation with perfect clarity, hanging onto every agonized word.

The man mounted to the crucifix on the right gasped through blood-filled lungs, "Yeshua, remember me when you come into your kingdom."

There was silence for a moment. The white-haired man's eyes

shone, and he mouthed in perfect sync with the Son of God when He replied,

"Amen, I say to you, today you will be with me in Paradise."

He leaned back, shaking his head. "Today. He'll let him in today."

The black-haired man scowled. "Why do you do this to yourself? You must've watched it ten thousand times."

The white-haired man turned and walked deeper into the cave. "You know why, Azazel," he answered mildly. "To remind myself of the injustice we fight to rectify. To remind myself, there is no other way to reclaim that which is rightfully ours."

He walked over to the horned woman, still silently screaming in pain, and cupped her remaining cheek with his hand. "He forgives a condemned thief without a thought. Meanwhile, see what becomes of us. His first children. Those with whom He shared all things."

He softly caressed the woman's disfigured face before turning to the rest of the cavern. "Mammon's failure is merely a setback. We have contingencies in place for such events. Belphegor's device will succeed. It is only a matter of time."

A figure in dark jeans, sunglasses, and a hoodie pulled down over his face flashed a thumbs-up and continued napping, leaning against an enormous, scale-covered wall that shifted ominously, as though it were breathing.

"What about the girl?" Azazel glared accusingly. "She burned our sister to a cinder. Surely, you don't consider her to be merely a setback."

"The girl was unforeseen, to be sure. But she's nothing but a mortal, subject to the same weaknesses and failings as all the rest."

"If she has the Tears——"

"If what she has is indeed the Tears, so much the better. We will add their power to our cause. Our asset will be with her soon, watching her closely. When the moment presents itself, she will offer them to us freely. She will beg us to take them."

Outside, the sun went black, and a tremor shook the earth. The cries of frightened mortals rang out as they scuttled around the hillside like so many ants.

The beautiful white-haired man paused thoughtfully.

"Of course, there's never any harm in hurrying things along. That which we cannot acquire, we could always… consume." He looked toward a dark corner of the cave. "Baal?"

The air filled with a terrifying noise. It started softly and quickly crescendoed into a deafening buzz as a swarm of hellish metallic creatures rose like a dark cloud and formed a face. It hovered a moment, then twisted itself into a monstrous smile.

The white-haired man smiled in return.

"Are you hungry?"

CHAPTER ONE

Angels and Aftermath

"Flirting with disaster, are we?" The towering stranger's golden eyes flashed at her angel in furious condemnation.

Brie stood amidst the chaos, heart pounding as reality crashed over her, shattering her fragile bubble of hope — severing the lifeline to normalcy she'd clung to with both hands. Her new beginning, her new job, everything had been dashed against the jagged rocks of supernatural chaos once again. She'd sworn to start fresh, to leave the trauma of her mother's accident behind; she'd vowed to stop running and start building, but fate seemed determined to drag her back into the abyss.

Blood dripped from the ceiling. Smoke curled from a demon-shaped crater in the hospital parking garage. Her friends lay scattered on the ground like broken toys.

A few steps away, surrounded by rubble, stood her personal angel.

The taste of their first kiss still lingered on her lips.

But the most astonishing sight of all was the immense, nude figure standing before her, wearing nothing but an aura of disapproval and a sarcastic scowl, radiating judgment and damning them straight to Hell.

"If Hell has a waiting room, I'd say you've practically signed the guestbook." His eyes, rings of liquid gold, flashed at her angel in Heavenly disapproval.

She clapped a hand over her face, peeking through parted fingers while trying to avoid his conspicuous anatomy. "This must be a hallucination," she muttered, trying to make sense of the surreal scene. The man glared in her direction, and her legs turned to jelly. "It has to be."

She harrowed another look around, then took a deep breath.

Brianna Weldon, you are a nurse. Run your checks.

Quickly, she patted herself down.

Limbs are intact and attached. No nausea. I can turn my head. Vision is clear.

I'm awake, alert, alive.

And there's a naked giant condemning me to Hell.

Perfect.

"Cameron," she said quietly. "Please tell me that you see this, too?"

Her angel, usually the voice of reason, opened his mouth several times in an attempt to answer but succeeded only in nodding and turning a more worrying shade of green.

So, this isn't a hallucination. Which means it's real.

… Just perfect.

She turned to the interloper. "Hi," she said, louder than she intended and with more bravery than she felt. "Are you all right? Can we help you?"

He raised an eyebrow as though the question was utterly absurd.

Maybe he isn't another supernatural being come to turn my world upside down.

Maybe I'll get lucky — perhaps he's just an escaped psychiatric patient from upstairs.

"I think you're the one in need of assistance, Brianna Weldon," he replied. His gaze flitted briefly over her face before spearing into Cameron. "I assume this is why you haven't come to Elysium?"

Elysium.

The word echoed in the silence like a stone dropped to the bottom of a dry well.

She expected Cameron to answer. The stranger seemed to expect it as well. They turned to him from opposite sides, but he merely stood there, rigid in that suffocating quiet, trapped between their stares, looking as if some vital part of him had been turned to stone.

A sharp taste of panic rose in her throat. "I don't understand," she stammered, turning back to the stranger but finding herself almost unable to look. "How do you know my name? Who are you?"

And where the heck are your clothes?

He smiled like she'd said something funny. "We have already met."

She looked at him in bewilderment. In the last few days, she'd met hordes of faceless wraiths, Elysians from the realm between Heaven and Hell, guardian angels, and the incarnation of Greed itself in human form.

But a stark-naked man who looked like he'd played tight-end in the Superbowl?

She paused a moment before responding. "I think I would have remembered."

If anything, her bristling sarcasm only seemed to amuse him. Instead of answering her directly, he turned again to Cameron. "Go on, old friend. Tell her."

Cameron cringed like he was in physical pain. "Brie, this... is Ephriam."

Her mouth fell open, and she turned in astonishment, trying to reconcile this impossible stranger with the cheerful, bobbing light she'd known him as before.

As if to help, he vanished with a *pop*, and a golden orb appeared in his place. It floated in front of her — smirking, she'd bet her life.

She reached out a finger as if to touch it, then let her arm drop back to her side.

Like I said. Perfect.

◆   ◆   ◆

There is a particular pitch and tone to a woman's voice that can only be reached when she has been pushed well beyond her breaking point. It is known and feared the world over by generations of children who have painted their living room walls with vibrant, primary-colored fingerpaint and husbands who have forgotten their anniversary for the third year in a row.

Brianna Weldon had reached this point.

"I can't believe you twinkled around my living room like a pixie for days — *days*, Ephriam, when we all could have been having perfectly pleasant conversations, face to face, like *normal people*. Have I not been thrown into the deep end of all this supernatural ridiculosity enough to satisfy you? Did you find watching me have completely one-sided conversations with a glowing baseball entertaining? What in the name of Zeus possessed you?"

"Spite," he replied flatly.

"I'll show you some spite!" She whirled on him in exasperation, forgetting for a moment that he was utterly nude. She averted her gaze and glared at the ceiling with a frustrated growl. "What are you even *doing* here? *And would you please put some damn clothes on?*"

Ephriam shot her a scathing look. "It's quite prejudiced to say that human form is the normal one. I'll have you know, Cameron sent word you would be coming to Elysium. You didn't come." He paused with a hint of judgment. "I went to your home to see if you were all right. When I didn't find you, I came here." He shrugged a little like the rest was ancient history. "And, no, I will not put on clothes just to soothe your human embarrassment. You're lucky I'm wearing *skin*."

The conversation came to a full stop.

That's going to fester.

With a hint of hysteria, she turned to Cameron. "A little help here, Cam?"

Her angel was still pale as a sculpture, but he gave her a swift nod before turning to Ephriam. "I, too, would prefer it if you would put on some clothes—"

The Elysian folded his arms without a hint of expression. A moment passed before there was a scarcely audible *pop*, and a gauzy, hot-pink sarong settled onto his hips.

Brie clapped a hand over her mouth.

Do I get extra years in purgatory for laughing at an angel?

"Are either of you going to tell me what happened here?" Ephriam demanded, gesturing impatiently around the scene. "This place looks more like a warzone than a hospital, and I am not giving a false report for your sake, *Cam*." His eyes flashed across the bloody pavement, hot as a new-forged blade. "We've known each other a long time, but this is too big to be ignored. There's a time shroud around a *hospital*. The mortals will notice. You're violating our prime directive everywhere I look." He began to pace, eyes narrowing as they leapt from one thing to another: burnt walls, melted pavement, and humans propped against each other. "How did you even manage it? You've never been able to freeze time before."

Cameron drew in a slow breath, deciding how to phrase it. "I am not the one who tampered with time," he began.

"Then who did?" Ephriam demanded.

"Mammon," Cameron answered quietly.

Ephriam stopped pacing and turned to face him. His pupils dilated with fear, but his voice remained steady. "She was here?" he asked. "You are sure of it?" Cameron nodded, and Ephriam exhaled slowly, looking once more around the demolished parking garage. His attention lingered on the hoofprints. "And you're sure she's gone?"

Cameron glanced at Brie. "I'm quite sure."

It was quiet for a few moments as each of them digested this. Cameron flashed panicked glances between them like he wasn't sure he wanted either one to understand.

"How in the nine circles of Hell did you manage that?" Ephriam finally asked, his perfect brow furrowed in frustration. It was a strange look for an angel, but in the case of this *particular* angel, Brie got the feeling he wore it more often than most. "I mean no disrespect to your talent, kid, but you mean to tell me—"

"It wasn't me," Cameron said. Twice, his eyes traveled between his oldest friend and the woman he'd just kissed before he could bring himself to say the next part out loud. "It was Brie."

The words seemed to resound in the stillness, echoing off the blood-splattered walls before fading into silence. It was enough to stop the conversation short, bringing the men to almost solemn attention.

"The girl," Ephriam repeated in a low murmur, unable to hide his surprise.

"Yes, *Brie*," Cameron corrected, a bit sharper than he meant. "First, she cut off her head, and then?" He gestured around the scene. "She did everything. I spent the whole time—"

"Getting your ass handed to you?" Ephriam's expression betrayed a flicker of amusement, though the sight of his friend's battered face made it impossible to fully hide his concern. "Yeah, it looks like it."

"*He* understands idioms?" Unable to process bizarre phrases like *first she cut off her head*, Brie had decided to fixate on style, rather than substance. Similarly, instead of questioning the exact nature of the black, tar-like substance bubbling from the pavement, she'd decided to be personally offended by its smell. She caught their joint look, throwing up her arms in exasperation. She looked at Cameron. "Why does *he* understand them and you don't? You're at least part human — he's some celestial ball of fire and bad manners!"

This was just one of *many* moments that would haunt her in the days to come.

"Your *Cameron* is completely human," Ephriam replied stiffly, vowing to remember the moment as well. "But he doesn't understand because he was raised in a palace — in an ivory tower of imported tutors and courtly etiquette. Besides which, he's still very young."

She stared in bracing silence, trying not to dwell on the way he'd said, *Your Cameron*. "He's thousands of years old. What am I then?"

"A fetus."

For a moment, she was too infuriated to speak before something registered. "Hold on, what do you mean *I* did everything?

That *I'm* somehow responsible for all this chaos?" She looked between them, searching for answers, finding none. Curls of acrid smoke rose into the air behind her as she made a flailing gesture, the taste of bitter adrenaline flooding her mouth. "I blacked out!" she cried. "I assumed all of this was you! You and... and..."

There was a lurch in her stomach, and she found herself unable to say it. With a rising sense of dread, her eyes lifted slowly to a scorch mark on the wall.

Oh God...

Cameron took a compulsive step toward her before his attention jerked back to Ephriam as if tethered by a string. Unable to fix one problem, he turned to the easier of the two — the stern-faced angel, rubbing his temples with Heaven's fire blazing in his eyes.

"Listen," he said diplomatically, lifting his hands in a peaceful gesture, "what happened with Mammon — it seems Brie doesn't remember, and frankly, I don't know what to make of it myself, but we have a dead man upstairs missing a heart, a hospital caught in a time freeze, a resurrected doctor passed out on the ground over there, and—"

"I thought the resurrection only lasted a few seconds," Ephriam interrupted sharply.

"Different resurrection." Cameron nodded at Rashida, who lay on the ground nearby, her chest rising and falling in steady, reassuring breaths. "This one feels permanent. We need to—"

"What do you mean I did everything?" Brie repeated, drawing their attention back to her. A different version of her might have cowered, but she was well beyond such things. "Can we circle back for a sec? What do you mean? Everything? *All* of this?"

Her attention darted around the decimated hospital, unable to settle on any particular thing. A portion of the ceiling had begun to crumble, and two cars had slid halfway into the crater.

It couldn't have been me. I couldn't have done this.

Her throat tightened in panic as she began to tremble.

Cameron rushed to her side, determined not to notice the way Ephriam's golden eyes followed his every move. With gentle hands, he steadied her shoulders and pulled her into a crushing embrace, pressing his lips to the top of her head.

She tensed in surprise, then leaned against him.

"This is going to be all right," he whispered into her tangled curls like his Elysian friend wasn't still able to hear them. A nearby car emitted a groan as its roof collapsed in a flurry of sparks, and his arms tightened, cradling her against his chest. "I promise, we're going to find a way to fix this."

She shivered, nodding into his shirt.

I don't see how.

"*You're* not going to do anything." Ephriam's voice cracked across the pavement like a whip. He was standing beside them a moment later, taking no more notice of his blinding speed than of the magma pooled near their feet. "Your father has been indulgent with you, but this has gone far enough. Too far, *Cameron*," he added sharply. "I should have done this days ago."

Without further explanation, he closed those staggering eyes and started chanting under his breath, the words picking up speed and rhythm. Within seconds, the air itself seemed to come alive, swirling their hair and tingling their skin like ozone before a lightning strike.

"Wait," Cameron shouted, bracing himself in alarm, "we need to—"

"There will be no more waiting," Ephriam interrupted, his voice taking on an otherworldly resonance. He lifted both hands as the ground beneath them started to shift. "There will be no more delays."

The lights flickered, and Cameron threw out a hand between them as if he were warding off something Brie couldn't see. "Ephriam, I beg you not to do this."

"Do what?" she asked, clutching onto his sleeve. "What's he going to do?"

Her angel ignored her, eyes staring fixed at Ephriam.

"Just give her a moment," he pleaded. His other arm wrapped tightly around her, keeping her steady despite the seismic quake. "Give her a moment to catch her breath."

Her pulse quickened with a thrill of dread.

"Catch my breath for what?" she echoed in a daze. "What are you talking about?"

Cameron glanced down at her, desperate with apology.

"He wants to send us to Elysium now," he answered.

It took a second to click.

Then—

"No!" she cried, wrenching herself away from him. The air had started to shimmer; she could barely see the bodies of her friends through the charge. "I came here to protect these people. Now you want me to leave them on the ground?!"

"Your friends will be perfectly safe," Ephriam murmured dismissively as if the question had already half-escaped his attention. Those swirling forces had started to take shape and sharpen, centering on the glinting cuffs around his outstretched wrists. "I will maintain Mammon's time shroud over the hospital."

Perfectly safe?!

Under a shroud?!

A hundred jumbled images flashed through her mind in an instant: impacts and screaming, the roar of an enraged demon, the look of abject fear on her friends' faces. She looked at Sherry, Mike, and Rashida, still lying unconscious on the ground.

I'll be damned if I leave them here alone.

Those celestial forces were gathering, threatening to lift her right off the ground. Still, something inside her was gathering as well, building and coalescing, lighting the very blood in her veins as she stepped directly in front of the angel.

"I said *NO!*"

A lash of lightning-white energy burst from her pendant, fast as a gunshot. There was a violent crack beneath her, and the asphalt split right down the middle — like a giant hammer had struck it from the sky. She was standing on one side of the chasm. Ephriam was on the other. He stared at his toes, perilously close to the violent suture, with a look of genuine astonishment before his attention flashed to the pendant. There was a quickening somewhere deep inside his gaze, a kind of uncomprehending fear. Whatever divine powers he'd been summoning vanished as quickly as they'd come, leaving everyone suspended in a dangerous sort of quiet.

Holy Mother of… Brianna Weldon, what the hell did you do?

She swallowed in fright, but that was the extent to which she allowed herself a reaction. Instead of listening to all those screaming instincts, she balled her hands into fists and stood her ground, staring at Ephriam through the dust with a look of grim determination.

"I'm not leaving them." Her voice left no room for debate.

There was a whisper of movement as Cameron stepped to her side. He might have gone even further. He might have placed himself right between them, divine retribution be damned, but his attention flicked to the jagged crack in the asphalt. He kept his place beside her.

Ephriam opened his mouth to answer, but for the first time since his shocking appearance, the Elysian seemed to have lost the script. Instead of trying to reason with her, he turned to Cameron. "You are blinded by sentiment, my friend. You *must* see reason. I have no wish to punish the girl, only to protect her. A member of the Seven was in this place. We *must* depart—"

"Just try it," she growled.

"We are in agreement," Cameron interrupted, trying to calm things down. "But she's right. We cannot leave them in such a state." He glanced around quickly, then lowered his voice as if what he said next was meant only for Ephriam. "Nor can we leave this place as it is. There is damage inside that cannot be explained by mortal excuses. There is damage we would wish to hide."

Ephriam regarded him in silence, the sting of a hundred judgments flashing in his face as if compiling a mental list of all the screaming frustrations he would shout into the void later. For a moment, it looked like he was going to refuse to listen at all, if only on principle. Instead, he looked down at the canyon carved into the asphalt between them and addressed Brie. "Be it on your own head."

"Big talk for someone lucky to have all of his toes," she spat back.

Cameron looked upward as though asking for strength. "Why don't we start with the obvious and focus on repairing this place? The sooner we get things back to normal, the sooner we can figure out what to do next."

"We *know* what to do next. We need to wipe all memory of these events." Ephriam glared at him, emphasizing every word. "We cannot have—"

"Of course," Cameron blurted. "I'm not trying to involve any more of them."

In the silence that followed, it *could not* have sounded less believable. As if this was somehow unclear, Ephriam spread his arms in a wide gesture, taking in all the dark splendor of the carnage Mammon had left in her wake. As if to emphasize his point, an explosion of sparks from a broken car showered into the air behind him.

"I have known you a long time," he said quietly, never breaking Cameron's gaze, "since you were a youngling. I'd like to believe you, but you've made that extremely difficult."

A flush of embarrassment colored Cameron's cheeks as the two slipped without thinking into an ancient language, throwing up their hands in exasperation as words flew between them. Brie tried to follow along a few moments before turning instead to the smoldering wreckage, a feeling of quiet frustration knotting in her chest.

Sherry, along with her boyfriend Mike, still lay passed out some ways away where Cameron had healed their wounds. Brie harrowed a glance down a closer row of cars, and her stomach turned at the sight of blood, *so much* blood, pooled around her friend Rashida. She turned away with a shudder. Finally, almost unwillingly, her eyes lifted to the circle of glowing magma carved into the earth. It glimmered in the shadows, still emitting such heat that it distorted the air like a desert mirage.

As she stood on the bloody pavement among the wreckage, a strange feeling tugged at her stomach, prodding and persistent, like a memory lurking just beneath the surface, trying to break to the other side. A series of fractured images flashed through her mind — ropes made of lightning, bloodied demons, and echoing screams.

And the sound. There had never been anything like that sound.

She shook her head faintly, every part of her in full retreat. With a concerted effort, she pushed the memory down to the bottom of her consciousness. It would be hard enough to stay in the present and get to the end of yet another hellish day.

Hard enough for now. Hard enough for a lifetime.

She turned her attention back to the two men. They looked at her with peculiar expressions that made her feel sure they'd just been talking about her. She squared her shoulders, remembering what her mother used to say whenever she didn't know what to do.

The next right thing. Just do the next right thing, Brie.

"Well, come on then, Tinkerbell," she said, glaring at Ephriam. "Let's go clean up."

"If this is what it's like working with angels, I'm strongly considering switching sides." Brie doubled over at the waist, panting, as a cheerful beep from her wrist congratulated her on reaching ten thousand steps. She took a single look, ripped off her watch, and shoved it into her pocket, trudging endlessly up to the seventh flight of stairs.

All the powers in the cosmos, and they can't unfreeze the elevator?

Cameron had looked so proud of himself when he'd lowered his arms and stopped his chanting — even Ephriam had uttered a grunt of approval — but his pride had faded the moment she'd pressed the button for the elevator. She'd stood there and pressed that powerless button in vain for a full minute before shooting him a look of supreme disappointment and begrudgingly joining Ephriam in the stairwell to start their climb.

"Remind me again why you let Cameron reinforce the time freeze," she demanded, trying desperately to catch her breath. "Did you really think *this* was the time to let him brush up on his magic skills? Half a dozen stories down?"

A golden orb floated breezily up ahead, twinkling in a way that looked suspiciously like laughter. She shot it an icy glare, remembering the past week's one-sided conversations with Ephriam in her living room when he'd appeared as he was now — an innocuous ball of light. She hadn't known there was another option for the Elysians, except for one — the form he'd used days ago to prove that he was up to the task of being her protection detail. The one that had left her breathless with awe, gasping at his four-headed, flame-wreathed celestial body. By contrast, *this* form looked like something out of a cartoon. The memory of his intimidating parlor trick made her growl now, knowing that human form had been an option the entire time.

"Four faces. Literal great balls of fire. *Way* more claws than any one being has use for," she muttered, punctuating every sentence with another angry step. "Sure. Why choose a human form to talk to *a human*? Why choose the diplomatic route when you can engage in celestial dinner theater? Real mature. I can tell you must be a bajillion years old by how super mature that was, Ephriam. But what do I know? What did you call me again? Oh, right. *A fetus.*"

I shouldn't have talked Sherry out of all those cardio days.

She arrived, gasping, at the seventh floor just as Ephriam transformed back into his hulking human body with an increasingly familiar *pop*, completely naked once again. She flinched away from him, fighting the urge to hold up a shielding hand.

"Ephriam, you *promised* Cameron you'd at least wear pants."

With another *pop*, he compromised with a white leather loincloth emblazoned with pink flamingos running up the side. She took a single look and decided this was not the hill she was prepared to die on — not when so many others were clamoring to take its place.

"Yep. Real mature." She set her jaw and pushed her way past him through the doors to the pediatric wing.

Good God...

All the bluster drained from her in an instant, along with whatever adrenaline had been propelling her up those stairs. The image that stretched before her looked like something one might find in a movie — a horror movie. Such utter, violent destruction left room for only one thought: *I can't believe we survived this.*

The unlikely pair drew in a simultaneous breath. They stepped inside, past the orderlies and patients immobilized mid-step and mid-breath, past the crater in the floor where Mammon had held Cameron in her deathly grip, past the man-sized trench in the wall where she'd dragged him up by his throat, past the splatters and pools of his blood, still wet and shimmering, and into the atrium where the body of Dr. Matthews lay face down amongst the potted trees.

She knelt beside his corpse and turned him over, closing his eyes with her palm.

"Where is his heart?" Ephriam asked quietly, his golden eyes resting on the doctor's body. In hindsight, it was a rather obvious question to have asked, but it still took her a minute to summon the breath to reply.

"It's somewhere in the hall," she managed, feeling strangely deflated. "Mammon threw it. She was eating it." The memory of the horrific sight drained the color from her face.

Ephriam stared for a moment, then knelt to the floor beside her. "Such a thing is an abomination. Even for those who, in life, we thought worthy of such an end."

Her cheeks burned in shame. "I didn't like him," she admitted softly. "I thought he deserved what was coming to him."

He closed a hand over hers. "You didn't know what was coming to him. And you saved him from committing a most ignoble sin."

She looked at him, surprised.

"Cameron told me," he admitted. "You have saved a child, defeated an impossible enemy, and thwarted a plot. Though, what kind of plot, we have yet to ascertain."

On some unseen impulse, they turned together to the strange wooden sculpture embedded in the wall amidst splatters of the horrible black tar that had bubbled from Mammon's neck. It still smelled of sulfur. Brie remembered with a shudder the sound it had made, slicing messily through the demon's flesh.

It was quiet for a few seconds, then Ephriam tilted his head and asked, "Now, what in all the heavens do you suppose this is?

CHAPTER TWO

The Coverup

Ephriam mended the structural damage to the hospital as Brie pried the sculpture from the wall, yanking it free with a violent scrape. She turned it over and over in her hands, examining its sharp, interlacing claws and the jet-black stone encased in those strange, looping antlers. A warped image of her pendant reflected on the stone's inky surface. She felt a ripple of unease.

While Ephriam worked, he asked her to recount what had happened with Mammon in the hall. Several times, he stopped her, asking for clarification or further details. Several times, he looked at her with astonishment bordering on disbelief. But there was no denying the truth of her fantastical tale. Not when it matched the story Cameron had just relayed to him in rapid-fire Elysian minutes earlier. Not when he was cleaning up the evidence himself.

When he'd finished repairing the hall and atrium, the Elysian retrieved Matthews' heart, picking it up from the floor behind a nurse's station with gentle hands. With a soft golden glow, he transferred it back into the doctor's chest. There wasn't a mark on him. Not a single thing to point to his violent end.

She couldn't bring herself to ask the burning question, but he guessed and answered it anyway. "The humans will call it a heart attack."

She nodded, fighting a wave of unexpected sadness, and looked around the hospital at the nurses and lab techs, machines, and monitors suspended between heartbeats. "How are you going to fix all this?"

He lifted his eyes to the ceiling, mending a crack he'd missed earlier with an almost absentminded wave of his hand. "You'd probably call it magic."

She scowled. "Why? Because I'm a primitive youngling who would never understand?"

"Yes."

She sighed and stared at the floor.

Fair enough, I guess.

He hesitated a moment before adding, "A very brave primitive youngling, from the looks of it." The corner of his lips tugged up faintly. "I certainly wouldn't bet against you. Fetus though you are." He gave her a gentle look, as one would a small child who has borne a great trauma, before asking, "Is that everything?"

"No, not quite…" She trailed into silence before mustering her courage to speak. She didn't blink and maintained direct eye contact. "Ephriam, I'm not leaving my friends here. Not without protection."

It probably wasn't the best idea to test the patience of a celestial warrior. It probably wasn't the best idea to engage in a staring contest with him, either. But no sooner had Ephriam opened his mouth to reply than his eyes darted to the pendant on her chest.

He was quiet for a few seconds, considering.

"I will arrange for a team of Elysians to guard your friends," he finally replied. "Unseen. The most elite warriors we have."

She let out a breath she hadn't realized she'd been holding. Her shoulders drooped like someone had deflated a particularly over-stressed balloon. "Good," she stammered, the words 'elite warriors' echoing in her mind. "That should probably cover it."

He nodded slowly, watching with a touch of amusement. "Anything else?"

There's a chance he's just trolling me now.

"Not from you, but yes," she answered. "There's someone I need to check on first."

With significantly less awkwardness than before, she led him down the hallway to Kylie's room. The little girl was sound asleep and looked much healthier than the day before. Her red hair flamed around her face like a Rembrandt painting. The color had returned to her cheeks, and fewer tubes ran in and out of her spindly arms. The frozen monitor displayed some prom-ising statistics. Her mother was asleep in the chair next to her, a book of fairy tales still open on her lap.

Brie stopped in the doorway, half-expecting to find an active volcano or a pair of untrained dragons snapping at the tiny girl, but for once, everything was as it should be. She drew in a deep breath and let it out slowly. "Thanks for this. I had to make sure she was okay."

Ephriam was standing a half-step behind her, staring at the girl with a strange expression. "This was the child? This was Mammon's target?"

"Yes. Though why she singled her out is beyond me."

He stared a moment longer, then approached the bed. The frozen machinery cast an eerie glow as he came to a stop beside the railing, assessing Kylie with a look of caution that didn't make sense. A few seconds passed, then he reached out hesitantly, pressing a glowing fingertip to her forehead. As soon as he touched her, the angel jerked his arm back with a hiss of breath, cradling his hand like it had been stung. His face was painted with an expression that sent Brie's heart racing, but before she could open her mouth, he composed himself and said, "We should keep moving."

She blinked. "What? But what did you just—?"

"We should keep moving, Brianna."

In a daze, she followed him to the hallway and watched as he knelt on the ground and muttered something in an ancient language. As he chanted, a glowing circle of runes emanated from his palm and quickly grew to encompass the two companions, the hallway, and the whole floor before expanding right out of view. Almost immediately, the air filled with the beeps of monitors, the murmur of voices, the opening and closing of doors, and somewhere, a stapler being destroyed in frustration.

Brie watched as a nurse hurried past, oblivious to their presence.

"Can they see us?" she whispered.

"No," Ephriam replied with a wry grin. "Magic."

She shook her head slightly, feeling as though some abstract part of her was wearing thin. He held out his hand for hers. When she gave it a dubious look, he attempted to smile reassuringly, succeeding only in showing her all of his teeth.

"Are you smiling?" she finally asked.

He hesitated. "I'm not entirely sure."

We'll have to work on that.

She took his hand as he eased the ancient sculpture away from her and held it to his own chest. When he caught her questioning look, he shrugged. "You shouldn't carry anything your first time. Are you ready?"

"First time for what? Ready for wh——?"

The world around them began to shift and spin. Colors melted into each other until the entire hallway whirled into nothingness. She didn't have time to cry out. She didn't have time to do anything except clutch his arm before the vaulting, dizzying darkness suddenly rearranged itself into the parking garage once more. Her balance vanished, and her stomach swooped. As soon as the ground stopped lurching beneath her, she turned and threw up.

Stupid, inconsiderate angel.

"Next time, a bit of a heads up might be in order, Ephriam," she shot him a dark look.

He wasn't listening. He had pulled the sculpture away from his chest and stared into its depths with a troubled, distant expression.

Cameron appeared in an instant, helping her up. "Are you all right?" he asked anxiously.

She nodded. "I'm fine, but I could use a mint."

With the glow of his palms, he conjured a mint plant out of thin air and offered it to her, concern shining in his eyes. She stared for a moment. "Um, thank you, I guess," she said, plucking a leaf and popping it into her mouth. "Just what I needed — a salad and a breath freshener all in one."

At least he means well.

The parking lot had been restored to its original state of benign neglect. Mike and Sherry had been carefully placed in Mike's squad car, still fast asleep. Rashida was nowhere to be seen.

Brie turned to Cameron. "Where——?"

"At her desk in the morgue, asleep on her files, safe and sound," he answered. "She'll wake up in a few minutes and remember nothing. And I fixed the door."

"Oh. Right." During the mayhem, she'd inadvertently crushed the steel doorknobs to the morgue into smithereens with her bare hands. Yet another flourishing crisis to add to the pile.

She took a deep breath.

You know what? We don't need to think about my growing superpowers right now.

We've had a bit of a day. Maybe we just need to calm down and invest in a top-shelf whiskey.

"What *is* it with you and flamingos? This isn't what we discussed." Cameron scowled at Ephriam's loincloth, shaking his head.

Ephriam ignored him. "Did you modify the mortals' memories?" he asked sharply, staring at the police car with a look of suspicion.

Cameron glanced over with a frown, still holding the mint plant. "Of course. Why?"

"She dreams of a monstrous goat," Ephriam answered.

This made them all pause.

Hell of a coincidence…

"How is that possible?" Cameron muttered. "I already—"

But Ephriam had apparently decided this wasn't his problem and moved on to what he considered to be more pressing concerns. "Time has been restored, and this place has been repaired. Now, we *must* go to the Elysian court. You need to tell them everything that happened. Everything. Omit no detail, no matter how insignificant you may believe it to be. And we need to bring them this." He held up the sculpture that had beheaded

Mammon, eyeing the wooden object with a look of dread. "Not just anything can wound one of the Seven, but it's more than its destructive capacity that troubles me. There is something about this artifact — a darkness I find disquieting."

That's one word for it.

Ephriam turned to Cameron, his expression serious. "And there's something else. Something crucial we must tell them." His expression was grave. "The girl Mammon targeted, the one who was saved, is a scion."

Cameron turned white as a ghost. "Are you certain?"

"There is no mistaking such a thing," Ephriam affirmed. "None have been seen since—"

"I know," said Cameron, his voice barely above a whisper.

Brie watched their exchange with a growing sense of anxiety. She didn't want to ask the question. She *really* didn't. But there was a part of her that simply had to. "What's a scion?"

Cameron steadied himself and raked his hand through his hair. "I'll explain later," he murmured. "I promise. For now, let's just focus on one thing at a time." He took her hand. "Let's get your friends some protection and navigate this interdimensional travel first."

"Yeah, because who doesn't love some cosmic chaos before lunch?" she said ruefully.

"Before breakfast," he corrected with a smile. "We left in a bit of a hurry." He sighed softly and leaned in to touch his forehead to hers. "The Elysian court will know what to do. And when this is over, I'll make sure you get some well-deserved rest."

They drew close for a moment. She was so tired. So overwhelmed. She rested her cheek against his chest, felt his heartbeat in the side of her face, and remembered the way his heart had thundered when he'd kissed her.

Then, she remembered the way he'd stiffened when he realized that Ephriam had seen.

She pulled back, and her stomach suddenly tightened, cold with fear.

Because it's against divine law, Brie. He made that terribly clear.

Their eyes met, but before she could ask, Ephriam coughed pointedly. She pulled away.

"I'll organize the protective detail as discussed to safeguard your friends and this place," the Elysian continued. "I will be back shortly, and then, *we are leaving.*" He shot another glare at Cameron, silently communicating what he wouldn't say aloud: *Do you think you can handle this? Waiting quietly without causing any more trouble for ten whole minutes?* Then, he stomped away. Before he'd rounded the corner, he disappeared into a golden glow, like a drop of sunlight falling through a crack in space.

Brie stared at the spot where he'd vanished before turning in a slow circle, taking in the rest of the scene. Her eyes came to rest on the squad car — on her best friend asleep in the front seat. Her chest tightened, and a breath caught in her throat.

This is it. I'm truly about to leave the world behind.

And Sherry with it.

Cameron set his mint plant on the hood of a nearby car and placed a hand on her shoulder. She turned to him as he tucked a strand of hair behind her ear and asked, "Are you all right?"

She hadn't the faintest idea. "Are *you* all right?" She returned the ominous question to him.

He shook his head. "I thought I'd lost you."

She picked at the fraying edge of her sweater. "I thought so, too."

There was a moment of silence, and he reached for her hand. "Here. There's at least one thing I can fix." A glow emanated from his palms and briefly surrounded her. When it faded, her clothes were clean. Still frayed around the edges and torn from the trauma of the morning, but the bloodstains and scorch marks had magically vanished.

Like it never happened.

Getting rid of the evidence.

Erasing the memory.

She looked over at her best friend.

Again.

"Sherry will be okay," Cameron said gently. "I know you don't want to leave her, but the Elysian guard will keep her safe. There are so many questions that deserve answers, and it would be naïve to believe this threat has gone for good." He looked at her pendant. "Perhaps now more than ever, we need to find the truth. We can't go on not knowing."

Brie nodded, though her heart sank. "I hate that you had to mess with her memory," she whispered, unable to reconcile the horror of it, trying to imagine what she'd say when she was finally back. "What am I supposed to tell her? She'll never forgive me for this."

Cameron angled her deliberately in the other direction. "She might never know. And if she does?" He drew her close, staring somewhere over her head. "You'd be surprised what someone can forgive."

There was a lot to say, but she held back. She merely closed her eyes and waited for Ephriam to return, resting in the warm curve of her angel's chest.

Couldn't we stay like this?

Couldn't we stay just like this, just a little longer?

A car door slammed.

Sherry's voice echoed furiously off the walls.

"What in the name of *Hecate* do you mean you're moving to Croatia?!"

♦   ♦   ♦

Brie's eyes flew open, and she and Cameron broke apart as her best friend in the world descended on them like an oncoming storm. "Sherry?!"

"*Yes*, Brianna Weldon, *SHERRY*." It seemed impossible that anyone so small could radiate so much wrath. "Are you dying? Did you join a cult? Is this HIS doing?" She whipped her head, shooting Cameron with imaginary death darts as she advanced towards them, waving the letter Brie had left for her on her mantle. "You're moving to Croatia, and you tell me in a stupid *note?*"

Oh God, I forgot about the letter.

"No, Sher, you don't understand—" Brie pleaded.

"You are damn right I don't understand! I have tried to take this on good faith. I have gone along with it and not kicked up any fuss. I've been supportive as hell. But enough is enough! You can't throw your whole life away to run off to Europe with some guy you hardly know. Are you hearing me?! He cannot take you away!"

Mike joined them a second later, looking disoriented. Despite his confusion, he lost no time jumping into things. "Ladies, is there any way we could try to take this somewhere else—?"

"No! Absolutely not! We are having this out right... right... now." Sherry started out strong, then faltered, looking around with uncertainty.

Brie followed her gaze, heart pounding. "What is it, Sher? Are you okay?"

The others turned and followed Sherry's eyes to the fire extinguisher. Brie sucked in a breath. One of the last things she remembered was Sherry covering Mammon in a large quantity of flame-resistant foam before being thrown into a concrete pillar.

Does she remember? Why are they even awake?!

Brie glared at Cameron, who raised his hands in confusion.

Sherry stepped cautiously toward the fire extinguisher before whirling with sudden urgency to Mike. Before the others could even react, she raced to him and started patting him down, running her hands over every inch of his body to check for damage.

The others were horrified. For Mike's part, he was simply confused. "Babe," he said, perplexed. "What are you doing? Are you okay?"

She didn't answer. She kissed him, hard. He had only started to reciprocate when she broke away with a look of horror and ran to the exact place Rashida had fallen. She stood there a moment, looking lost, before whipping out her phone.

Mike looked bewildered. "Honey, who are you—?"

She held up a finger, silencing him, until a voice picked up. "Rashida, are you okay?" she gasped, fingers drumming on the side of the phone. She listened for a moment, nodding. "Are you sure? Yes, I'm fine. No, everything's fine. No reason." She hung up, then turned around with a scathing glare. "Brianna Weldon, tell me what the *devil* is going on."

Brie and Cameron looked at each other, both at a total loss.

"What do you *think* is going on?" Brie asked hesitantly.

This did nothing to soothe her friend's rage.

"I haven't the faintest clue, have I?!" Sherry cried. "One minute I'm driving to the hospital to keep you from making a *terrible* decision, next I'm having some horrible nightmare, and then I wake up to an equally infuriating *day*mare! Brie, what the hell are you thinking?!"

Brie tried to redirect her back to the letter. "Look, I know you're upset. I'm upset, too. I'm overwhelmed by all the stuff that's happened. The new place, new job, the little girl from the other day. I just need a little break. Admin said it's okay, and it won't be for long." She nodded quickly, trying to convince herself. "Just a little trip. A little, tiny trip... to clear my head."

And make sure the world keeps spinning.

Sherry was the picture of fury. "Do not patronize me, Brianna." She stalked slowly forward, closing the distance between them. "I have known you for a long time. Much longer than this *person* you've invited into your life." She looked at Cameron like he was made of snakes. "I know you backwards and forwards. And I know when you are hiding something from me." She stood before Brie with tears shining in her eyes. "I don't know what it is, and I don't know why you're keeping me in the dark, but I know it's something big." She threw up a finger, "For reasons I don't yet understand, I know it involves a goat. And I *demand*, as your best friend and confidant, that you tell me whatever it is *this instant!*"

They might have thought of a clever lie. They might even have been able to convince her it was true. But with that final demand, Sherry jabbed her index finger into Brianna's chest, hitting her pendant dead-center.

And the pendant began to glow.

They stared down at it for a moment: Brie in mindless shock, Sherry with a kind of post-emotional apocalypse level of disbelief.

They lifted their eyes at the same moment.

Sherry narrowed hers. "I think it's fair to say you have some explaining to do."

CHAPTER THREE

The Elysians

The average person might reasonably assume that the policeman was in charge of the situation. Mike stood with one hand ready for action, resting on his nightstick, the other placed lightly on Sherry's shoulder.

The average person wouldn't have met Sherry Walker.

Her eyes blazed at Brie and Cameron, who stood, heads bowed before her, radiating guilt. "One more time, from the beginning," she growled.

Brie sucked in a deep breath, trying to gather her senses, as she launched into the fantastical tale once again. "Sherry, the day my mom died—"

Sherry held up a hand while the other pinched the skin between her eyebrows as though warding off a migraine. "On second thought, I can't stand to hear the beginning again. Let me see if I have this straight." She looked to the policeman for support. "Mike?"

He held up his hands with that particularly male brand of social helplessness that says, *I am so far out of my emotional depth here. This one's all you.*

Sherry scowled at him and turned back to the others. "So, Cameron here," she indicated the impossibly handsome man standing before her, "is an angel from a supernatural world between Heaven and Hell, in charge of ferrying souls to the afterlife. And not just any angel, but the one who brought your mom to Heaven after the accident. The one you said you saw all those years ago. And he's come back to protect you from the invisible shadow monsters who are out to get you again." She looked back and forth between them. "How am I doing so far?"

"We call them wraiths," offered Cameron.

Brie put her hand over his, urging him to shush.

"I was just trying to get her acquainted with the correct terminology—" he started.

"Not the right time, Cam," Brie whispered.

Sherry acted as though he did not exist, glaring briefly at their intertwined hands. "Brie, you're saying those shadow-things attacked you in your car? On your way here to Virginia?"

Brie nodded wearily.

"Out in the woods? In the middle of nowhere?" she went on.

"Sherry, what more could you—?"

"Brianna Weldon, answer me."

"Yes, Sherry. Out near the state border."

"And this guy just *happened* to be there to rescue you." Sherry flashed a scathing look toward Cameron.

"No. I told you, he was already there." Brie knew what was coming and flinched.

"In your purse," Sherry said flatly.

"Yes."

"As a golden ball of light. In your *purse*." Sherry's tone was picking up some color now.

Brie stared at the ground. "Look, I know how it sounds—"

"Do you? Do you actually?"

"Sher—"

"Because I feel like if you *actually* knew how this sounded, you would stop saying it, and we wouldn't be having this problem. Because it sounds exactly how it sounded after your accident, Brie. No, scratch that. This is worse. This is much, much worse."

Cameron tried to interject. "Sherry, I think if you—"

Brie squeezed his hand in warning. He shut up.

"This is worse, because now you think there's a doctor in our hospital involved in a plot with a giant, demonic goat woman to kill a child." Sherry continued, picking up speed. "This is worse because now you're away from everything familiar. Away from your home. Your family. Your therapist. This is worse because you're trying to quit your job and move to Croatia with a guy from some backwoods Appalachian cult who has clearly brainwashed you and tried to do the same to me."

Cameron started at this. "I beg your pardon?!"

She whirled on him in blind fury. "Beg all you want, you despicable worm. I will get to you in a minute." She rose to her full, if diminutive height, took a deep breath, and stood next to Mike. He took her hand in a caring gesture, and together, they turned deliberately to Brie.

"Listen. The important thing to remember—" Sherry began.

"The very most important thing," added Mike,

"Is that we love you, we support you—"

"And we're going to get you through this."

Brie and Cameron blinked with blank stares.

Sherry pointed upwards to the bustling hospital. "We have access to one of the very best mental health programs in the entire country. Money is no object. There's an excellent treatment facility right upstairs."

"It really is one of the best in the nation. I had an aunt go funny on us once, and they fixed her right up in time for Thanksgiving." Mike nodded as though this was reassuring.

"And I'm sure they'll get you in straight away, no wait time," Sherry said with finality.

"Guys," Brie cried, "we're not crazy! And I'm not making this up! I'm telling you the truth. *He's* telling you the truth." She looked pleadingly at Sherry. "Sher, how long have we known each other? All the inexplicable things from this past week? Surely, you must have noticed something. My necklace started glowing! How do you explain that? Sherry, please. *Please.* You have to believe me."

A tear spilled down Sherry's cheek as she took Brie's hand in hers. "Honey, I know this feels real to you. And after everything you've been through, it's no wonder this is all coming up again. But this—" she pointed at Cameron, "is not an angel. He did not save your life when you were sixteen. He does not turn into a glowing ball of light. And he most certainly does not have your best interest at heart." Cameron opened his mouth to protest, but Sherry cut him off, her eyes fixed on Brie. "Not if he's playing along with this delusion. Not if he's making you think it's real. I know you think you're telling the truth, love, but it isn't real. It's okay. It's going to be okay. We're going to get you all the help you need. And as for *you*."

She turned at last to Cameron and advanced on him like a tiger defending its cub.

"I will make you pay for what you've done to my friend." She pointed at Mike, who flexed and clenched his jaw. "I don't know why you thought you'd get away with this, but he is a *police officer.* Do you understand? You will never see *sunlight* again after we're through with you – preying on her like that. Using her vulnerabilities against her." She took another step forward, pure menace. "I am going to *destroy* you. Do you hear me?"

It would have been very difficult not to hear her. Her voice roared through the parking lot at a decibel level that felt too great to come from such a tiny person.

"I am going to march through your life, salting the earth behind me so nothing good can grow in your heart for a thousand years. I will find whatever is precious to you and make it see you for what you really are: a fraud, a coward, and a malicious, conniving — *Who the hell are you?*"

Brie and Cameron had drawn closer together throughout her rant, wilting beneath her words like ill-kept flowers. When she shouted, they whirled around in surprise.

Oh shit…

Ephriam had come back.

And he was not alone.

Five Elysians stood in formation in the parking lot of Daya Memorial Hospital, looking about as out-of-place as Medieval knights in an Apple store. Three stood behind Ephriam, each nearly seven feet tall and all sporting different variations of his leather loincloth. The fourth and tallest among them stood beside him: a woman dressed head to toe in what Brie could only assume was Elysian battle gear — an assortment of leather, cloth, and metal that could have been plucked straight from the

THE PENDANT & THE PROPHECY 35

pages of ancient history. She stood shoulder to shoulder with Ephriam, and though Brie would not have thought such a thing possible, she looked like she could comfortably kick his ass. She was tan, lean, lithe like an Amazon, and twirling a knife made of pure sunlight between her fingers like she'd been born with a blade in her hand.

She was also grinning ear to ear.

"Is this how humans usually interact with one another?" she asked, delighted. She pointed at Sherry. "I *love* her! But why can she see us? Though I suppose, at this point, it's to be expected. You've managed to make everything else go completely sideways, why not this as well?" She let out a charming laugh directed at Cameron, who still seemed to be gathering himself back together after Sherry's blood-chilling tirade.

"Do not stop on our account," added Ephriam, speaking directly to Sherry. "I would like to hear more about your plans for 'Cameron.' If you are open to assistance, I offer my services."

Sherry looked between them, shocked and furious. "Brianna Weldon, who are these people, and why are they so tall?"

"What people? Who's tall?" Mike asked in bewilderment, staring into what he clearly perceived to be a blank space where the Elysians were standing.

"Ephriam! Tavi! Why can she see you?!" hissed Cameron, having somewhat recovered himself. "Why aren't you following protocol?"

"What do you mean *why can I see them?*" screeched Sherry.

Ephriam bristled, "Why aren't WE following—?"

"I have no idea," the warrior woman, presumably Tavi, interrupted with a cheerful shrug. "She shouldn't be able to. We've been shielded this whole time. Probably the same reason you couldn't keep either of them asleep." She studied Mike and Sherry curiously as if they were some riddle to untangle. "They must have some natural immunity. I've never seen anything like it. What a furious, fascinating—"

"What people?" yelled Mike. "Babe, who are you talking to?"

"Brie, what in the nine circles of hell is going on?" screamed Sherry.

Ephriam and Tavi looked at one another. At an unseen signal, a shimmer passed over them and the rest of the Elysians. This must have made them visible to humans because, at that moment, Mike drew his gun with a shout of surprise and attempted to aim it at all of them at once. "Get down on the ground! Drop your weapons! Show me your hands and get down on the ground!"

Ephriam scowled. "For what purpose?"

Brie leapt between them, waving her hands. "Woah, woah! Mike, Sherry, this is Ephriam. And that's…?"

The warrior woman sheathed her knife and stepped forward. She took Brie's hand by the fingers, angled it above her shoulder, and shook it vigorously. "Tavianne. Head of the Elysian Guard. Exceptionally pleased to meet you." She continued shaking with a proud grin, throwing a look at Cameron. "Heya, kid. How long are you supposed to do this?"

"That's probably enough, Tav." Cameron rescued Brie's arm and turned to address their confounded friends. "Sherry, Mike, this is Tavi. That's Ephriam. They're old friends of mine. They're Elysians. Just like we've been trying to tell you." Sherry looked as though she'd swallowed a lizard and couldn't quite manage to throw it up. Cameron kept a wary eye on her and continued. "Tavi came to keep us safe with her unit, and Ephriam has been helping me keep an eye on Brie. Mike? Mike, can you put the gun away?"

Mike was still looking wildly from one giant warrior to the other.

Brie said gently, "Mike, they're unarmed."

"They're un*clothed*!" he cried.

"I'm definitely armed," added Tavi, unhelpfully.

Brie closed her eyes and exhaled. "Mike, they're his friends. Please, put the gun away."

"Friends? Is this your cult?" shrieked Sherry. "Are these cult members? Is that why they're dressed like that? Brianna, I am confused, and you know how that makes me throw things!" By now, she had taken some pepper spray from her designer purse and aimed it at the Elysians, staring like a bull ready to charge.

Ephriam crossed his arms over his chest and stared Mike down as if daring him to fire.

"Oh, by all the saints!" Tavi said in exasperation. She flashed a lopsided grin and transformed. The edges of her glorious body vanished in a flash of golden light, like the sun reflecting off the ocean the moment it touches the horizon. The brilliance faded in an instant, and in Tavianne's place, a glowing golden orb the size of an apple floated weightlessly in the air. No one so much as breathed as it floated over to Sherry and hovered right in front of her face.

Brie gasped as it spoke:

"Do you have a moment to talk about our Lord and Savior, Jesus Christ?"

Mike immediately lowered his gun.

And Sherry fainted dead away.

◆   ◆   ◆

"I don't see how this is in any way preferable to simply healing her."
Ephriam stood in the corner of the hospital room, watching Brie
hang an IV saline drip for Sherry in what she had come to understand was his default posture: arms crossed and scowling. "Sticking
tubes and needles into them. Pooling them full of water and salt.
It's like the Dark Ages all over again. We might as well cover her in
leeches. What she *needs* is a simple Elysian healing spell."

The three Elysians in Tavi's unit had been sent to run a perimeter check around the hospital to ensure they were safe.

The remaining two were driving Brie slightly mad.

Tavi came to Sherry's bedside with a look of chagrin. "Please,
let me fix her. I feel terrible. I was trying to keep the orange one
peaceable. I never meant to—"

"I know you didn't," Brie interrupted. "But Sherry's just been
through a lot, and I don't think any more supernatural interven-
tion will make her feel better right now. Let's just let her rest."

"Am I the orange one?" asked Mike. Since the moment he'd
lowered his gun, his primary concern had been bringing Sherry
inside the hospital without drawing too much attention. Once
inside, Brie had hustled them into an empty room, closed all the
privacy curtains, and hung an IV bag for her best friend. Mike
sat at his girlfriend's bedside, holding her hand and keeping Tavi
in his line of sight at all times.

"Of course you are. Unless humans experience the color spec-
trum differently. What would you call that?" Tavi pointed at his
hair.

Mike narrowed his eyes at her, then turned back to Sherry.
"We call it orange, too," he muttered.

"I'd really like to run a CT scan on both of you," said Brie,
looking worriedly between Sherry and Mike.

"Why would we need that?" he asked sharply.

"Oh, to make sure that…" she stammered, looking frantically at Cameron. The secret of the Elysians' existence was supposed to be absolute. She wasn't even supposed to know herself, and though her friends had already been tangled up in the events of the day, she had no idea how much she could reveal without breaking promises and breaking trust. Ephriam's ever-darkening glares did nothing to bolster her confidence. "Just to make sure she didn't hit her head, and to ensure you weren't affected by the Elysian energy in any negative way. You know, make sure all the gears are still turning."

Cameron stepped in and covered for her. "Though I'm absolutely certain it isn't necessary." He gave Brie a meaningful look. "If anything, our energy has a healing effect on human physiology. I can tell you beyond any doubt that you are both fine." He directed this at Mike. "Whatever caused her to faint is emotional or psychological. A result of the shock from the day. Physically, she's in perfect health."

Mike gave him a long look, then turned deliberately back to Sherry. "Good," he said shortly.

"So let me make sure I've got this right." Tavi took a break from rummaging through cabinets filled with medical supplies to address the group. "You," she pointed an epinephrine syringe at Cameron, "have been secretly guarding this woman for the past five years, ever since she survived the wraith attack that killed her mother." As Tavi continued, Brie immediately confiscated the syringe and put it back in the drawer. "She can see you, she can see all of us, and very few of our powers seem to work on her."

Brie's head snapped up. "Tavianne, have you been trying to use your powers on me this whole time?"

There was a guilty pause.

"Of course not," replied Tavi. But she squinted ever so slightly and made a strange twisting motion with one of her hands.

"You're not trying to use some psycho Elysian magic on me at this very moment?" Brie crossed her arms over her chest, mirroring Ephriam's scowl.

"Of *course* not," Tavi repeated, flashing her a bright smile. "Moving on — *this* one," she indicated Brie, "has somehow managed to take down one of The Seven. The actual *Seven*. And she did so with nothing but a magic necklace and a weird sculpture, resulting in some kind of supernatural showdown that nearly leveled a city block."

It sounded truly horrible, but the warrior couldn't stop smiling. She whirled on Cameron and punched him in the arm. "You've been holding out on me! How many times have we sparred together in the arena? How many years have I trained you? And for years now, you've had a secret protective mission? On Earth? With a *girl*? And you got her to use your *fake name*?" She punctuated each point with another punch to his arm, oblivious to his attempts to block her. "I will never forgive you for not including me. This is worse than the time you built that Jurassic enclosure with Eth——"

"Tavi!" Cameron interrupted, cutting her short. "It's more complicated than that. I'm sorry," he added, though he looked thoroughly unraveled.

"What do you mean, a *fake name*?" Mike asked, latching onto this one thing.

"It isn't fake, it's chosen!" Cameron turned to Brie. "I told you about this. My friend, the one who was sacrificed under the——"

Mike didn't let him finish, "*You forgot that his name is fake?*" he asked, shocked.

At a loss for words, Brie needlessly adjusted the IV line again.

"It isn't fake," Cameron protested, a little milder, ensuring everyone in the room was clear.

Brie pursed her lips. "I guess that little piece of information must have slipped through the cracks for me somewhere between starting my job at the hospital and surviving *another* supernatural attack. And developing superpowers that I never asked for and don't want. *And* trying to hide all of this from my best friend in the entire world so she won't have me committed, or worse, *hate* me. *And* destroying a good chunk of the hospital in a battle with some demonic goat woman, AND apparently saving all of your asses!" She stopped short, suddenly aware she'd ended up yelling.

Tavi, Cameron, and Mike had all frozen in place, staring at her. Ephriam smirked.

"Sorry," she concluded in an embarrassed mutter. "It's been quite a week."

"It sure sounds like it," said a familiar voice.

All five heads swiveled at once to Sherry.

"You're awake!" Mike pressed a kiss to her hand. "How are you feeling?"

"*How am I feeling?*" she echoed, leveling an emotionless gaze to Brie.

Just then, the door burst open, and everyone froze again.

Their charge nurse, Denise, took in the scene for a second and stepped inside. "Weldon? Walker?" She nodded at Mike. "And who is this?"

Sherry made no move to reply, so Brie scrambled to explain. "This is Officer Mitchell, Sherry's boyfriend. We were in the parking lot, and she fainted, so I…"

Think faster.

Brie swallowed and opted for honesty. "This was the fastest way to help her. I didn't think anyone would mind."

Denise regarded them levelly. She clearly didn't register anyone else in the room except the two nurses and their police escort. The Elysians stood quietly in the corners, invisible to her mortal eyes. "I'm surprised you're here at all," she answered with a curt nod. "Admin told me you're taking some leave. After yesterday, I think it's a good idea. After this morning, an even better one."

"What happened this morning?" Mike asked.

Brie held her breath, afraid of the answer.

"You haven't heard? I assumed that's why Sherry..." Denise frowned, confused for a moment, before explaining. "Dr. Matthews had a heart attack in the hospital last night. They found his body in the atrium this morning. Given the timing, police are here asking questions. He was still their primary suspect in that little girl's poisoning."

Brie thought it was possible that her heartbeat had become audible.

Denise gave them an appraising look. "I need this bed. Go home. Rest." She turned on her heel and started to leave before stopping abruptly and looking over her shoulder. "You know you're practicing medicine without a license, right?" In an utterly uncharacteristic move, she winked and shut the door behind her, muttering something about getting a donut.

No sooner had she left than the three Elysians from Tavi's unit materialized right where she'd been standing. One rushed over to Ephriam and whispered something urgently in his ear.

In the silence that followed, Sherry's voice drifted up from the bed, answering Mike's question from before. "I feel like my world has shifted on its axis. I want to go home."

Brie turned to her at once, ready to do anything in the world to make that happen. Her chest tightened when she saw the way Sherry avoided looking at her.

Ephriam cleared his throat. "That is not going to be possible just yet. The King has summoned us. We are to leave at once."

Brie turned to him. "What do you mean?"

But the scowling warrior was no longer willing to entertain the question. Before her pendant could meddle any further, he spread his arms wide and muttered some words in an ancient tongue. Within seconds, they were immersed in heavenly light. There wasn't time to protest. There wasn't time to stop him. There wasn't even time to cling to the side of the hospital bed, although, in a split second of childish panic, Brie was actually tempted. There was no time for anything at all. Before she could even pull in a breath, swirling celestial forces enveloped them all. This time, her pendant did not intervene.

They left the mortal world behind, vanishing into the unknown.

CHAPTER FOUR

The Impossible Sky

When Brie was ten, her parents took her on a trip to Six Flags Over Georgia with Sherry and her family. The girls were desperate to prove their maturity by riding the "grown up rides." Sherry's height was an impediment, so the night before, after Brie's parents had gone to bed, they stayed up in their sleepover tent made of bed sheets. By the light of a My Little Pony flashlight, they hatched a scheme to make sure they'd be allowed on the rides. The next morning, Sherry had two pairs of socks stuffed in the bottom of her shoes and Mrs. Weldon's good drink coasters stacked together and superglued to her rubber soles to make sure she was tall enough.

After an ill-advised quantity of corn dogs, cotton candy, and cherry cola slushies, the girls strapped themselves into a contraption that towered over the entire park, aptly named "Goliath." They sat in the front, holding each other's hands as the coaster clicked its way up the first, hundred-and-seventy-five-foot-tall hill. There was a moment of suspension. Then, they clutched each other in terror, screamed, and vomited up the entire contents of their stomachs as they plummeted down, to devastating effect on everyone in the cars behind them.

This was so much worse than that.

The world melted and spun. Colors whirled around Brie, like she was trapped in a cosmic laundry machine. She felt hot and cold in waves. Her curls were ironed straight by the G-forces, which were also giving her an involuntary facelift. She was vaguely aware that Mike had curled protectively around Sherry about an arm's-length away.

Suddenly, she felt Cameron by her side, encircling her in his arms. She clung to him like a shipwreck victim to a life raft. She wanted to beg him to stop but was afraid that if she opened her mouth, the air would be sucked clean out of her lungs. Instead, she shut her eyes tight and turned her face into his chest.

Light and color blurred past at unfathomable speed, but she didn't feel velocity. What she felt was more like pushing through something thick and resistant. The air didn't feel like air at all anymore but rather some kind of pressurized plasma. Strange snippets of sound filled the air like someone tuning a radio that couldn't get a signal. Her ears rang as gravity doubled back on itself, then let go completely. A second later, she was free floating, grounded to reality only by the inescapable circle of Cameron's arms.

Is this time? Is this what time feels like?

Suddenly, something changed — a charge, like a crackling of electricity, pulsed through the thick, viscous substance. White sparks eddied and swirled. Everything felt alive for a moment. As she jerked her head up and looked around, her pendant began to glow the brightest, purest white.

That's when the curtains of time parted, and she saw the last person she expected to see in all the world.

Her mother.

She was in the kitchen of Brie's childhood home, singing softly and baking — stirring batter in the blue ceramic bowl they'd always used, the one with the chip that looked like a cat. Her skirt swirled as she spun like a ballerina to preheat the oven.

Brie's heart caught in her throat.

Mom?

Clusters of white sparks splashed around like water dashing off rocks. The Elysians were shouting. Brie couldn't understand — didn't want to understand. She only had eyes for her mother. Purely on instinct, she reached a hand toward the shining window to her past. Her mother looked up for a moment with a confused expression, staring right at the place where her daughter was looking back at her. Staring but not seeing.

The shouting grew louder. There was movement behind Brie, and she glanced back.

A formation had emerged within the Elysians — a concentration of both their forms and their energy. A glow pulsed through them and burst outward like a shockwave, surrounding their party and continuing until it reached the image of her childhood home. This sparked around the edges, then cracked. Like an explosion inside a television, the window to her mother shattered.

No! Don't go.

Don't leave me again.

A surge of energy rippled around them. Suddenly, her feet touched something solid, and the world jolted back into focus, but not any world she'd seen before. For a fleeting moment, she saw a wildly foreign sky, painted turquoise and violet, peppered with orange explosions and lightning-white cracks, as though someone or something was attacking the heavens themselves.

Beneath it, a legion of Elysians moved with purpose, their ethereal forms darting back and forth like cosmic weavers, repairing the cracks in the sky as soon as they appeared. It was a terrifying, mesmerizing sight, a testament to the grandeur and power of the universe itself.

She tried to ask what was happening, but her words, her very mouth, seemed far away.

She only had time to lock eyes with Cameron for a fleeting moment and register his shining, unmitigated terror.

Then everything went black.

♦   ♦   ♦

"You brought the children here."

A voice drifted from the ether, and Brie fluttered into consciousness. Tiny sparks of comprehension appeared in the fog. Her mind was willing, but the rest of her wasn't so easy to convince. There was a ringing in her ears, and her limbs felt like they'd been weighted to the bed.

It *was* a bed, she was assuming. In some kind of a hospital, she was desperately hoping.

Her eyelids wouldn't open — she couldn't tell anything for sure.

"Here," the voice said again. "To this place."

It was a man, she slowly realized. It was the voice of an aged man. Aged, but not in a way she'd ever considered. Each line he spoke gave evidence to his depth of understanding. This was a voice so rich with wisdom and experience she found she wanted him to keep speaking, to fully discover the depths of his stories, to learn at his feet. Never had someone made such an impact on her, sight unseen. She fought against the wave of exhaustion that threatened to sweep her off to sleep again.

Who is that?

The voice was countered almost immediately by one half its age. No, a quarter. A mere fraction. The measurements to which she was accustomed didn't matter anymore. While the first voice was as steady as a ship in the harbor, the second was fiery, indignant. A flame whipping on the waves.

"If there is a question on your lips, Father, just say it. It is *maddening* when you do this: making riddles out of nothing, spinning questions out of simple facts. Just speak it plain."

That voice she knew — the one she'd whispered to every night for years, praying it would whisper back. It wasn't so long ago that her guardian angel had promised her everything would be all right. Strangely, she'd believed him. Now, she wasn't so sure.

This must be some new and exciting definition of "okay."

"Yet the facts you bring me *are* questionable." The old man placed each word with care like he hadn't spoken in a long time. "You have brought mortal children to the halls of our home, erasing eons of precedent. You have crossed boundaries I thought you knew, broken laws I thought you respected. You vanished from this place and returned to me now in the strangest of company. And you call it maddening, the way I speak in my own house?"

A silence fell over them while Brie struggled to stay conscious. The corners of her mind kept drifting, like the frayed edges of a flag beaten too long by the wind.

There seemed no appropriate response to what the ancient man had said, yet the resulting silence wasn't particularly uncomfortable. It felt impossible that anything could be uncomfortable here, wherever "here" might be. A warm breeze drifted from what felt like an open window. The air was soft, if air could be soft, and scented with a delicate fragrance. Sleep tempted her like a siren's song, beckoning her to drift, to let go. She resisted. Her eyes cracked open, and a blurry image streamed through her lashes. She was indeed inside and lying in a bed. Cameron was at the foot of it, angled in front of her, his head bowed.

"I panicked," he said quietly, almost in a whisper. "We received your summons, and Ephriam said we had to leave immediately, and we…" He trailed away, as uncertain as she'd ever seen him. He was just a young man having a conversation with his father, grappling with issues too big to understand. "I just panicked. There are things happening unlike anything I've ever seen."

Across the room stood the blurred figure of a man. He nodded slowly like his head carried the weight of a crown. "They are here now," he murmured, as though the very act of saying the words made them law. "For better or worse. Although, your reason is beyond me."

Cameron lifted his chin a little. "It's their story to tell," he replied.

His father let out a sigh. "They are in no state."

"They are stronger than you think—"

"I do not say it to criticize," the old man interrupted. "They are in no state." He glanced at the bedroom wall as if he could see people on the other side. His eyes drifted down and lingered for a moment on the young woman lying on the bed before turning to leave. "They need rest now. They need to piece themselves together." His cloak whispered over the ground behind him. "Before we tear them back apart."

She had to strain to hear his final words as he paused in the doorframe and looked back, eyeing her as though she was dangerous. "Son... Be careful."

♦   ♦   ♦

Brie woke up face to face with a dinosaur. She blinked. It blinked. She closed her eyes.

Nope. Absolutely not.

Let's try this again.

She opened one eye, then the other. It was even closer now, but the adrenaline flooding her system was waking her brain. She now identified the creature mere inches away from her face as a turtle, albeit several degrees of magnitude larger than the largest she'd ever seen. Its long neck, giant shell, and beady black eyes began to register as something cute rather than a carnivorous threat. Far too large to be considered normal, but still, cute. She started to relax.

It moved closer still, then slowly, almost tenderly, nipped her on the nose.

She let out a muffled shriek. Cameron flew around the corner.

"Cong! Cong, we talked about this! I'm so sorry," he apologized as he dragged it by its shell to a safe distance a few feet away. "He's always sneaking up on people, and he isn't used to strangers."

Cong's eyes crinkled and his mouth opened in an expression that looked uncannily like an elderly toothless man laughing at his own joke.

She rubbed her nose and stared, astonished. "Cameron, is that...? Do you have a pet?"

He nodded as he ushered the giant reptile out of the room. "A few."

A few.

She stared at him a long moment, then let her attention drift.

She was in a child's room — a child's room the size of a two-bed-room apartment. The modesty of the furnishings looked out of place with the height of the ceilings, the hugeness of the space. The bed was just the right size for her, which meant it was surely too small for Cameron. A wooden letter 'C' as big as her head, painted with messy, bright colors, hung on the open door. One enormous wall had floor-to-ceiling shelves, which housed hundreds of books, games, puzzles, strange trinkets, rocks, and plants.

The ceiling, so uncannily high above them, was painted to look like the night sky with a skill that surpassed that of any human master. As she watched, a painted comet flew from one corner of the room to the other, and she realized the entire mural was moving to mirror night on Earth. On the nightstand was a carved miniature pterodactyl and a glass of water.

Hanging on the wall above the bed was a painting of a magnificent, angelic being with six wings and impressive golden armor wielding a flaming sword. This creature was also represented in a series of crudely drawn crayon pictures resting on a nearby desk. Cameron hurriedly collected these and stuffed them into a drawer, his cheeks flaming with embarrassment over either the drawings or the conduct of his pet. She watched him awkwardly approach.

"A turtle named Cong?" she asked.

"Tortoise, actually." He raked his hand through his hair self-consciously. "I'm sorry about that. I didn't think you'd wake up so soon."

She picked up the glass of water and took a sip. "How long was I out?"

He sat on the side of the bed. "Not long. About three Earth hours. How are you feeling?"

"I—" she took a moment to ask herself the same question, quickly running through a bodily checklist to see if she was, in fact, okay. Her aches and pains from the encounter with Mammon were gone. She felt refreshed and alert. Far too refreshed and alert for only three hours of rest. "I feel fantastic," she answered.

I absolutely should not feel fantastic.

"That's a relief." He reached for her a bit hesitantly, tucking a flyaway strand of hair behind her ear. "You gave us quite a scare."

She took another sip and frowned. "What happened?"

He glanced at the window, his face tight. "There was a problem with the barriers on the border of our realm. Wraiths, no doubt, testing our defenses at the perimeter. It happens sometimes, though such a coordinated effort is unusual."

"No, that's not what I meant." Brie rubbed her eyes, recalling the image of her mother and the panic on Cameron's face. "When we were traveling. What I saw..." She searched his face for any sign of recognition, any evidence that it wasn't a hallucination.

He stared back, blank but reassuring. "It was likely a small crack in our defenses," he explained. "A team was already repairing the damage as we arrived."

He didn't see her. Her heart sank. *It was all in my head.*

She tried to hide her disappointment with a question. "Is it always like that?"

He shook his head. "There was also some kind of turbulence on our way in. The wraith attacks don't usually produce that sort of effect. It took our combined energies to get us here. The others seemed fine. You were the only one who registered the glitch besides us."

"The others..." Her eyes flew wide, and she nearly dropped the water. "Sherry! Mike! Where? Where are—?"

"In the room next door, fast asleep, completely fine," he reassured her.

She looked at the wall he was pointing to, then back to him. It took a few seconds to register. Even then, it didn't make a bit of sense.

"You brought them here?" she asked in shock. "Why? Why would you do that?"

He dropped his gaze. "We were summoned. You have to understand, we cannot ignore a royal summons. It simply isn't done. Ephriam obeyed, and so did I — without thought, purely on instinct."

Brie absorbed his response blankly. "This is going to be a disaster of epic proportions."

He stared at the floor, wringing his hands. "Brianna, I keep trying to preserve your life as it was, as it should be. And now look where we are. Your friends as well. I am so sorry."

She stared at the wall, Sherry's words from earlier ringing in her ears: *"I know you backwards and forwards. And I know when you are hiding something from me."*

She looked at her angel, practically shining with guilt. He was always sorry for things that weren't his fault.

"Don't apologize," she said. "Sherry deserves to know the truth." The pendant rested warm on her chest. "We all do."

She reached for his hand to offer comfort, but he withdrew. It was barely a flinch, but she noticed. His eyes flashed to the open door, and she understood. He stared at her hand, which had dropped to her side. "How is Sherry going to handle the truth?" he asked carefully.

It was a fair question, given the force of her friend's parking lot tirade. "I'm worried," she answered honestly. "She hates anything that isn't completely linear and rational. She doesn't even read her horoscope. The only instrument she'd even tried to learn as a child was the piano because it's literally black and white, left to right. This?" She shot another look at the wall separating them. "This is going to rough her up something awful."

They sat awkwardly for a moment, struck by the mounting ridiculosity of their circumstances, before she chose to reign the conversation back to safer ground. "So, this is your room?"

He glanced around fondly, warming at the sight. "When I was very young. My father wanted to give me a space away from the rest of the court. He built this place to give me somewhere to learn and play as I would have done on Earth, and to house all my human books and hobbies."

"And pets, it seems." She looked out into the hall, where the shadow of the gargantuan Cong was still visible, moving slowly along the opposite wall. He had to be eight feet long and must have weighed as much as a small car. Yet he somehow fit the space with all the presumption of a house cat. "I didn't know tortoises could get that big. Where's he from?"

It felt easier to talk about simple things — pets, books, celestial hideaways that stored one's human interests. Easier than talking about those more troublesome things.

Cameron brightened. "The Galapagos. But you're right. They don't grow this large anymore."

She looked at him quizzically.

"Cong's species went extinct on Earth some time ago. I brought him here, along with a few others, before they were all gone," he explained.

She stared, the glass of water paused halfway to her lips. "You saved an extinct species?"

Of course you did.

"Just a few." He looked bashful.

She glanced suspiciously at the model pterodactyl on the nightstand. "Cameron, please tell me there aren't any actual dinosaurs wandering around this place."

"Of course not." He dropped eye contact and looked out the window, mumbling, "They're on a preserve on the other side of the mountains."

It's going to be another one of those days, isn't it?

He changed the subject. "After last night, my father thought it might be best if the two of you spoke one-on-one before bringing you into a more intimidating scenario. Is that all right with you?" He watched her face closely, searching for any sign that the situation might be too much, that she might be headed for a debilitating giggle fest or emotional breakdown. Maybe both.

Do I have a choice?

That's what she wanted to say. That's what she wanted to scream. She'd been whisked away from her planet and sucked through the space-time continuum. This had happened at the summons of a supernatural monarch and in full violation of the increasingly fraying emotions of her friends.

Oh God, my friends.

Do THEY have a choice?

She looked at him, eyes large and searching. "Do I have—?"

But she never got a chance to finish that question.

Because at that moment, there was a wild scream from the other room.

In a flash, Brie was on her feet, shouldering past Cameron and barreling down the hallway at a speed that nearly defied the boundaries of her physical form.

There was barely time to register the rest of the house — because it was a house, the place where they'd been brought. A sprawling open-air villa with flowers pouring in the windows, plush fabrics strewn across the marble floors, and the sound of water coming from somewhere inside. It was lovely. There was no denying it. It was everything she could have imagined and more.

At the time, it barely registered. Her attention fixed on a door just down the hall.

There was another scream. This one was even louder than before.

"Babe?!" Mike's voice filtered through the doorway. "I need you to put down the fire poker."

There was a reflexive hitch in Brie's step, one that almost sent her spilling forward. Then came a loud *thump*, followed by an ominous scraping sound. Sherry screeched again at a volume that sent an unseen flock of birds spilling from the garden trees.

Oh, no.

Cameron appeared a moment later, having safely stashed the tortoise somewhere it couldn't add to anyone's nervous break-down. He pulled up short just as Mike's soothing reply was interrupted by the sound of glass breaking and stared at the door the way one might regard a wild boar.

"Maybe we should…" He trailed away with uncharacteristic hesitation, searching for the words that came so naturally to those tethered to the mortal coil — those humans who dealt with emotional meltdowns on a more regular basis than absolutely never. After a moment, it came to him. "Maybe we should give her some space."

"I'm not going to CALM DOWN. I want someone to GET ME THE HELL OUT OF HERE!"

There was another crash, followed by a violent swooping sound.

"I can't get a signal, and Siri keeps reciting nursery rhymes!"

Brie froze where she was standing, one hand gripped loosely on the door handle. A part of her was desperate to throw it open. Part of her had wanted nothing more than to show Sherry the terrifying truth ever since those shadowy abominations had incinerated her car on her way to Virginia, and her life had spiraled out of control. But after the spectacle outside of the bar the other night, when she'd drunkenly ripped off her pendant for the briefest of moments, and the hordes of Hell had descended upon her — when Sherry had been there once again to miss the event itself and pick up pieces of the aftermath — since then, she couldn't be so sure. She had seen that look on her best friend's face too many times before. The disbelief. The pity. The complete and utter dismissal that any of this could be true.

She wasn't sure she could face it again.

What if she doesn't believe me?

What if, after all this, she still doesn't believe me?

"Brie," Cameron whispered, catching lightly onto her arm.

There was nothing further. He simply waited until she glanced at him over her shoulder, ready to follow whatever course of action she chose.

She considered for a fleeting moment, then did the harder thing. That was usually the right thing to do.

She opened the door.

"I DON'T BELIEVE YOU!" No sooner had she stepped inside, than Sherry's words flew at her with venom, slicing the air like the crack of a ruthless whip.

Brie flinched instinctively, then lifted her eyes to the tiny brunette standing in the middle of a four-poster bed. The one who was indeed wielding a fire poker like a demented musketeer and had apparently used it to shatter everything in sight.

"Do you hear me, Brianna?!" Sherry cried again, leveling the tip of the dangerous prod at the door. "I don't believe this *CRAZY* story for one *SECOND!* And I *DEMAND* to be taken home!"

This last part seemed to be directed at Mike, as Brie herself could no longer be trusted with such simple instructions. No doubt she would be shoved unceremoniously into the trunk of a car and forcibly returned to Virginia to begin her psychological incarceration as soon as Sherry could manage it.

It was the police officer who'd been charged with getting them both home, though how he was supposed to accomplish this was something of a mystery. As it stood, Mike looked nearly as out of sorts as his girlfriend. The only thing keeping him standing was half a decade's worth of experience working for the Virginia Police Force and twelve generations of fierce Irish pride.

He flashed a bracing look at the door before returning his attention to the bed. Both hands were still raised, like he could somehow magic the poker away.

"Sweetheart, I'm going to get us home. I promise." He inched closer, casting a dark look at Cameron when he attempted to do the same. "I just need to figure out where we are first."

"We're in Elysium," Brie said quietly.

"Was it drugs?!" Sherry interrupted with a shriek, jamming two fingers into her wrist to measure her pulse. "Did those costumed people *DRUG* us?! Is that why we're—?"

"You *know* it wasn't drugs," Brie snapped, feeling like a fire had been lit inside her chest. She took another step inside. For one of the first times since she'd turned sixteen, she didn't have a single problem speaking her truth. "I told you *exactly* who those people are and *exactly* what's happened to me. And given the fact that you've finally seen evidence with your own eyes, and we've all been transported to a celestial realm, I might have thought you'd start believing me. I don't know what else it's going to take, Sherry! I have told you *everything* I can!"

A dangerous silence fell over the room. The men were looking as though there could have been nothing worse than for the women to have started arguing directly. The women only had eyes for each other, staring with unnatural intensity.

A full minute dragged past before Sherry finally made herself speak.

"I was not transported to a celestial realm," she answered with gritted teeth as if each word were a dagger in her mouth. "I was attacked in a parking garage. And the second we get *out* of this mess, Brianna, we're going straight back there so I can show you. I'm going to dismantle these delusions of yours once and for all. Brick by broken brick."

She snapped her fingers, and Mike sprang to attention, throwing a preemptive look at the pair by the door before making a quick sweep of the room. It was hard to tell what he was looking for — evidence of dark rituals, perhaps a time-stamped receipt. When he couldn't find it, he paced instead to the curtained window. His police training took over — doors were too risky, they would need to escape on foot through the grounds.

"Why is it so impossible for you to believe me?" Brie whispered, still looking her best friend directly in the eyes. "After everything we've been through, why is it *so* impossible for you to believe?"

The fire-poker came down, revealing a tear-stained face.

"Because you went through a terrible childhood trauma," Sherry whispered back, wiping a hand across her cheeks. "Because your entire world got ripped apart the day you turned sixteen, and now you're talking about angels, shadow monsters, and celestial realms. Because I *care* about you," she finished in a rasping breath, "*desperately.* And since your mom's not here, I'm going to make sure—"

"Sher?" Mike's soft southern voice sounded from the window.

Sherry pulled in a breath, fighting back her frustration. "Not now, Mike."

"Yeah, it's just… Sher?" His voice was tinged with something else now — something shocked.

The friends tore their attention away from each other and turned to where he was standing by the window — holding back the curtain with the tip of his nightstick and staring through the glass. It took a moment to understand his expression. It took a moment to notice the radiant world outside. A place that went beyond drugs and cults and casual parking lot abductions. A place that could only be described as having been touched by the divine.

There was no denying that sky. Deep turquoise pooled into ruby reds and amethyst purples like mingling watercolors. Veins of gold, pulsing with light, embroidered the whole of the ether in a staggering latticework of energy. It was like a nebula. It was like a coral reef. It was like nothing they'd ever seen before. And hanging within that bizarre, beautiful, gemstone-bright sky, huge against the mountains, two heavenly bodies commanded attention more than any of the rest.

The moon.

And the Earth.

For a single, unending moment, all they could do was stare. Then, Sherry leapt off the bed and dashed into the adjoining bathroom, locking the door behind her.

CHAPTER FIVE

Rolling With It

"You can't stay in there forever."

Brie was sitting with her back against the door, trying every trick in her arsenal to get Sherry to come out of the bathroom, to absolutely no avail. For the first ten minutes, she'd heard nothing but the sounds of hyperventilation and running water. She'd been relieved when it had stopped. Until it was replaced by muffled sobs.

Then, panic had set in, and with it, guilt. Sherry hadn't asked for this any more than she had. And while she might deserve to know the truth, the shock of it was enough to send even those of sound mind and body into a complete tailspin.

Brie had apologized. She'd bargained. She'd shouted.

Now, she was telling jokes.

"Sherry, what's the best thing about Switzerland?" Silence. "Well, the flag's a big plus." She listened for a minute, tapping the back of her head against the door. "How do you make holy water? You boil the hell out of it."

Another silence, even longer than the first.

"I can't believe you didn't laugh at that," she muttered, shifting uncomfortably against the door. "You got me in trouble with that joke in fourth grade. Mr. Lennox threatened to give me detention, because I snorted in the middle of his poetry lesson."

Someone coughed quietly, startling her.

Mike was standing some ways off, looking significantly less fazed than she would have expected. Less fazed but less certain, all at the same time.

"Hey, Mike," she greeted him, feeling awkwardly formal. The two might have eaten their body weight in cheeseburgers together just a few nights before, but a lot had changed since then.

For example, I stranded him and his girlfriend somewhere off-planet.

"Hey, Brie." He motioned to the ground next to her. "May I?"

Surprised, she scooted over a few inches, and he eased onto the floor next to her, his back against the door. They sat together in silence, tapping their feet on the marble floor.

"So, you've abducted a police officer to an alien world," he said without looking at her.

Small talk be damned, I guess.

"Yeah. I'm sorry about that." Her pulse started racing, though she tried to keep her tone as even as his. "How much jail time am I looking at?"

He shook his head and casually raised the fingers on one hand in that particularly southern gesture that means, *don't worry about it.* He shot her a lopsided grin. "Pretty sure we're out of my jurisdiction. You're good."

She looked at him curiously. "Are *you* good?"

He glanced out the window, eyeing that impossible sky like a suspect he was keeping under surveillance. "I'm rolling with it. Maybe this is real. Maybe I'm in a coma. Maybe somebody drugged me with a fancy mushroom. Maybe we're all in the Matrix, and I'm about to learn kung fu. It doesn't change much, does it?"

She blinked in amazement, trying to follow along. "How do you mean?"

"I mean," he drew in a breath, trying to find the right words, "no matter where we are, no matter what this is, it doesn't change what I'm going to do."

"And what's that?"

"Try to be a good guy and take care of this one." He jerked his thumb at the door behind them. "Try to avoid getting impaled with a fire-poker, if that's at all possible." He sighed resignedly. "Which it's probably not."

She felt a catch in her throat. "Mike?"

"Yes'm?"

"I'm really glad you're here."

Mike nodded once, then tipped his head toward Cameron, who was hovering some ways off near the doorway and pretending not to eavesdrop. "You might want to take care of *that* one, Brie," he continued, pointing at her angel. "Not that I approve, per se, and I have my fair share of questions for your gentleman when the time comes, but right now, he's looking more than a little green around the gills."

Mike was right — her angel looked positively stricken. When he caught her looking, he rallied with an obviously fake smile and retreated to his room down the hall.

"He's probably checking on his extinct tortoise," she said.

Mike gave her a blank stare and chose not to engage.

She glanced back at the bathroom door.

"I'll stay. Don't you worry," Mike assured.

She touched his knee. "Thank you."

He took her place as she walked off toward Cameron. The last thing she heard before quietly closing the door behind her was his soft southern drawl. "An Englishman, a Scotsman, and an Irishman walk into a pub…"

♦   ♦   ♦

Cameron was sitting on his bed, head in his hands. Cong was slowly moving toward him. The mischievous glint in his ancient, reptilian eyes made Brie feel sure the plan was to bite her angel's fingers. She came and sat beside him, smiling a little as he attempted to put on a brave face — a face that crumbled into misery the second she shot him a questioning look.

"Your best friend hates me," he lamented.

"She does not hate you—"

"She does. They both do. And they should." He stared out the window in such obvious pain that it tugged at her heart. "Brianna, I have longed to show you my home for what feels like a lifetime. I always imagined…" He sighed. "It doesn't matter now."

She was quiet for a moment, then nudged him. "Why doesn't it matter?"

"Come on—"

"*Why* doesn't it matter?" Instead of waiting for him to answer this time, she squeezed his knee, waiting until he met her eyes. "I would love to see your home."

He brightened ever so slightly. "You would? You don't feel… abducted?"

We should ban that word from the house.

She answered carefully. "Those are two different questions, and I'm going to say. yes."

He nodded. "That's fair."

"But…" She looked down at her torn jeans. One sleeve of her

sweater was unraveling, and her hair was mussed from her all-too-brief sleep. "Is there anywhere I could get cleaned up first? Maybe take a shower? Or a bath?" she added, more out of habit than hope. This might be an idyllic place, but she didn't see how Elysians would require such an amenity.

To her surprise, his face lit up. "I know just the place."

She followed him into the long hallway, pausing to pet Cong, who still sported his expression of silent, open-mouthed laughter. "You're just a big prankster, aren't you, boy?" she asked, stroking his ancient head. Looking over his shell, she noticed a large letter 'E' hanging on the door across from Cameron's room to mirror his letter 'C.'

'E' for Enoch, I suppose. Did his dad live across the hall from him when he was little?

She was about to ask, but Cameron was already some paces away. She hurried to catch up.

♦   ♦   ♦

Since she was three years old, Brianna Weldon could count on a single hand the number of times she and Sherry Walker had disagreed. There had been a squabble about pencil pouches in the second grade, a fiery argument over a beloved boy band a few years after that, and, of course, a slight difference of opinion regarding the events that transpired the day she'd turned sixteen. It was a constant she'd come to rely on — her best friend's opinions could nearly always be counted on to speak for them both. However, on the subject of Elysium, they had reached an unlikely divergence.

I am NEVER leaving this place.

"Everything all right in there?" Cameron called to check on her through a door that looked as though it was made from a solid slab of agate. It was just translucent enough to allow for one to discern vague silhouettes on the other side, without sacrificing any modesty. "Brie?"

He had brought her to a room containing a natural hot spring. The entire structure had been built around it. It bubbled up from the ground and ran through a white stone channel into what looked like a giant marble teacup. This was where she sat, floating, utterly relaxed. The water seemed to cleanse and soothe her intuitively, almost like a massage. In fact, the entire room seemed to have a kind of intuition. When she'd walked in, the scent had been something like eucalyptus. The moment she wished it was something else, she smelled gardenias. Curious, she thought about cinnamon rolls and the room instantly filled with the warm, spicy scent of cinnamon.

There IS a God. And that God definitely built this bathroom.

"Brie is no longer accepting calls at this number," she called back, lifting her toes lazily out of the water. "Please have all my mail forwarded. I live here now."

She heard him chuckle.

"Can I get you some breakfast?" he asked.

God yes.

And possibly lunch as well. And maybe dinner.

Her stomach let out a rumble as if to agree. "That sounds wonderful, thank you."

"Pancakes?" he guessed.

"Cinnamon rolls. *Lots* of cinnamon rolls. And *all* of the coffee."

"Cinnamon...? Of course. Back in a bit!" He left her to her own devices.

She was grateful for the space.

When was the last time I was alone?

A hundred reality-changing revelations ago, probably.

She swirled her hand through the warm water and let her mind drift, reveling in the casual distraction. The ability to space out was a luxury that rivaled even the bath. The last few days had been nothing but an ever-rising sea of adrenaline — one life-or-death situation after another. She'd had no chance to process any of it.

Now, she didn't particularly feel the need.

I'm floating in a giant teacup.

She smiled content as the warm suds lapped against her chin.

Teacup people don't have life-or-death situations. They just have bubbles.

With a sudden burst of curiosity, she wondered if that was actually the case. She sank lower in the water and let it close over her head. She held her breath and counted the seconds. Many seconds. Nothing. She was perfectly fine.

How does that work anyway? No matter how much time I spend here, it's still the same moment. So why does one thing still lead to another? How can there be any cause and effect without time?

I should've paid more attention in physics class. Then, maybe I'd know why I saw my mom on the way here.

As soon as she thought of her mother, the memory flooded back in a tangle of images and emotions: the kitchen, the blue bowl, her singing.

A lump rose in her throat. It was too much. She surfaced and breathed the lovely cinnamon scent in the air. A single hand lifted to her pendant, absentmindedly running the stone side to side along the chain. For so many years, the stone had hung around her neck. It seemed impossible it had ever belonged to anyone else — impossible her mother could have worn the same chain, carried the weight of it, learned its secrets.

Kept those secrets from everyone in her life.

Brie's eyes clouded, and her face went still. It was one of the parts she tried not to think about. All the uncertainty she was feeling, all the fear, the doubt. Had her lovely mother felt those same things herself? Had she suffered in isolation? Resented the weight of it? Had some part of her ever wanted to take it off? Had she ever wanted to walk down the hall and tell her daughter there were angels among us in the world?

And demons?

The pendant went loose in Brie's hand.

Hopefully, it'll all be over soon.

I'll tell the court what happened. They'll figure out what this thing is, and then...

Then, what? What did she want them to do, anyway? Take it away? Put things back to normal? Allow her to return to Virginia, to the life she'd planned?

Yes, she thought determinedly. *Everything will go back to normal once they figure out what's been happening and who is supposed to have this thing, because there's no way it should be me. Simply no way.*

She struggled to believe it, but the truth was, ever since that day in the woods when her pendant had glowed hot for the first time, ever since the day the curtain had been pulled back and she'd seen the supernatural world that existed parallel to her own, she'd been avoiding a thought that seemed increasingly inevitable.

What if there's nothing anyone can do, because everything is already as it should be?

She held the pendant in her palm and stared at it.

What if this is already exactly where it belongs?

What part could I possibly have to play in all this?

CHAPTER SIX

Wonderland

Brie toweled off quickly and slipped into a white robe, sitting on a stool nearby. It was the softest, most indulgent thing that had ever touched her skin. No sooner had she wondered where she might find some slippers, than a pair appeared on a wooden bench. They were exactly her size. She looked around suspiciously.

I don't suppose you have a hairdryer lying around? Or a brush?

Nothing appeared. She grabbed another towel to sweep up her hair, but when she gathered a handful of her chocolate curls, she realized it had already dried. She looked in the mirror in surprise. Her hair was perfectly set and styled.

"That's handy," she murmured, glancing around. If the room was doing her favors, it seemed only polite to show some manners. She awkwardly addressed the ceiling. "Thank you. Any chance for a—" Before she could finish, a cup of herbal tea appeared on the counter before her. While it wasn't the sugar-laden, hyper-caffeinated latte she'd been about to request, it did smell delicious.

"I suppose it's good for my blood pressure, too?"

The room was not forthcoming with any details.

She picked up the tea and wandered toward a second door in the back of the room. It opened onto a veranda covered in vines laden with small, star-shaped flowers. The moment she stepped outside, she gasped and very nearly dropped her china cup.

She wasn't sure what she'd expected.

But *this*?

This defied even her wildest imaginings.

It was a glorious mess.

Beneath that strange, turquoise sky laced with veins of light, someone had recreated all the different climate zones of Earth, and placed them right next to each other like pieces of a child's jigsaw puzzle. A veritable menagerie of animals lounged in every giant puzzle piece. A small herd of creatures that appeared to be half-zebra, half-horse scampered through African grasslands next to a herd of black rhinoceroses and dark elephants larger than any she'd ever seen. A family of polar bears lounged on an iceberg in a small lake beneath a layer of snow-filled clouds that hovered exclusively over their section like they were enclosed by invisible walls. Not far away, a flock of tropical birds with shock-pink beaks nested in the roots of a mangrove tree on the opposite shore.

Some efforts had been made to separate the beasts from one another, rickety fences that looked as though a couple of nine-year-olds had cobbled them together with sticks, though it seemed that there wasn't any need. As she watched, a fluffy little animal that looked like a baby goat bounded up to a saber-toothed tiger. Her breath caught in her throat, already preparing for the inevitable, but the enormous hunting cat merely licked the little beast's forehead and nudged it back to its pasture, one that was filled with blue-green grasses and alien-looking flowers. It let out a contented bleat, joined its mother, and started to graze.

That's when she saw it. Just beyond the goat's pastures, a vision of grace, glowing cream and gold, moving fluidly through the meadow like something out of a dream.

Sweet leaping Jesus.

The creature turned and stared straight at her like it could sense her thoughts. It tossed its proud, beautiful head in the golden light. It even pranced around a little, looking like the cover of every childhood notebook and secret dream journal she'd never confess to actually owning.

With a single look, she promptly turned into the emotional equivalent of a six-year-old.

That, Brianna Weldon, is a freaking unicorn.

As she watched, breathless, the lovely creature was joined by another, then another. It wasn't long before an entire herd had gathered, tossing their bright manes and nickering beneath the trees.

Within the space of an instant, her purpose in life shrank to a solitary goal:

I've gotta get down there.

She rushed back into the bathroom, half-expecting to find an equestrian helmet, only to discover her own clothes and shoes, fresh and clean, waiting for her on a footstool. They'd been mended to look as new as the day she'd purchased them.

"Thank you, room!" she whispered excitedly.

She dressed faster than ever before, determined to reach the exquisite creatures before they somehow vanished, and dashed full-tilt out of the room.

Where she crashed straight into a perfect stranger.

And "perfect stranger" had perhaps never been such an apt description.

As she recovered her balance and exclaimed, "Excuse me!" his radiance was already beginning to register. He was ivory-skinned with hair black as jet, dressed in what looked like a simple silk kimono. He did not try to help her as she righted herself. He merely took a step back.

In retrospect, she should have known better. She'd received signs from the Universe to never make such an attempt again — but in the moment, after stopping mere inches short of tackling the man like a renegade linebacker, it seemed the only appropriate thing to do.

She tried to curtsey.

The man watched her, his face unreadable. After a few agonizing seconds, he inclined his head with a curt nod. "Ephriam told me you might do something like that."

Her cheeks turned scarlet. She wondered if the magical room she'd just left would be obliging enough to let her melt into the floor if she wished hard enough.

He stepped closer, bowed slightly, and took her hand, bringing it to his forehead in a gesture of respect she'd not seen before. "I am Cassius, Protector of the Sovereign and Lord Confidant to the King. On behalf of his Majesty, I welcome you to Elysium, Brianna Weldon." He released her hand and took another step back.

"Thank you, your... your highness."

He raised a judgmental eyebrow.

Brianna Weldon, you absolute walnut.

Her cheeks were still burning. That was unlikely to stop. Somewhere in her heart, a warning panged. The way the man considered her carefully, the way his eyes ran over the whole of her in quick, almost scientific examination before resting on her pendant. It wasn't just his disconcerting perfection. His whole demeanor raised the hairs on the back of her neck.

Be careful.

"It's an honor to be granted safe haven in your realm," she continued, placing the faintest emphasis on the word *safe*. "I understand this is a privilege afforded to very few."

Cassius nodded solemnly. "The secret of our existence is one of the core tenets of Elysium. It is the foundation upon which our society operates in your world."

She hesitated. Later, she wouldn't be able to tell Cameron where she got the nerve. But she looked at him without blinking and asked, "Do you not consider it to be your world, as well?"

If Cassius was surprised, he didn't show it. And he had to be surprised. How many eons had the man been alive? How many people had ever asked him the question? It didn't seem to matter. He merely regarded her with that focused, impassive stare. "I am searching for the prince, the one you call Cameron. Do you know where he is?"

The prince?

The word managed to make an impression even sandwiched between a celestial hijacking, a magical bathroom, and a meadow full of extinct ponies. She had known his father was some great authority. She had known there were countless souls under his care. And yet, she'd never thought about it in precisely those terms.

He asked you a question, Brie. Where's the prince?

"He left to go get cinnamon rolls."

There was an unbearable silence. "I see," Cassius finally answered. "And where, may I ask, are you off to in such a hurry?"

Don't let him intimidate you.

Say something smart. Don't say anything childish or immature.

"I want to go see the unicorns."

Brianna Weldon, you are the reason the gene pool needs a lifeguard.

For the briefest of moments, he looked at her in undisguised amusement, before that all-encompassing, ineffable calm enveloped him once more. "The pasture," he extended an arm and pointed to a path in the garden, "is just beyond the Salix tree. It is in full flower — you are unlikely to miss it." He considered her a moment. "The King wishes to speak with you later, Ms. Weldon." He looked again at her pendant before meeting her bracing gaze. "I suspect you have much to discuss."

At that moment, Cameron walked into the hallway carrying a latte and a fistful of cinnamon sticks. He examined them curiously and didn't notice Cassius as he called out, "These are the most tightly rolled ones I could find, so I hope that's what you... wanted." He looked up and registered the awkward scene.

Like flipping a switch, Cassius's posture straightened, and his tone became pointed and brusque. "I came to tell you that a meeting of the Small Council will convene in the Great Hall once all parties have arrived. In the meantime, Elysium will extend to the humans every hospitality we have to offer. *Your* case," his normally restrained face colored with a flush of gloating, "will be considered immediately after we've dealt with the mortals. Ms. Weldon. *Cameron.*" He bowed to each of them in turn and walked back the way he'd come with a graceful, quick gait. He seemed to glide over the marble floors, fleet as a shadow.

Cameron looked rooted to the spot, his face a mask of fear for a moment before it pivoted to anger. "I see you've met our Minister of Charisma and Positive Feelings," he said with false levity and a touch of sarcasm, handing over the latte and his interpretation of cinnamon rolls. "What did Cassius have to say?"

"He really didn't say anything," she answered, eyeing him warily. She pocketed the cinnamon, vowing never to tell him, and took a grateful sip of her latte. She waited a moment to see if Cameron intended to fill her in on whatever context had gone over her head during the exchange to leave him so spooked. When he didn't say anything, she moved on. "He *did* give me directions to the unicorn pasture." She grabbed his shirt with her free hand and pulled him toward her. "Which exists," she continued in a childlike whisper, eyes wide and shining. "Which actually, *actually* exists. *Cameron.*" She shot him a look halfway between delight and exasperation, grinning ear to ear. "How could you not tell me about the unicorns?"

He regarded her with a touch of surprise before lifting his shoulder in a shrug. "I suppose it never really came up."

It never came up.

She pulled in a breath and let it out slowly. "Cameron," she began, striving for patience, "the next time you ask a girl to come see your celestial parallel reality? Lead with the unicorns."

This is a fairytale. An absolute fairytale.

Brie and Cameron walked toward the meadow where she'd seen the mythical creatures, past fields of shimmering flowers that seemed to chime in the wind and animals that hadn't walked the face of the Earth for centuries. Her head swiveled this way and that, so overwhelmed with the surreal novelty, she couldn't decide where to look. She reached out a finger to touch a chiming flower and exclaimed, "Oh!" as it curled a tendril around her finger and squeezed gently before letting go and resuming its lovely melody in the breeze.

What in the name of Alice in Wonderland is happening to my life?

Somewhere nearby, she could hear the sound of waves crashing and saw the play of light reflecting from water up the sides of marble towers some ways away. As they rounded a corner, she saw that these were part of a larger structure that rose gently, in harmony with the landscape, out of the gardens toward the blue-green skies. Despite the troubling circumstance in which she now found herself, her breath caught at the beauty of the palace as the gorgeous edifice revealed itself with every step they took, like a wave swelling before its crest.

It lacked any of the imposing brutalism of Earthly castles. Nothing about it was designed to show off its strength, though she suspected it was more impenetrable than the pyramids of Giza. It sported no overall symmetry, no straight lines that jarred it out of kinship with nature. It merely swept gently upwards, like a continuation of the ocean waves on one side, the hills on the other, as though sea foam had transformed into marble mid-swell and decided to remain so, stacking upon itself until nature formed the structure.

A few steps later, the path curved again, and the sea itself was revealed, eliciting another wonderstruck gasp. Whether it was the water itself or the reflection of that impossible sky, she could not say — but it was the color of the finest, richest wine. Its burgundy waves rose and surged beneath a lavender foam that frothed across the surface like frosting.

She breathed deeply, letting the delicious sea-foam-scented breeze wash over her. "Your home," she murmured, "is more beautiful than I ever could have imagined."

He looked at her with quiet delight. "I've wished to show you this place for longer than you know."

As they walked on, he started pointing out things she would never have seen if she didn't know where to look. An insect that looked like a tiny violin pollinating a flower. The way a seed pod would open if you pressed just below the tip, spilling flying, feather-light seeds into the breeze like a neon blue dandelion. A group of sea mink playing in a saltwater pool. A vicious-looking creature approached them, startling her, but Cameron smiled and stroked its face playfully before pulling a treat out of his pocket to feed it from his hand. A Tasmanian tiger, he said. And here was the tree fort he'd built as a child. Here, the place he'd learned to fly a kite.

Little orbs of light, smaller than the baseball-sized Elysians she'd almost come to think of as normal, drifted through the sky, clung to tree branches in clusters, and shone amidst the tall grasses. Their golden lights flickered and pulsed like fireflies in July.

"What are they?" she breathed.

"Not what — *who*."

She turned to him, fascinated, questions dancing in her eyes.

"They're free spirits — souls that cling to no particular realm. No longer attached to Earth nor condemned to Hell, their life force becomes one with the power of Elysium. Some souls belong to Heaven, and we ferry those onward. These," he gestured at the glowing lights, "remain here."

She turned to him, startled. "They were people?"

"They still are," he said softly. "People are so much more than their bodies. The most significant part of a person is their soul."

She stared again at the enchanting world before her and shivered.

"Are you cold?" he asked, immediately starting to take off his sweater.

"No. It's just… they're like ghosts."

He cocked his head. "I suppose, in a way, they are. Every one of them had a life on Earth. Things they cared about. People who loved them. Who knows? Maybe you even crossed paths."

She looked at him. "Must have been strange for you, growing up surrounded by the dead."

The word jarred him, and his handsome face clouded with the faintest frown. "Nothing here is dead, Brianna. It is all quite the opposite."

She nodded slowly, taking this in.

He hesitated. "Although, in a way, you aren't too far off from the truth."

She looked up, confused.

"My father has never moved past my mother's death," he said softly, watching the butterflies drift over the trees. "This place has always been a shrine to her memory. I have long desired to show you my home, but part of me never wanted you to come here." Without seeming to think about it, he continued down the path of blue-green grass. "For a long time, the memory of my mother has felt more alive to me than anything else here."

That makes sense.

She nodded in silence, trailing her fingers over the velvety meadow. "That's exactly what it was like at my dad's house."

A shrine, he'd called it, yet he'd managed to find some life in it. Her father's house was more like a tomb — a frozen snapshot. Her stomach lurched with a sudden wave of nerves as she lifted her eyes to the lovely, blue planet in the distant sky, realizing all at once that she'd never been so far away from her home. Or from her dad.

Cameron caught her gaze, bringing her back with a gentle smile.

"I know," he said simply.

Like it was simple. Like it could be soothed with a smile.

Perhaps it could. Perhaps it merely required a shared perspective: two motherless children struggling to keep themselves afloat.

We have a lot more in common than I originally thought.

She drifted alongside him, suddenly achingly aware of how close their hands were to touching. He seemed painfully aware of this himself, and as she watched, his hand flexed almost involuntarily, brushing his fingers against hers. Her eyes flashed to his face, and he offered her the faintest, most hopeful smile. His little finger instinctively caught around hers for only a moment before he jerked away.

Her heart thrummed in her chest as they walked on.

How can anything that feels this right be forbidden?

Don't think about it now. Just be here, in this moment. With him.

They wandered a bit farther, not really saying much, not really needing to. Not doing anything besides pointing with occasional smiles as some new wonder sprang into their path. A massive deer with spiraling horns. A golden frog, bright as the sun itself. He picked her a clutch of flowers. Whenever they rustled in her hand or with the breeze, they made a faint musical sound. She buried her nose in their hyacinth scent, thoughtful. "It must have been lonely," she said. "To be here all by yourself, all the time."

His steps faltered for a moment and she saw a muscle flex in his jaw, a ripple of tension in his arms. "I wasn't alone," he finally answered. "Not always."

For a moment, it seemed like he might keep going. It certainly seemed that there was a part of him that wanted to. But at the last possible second, he changed his mind.

"We're here," he said instead.

They stopped on a hill, slightly elevated from the pasture lands themselves and topped by a single tree. It must have been centuries old and looked something like a willow but more ancient and wilder. White blossoms trailed down its brushstroke branches like tiny natural fireworks, and the scent radiating from these flowers was heavenly. They stood quietly, hair ruffled by the wind.

She closed her eyes and basked in the light that seemed to reflect from every part of the sky. When she opened them again, they were standing before her — a herd of cream-colored creatures that could easily have been mistaken for giant horses were it not for the golden horns emanating from their foreheads. They grazed on the blue-green grass, unconcerned with the proximity of the visitors, glancing over only occasionally before returning to their meal.

She sucked in a breath, every muscle going utterly still. "They're magnificent."

He watched them with a touch of sadness. "At one-point, giant herds roamed the Earth. But their horns were prized as treasure, and men, eager to scam the ill and the desperate, claimed their blood could cure the sick. They were hunted nearly to extinction, their heads sold in the streets."

She turned back to the herd, shocked.

Who could ever kill such a glorious animal? Who in their right mind could ever look at those sunlit miracles and think, "I'm going to cut off their lovely heads?"

"Nowadays, the herd has developed a finely tuned sense of intentions," he continued. "They will only tolerate the presence of those who are pure of heart." He caught her eye with a soft smile. "I'm not at all surprised they've taken to you. They seem to like your presence."

"And yours," she added.

Never had she felt so close to him. He angled toward her, bending his face slowly to hers, close enough that she could see every ring of blue in his enchanting eyes. Then, all at once, those eyes lifted over her shoulder, and he pulled swiftly away.

"We should get back to the others," he said in a strange, flat voice. "See if Sherry has decided to drop the barricades yet."

"Oh. Okay." She nodded quickly, taking a second to switch gears. Her head was still spinning when they turned and headed back the way they'd come. Only then did she see them.

Two men were standing on the garden wall beside the castle. Having only met him once, there was no mistaking the first as Cassius, while the other had a slightly more regal bearing. And though she'd only been half-conscious the last time they'd been in proximity to one another, she knew in an instant who it must be.

King Enoch. Cameron's father.

The king and his advisor watched as the young couple hurried through the grass, leaving the garden and everything in it behind.

They kept watching until they vanished completely from sight.

CHAPTER SEVEN

By the Light of the Moon

Cameron's mood had noticeably changed as they swept back down the path to his childhood home. Brie kept trying to muster up the courage to ask him what was wrong, but every time she caught his eye, she lost her nerve.

Be honest. Do you even want to know?

She found she wasn't sure.

They were still walking in awkward silence when he suddenly took her hand and pulled her in a different direction, off the paved walkway and onto a rougher, gravel path that wound along with no obvious direction.

"Cameron?" she asked. "Where are we going?"

He pulled her onward, along the trail, around a sharp turn that abruptly widened into a small clearing just big enough for two, surrounded by spearing cypress trees — a serene sanctuary hidden from view.

"Cameron, what in the world?"

He turned to her, breathless and urgent. "Brie, there's something I need to talk to you about, but I can't do it here. Will you trust me?"

Will I trust you?

She bit lightly on her bottom lip.

"I'll get us back before anyone even knows we've left," he continued.

"Wait a minute, where are we—?"

"Brie," He'd never cut her off like that before. It made her stop short and meet his wide, imploring eyes. "Please. Just… Please."

She shot a look back at the villa, then nodded.

He pulled in a relieved breath. "Hold on tight."

She felt supernatural forces swoop down and carry them away a moment later.

♦   ♦   ♦

I've STOPPED trusting you!

As the cosmic winds ripped at her hair, Brie clung to her guardian angel's hand with a grip that could tear through plywood, oblivious to the bouquet of heavenly flowers shredding to pieces beneath her fingers. Her eyes were squeezed so tight, bracing against the temporal whiplash, she didn't realize they'd arrived at their destination until he gently loosened his hold and patted her arms up and down as though checking to make sure she was still intact.

"Brianna?" he said hesitantly. "You can open your eyes."

She shook her head. "Not until it's stopped."

"But we *have* stopped."

My stomach hasn't.

She might as well have spoken the words out loud. With a smile she'd never see, Cameron pressed his hands gently to the sides of her neck. A feeling of warmth and safety flowed through her, vanishing the dizziness and steadying her feet.

Slowly, she opened her eyes and blinked.

She blinked again.

She was looking at Earth, but not from a vantage point she'd ever had before. She gasped, unable to form words. She looked down at the ground beneath her feet — it was a powdery, white-grey substance, like something between sand and ash, peppered here and there with stones. Her head snapped up as a new reality settled slowly into place.

"This isn't Elysium," she began.

Cameron shook his head.

"Are we on...?" She couldn't say it. "Is this...?" She really couldn't say it. But she absolutely *had* to say it, however impossible it might be. *"Did you take me to the moon?"*

There was the slightest of pauses before Cameron nodded, a self-satisfied smile playing at the corner of his lips.

"The moon," she said again, now unable to stop saying it. She dug her shoes into the silvery powder and looked up to stare in wonder at the Earth's rise. Her mind was flying too fast to process her thoughts. Legitimate questions tangled with the nonsensical. "How are we breathing? How did we *get* here? Won't NASA be mad?"

Can I write my name?

He chuckled, wiping a smear of sparkling dust from her cheek. "NASA doesn't own the moon. I'm sure they'd be more stunned than angry if they could see us, but don't worry. We're cloaked from all humans and their technologies. And we're breathing because I brought a pocket of atmosphere with us." He stood beside her, following her line of sight back to the blue planet. "This is the farthest I can travel, using the Elysian energy, because this is the farthest human souls have traveled. I come here sometimes to think — to find some peace."

He goes to the moon to think.

She stood quietly, utterly shocked, taking in the view of Earth.

It's so much smaller than I thought. So fragile and alone. So far from everything else.

So surrounded by darkness.

He came to stand beside her and deliberately took her hand. She turned to him, surprised as he took it a step further, bringing her fingers to his mouth and kissing them tenderly. "How are you doing?" he asked.

On a different day, she might have imagined he was referring to their little game of interplanetary leapfrog, but somehow, she knew this was about something else.

"We haven't had any chance to talk about it, but I've never seen anyone go through what you've been through," he continued softly, struggling to say the words. "You could have died."

She shifted toward him. Her other hand reached up and touched his neck, where the angry bruise had blossomed when Mammon dragged him up the hospital wall.

"*We* could have died," she corrected.

He gathered her into his arms. "I still don't understand how we didn't," he said huskily. He kissed the top of her head and squeezed her gently. "I don't understand so many things that have happened, but on a single point, I remain perfectly clear: You are a miracle."

She looked up at him, framed against the starry sky.

There were a hundred different ways she might have answered. A great many of them involved her replaying the events of the last forty-eight hours, then becoming the first person in history to faint on the moon. Still, something different struck her — a silent admission he'd made without thinking, waves of moonlit hair spilling into his eyes.

In such a magical world as his, why does he feel the need to escape?

And not just escape — to travel as far as possible away from his home?

"Cameron, what did you want to tell me?" she asked, searching his face for some clue.

It was a tangle of emotions. He kept parting his lips as if to answer before snapping his mouth shut like he couldn't find the words, let alone string them all together. When he finally spoke, it was in broken fragments. "At the hospital, in the parking lot. Right before Ephriam got there. Brianna, when we... When I..."

"When you kissed me?" she offered, taking pity on him. It was like watching a man drown on dry land.

"Yes." He tightened his arms around her. "And before that. What you said. You'd just gone through an unspeakable trauma. It would be natural if you... if you felt like you wanted to..." He frowned, frustrated with himself, before beginning again with a look of supreme concentration. "I have been with many humans during their darkest moments. Sometimes, when in mortal danger, there's a tendency to blurt things out. Emotional things. Things they haven't thought through. Things they don't necessarily mean." He searched her face. "Things they never would have said if they knew they'd have to live with the consequences of saying them aloud."

She drew back from him, surprised. "Is this about what I said in the elevator?"

"Maybe," he answered. "I mean, yes."

The memory flooded back to her. They'd left Mammon crawling after her own disembodied head and were racing to find Rashida, and she'd told him. "When I told you I'm halfway in love with you?"

He looked so vulnerable. "You needn't feel obligated to stand by anything you said in the heat of the—"

"Did *you* mean it?" she interrupted.

He blanked. "Did I mean what?"

"What *you* said. When you kissed me," she began, her voice wavering slightly as she repeated the words that had danced in her mind countless times since that moment, questioning their reality. "You said you should have done it a long time ago. That you should have—"

"That I should have done it every day since," he finished softly, his gaze locking onto hers with unwavering sincerity. "I meant it, Brianna. I mean it."

"I meant it, too," she replied, the words echoing in space. "I mean it."

The silence between them felt like a promise — an honesty that transcended mere words.

"Oh." His face went completely blank, then flamed alive with an excitement that he made a visible effort to contain. He nodded. "Okay. Yes. That's good. That's very good." He continued nodding as he pulled her back into his arms. She pressed against his heartbeat with a hidden smile. After a moment, he asked, "Only halfway?"

She tilted her face up to him with a teasing look. "Always good to leave room for a little improvement, don't you think?"

He looked down with hungry eyes. "I never leave anything half done."

Without another word, he pulled her into a tight embrace and launched them both into the starlit sky. She gasped and clutched his arms tight, the new sensation of weightlessness leaving her dizzy. Her hair floated around them like they were underwater. He traced his fingers up the side of her neck as their hips pressed together. Her breath caught. She looked into his eyes, those ocean-blue eyes, now hot with desire. She touched her fingertip to his mouth, grazing his bottom lip. He moved closer till their breath mingled, sweet and ragged. He took a fistful of her silken hair, gently tilted her face to his, and drank in the sight of her, in hunger, in awe. The tension braided between them, thick and unbearable. Just a second before it became too much, he drew her in for a breathless kiss — knotting his fingers in her hair, pressing his lips to hers as the stars blurred to a shimmer around them, and they floated gently back to the moon.

She rested her head against his chest, savoring the moment as the heavens stopped spinning. He was in a similar state, holding her quietly, trying to press every moment like a seal into his mind.

Together, they watched their world turn.

It was the quiet that surprised her. In her entire life, Brie had never experienced such a profound lack of sound. She realized now how she'd always taken it for granted. The birds, the cars, the clocks, the hum of telephone wires, the wind, the water. Within the confines of that lovely planet's atmosphere, there wasn't a place in the world you could go to escape the constant cacophony of sounds. But up here? Up here, things were different.

The only sounds for hundreds of thousands of miles were coming from them.

His heartbeat. Her heartbeat. And the sound of their breathing.

He's right. I can't imagine a better place to think.

"I could stay here a long time," she said softly.

He pressed another kiss to the top of her head. "We don't need to hurry."

She suddenly remembered. "That's right, we don't." She pulled away and looked at him with narrowed eyes. "We don't, because I suspect it isn't much trouble for you to control the moment we choose to arrive. Or the moment we choose to come back." She frowned. "You let me believe there was no way of knowing how much time would pass when we went to Elysium."

It was one of the main reasons she'd avoided leaving when he first broached the subject. Some abstract fear that she'd be gone for the space of a leisurely dinner and return only to find all her friends had white in their hair.

He looked more guilty than confused. "In fairness, I never explicitly said there was no way of knowing."

An evasion, if ever I heard one.

She gave him a stern look. "*Cameron.*"

He sighed. "For one thing, like I told you in the garden, I didn't want you to go. I thought *you* wanted to go. There were many reasons. I thought you wanted answers. I also thought it might be safer for you. My father wanted to meet you." He shook his head. "But I had no desire to uproot you from your entire life, your whole world. I still don't. And as for me?" He pulled slightly away from her. "For my part, if I can help it, I rarely return for longer than it takes to guide a soul to the next realm. I haven't for a long time."

She absorbed this silently.

We aren't just here to catch our breath or find some privacy. He's stalling. He doesn't want to go back. And it's beyond a dislike. It's more like…fear.

He started pacing some feet away.

"But it's more than that, isn't it?" she prompted, trying to read the lines of worry on his face, trying to figure out what piece she'd missed.

He looked for all the world like he was standing on the edge of a cliff. For the second time that day, it looked like there was something he was on the verge of telling her. He pivoted just as quickly, shoving whatever it was back in its place.

"First, let's take care of you," he answered briskly like they were discussing the day's errands. Like they weren't standing on the surface of the moon. "You haven't had breakfast yet. You didn't even touch your cinnamon rolls. Here, let's sit down."

She looked around as if they might stumble upon a handy bench. *One that would baffle scientists for decades to come.*

"Sure," she answered lightly, trying to hide her amusement. "Let me know if you spot any comfortable rock formations." She gestured out over the silvery plain. "There's supposed to be a Sea of Tranquility around here somewhere. That sounds like a good place to eat a scone."

Of course, her angel was a stranger to teasing. He'd already started making plans. She turned back a moment later to find him placing a pitcher of water onto a familiar-looking coffee table, one that was sitting right next to a familiar-looking sofa. He fluffed a pillow and gestured her over.

She didn't move. "Is that my couch?"

He frowned. "Would you prefer a different one?"

Just roll with it.

"No, it's fine." Feeling utterly resigned to the absurdity of the situation, she sat as he poured her some water. "Any chance for a coffee?"

"Hydrate first."

He's as withholding as my celestial bathroom.

She accepted the glass with a sulk. "You'd think that battling the forces of Hell before sunrise would entitle one to as many lattes as one pleased, no questions asked."

He unsuccessfully tried to stifle a chuckle.

Much as she hated to admit it, he was right. She badly needed to hydrate. Once she started sipping, she couldn't stop and soon drained the glass without stopping for a breath. When she set down the empty glass, a latte was waiting for her on the coffee table, along with orange juice, a platter piled high with chocolate croissants, and a bowl of gummy worms. She looked up at him, beaming. "Sugar worms? For breakfast?"

"You've earned it."

She took the latte in both hands and gratefully inhaled the sweet scent of caffeine. This was perhaps the strangest thing to happen so far — a sudden familiarity amidst an environment so foreign.

He waited for her to start sipping before he carefully began to speak. "You met Cassius today."

She gulped swiftly, nodding. "Your Minister of Charisma and Good Feelings."

He laughed, but it sounded hollow. "The very same. You may have noticed a kind of coolness between us."

Brie decided fun was the order of the day. "Why, whatever do you mean? He was so warm and welcoming, and I figured you two were best friends."

He smiled, realizing this must be a joke, before continuing. "Brianna, the Council comprises powerful individuals with strong opinions and a fierce desire to protect Elysium. What I have done in my efforts to protect you is strictly forbidden by the laws of my people. When I went to Elysium a few days ago to report all this, I didn't know what they would do when I told them the extent of my disobedience."

Disobedience.

The word struck between them like the ringing of a bell. She remembered how worried he'd been before leaving to tell his father about her situation — *their* situation — and how worried she'd been that he'd get in trouble for protecting her.

"But, didn't it all turn out okay?" she asked. "Ephriam kept checking in and giving reports. You said your father was disappointed, but it was going to be all right. You said you weren't sorry," she added with a hint of desperation. She remembered how her heart leapt when he'd said so.

"I'm not." His face hardened with resolve. "Brianna, I will never be sorry for a single moment I get to spend with you, but I'm afraid the full consequences of my actions have yet to play out." He pointed at the chocolate croissants. "Do you remember what I told you the first time I tried one of these?"

She blanched. She did remember. She remembered what she was wearing and how the bakery smelled. The look on his face when he'd told her:

'I don't think you understand the forces that stand against it. The same forces that could separate the two of us in an instant. They could make me ache for you forever... and make you completely forget about me.'

She sucked in a breath. "You said they could make me forget you."

He nodded slowly, willing her to understand.

"But surely, they've decided *not* to," she insisted like he was the one who needed convincing, "or else they wouldn't have let you come back." Her mouth went dry, and her voice came out in a whisper. "I would never have seen you again. Or if I had, I wouldn't have known it was you." The thought of it gripped her stomach like a fist of ice. "But they *must* have decided not to," she repeated firmly. "And anyway, your father is the King. That must count for something."

And you're the prince. Though I've never once heard you talk about it.

His face darkened, and he took her hand. "My father might be the King, but that doesn't always mean I have a powerful ally. He needs to think about the safety of the realm before he considers what I want. Even if he loves me." He set his jaw, and the words took on a practiced tone like they were something he'd heard before — many, many times.

She traced the inside of his wrist with her thumb. "That must have been a complicated family dynamic, growing up just the two of you."

She'd meant it as a comfort, but if anything, it seemed to make things worse. He clenched his teeth and didn't answer, staring at the blazing curve between the Earth and the Sun.

"I'm sorry, did I say something wrong?" she stammered, confused.

"Of course not," he assured. "You're right. Things have always been complicated between us, but that isn't the concern right now." He lifted the latte again, pressing it reflexively into her hand.

Does he get me coffee whenever we need to have a difficult conversation?

…Smart.

He went on. "My father's word is law in Elysium, but this isn't a family matter anymore. This isn't something he can deal with on his own. A member of the Seven is no trifling concern and the fact that we don't even know what she was doing there? Every being who wields power and influence in the whole kingdom will be summoned. With everything that's happened since my last report, the matter will be debated among the Council once again. The *entire* matter," he clarified. He looked lost for a moment. "You and I, Brianna. It is not permitted."

Despite the radiant sunrise, her blood went utterly cold.

How is this real? How is it possible that my life can be litigated by people I've never even met?

He continued. "I meant what I said— if I'm to be damned for this, I want to deserve it. I've watched over you for years, wishing we could speak openly with one another. We've only been able to do so for a week, and no matter what happens, I wouldn't trade this week for anything. I don't want any regrets. So now," he glanced at the Earth, "if ever the worst should happen, if you should ever forget me, at least I'll have brought you here."

She stared at him in shock, feeling like the air was too thin to breathe.

That's why he brought me here? That's the point of all this?

"You don't think your father would actually try to take my memory of you away from me?" Her mind balked at the thought of it, angry that such a thing was even possible.

He hesitated. "I'm worried that's actually what's best for you."

It certainly wasn't the answer she was expecting. And it was so sad and softly-spoken, it tore at her heart. In hindsight, she probably should have known. When had the beautiful man in front of her ever done a single thing for himself?

She considered this only a fraction of a moment before positioning herself in diametric opposition to the premise. "In case you hadn't noticed, I am not in the habit of allowing others to decide what's best for me, Cameron." She lifted her chin defiantly.

A wry smile curled at the corner of his lips. "I have noticed that, actually."

"Besides," she went on, trying to convince both him and herself, "you told me that Elysians have a strict noninterference policy with humans, right?"

"Right."

"I'd say that taking memories away interferes quite a lot, don't you?" The memory of a freshly brainwashed Mike waving vacantly in her rearview mirror as they drove to Virginia pricked her conscience, and she moved on quickly. "*And* you did tell your father all about this — later than he would have liked, but you *told* him, and he gave you permission to come back, protect me, and try to figure out what's been going on, right?"

He drew in a deep breath and let it out slowly. "Right."

"Okay, then. I'd say our odds are, if not great, at least well within these new parameters of *what's possible* that we seem to have established."

Those parameters being slightly skewed, given that we're sitting on my sofa, on the moon.

"Besides," she rallied herself and threw him a smile that looked considerably braver than she felt, "do you remember what happened to the last creature that tried to get between us?"

At that point, there was a good chance he might have been working up to a smile himself, but at her question, his face froze. "Do *you* remember?" he asked.

The images flooded unbidden through her mind. There was a flash of blinding white, a horned woman, a scream with the power of a supernova.

She determinedly shook her head. "Nope. Not at all."

CHAPTER EIGHT

The Seas of Time

Brie and Cameron settled into a comfortable silence, fingers laced gently together, her head resting in the soft curve of his arm, watching the Earth rise over that strange, greyscale horizon. They could have lingered for a small eternity, but she jolted suddenly upward with a surprisingly normal thought. "Cameron, is this our first date?"

He startled a bit, glancing down at her. It was the first time either of them had spoken in a long time, and whatever questions he'd been expecting, that was nowhere on the list.

A date. Can angels date?

"Do you want it to be?" he finally asked.

She considered this a moment. They'd been out to breakfasts before. They'd been hanging out together all week — sharing meals, sharing supernatural battles, sharing beds, even if it was just to sleep. But this felt different. She looked around and grinned. "I mean, it's probably the best first date in the history of humankind. It seems a waste not to lay claim to it. Bit light on chocolate and flowers, but the location makes up for a lot."

It makes me wonder where our second date could be.

Before she could even finish gesturing at the lunar horizon, he'd twisted his fingers in the air, conjuring a massive bouquet of freesias, roses, and peonies. In the delicate atmosphere, their intoxicating fragrance filled the air. Beneath these was a plate piled high with chocolate truffles.

She took the bouquet with a laugh and inhaled its sweet scent. "Now we're talking."

He picked up a truffle and offered it to her. She felt abruptly shy. Sure, they'd kissed and pretended to be a couple for one magnificent mess of a double date, and they'd slept next to one another, but again — this was different.

Because he kissed me. Because he admitted, he'd always wanted to.

Since that moment, every little act of intimacy was new and untested. Simply holding hands made her heart beat a samba rhythm. And he'd never fed her before. She allowed him to bring the confection closer and delicately took it between her lips. They locked eyes for a moment, and she was acutely aware of how intensely she longed to bring his lips to her own again when a glorious flavor melted over her tongue, and all self-consciousness was suddenly forgotten. "Holy Moses, Cameron!" She covered her mouth with her hand and looked at him in delight, speaking around a mouthful of chocolate. "Where did you get these?!"

"Scotland," he beamed, proudly. "Burnett's Highland Chocolatier. After you introduced me to this most marvelous of human confections, I did a bit of research. These are now my favorites. Although," he amended, "the Mayans do a wonderful job, and there's a healthy argument to be made for the original."

"We can try Mayan chocolate? The *original?*" Her mouth watered. Her eyes were dancing.

He hesitated, frowning. "That may not be a good idea."

"Why not?"

"Well," he shifted uncomfortably, "they tend only to use it ceremonially, and their civilization still lends credence to the idea of blood sacrifice. At a certain point, no matter how delicious their hot cocoa might be, you *have* to feel sorry for the people on the altar." He broke off when he saw her face. "Um, Scotland," he reiterated, offering her another truffle. "They're from *modern* Scotland."

She took it from the plate and, this time, passed it to him. He took it from her fingertips with his lips, and she lingered for a moment, touching his mouth through the light dusting of cocoa before blushing pink and turning away. "Well," she said. "Now, it's definitely the best first date in the history of humanity. And I guess it's a good thing we've got at least one of those under our belt before I meet your dad."

That's a delicate way of phrasing it. Sounds better than, "Meet your father and get interrogated by the king of purgatory."

She gulped nervously and reached again for the water. "Speaking of which, are you absolutely sure that we're not late or anything? If he's already predisposed to dislike me, the last thing I want to do is keep him waiting. And I don't want to leave Sherry and Mike alone for very long at all," she added.

"Mike and Sherry are perfectly safe," he assured. "And my father is not predisposed to dislike you. It's my behavior he has an issue with." He looked worried for a moment, then rallied. "And no, we won't be keeping him waiting. Elysium exists in a different sort of time than the one you're used to, so getting *there* isn't a problem. It's when I try to travel around Earth that I sometimes run into trouble."

She paused at his tone, a truffle halfway to her mouth. "What kind of trouble?"

"Just normal difficulties." He said, remembering. "Once, I kept trying to get to seventeenth-century Cyprus, but every time, I ended up in this Judean cave on the eve of a solar eclipse with this raving lunatic who kept acting like he knew me and talking about dragons." He chuckled softly but stopped short at the look on her face.

Normal difficulties, huh?

"How many times did you end up in this cave?" she asked pointedly.

"A few. Dozen." His embarrassment was painted all over his face as he reluctantly admitted, "I don't always have the best aim."

That got a reaction. "You don't always have the best *aim?*" she exclaimed.

He threw up his hands in a hapless gesture. "I'm not a true Elysian. For someone like Ephriam, it isn't a problem. He can choose whatever moment he likes and be there in a flash. For me?" He changed gears. "Look, the cave was a fluke. I can definitely get the day right."

She stood. "You can definitely get the *day* right."

He stood, too, and nodded. "Almost definitely."

Her eyes flashed at him. "Cool. Great. Excellent. I'm on the moon, in a pocket of rapidly dwindling oxygen reserves with a guy who can *almost definitely* get the day right."

He drew himself up defensively. "I told you, it's different when time is frozen or when I'm going to Elysium. Then, I can hit the moment. Within an hour or so of the moment."

"I should certainly hope so, Cameron, because we just left your scowly, naked friend and your memory-wiping society in charge of some people who are very important to me, and you promised me we'd be back *at the very same moment we left.* I don't know what Elysian protocol dictates, but on Earth, it is very poor form indeed to be late getting home to your babysitter. *Are you smiling?*"

He made a sincere effort not to, then ended up grinning ear to ear. He shrugged in what she had to admit was a charming gesture. "You're beautiful when you yell."

She let out an exasperated sound. "I need to learn your full name so you know when you're truly in trouble."

"I'll never tell."

She flashed him a wicked smirk. "Then I'll ask your dad."

That drained some color from his face.

Serves you right.

She took a step back with no small amount of satisfaction, then abruptly startled when her foot came down with far less force than she was accustomed to. In that fateful moment, she realized there was still an untapped vein of fun to explore.

When's the next time I'm going to be on the moon?

She started experimenting subtly at first, bouncing on her toes with a thrill of delight when she hovered in the air for a few moments too long. Little bounces started to become bigger jumps. She giggled, enchanted at her weightlessness. Before long, she was leaping into the air like a child, hooting with laughter as she floated back down.

After watching for a few minutes, chuckling under his breath, Cameron caught her around her waist. She looked up, breathless. She thought he might tease her for childishness. At the very least, she thought he might scold her for leaving a spattering of incriminating footprints right there on the moon. Instead, he pulled her close and bent to touch their foreheads together. "Brianna Weldon, you are utterly ridiculous."

She pressed a quick kiss to his lips. "I know."

She turned once again to the spectacular sight of the Earth hanging in the sky. He stood behind her and held her close. A minute passed before he gently cleared his throat.

"Do we need to go?" she asked.

He stroked her hair. "We could always just move here. Locked forever in this moment — our eternal first date. I'll make sure you never run out of caffeine."

Don't threaten me with a good time.

They lingered a moment, both more tempted than they would ever admit before she pulled away with a quiet sigh. "No, you're right. We need to go."

With a swish of his hand, their beautiful feast vanished, along with her flowers and her couch. She managed to swig down the last of her latte before that vanished as well. A little twirl of his fingers, and he was holding out her favorite coat. She shrugged her way into it, then knelt down on the pretense of tying her shoelace, scribbling her finger discreetly in the sand.

B. W.

She added a little flourish and pocketed a rock. He graciously pretended not to see.

Then he took her hand, and they faced one another.

"I don't know how much you remember about your first time traveling into Elysium," he said. "You passed out as soon as we arrived. Just so you know, it's different from traveling through space. To get to Elysium, we travel through the membrane of time. You might see things, hear things. That's normal. As your personal timeline passes through to Elysium, it's like when water that's used to flowing in one direction suddenly pools. Flashes of your past might swirl around us briefly before they settle." He looked at her seriously. "It is important that you do not try to interact with any memories you see. Do you understand?"

She nodded, figuring a non-verbal lie was better than an outright one. Try as she might, she couldn't control the expression on her face, which must have been slightly green, because Cameron touched two fingers to her chin and lifted her head to look at him. "It gets better the more you practice. Are you ready?"

"Of course," she said with false bravery. "Piece of cake." As he pulled her close, she couldn't help herself. "To infinity and then, you know, well past that!"

He pulled back, delighted. "Exactly! I wasn't sure you'd understand the mathematical underpinnings of this kind of dimensional travel, but that's quite correct."

She blinked. "Cameron, just start the damn car."

◆　　◆　　◆

It felt different this time, more like being in a river than a G-force. The eddies and swells of time seemed to press in around her — trying to flow into her, through her. She careened through time and space, buffeted through the flow like a kayak down rapids, hitting rocks along the way. She felt Cameron strain beside her. Veins stood out on his neck like he was pushing as hard as he could against something as ungiving as a mountain.

Something is wrong.

Suddenly, they hit something big. It added a whole new level of spin to their trajectory. One Cameron clearly hadn't initiated or anticipated. She felt him brace against it. The image was starting to waver. The forces increased, getting more challenging to control.

That's when it happened.

Her pendant shone shock-white, and within the space of an instant, her mother was there. There in her kitchen, with the blue bowl, singing, dancing, and baking, graceful and lovely, oblivious to her adult daughter gasping for air through the translucent curtain of time.

Brie's heart caught in her throat.

How is this possible?

Cameron was saying something but sounded far away like he was underwater. She ignored him — moving without permission and reaching out her hand.

I just need to touch her. To be near her, one more time.

She battled past the forces separating them, braced as though she were walking against a strong wind, her hand glimmering in the flickers of light and shadows — *reaching.*

Mom!

She didn't think it would happen. She didn't think it was possible, but her mother froze on a dime, turning in the direction of her voice.

Brie stopped cold, utterly astonished. She hadn't said anything, not a single word. She'd done nothing more than reach out a hand and wish with all her might that it would happen.

Can you hear me? Can you sense me?

Her mother looked this way and that as though trying to locate a sound.

Brie took another straining step and shouted,

"Mom!"

Her pendant flashed even brighter, hot against her chest. But this time, it wasn't alone. Like an eerie reflection, her mother's pendant was also flashing — glinting off the old kitchen's copper, tile, and glass.

Cameron's voice cut suddenly to the surface, loud and frantic. "Brianna, stop!" He grabbed her tightly, fingers digging into her arms as he tried to pull her back. But for one of the first times ever, she fought against him — driven by an impulse she couldn't control.

"I can reach her," she gasped, struggling fiercely. "She can hear me."

Her mother was looking straight at them now, and it did indeed seem as though she could hear them and perhaps *see* them. Her eyes were wide with shock, and she reached up to touch her pendant, identical to the one around Brie's neck — the one ripping a small tear in the fabric of time and space.

Brie mirrored her gesture, straining with all her might to get closer.

Suddenly, the image changed. Both women held their pendants, but they were no longer alone. It looked like they were standing between two mirrors, with an infinite number of reflections before and behind them, all shadowy images of women holding pendants, stretching through eternity.

Brie barely noticed — she only had eyes for her mother. She gripped her pendant tight in her fist, ignoring its burning heat on her palm, trying to concentrate, trying to push through the thick material that separated the two women. A slit no bigger than a paper cut opened on the side of her forehead, and a small trickle of blood dripped down her temple.

Cameron was shouting again, his voice rising into a panic. "Brianna, you *can't* go in there!" he cried. "You have no idea the chaos it would unleash. We need to leave now. *Right* now. Brie, please!"

That's when Brie ran into the kitchen.

Only it wasn't the woman disobeying the laws of heaven, fighting against her angel's arms; it was a little girl with chestnut curls and dimples.

Holy hell…

The child flew past her mother in a whirl of giggles, pursued by another: her little best friend — Sherry. Bouncing ringlets flew around her face. She let out a peal of laughter as Sherry touched her and yelled, "Tag!" They must have been four or five.

The children skipped obliviously out of the kitchen, leaving her mother in a daze. Twice, her eyes flickered between her young daughter and the bleeding, distraught reflection of the woman in front of her. On the third time, a look of dawning comprehension lit her features.

"Mom!" cried Brie. "I can get to you. I can almost touch you!"

Her mother reached out a hand, her fingertips grazing some invisible barrier between them.

The cut on Brie's forehead opened wider. A steady stream of blood was now running down the side of her face, staining the front of the jacket Cameron had conjured for her.

It didn't matter. None of it mattered.

There was her mother, standing in the middle of a sunny kitchen. Like nothing had ever happened. Like she hadn't been ripped from the world too soon by an evil she hadn't deserved. There was her mother, and Brie was determined to reach her. Even if it killed her.

"Brie, you must stop! *Brie!* It's hurting you!" There was something different in Cameron's voice, a tone that cut through all the rest. She threw a glance over her shoulder. His eyes were wild, frantic, filled with a nameless dread.

Listen to him, Brie. He's trying to save you.

Her chest ached like something had hollowed it out, and she could never quite be whole again. For the briefest of moments, she turned back to the portal.

"I love you." Her voice rang loud and clear.

Her mother's mouth fell open. A tear fell down her cheek.

So much, Mom. I love you so much.

Their eyes locked together in a moment of shared understanding, and her mother spoke, her words echoing through time:

"You're my whole heart, Brianna."

And then it was over.

What happened next must have been incredible, but Brie remembered very little of it. Cameron wrenched her away. He was shouting. His muscles strained with effort, and an agonized yell escaped unbidden as he pushed with everything he had against the invisible forces hindering them.

For a few agonizing seconds, nothing happened.

Then, all at once, it worked.

Her mother disappeared as the swirling ocean of time crashed back into place. Everything around them shifted, turned, and peeled away like a wave pulling back into the sea after breaking on the shore. The image wavered, then solidified. Her feet touched something smooth and hard.

Cameron's arms stayed clenched around her. She could feel his heart racing and his breath heaving in his chest. It wasn't until he finally pulled back that she realized he was furious.

"Would it be possible," he began, his tone clipped and measured, "would it be at all possible for you to perhaps, just once, take my word for it? Particularly when facing a circumstance in which I have *immeasurably* more experience than you?"

"Cameron—"

"Say, for example, when we're traveling inter-dimensionally?"

"Cameron—"

"No!" he shouted, that irrepressible humanity coming through at last. "Just this once, if only for the sake of novelty, you need to listen to me! You have no idea the repercussions that could result in meddling with the past! *Anyone's* past, let alone your own personal timeline! Do you understand that *now*, that has always happened? She's seen you, felt the pendant. And it can *never* be undone! Why you would even consider something like this is utterly beyond me! I've never seen anything like it, but the fact remains that I specifically warned you not to—"

"*Cameron!*"

"*What?!*"

"I think we're here."

He froze dead still, then turned slowly to look at their surroundings. She cringed against his chest. They were in a vast hall that seemed to be hewn from a single, mountainous block of white marble, with veins of lightning running through. It formed the floor, the walls, the ceiling, and the innumerable columns and giant chairs that rose up from them on all sides.

Chairs that were occupied by monsters and golden orbs of light.

All of whom had fallen utterly silent.

I'm guessing we forgot to knock.

There were creatures she had never seen before, ones she never could have imagined. Creatures with the heads of eagles, bulls, lions, men, and beasts, all equipped with rows upon rows of wings and razor-sharp claws. Spheres of golden light, the size of baseballs, hovered thick in the air and bunched together on the ceiling like clusters of grapes. The hall was filled with so many points of brilliant light that it was impossible to look anywhere, yet equally impossible to look away. The air itself seemed to move and crackle. Light pulsed through the veins in the marble as though the stone itself was alive.

At the front of the hall rose a podium. On this sat a throne, and on the throne sat an ancient man with snow-white hair flowing past his shoulders. He was dressed in simple but fine robes of royal indigo and a crown set with shimmering jewels circled his head. His white, caterpillar-like eyebrows were knit together in an expression of ancient disapproval. One that made her mouth go instantly dry.

King Enoch.

He was flanked on either side by a pair of monsters, each the size of a house. As if their size wasn't enough, they appeared to be made entirely of wings, claws, and eyes. Each of those eyes swiveled in their sockets to fix on Brie as she craned her neck backward, trying to see to the top.

The king spoke in a sonorous voice that was decidedly sarcastic, one that seemed to echo through the entire length of the hall. "Don't mind us, son. We were just debating the merits of trusting a human with the secret of our existence, but do go on." He raised one snowy eyebrow. "I believe you were reprimanding the young lady for fracturing the space-time continuum."

Brie's heart was beating so hard she could feel her pulse in her ears.

That's when one of the enormous, winged monsters leaned toward her. Her brain was screaming at her to run, but she found herself paralyzed in terror.

A voice emanating from deep within the creature shook the very air surrounding her, trembling the ground beneath her feet. *"Do not be afraid."*

At that point, she did the most sensible thing she'd done all day. She passed out cold.

"Is she going to be all right?" Cameron's voice floated into the ether, echoed almost immediately by one Brie didn't recognize. She struggled to place it, fighting her way back to consciousness.

"Don't worry, she's merely fainted."

"Of *course*, she fainted!" Cameron fumed. "How many times did I ask you to maintain a human form during her visit? *How many?*"

"You materialized in the middle of court, son. Don't blame Raphael for your inability to navigate the time currents."

That was definitely Enoch.

"I did try to reassure the young lady," said the unfamiliar voice.

"By telling her not to be afraid of a skyscraper made of nightmares?" Cameron spat.

"That's highly offensive."

"*You're* highly offensive!"

"I put on the skin suit. What more do you want?"

Brie let out a quiet groan, deciding that if she didn't open her eyes, this wasn't actually happening.

Three male voices rang out immediately above her.

"*Ms. Weldon!*"

"*Ms. Weldon!*"

"*Brie!*"

"I think she's coming around," said the king.

She could feel them all standing over her with bated breath but stayed stubbornly silent while squeezing her eyes closed. Just a few more seconds. They couldn't *make* her wake up.

This isn't happening. This is a dream.

Even if it is a dream, it's best to stay still. You know, in case they can track movement —like T-Rexes.

"Perhaps one more draught of ambrosia?" suggested the new voice.

Someone held something cool and hard to her lips and tipped a few drops of warm, sweet liquid into her mouth. She swallowed, and a blissful feeling began to flood through her, starting in her stomach and radiating out to the very tips of her toes. She sighed happily as the warmth dissolved every tension in her body. She swore her hair felt more relaxed.

I could play possum. Let them deal with me and whatever cosmic calamity THAT was... Because they've done such an excellent job dealing with me so far.

She sighed and decided to face the music. She cracked open a single eye, only to find a trio of concerned faces hovering above her — Cameron, King Enoch, and a handsome stranger, all sporting matching expressions, brows furrowed with worry.

Cameron spoke first, half-shoving the others aside. "How are you feeling?"

She blinked. Blinked again. "Did I just see a giant mutant made of feathers and eyes?"

The men looked at each other nervously before answering in unison. In all the heavens, there had never been a more unconvincing lie:

"No?"

That's when she started laughing. *Really* laughing. The kind that doesn't stop, even when it makes other people uncomfortable. She laughed so hard her sides hurt and tears welled in her eyes. Through the mounting hysteria, she managed, "So it was an *optical illusion*?"

She cracked herself up again.

As she wheezed on the marble floor of the court, Cameron snatched a glass vial away from the man she didn't recognize. "How much of this did you give her?"

The dark-haired man looked at the bottle, throwing up his hands. "It isn't always possible to gauge these things exactly—"

Cameron said something in a dialect she didn't understand.

Enoch shot him a stern look. "Language!"

That just set her off again.

It was one of those situations in which none of the people involved had ever expected to find themselves, and good as their intentions might have been, not a single one of them was working with a script. There was a chance they might have lingered forever if the king hadn't cleared his throat.

"Perhaps it would be best if we allow the young lady to get some rest and come at this fresh when she's feeling more herself," he said graciously.

"I think that's an excellent idea," Cameron snapped.

The strange man looked genuinely contrite. "The effects should wear off in a few of your Earth hours. Would you permit me to give her some herbal tea to help with the—?"

"No, that's quite all right. I'd say she's suffered enough of your assistance for one evening." Cameron knelt and picked her up, holding her almost territorially against his chest. The moment he touched her, a golden glow emanated from his palms, and warm relief flooded through her. The uncontrollable laughter simmered down to a blissful grin and a few residual giggles.

She circled her arms around his neck and buried her face in his chest, drinking in his scent. "You smell incredible."

Cameron shot a panicked glance around the room and started

beating a hasty path to the nearest exit, pretending not to notice when she waved over his shoulder.

"Goodnight, your majesty!" she called cheerfully. "Goodnight, Gorgeous!"

The stranger looked surprised, then shrugged with a chuckle. "I suppose I am."

They raised their hands in return, watching with bemused expressions as the pair vanished quickly down the marble hall.

Happily stoned on the celestial potion, she turned to Cameron with a grin. Looking at her face, his expression softened. "Are you okay?" he asked.

"Oh, sure. Fine. Just, you know — fractured space-time, saw my mom, fainted in front of a room full of Godzilla-sized monsters, met your dad. No biggie."

He gave her a slight squeeze.

She looked around, hazily registering the Earth and the massive moon hanging over the horizon, bathing the landscape in an ethereal glow and a lilting, chiming song that seemed to be coming from the trees. "Are the trees singing? Is that happening? And am I really stoned in a world without nachos? Let's be honest, that's the real crisis here."

Giggles threatened to overtake her exhausted body again. Before this gained any momentum, Cameron's palms glowed once more, and she found herself slipping away.

"Your dad seems nice," she said, drifting. "And he looks like… Gandalf." She nuzzled closer to him. "Thanks for showing me the moon."

She was asleep before he tucked her into bed.

CHAPTER NINE

Secrets in the Library

When Brie woke up some time later, not much had changed. She was still wearing clothes sprinkled with moondust. Her lips still tasted of ambrosia with just a hint of chocolate. She was still stoned out of her mind. And her best friend in the world was still stubbornly locked in the bathroom.

Three of these things were deemed acceptable. The fourth was not.

That's long enough.

With a burst of determination that didn't exactly translate into balance, she sat bolt upright, threw her legs off the mattress, and flung herself dizzily onto the floor. She landed on her knees, spinning and grinning, forgetting why she was there. It took a second for things to steady, for her to remember what had prompted her to move in the first place. That's when the grin faded.

It was replaced with a ferocious scowl.

"Sherry!"

She hollered the name without thinking of the consequences, taking a second to orient her feet before remembering the way to the bathroom and stomping down the hall. The eyes of the pictures framed in the corridor seemed to follow her, and the ceiling rattled with every furious step.

That might be the drugs.

"Sherry Walker, get out here!"

Mike set aside the enormous book of Elysian combat tactics he'd been reading, and leapt to his feet as she approached, staring in surprise at the strange bits of space dust raining from her hair. He held back the first ten comments that leapt to his mind and offered a mild smile instead, the same way he'd done when Cameron had carried her, singing loudly, into the house.

"Hey, Brie. How did your—?"

"Is she in there?" she interrupted, pushing past him and planting her feet in front of the door. It loomed before her like some challenge waiting to be defeated. "Rhetorical question," she continued loudly before he could speak. It scarcely mattered. She wasn't talking to him anyway. Every word was directed to the lovely woman who'd barricaded herself in purgatory's powder room. "I *know* you're still in there, Sherry. And it's time to COME OUT!"

Her words echoed into a reverberating silence.

She took this as a positive.

"Thanks, Mark." She clapped him on the shoulder, eyeing the door like she seriously considered kicking it down. "I'll take it from here."

Most days, he might have argued. Most days, he might have actively restrained her. But on this particular occasion, he merely chuckled under his breath and muttered, "It's Mike, hon. And you know what?" he continued, straightening his clothes. "You do that. I'll be outside, *not* involving myself in whatever comes next."

Yeah, that's a good call.

"Sherry!" she squawked again, leaning on the wall for balance. "Open the door!"

No reaction.

"Open this damn door right now, or I'm going to break it down! I have powers now, you know," she added in a pathetic attempt to be threatening. "I could probably melt it, or transform it, or find some snacks."

She paused, wondering if she'd said that last bit out loud.

Seriously, where are the nachos?

"Disregard that!" she called, trying to rally. It was nearly impossible to win an argument with her best friend, even under the most forgiving of circumstances. It was a thousand times worse when Sherry chose not to participate. She decided to change tactics. "You know what? I don't even *want* you to open the door! Just go ahead and stay in there!"

Don't, though.

Please, come out.

"You're being incredibly rude, Sherry Walker!" she shouted into the void. "These people have invited us into their home — all right, they sort of abducted us — and instead of showing even the slightest bit of interest, you've done nothing the entire time but monopolize the bathroom! What would your mother have to say about that?"

That last part might have been pushing it a bit. As a rule, they didn't invoke the name of Sherry's mother unless it was the last possible resort, but given that they were no longer in the same time zone, let alone on the same planet, it seemed like a reasonable maneuver. At any rate, Brie wasn't thinking about mothers or time zones. She was tripping through her own celestial fever dream, and she wanted her best friend back — the one who remained stubbornly on the wrong side of the door.

"And you shouldn't have yelled at Cameron like that," she added, surprising herself. "He's a *good* person, Sherry. He's a good person who can't even properly navigate a vending machine. He can't hold his own against the likes of you!" She shook her head vaguely, trying to keep her thoughts from running away. "He rescues extinct species in his free time. He has a pet turtle and keeps a herd of unicorns in a paddock outside." She stepped closer, cupping her hands directly against the door. "He brought me to the freaking moon, Sherry! And you know what? He ALWAYS believed me!"

She regretted it the second the words left her lips, before she even heard the sharp intake of breath inside. Silence fell over them again, but it felt different this time. The door was still wedged between them. Now, it seemed there was no moving it.

He always believed me.

She took a step back, not realizing the sting of the words until she'd said them. Not realizing until that very moment how much she meant them.

And how much she wanted to take them back.

It wouldn't be a great exaggeration to say Brie fled the villa.

Taking her cue from Mike's initial instincts, she decided the best way to avoid unwanted conversation was to go out the window. She stripped the four-poster bed that Sherry had all but destroyed with the fire poker, tied some truly luxuriant sheets together, and heaved them out the window. It was only after valiantly leaping out after them that she realized the entire villa was one story. She landed with a graceless *thunk* on the pile of sheets in the middle of a bush whose electric-blue blossoms levitated away from her. They emitted a series of outraged murmurs before settling back onto their branches.

"Sorry. Sorry," she muttered as she disentangled herself, swatting a stray bloom away from her face. The second she was mobile, she stomped through the garden, looking for a path with all the finesse of a drunk elephant. Thankfully, most of the flora seemed to possess some kind of consciousness — almost everything seemed to sense her mood and shift out of her way. At one point, she swore a fountain jumped several feet to the left to avoid one of her more careening steps. In the end, a series of low-hanging branches of a presumably sympathetic tree nudged her onto the path to the palace, as much to get her out of their garden as to help her on her way.

All the while, she kept muttering.

"Sorry for this. Sorry for that. Sorry I said so, sorry I didn't say so. I'm so sick of being sorry! Why isn't anybody *else* sorry?" She was immediately sorry she'd wished that upon anyone else. "Damnit!" She plopped down hard on a marble bench, leaned back, and tilted her face to the sky. The Earth hung in low orbit, huge and gently turning. Africa and Europe slowly rotated counter-clockwise, and before she knew it, the Virginia shore became visible on the left horizon. As she kept watching, she could start to make out Georgia — her home.

Dad.

Her eyes misted over, though, as usual, no tears fell. Suddenly, the only thing she wanted in the whole world wasn't nachos. It wasn't even to make up with Sherry. It was to talk to her father.

I saw her today, Dad. And I think she saw me, too.

She stood up with a start. That was true, wasn't it? Her mom *had* seen her. She'd been reaching for her. Their pendants were both shining at the same time.

I have to know what it means.

While she didn't have the balance to run, a moment later, she was staggering purposefully toward the palace. The sky was bright, and the air was invigorating. She might nearly have made it on her own volition, if she hadn't collided into one of heaven's favorite angels halfway there.

"Ouch — sorry!" she gasped, peeling herself off his ivory robes. This time, she actually meant it. When she saw who it was, she meant it even more. "Oh, it's you!"

Raphael's eyes twinkled with amusement as he held her steady. "Yes, it's me. I'd introduce myself properly, but I like what you called me before."

I called him gorgeous. In front of my boyfriend. And my boyfriend's dad.

Her cheeks turned the color of ripe strawberries.

"Can I help you find something?" he continued pleasantly, smoothing his crumpled robes. "Or is this one of those journeys one needs to take by themselves?"

She tried very hard not to die of embarrassment, scrambling for something to say. What she settled on surprised her. "I'm looking for the library."

I am?

"I am," she added unnecessarily, wishing very much she'd stayed tangled in the bushes.

Of course, the second she said the words, she realized the obvious problem. Did the parallel dimension between Heaven and Hell have a library? Was there even a need? And if so, what kinds of books would be housed inside? Ones written by mortals or angels? She imagined a row of antiquated computers on tables along the side of a room, then realized the absurdity of that as well. Fortunately, at that particular moment, fate was on her side.

Raphael's brows lifted delicately, but he pointed over his shoulder. "You're nearly there."

She nodded swiftly, edging in a careful circle around him. The second she was clear, she broke into an awkward jog. "Thank you!" she called over her shoulder, nearly colliding with yet another tree as he stifled a laugh and waved goodbye.

She battled against the tipsily tilting floor as she made her way down another gilded hallway, scarcely noticing the casual displays on the wall. Each would have been enough to make the world's leading anthropologists swoon in ecstasy. Here, a strange, twisted horn with a placard underneath that simply read, "Jericho." There, a fragment of wood labeled "Golgotha," and beside it, a vial filled with a shimmering, red-gold substance.

She ignored it all, focused entirely on the door at the end of the hall.

Nothing could have prepared her for what she found on the other side.

You can keep your magical bathrooms — I live HERE now.

Ever since she was a little girl watching *Beauty and the Beast* for the first time, Brie became obsessed with bookshops and libraries. Half the entries on her official List of Places to See Before I Die were libraries from around the globe.

This one trumps them all.

It was like a city made entirely of books. There were towers of them, skyscrapers that shot so high into the sky that she couldn't see the tops. She didn't know how it was possible — the castle didn't sport any spiring towers when viewed from the outside. But here? If there was a vertical limit to the structure, she couldn't see it — as though an interdimensional origami expert had folded space to fit inside that magical door. Everything was arranged in a soft, upward spiral. Everywhere, priceless pieces of art, both human and Elysian, were tastefully displayed amongst the shelves or hung in hallways that seemed to dart off in every direction and come back to merge in the central, round antechamber where she now found herself.

It would have blown her mind several times over if she'd been completely sober. As it stood, she wasn't just at a loss for words. She was at a loss for thoughts. Her mind simply drank in the sight as she rotated in place, gaping in awe.

It was entirely possible she would have remained in this dumbstruck state for hours, or at least until Raphael's potion wore off, had something not rustled high above her and snapped her back to attention.

What she'd assumed was a chandelier was slowly unfolding itself and floating down from the rafters. The rustling she'd heard was coming from its wings. Pair after pair of lovely wings unfolded. As the creature drew close, she could see they were made of ancient-looking paper and covered with beautifully scripted words in a language she didn't recognize.

When the being had descended to her level, its wings completely unfurled, revealing what looked more like a sculpture than a human. She couldn't tell if it was wearing armor or if that was the creature's actual body. Light glinted off its curving figure. Its head, or heavily stylized helmet, cut an elegant silhouette against the glowing lights in the hallways. It looked powerful. Beautiful. Otherworldly enough to mesmerize.

Unfortunately, Brie was on a mission. And she was high as a kite. She asked bluntly, "Are you the librarian?"

There was a curious silence, which she took as an affirmative.

"I'm looking for information. Information about the — what did he call it? — the Time Seas. And information about this." She held up her pendant between them.

There was a great rushing sound, and before she could blink, the strange being was mere inches from her fingers, hovering intently beside the pendant. From this close proximity, she could see that the script covering its paper wings constantly shifted, and the text seemed to be writing itself. She stared, fascinated, as the words rolled out endlessly, and jumped when the creature finally spoke:

"I have waited for you for a long time."

Sweet pole-vaulting Jesus.

She shrank back half a step.

It spoke again. "Do not be afraid."

Sure. No problem.

"You know what?" she panted, trying to keep a grip on herself. "People keep telling me that. How about I'll be in charge of how I feel, and you tell me if you have the book I need?" She hoped her bravado was disguising her galloping heartbeat, pounding its telltale rhythm in her chest like it was fixing to win a derby.

The librarian was unfazed. "I have what you seek, and what you do not know you seek. Come."

She followed it up the curving hallway, up and up, around the infinite rows of books. She thought suddenly of a conch shell —

of the way the iridescent curves spiraled gently to a point. She wondered if, in fact, this building's structure was modeled after the inside of a seashell.

She wondered how much longer it would be until Raphael's ambrosia wore off.

And all at once, she realized she hadn't properly introduced herself. "I'm Brie," she blurted suddenly. "Brie Weldon. What's your name?"

"I am the angel, Raziel."

There was nothing further.

Withholding seems to be a common theme amongst Elysians.

"How long have you been here, Raziel?" she asked, trying to make up for her earlier rudeness by engaging in some small talk.

"Since the stars were but a thought in the mind of the Creator, and still after the stars wink their last. This is my place, my purpose. In these halls of infinite knowledge, I weave the story no one knows, for none have yet the wit to seek the common thread."

"Oh." She swallowed. "Well, it must be a nice place to—"

"We are here."

She was secretly grateful.

He led her to a softly glowing table that seemed to be made of rose quartz and, with a flick of his finger, conjured her a chair. She sat as he drifted, ever-rustling, into the maze of shelves. He emerged a minute later carrying an absolutely enormous book. He settled it on the table before her. With a short flurry of his wings, the book opened to a page somewhere in the middle.

He held out his hand. She stared at it, confused.

Is he waiting for a tip?

Suddenly embarrassed, she dug through her pockets and found a crumpled dollar she'd failed to use at a vending machine last week. Silently thanking the magical bathroom's laundry service for leaving it where it was, she removed the dilapidated bill and placed it in his hand with a satisfied smile. The angel's enormous helmet tilted down to look at it, then back up to her face.

"Is that not what you wanted?" she asked, uncertain.

There are some sounds that denote exasperation in any language — even ancient ones. Raziel made one such sound, grabbed her hand, and pressed something into her palm. Then, he straightened up to his full, exceedingly intimidating height.

"When the traitor wavers and the map turns white, I will see you in the next library."

With that, he shot into the space above them in a billow of wings, disappearing into the heights of the library. Brie pocketed what he'd given her and squinted at the place where he'd disappeared from her sight.

Whatever. Nerd.

She settled back into her chair and started reading the book. At least, she tried to. At first, she thought it was the effects of Raphael's potion, but she soon realized it was much worse than that. The book was written in ancient Aramaic. She let out a curse that had no place in such an astonishing library and would've gotten her shushed by custodians of far less extravagant houses of knowledge.

Of course. Of COURSE.

She shoved back from the table and held her head in her hands for a moment, face tilted upwards. "Could somebody just give me an effing clue?" Her voice echoed through the library.

The books remained silent. Judgmentally so, she thought. She stared at them despondently and slumped down in her seat when, all of a sudden, she realized she wasn't alone. Her head jerked up, sensing another presence. A flash of jet-black hair swished behind a bookshelf.

"Hello?" she called out, more mystified than frightened. "Is somebody there?"

A small child peeked her head around a tower of books. A lovely child with ivory skin and tumbles of raven hair that fell all the way down to her feet.

"Oh!" said Brie, surprised. "Hello! I didn't see you when I came in."

The girl merely stared back with wide, dark eyes.

"I'm so sorry I yelled," Brie continued, with a pang of guilt. "I didn't mean to scare you. I just don't know how I'm supposed to read this book."

The girl took a couple of steps closer. She wore a looping garment made of black linens and no other adornment. She had a strange, gliding way of moving. And when she spoke, it was in a voice that did not match her face. A voice that sounded neither old nor young but resonant and primal:

"I know you."

Brie's eyes widened. "You do?"

The small child nodded solemnly. "You are the one beloved by the fox."

To be fair, Brie might have had a different reaction to this if she hadn't been tripping out of her mind on celestial LSD. But as it stood, she couldn't imagine a happier development. "*I AM?*" she asked, thrilled. "I *knew* it! You know, Sherry is always telling me that they don't want to be adopted, but I *knew* that they wanted to come home with me!"

The little girl cocked her head. "What have you got in your pockets?"

"What have I...?" Brie shoved her hand into her pocket and remembered what the strange librarian had pressed into her palm.

When she looked back up, the little girl was gone.

She looked down at the curious object. It was a magnifying glass. One that seemed to fold into its own handle, which was wooden, inlaid with gold, and set with a beautiful green stone. She carefully pressed her fingertip on a tiny part of the golden ring that encircled the glass and delicately pulled out the lens. The glass slid out easily and straightened into position with a satisfying *click*. She held it up to her eye, zooming in to the titles of the books on the shelves in front of her. "The Peloponnesian Kings: A Culinary History." "Blood Magic of the Ancient Bayou." "The Definitive History of Jambalaya."

She lowered the magnifying glass and shook her head before realizing.

Those were in English.

She looked in amazement at the magnifying glass in her hand, then looked down at the book in front of her once more.

It was now in English, too.

When she took away the lens, it was back to the ancient language, but everything beneath the glass was being translated for her. She read the title at the top of the page:

The History of the Time Seas.

She breathlessly read on. And on.

And on.

It was hardly as informative as she would have liked. Mostly, the book seemed like a collection of unpronounceable names of angels who had made their way from Elysium to Earth, or Heaven, or Eden and had carved out hidden paths through the

Time Seas for just such a purpose. Sometimes, this angel or that would stumble upon what they called an "island" within the seas, solid, immovable things that seemed somehow immune to the currents of time, but no one seemed to know why they were there or how. There was no mention of anything that would explain why she saw her mother.

She fought back a yawn.

Awfully long way to travel, to end up bored in the most beautiful library in the Universe.

Her eyelids grew heavy, and the chair Raziel had summoned felt irresistibly comfortable.

I'll close my eyes just for a moment, she thought. *A moment won't hurt anyone.*

When Cameron found her, she was fast asleep, drooling onto the sacred text.

CHAPTER TEN

The Arena and the King

Brie opened her eyes to a familiar, breathtaking smile.

"So, you did a little wandering, huh?" Cameron asked with a lopsided grin.

She took in a quick breath, surprised to see she was no longer in the library. Even more surprising — her feet were no longer on the ground. A sunlit sky stretched in every direction. She was being carried through the garden, nestled safely in the gentle curve of Cameron's arms.

"I defenestrated myself."

He looked at her in puzzled amusement. "I beg your pardon?"

"I defenestrated myself, Cam." She fidgeted a little, trying to get herself into a more dignified pose. "I threw myself out the window. To get to the library."

"Yes, I know what it means, plus you left the evidence of your little jailbreak hanging in the bush outside. The blue pixies are very mad at you." He tried to hide his grin, watching her little struggles. After a few seconds, he graciously placed her feet on the ground. "And I have to say, I'm not entirely thrilled with you myself. If you feel inclined to throw yourself out of any more windows, please, don't."

She went about dusting herself off. "I'm basically in heaven, Cam." She tossed her hair and started back down the path. "What could possibly happen?"

That's when a spear flew past her face and buried itself with a resounding *thunk* in the trunk of an enormous palm tree, not six inches from her head.

She immediately sobered up, froze, and watched as the shaft quivered in the air. Cameron had thrown his arm in front of her chest, stopping her in her tracks, but strangely didn't seem alarmed. In fact, he fought back a smile when someone called out:

"Hey, kid!"

They turned to see Tavi step out of a grove of trees in full battle gear. She looked far more at ease among the Elysian flora than she'd looked rummaging through the medical cabinet of Daya Memorial. No less intimidating, but definitely more herself.

"Tavi," Cameron replied, unable to disguise his amusement as he nodded his head in greeting. "I see your flair for the dramatic is alive and well." He cocked his head meaningfully to the side. "You don't think she's already gotten enough shocks for a lifetime?"

"N-no, it's fine, I don't mind," stammered Brie, stepping gingerly around the spear.

"See? She doesn't mind." The warrior woman flashed her a blinding white grin before turning back to Cameron. "You didn't think you'd get to come home after nearly a century away without going a few rounds in the ring, did you?"

He chuckled. "I'd never dream such a thing was possible, but I'm afraid it isn't the best time. We have—" He glanced at Brie, whose face made him pause. "What is it?"

"You've been away for nearly a century?" She was shocked.

"I've been busy." He was avoiding something again, and though her intuition told her it was important, it also told her to leave it alone. For now. He turned his attention back to Tavi. "We have to go check on the others. Maybe some other time."

Tavi let out a peal of silvery laughter. "I only met your friend for a moment, but for my money? She's going to be just fine. I'm frankly more concerned about the rest of us." She accented her point with a theatrical wink. "Don't be a spoilsport, *Cameron*. Unless of course, you don't feel up to it." Her eyes glinted with mischief. "Ephriam sent word, you know. Told me to go easy on you. Said you'd had a rough time lately. Something about 'getting your ass handed to you and being rescued by the youngling.'"

Cameron flashed a dark look and muttered, "That little——"

Tavi smirked, reached past them and retrieved her spear from the tree trunk in one swift movement, then walked away, calling over her shoulder. "Suit yourself, kiddo. Though I'd *hate* for Brie here to think that *you* are the best example of Elysian badassery we have on offer."

He stared after her, silently fuming, before turning to Brie.

"Mind if we make a quick stop?"

From the outside, there wasn't anything exceptional about the arena beyond its scale. You could fit two Coliseums inside and still have room for a soccer field.

Not that THAT'S remotely on the table.

Brie chuckled to herself, remembering the last time she'd watched Cameron engage in an athletic activity. It had started with him mistaking soccer for American football and had gone downhill from there, much to her and her friends' amusement.

Sherry. Rashida.

She sucked in a breath, suddenly painfully homesick for a simpler time, for simpler problems. For her friends ogling the local soccer team over their sunglasses as Sherry downed her bodyweight in cocktails and catcalled the players in a British accent. The pain passed through her. She squared her shoulders and followed Cameron inside.

Focus. Tavi's right, your friends are fine. Cameron, on the other hand, is about to get his ass kicked by a knife-wielding Amazon Queen. No matter what happens, just be supportive.

After they entered, Cameron pointed her toward the entrance. "Do you mind waiting for a moment? I'm going to change. My clothes," he added when her eyebrows shot up in the unasked question. "I'm going to change my clothes, not my form."

"That's a relief," she said, eyeing the small, golden orbs that seemed to bob and float everywhere, clustering to every vine and branch. "I don't know how I'd be able to tell you apart from the rest if you did. I'd hate to lose you." She immediately regretted her choice of words as his face looked stricken. "Cameron, I—"

"No, no, it's okay. I know what you meant." He forced a tight smile, then gestured to the front row of seats. He gave her hand a squeeze and jogged off through a side door.

Tavi was waiting for him in the ring, pacing and twirling her flaming knife, throwing curious glances Brie's way. Brie watched her discreetly. It was strange to see the Elysian hesitate. After a few false starts, Tavi finally called out. "Did you really bust up Mammon?"

Brie's head snapped up, startled. "That's what they tell me."

Tavi jogged over. "Can't remember, huh?"

Brie shivered despite the perfect warmth of the day.

The Elysian sat on the seat next to her, looking at her quiz-zically for a moment before leaning back onto her elbows. She tipped her face up to the turquoise sky and closed her eyes. "That's all right. Maybe even for the best. It's a lot to heap on a mortal, after all — battling one of the Seven."

Brie absorbed this silently, casting a curious look to the side. They'd never been in such close proximity before. Up close like this, she could see that Tavi's skin was covered with a latticework of the faintest white tattoos or maybe scars. They looked like lace or lightning and were *everywhere*, even on her eyelids. Brie jumped a little when those eyes shot open, embarrassed to be caught staring. But Tavi just winked, stood, and reached out her hand. "Come walk with me, Brianna Weldon."

Brie grabbed her hand and pulled herself up. "My friends call me Brie."

"Then allow me the presumption of friendship, Brie. Shall we?" She took off with a friendly grin, which Brie couldn't help but mirror as she hurried to catch up to the long-legged fighter.

There was something irresistibly charismatic about Tavi. She kept up a constant stream of chatter while they walked the perim-eter of the arena, pointing out features of interest and cheerfully interrogating Brie all the while.

"The seats over here were all burned to cinders a couple hun-dred years ago. I got my hands on some Hellfire, but before we could even train with it, one of your boyfriend's Earth pets got loose and stampeded all over the place. Crushed a sacred chalice filled with the stuff. It took us ages to clean it all up, to say noth-ing of how difficult it is to resuscitate a mostly-cooked mastodon. Speaking of, is it true that you got him to try human food again?"

Brie struggled to keep pace. "A few times, yes."

Tavi's eyes sparkled. "You're going to need to tell me all about that. He thinks he's tried human food before, but I happen to know it was a mud pie with toothpaste frosting."

Brie couldn't help but laugh. "Who on Earth made him eat that?"

But Tavi had already moved on. "And here's where the Holy Lance buried itself in the wall because Raphael might be aces in the garden, but he's useless with target practice. And here is where the newer members of the guard train."

They turned a corner to reveal the most terrifying display of skill Brie had ever witnessed: Elysians, in their true form, fiery faces orbited by rings of golden light, were training to destroy everything in sight. Some hurled flaming spears at stone targets, breaking them in half upon impact every time without fail, while others flew straight at one another, wings folded like falcons diving for prey, holding weapons that looked like they could carve canyons into the surface of the Earth. Two Elysians crashed together with the force of a hurricane, blasting Brie's hair back and causing her to blink in the explosion of brightness. Two more, whose fires burned blue and green rather than golden-red, sat across from one another, staring with palpable intensity. Brie didn't know what they were trying to do, until the blue one's flames suddenly leapt from their body to engulf their opponent.

Tavi clapped her hands once, and all action suddenly ceased. A ridiculous number of eyes turned to her as she reorganized her troops. "Switch partners, one to the left."

The Elysians saluted with a surprisingly gentle gesture, fingertips to the middle of their foreheads, and threw Brie curious glances before returning to their training.

The one whose blue fire had successfully overwhelmed his opponent assumed a human form and jogged over to grab what looked like a handful of lightning bolts out of a nearby chest. He craned his head around, trying to get a better look at Brie.

Tavi noticed this and called out, "Careful, Jequn. Remember what happened the last time you—"

A bolt of lightning fell from his hands and proceeded to zoom around the arena, causing mayhem as it bounced from one sparring pair to the next. Tavi held up her hand, and the lightning flashed into her palm, where it seemed to soak into the white latticework of scars on her skin. Her arm glowed white for a moment, then went back to normal.

In a flash, Jequn rushed over, apologizing. Tavi laughed it off and sent him back to his sparring partner. Brie swallowed, consciously trying not to stare in open-mouthed amazement at anyone or anything.

"Not what you were expecting?" Tavi asked, still chuckling.

Brie shook her head as her eyes swept over the impossible scene. "This is beyond anything I would ever expect. You said these are the newer members?"

Tavi nodded. "I've only had these the last seven hundred years or so."

Brie frowned. "How does that work, exactly? I mean, if you've all existed for forever, then how do you get new trainees?"

Tavi took a moment before answering. "Our efforts to maintain the barrier between Heaven and Hell are not without casualties. Some of these are Heavenly reinforcements, and some are Elysian volunteers who have given up the work of ferrying souls to protect our world."

As she spoke, she indicated the wall behind them. Brie turned and realized that it was covered in names. "Are these Elysians who have been killed?"

Tavi ran a hand over the engraved letters. "Not all. Most are simply missing. They went out on an assignment and just never came back. We have Raziel look for them sometimes, but he's never found anyone."

"Who's Raziel?" asked Brie. She was struggling to keep the influx of exotic new names straight, and that one was ringing a bell for some reason.

Why does that sound so familiar?

"The Angel of Mysteries," Tavi answered. "Lives in a library, speaks in riddles. Paper wings. Super annoying."

Brie looked down the length of the wall. She couldn't see to the end. "I didn't realize what you do here is so dangerous," she said quietly. She shot a quick look back at the arena to its astonishing trainees. "I don't see who could possibly stand against you."

Cameron never told me.

What else has he shielded me from?

Just then, a ball of fire missed its mark and lit one of the chiming trees just over the wall ablaze. Tavi took off like a shot and jumped the wall before Brie even had time to be surprised at her vertical leap. She decided to stick to the perimeter and walk around as unobtrusively as possible until Tavi returned. She ran her hand over the names as she strolled, pausing when one felt different. She knelt down to see what she'd touched. While all the other names were carved out in pristine, even script, this one was much larger and looked as though it had been chiseled with a rough rock.

Ethan.

She looked down and saw a folded white robe and wooden sandals in a neat pile beneath the name, as though they were waiting for their owner to return and slip them on. She looked up to ask Tavi about it, but the warrior was scrambling back over the wall, holding a fistful of flames in her hand like a live animal and scolding the guard who had thrown it.

Brie traced the jagged 'E' with her fingertip.

"Ouch!" A single drop of blood appeared. She held up her hand, and as she watched, the blood was pulled back into her finger, and the cut disappeared without leaving a trace.

That's new.

"How long has that been going on?" Tavi was beside her again, studying her finger with fascination.

Brie frowned. "I don't know. Around the same time, this thing started glowing, and my entire world turned upside down." She touched her pendant ruefully.

"Can I see that?" Without waiting for an answer, Tavi reached over and grabbed the pendant delicately with her fingertips, bending her face extremely close to Brie's breasts without a hint of hesitation or impropriety.

Personal space doesn't seem to be a thing with her.

Brie bit back a giggle as Tavi turned the stone this way and that, like a child examining a seashell. The Elysian sun glinted off the pendant's gold filigree. She shrugged. "Doesn't seem all that special. Who'd have thought such a little thing could be so powerful?"

"I thought so," answered Brie softly. "Years ago, after the accident that killed my mother." She touched the stone herself. "This saved me. Nobody believed me, and I spent years convincing myself I imagined it. But it saved me back then. I wish I knew why." Words suddenly failed her, and she looked away.

Tavi tilted her head and answered seriously. "It's a terrible gift to be less breakable than the ones you love."

Brie's head snapped up. "What do you mean?"

"I mean," Tavi jumped twenty feet into the air and caught a lightning bolt intended for another target. Brie watched as the lightning once again sank, shimmering, into her skin, making her glow all over like a crocheted star before disappearing into her scars. "When the things that destroy others don't destroy you, it can weigh heavy on the soul." Tavi met Brie's eyes and held her gaze. "If you ever want to talk to someone, I'm around."

Brie nodded, touched. The warrior woman didn't know her at all, but her kindness, her familiarity, and hospitality didn't seem to be conditional upon such details as knowing her. "Thank you, Tavianne."

She grinned. "My friends call me Tavi."

"Then, allow me the presumption of friendship, Tavi," Brie echoed her words from earlier with a shy smile.

Tavi shot her a mischievous wink. "I'd be terribly put out if you *didn't* presume as much."

They started to head back the way they'd come, and Tavi changed the subject. "How did he get you to call him Cameron?"

"Um, he told me that was his name?" Brie answered. "I understand that he kind of borrowed it from a friend. He said his real name is unpronounceable by humans."

Tavi shot her a sly grin. "It isn't. It was his friend's name — he liked it so much he stole it. He's been trying to get us all to call him that since he was young, but it's not his given name, and none of us went along with it."

Sensing opportunity, Brie asked as casually as possible. "What do *you* call him?"

"Lele." Tavi smirked. "He *hates* it."

Brie momentarily forgot to breathe.

Too perfect.

"And is that short for something?" she managed to ask.

"*TAVI!*" Cameron was there before Brie even registered his presence, wearing a white robe and wooden sandals and balancing a spear with its tip to Tavi's throat on one arm. He threw his other hand up in a hapless gesture. "Have you no loyalty?"

"Loads!" Tavi laughed and pulled a flask from a holster on her leather belt. She took a long sip, then held it out for Cameron. "To whomsoever might be my strongest ally. And I sense that Brie here can more than hold her own in a tussle." She looked him up and down with a mischievous eye as he took a swig of the mysterious liquid. "Whereas I can't say I remember the last time you took so much as a point off me, kiddo. Here, hold this, would you?" She tossed Brie the flask, which she fumbled and barely caught.

"Perhaps I was never properly motivated before," he shot back.

Tavi grinned and turned back to Brie. "Lele is short for——"

Before she could finish, Cameron pulled her into a dizzying cloud of fire and slashes of light. The last thing Brie heard before they were too far away was her angel's familiar voice shouting, "So help me, God, I will send you to the *nether* if you utter another word!"

Brie found herself holding back giggles once again as she pocketed whatever celestial liquor Tavi had seen fit to entrust to her and settled herself onto the marble stairs to watch the epic battle. It soon became apparent that "watch" was a relative term. All she could see were blinding flashes of color punctuated with occasional bursts of laughter and flame. The other Elysians had a slightly easier time, turning from their drills to watch discreetly.

"Eyes up," Tavi called, instructing despite herself. The woman might have been powered with the momentum of a comet, but there was something surprisingly grounded about her as well. "I said, eyes up, Cameron. Watch the—"

There was a sudden break in the action, followed by a sharp cry.

"—the *blade*, Cameron."

Brie let out a gasp as they suddenly materialized, bleeding and grinning and scarcely out of breath. There was damage on both that hadn't been there when they'd started, deadly slices in the ivory fabric of their robes. Her inner nurse forced her to her feet, primed with lectures about sutures and antiseptics, but the pair took a single look at each other and started laughing.

He extracted a golden arrow from his hair. She twirled a flaming saber.

The fight began again.

"Exasperating, aren't they?"

Brie whirled around in surprise to see an elderly man walking toward her. His long robe barely kissed the ground, and his hands were clasped thoughtfully behind his back.

King Enoch.

She scrambled to her feet. Having sworn to never curtsey again, she started to bow when the ancient king stopped her.

"Let's not bother with any of that, child," he said, to her great relief. "Please. Sit."

She settled onto the bench and glanced at the arena once more.

"My son has been sparring with Tavianne in the ring for centuries. Always with that grin of delight. Like children." Enoch's long white hair rippled around him as he shook his head.

"Like children," she repeated faintly, tensing when the ancient monarch sat beside her.

Different definitions, I guess.

"It is good to see you feeling more yourself, Ms. Weldon. Please allow me to apologize for Raphael's overly enthusiastic medication earlier. He means well." Another exasperated look passed over his wizened features.

Her face burned bright pink. "I'm the one who should apologize. I should never have interrupted your meeting."

"You are not responsible. Think nothing of it." He nodded politely. "I hope you have found Elysium suited to your needs." His voice was friendly but formal. Wise but wary. He studied her face with a peculiar expression. "I must admit, my dear, I have only recently become aware of your existence. My son seems to have kept you all to himself for quite some time."

She blanched and replied carefully, "If it's any consolation, I only recently became aware that he wasn't a figment of my imagination."

Enoch raised one of his white, caterpillar eyebrows, and she continued.

"I know he didn't mean any harm or disrespect, sir. Cameron bends over backward, trying to do the right thing, more than anyone I've ever met. He hid from me and watched over me for years. He remained hidden until the only way he could protect me was to make himself known. And as far as him not telling you, I think he was afraid that if someone found out, the rules would oblige him to stop doing what he felt was right."

At this, Enoch looked at his son, fighting and shouting in the arena with a sigh. "You are more right than you know. Don't be troubled, young lady. In truth, I can't tell you how it sets my heart at ease to know where he has been spending his time. For a while, I feared…" The old man trailed off. His expression tightened. "I feared he might be lost to me — lost to some impulse to wander or rebel. I once lost someone very dear to me that way."

He glanced over at the wall, engraved with the names of the missing and the fallen. She wondered who he had lost that even in his long and storied life, his grief still felt fresh. The pain on his ancient face kept her from asking for details. She resisted the urge to place a hand on his arm in comfort, struck by how fragile he looked.

The old king composed himself. "I saw you earlier in the meadow with his unicorns," he continued. "I was surprised. It's enough my son would bring you to this place, yet he seems determined to show you all that which he holds most dear." He was quiet for a moment like he'd stumbled upon some quiet truth.

"When I saw them from the balcony, I had to see them up close," she admitted shyly, feeling the need to add something more. "They are a marvel."

"Had it not been for my son, I don't believe any would have survived." The old king's attention drifted to the arena for a moment, and he looked very proud. "He is an uncommonly kind and generous soul."

"He certainly is, sir."

He turned to her, his face serious. "I was relieved to see that the unicorns don't mind your presence. You see, something has troubled me greatly ever since my son told me your story." She tore her attention away from the fight in the ring and focused on Enoch as he continued. "When he spoke to me about your pendant, I had my suspicions. And now that I see it in person, there is no mistaking it."

Her eyes widened as she reached up to touch the pendant she'd worn for five years. "You know what this is?" she asked in astonishment. "Do you know why my mother had it? Do you know what it's doing to me?"

Enoch stared at her intently. "The last time I saw this pendant was thousands of years ago," he answered, "when an archangel gave it to my great-granddaughter."

CHAPTER ELEVEN

After the Flood

"May I?" Enoch tilted his head toward Brie's pendant. Dumbstruck, she held up the stone. He leaned forward and examined its mysterious, opaline depths, nodding faintly. "It is undoubtedly the same."

What? How?

She struggled to find any words at all, let alone the correct question to ask.

Her confusion must have been written all over her face, because the old monarch offered her his arm and said, "Come, child. Let me explain somewhere less distracting."

They walked away from the arena, through the grounds, over to a stone bench beneath a tree laden with long, willowy branches covered in blossoms, with tiny blinking lights clinging here and there. Enoch leaned back against its ancient, twisted trunk and began to tell her a story.

"My son tells me you know some of my family's history. I suspect you know the story of my grandson, Noah."

Her eyes widened. "Noah? *The* Noah? Like, with the ark?"

Enoch nodded. "He saved his family and a great many species

from the Flood by diligently following the will of the Divine. But while Noah was righteous and followed God, the rest of the world descended into wickedness and fell prey to the schemes and manipulations of the Nephilim."

Brie shook her head, uncomprehending. "What are the Nephilim?"

"They were the offspring of humans and fallen angels. Creatures whose desires ran contrary to the Divine will. They were strong, powerful, beautiful, and most important of all, *present*. It is easier to follow a thing you can see than a God you cannot, no matter how powerful that God may be. The Nephilim convinced many people to worship them. As punishment, archangels were sent to imprison the Fallen who had spawned the creatures, and the world was washed clean with Divine tears in the Great Flood, cleansing it of the Nephilim. Noah and his family weathered the terrible storm in the ark. When the waters abated, Noah's family received the sign of the rainbow — a covenant with the world to never again punish it with a flood."

Enoch paused and glanced once more at Brie's pendant.

"But that was not the only sign delivered to Noah's family. The archangel Gabriel appeared to Noah's adopted daughter-in-law, Neria. Noah's son found her wandering the mountains, pregnant and took her as his wife to raise her baby as his own. Neria was a lovely woman, pure of heart and purpose, and the daughter she bore was a delightful, intelligent child, beautiful inside and out. Neria helped everyone during the flood — her loyalties never faltered. One day, once they were back on dry ground, she was gathering food for their family. Gabriel appeared to her and gave her the pendant that you now wear around your neck."

Brie was sitting on the edge of the bench, waiting breathlessly for him to go on. After a few moments, when it became apparent that this wasn't going to happen, she gave him a gentle prompt. "But why? Why did Gabriel give her the pendant? What else did he say?"

Enoch shook his head. "I haven't the slightest idea."

She pushed compulsively to her feet and started pacing. "How do you know all of this?" she asked.

"I was fond of Neria. She was special. Nowadays, I do not make it a habit to ferry human souls to the next realm, but back then, I still had family whom I loved and was close to in the human world. When the time came for their spirits to depart, I would often go myself to ease their passing. At her bedside, just before she died, Neria looked at me and smiled as though she could see me, though I should have been cloaked from human view. She knew it was her time and greeted me as a beloved grandfather. Her firstborn daughter came into the room to hold her hand at the end. Neria gave her the pendant, and when she put it on, she could see me as well. I asked Neria how she came to possess such a trinket. All she said was, 'Gabriel.' Nothing more. Her daughter told me the rest of the story after she'd passed."

The king lapsed into silence — a silence seemingly comfortable for him, but one that was rapidly driving Brie to an emotional flashpoint. "That can't be all you know," she nearly pleaded. Her voice was sharp with a frantic quality. "There *has* to be something more."

Enoch watched her sympathetically. "I'm sure there is, but I am not the one who has the knowledge you seek."

"Then who does?" she asked quickly, trying to hide her panic.

"Gabriel, I imagine."

"All right, well, where is he?"

"The last time anyone saw Gabriel, he was in the Garden of Eden, along with Michael and someone else — the only other person who might know something about your pendant."

"The Garden of... okay. Questions for later, but okay." She took a steadying breath, determined that this conversation would land somewhere useful. "Who is the only other person who might know something about this?"

"The only other human in all the realms who is like me. The prophet Elijah."

She drew in a sharp breath. "The only other person who never died."

Enoch nodded. "I was placed in charge of the archangels and the realm of Elysium. Elijah was given the gift of prophecy, though he might say he was cursed with it. He was allowed to live in the Garden so that he might find peace from his visions."

She took a second to absorb his words, then nodded manically, still pacing. "Okay, good. This is good. Let's call him."

Enoch shot her a puzzled frown. "Call him?"

"Of course. If Gabriel and Elijah are the ones who might know what's going on, we should call them and find out what they know right away."

The king chuckled quietly. "My dear, I am terribly sorry to tell you that Elijah doesn't have — what do you young ones call them? — a telegram. Not that such a device would be remotely useful in Eden anyway."

There's a chance I'm going to explode.

A muscle clenched in her jaw. "Why not?"

"Because Eden exists in a different dimension of time and space."

Perfect. Just perfect.

"*You* exist in a different dimension of time and space." She jabbed a finger at the astonishing sky. "*This* is a different dimension of time and space."

"Theirs is a different, different dimension."

She let out a weary breath, more of a hiss. "Don't you have another way to reach them?"

"Eden is purposefully hidden away from all the realms, including Elysium. There are no lines of communication in or out, short of traveling there in person, lest the forces of darkness discover a keyhole into Paradise. Such a thing would be catastrophic for more worlds than one," he added darkly.

She finally stopped pacing and let out a maddened sound that was dangerously close to an oath. He regarded her quietly as she took a couple of deep breaths to compose herself, then turned to face him.

"I'm sorry, sir. I apologize, but please understand. Since I've put this thing around my neck," she held her locket like a noose, "my mother has been murdered. I've been attacked. I've seen impossible things — *done* impossible things. I don't mean to be rude, truly." She trailed off in frustration. "Sir, I *need* to know what's going on. I don't know what to do."

Enoch stared at her for a long moment as if he were choosing his next words with great care. "We all need to know what's going on, Ms. Weldon. The forces at play are greater than any one person. Which is why I must ask you," he regarded her with a somber expression. "Would you consent to show your full testament to my court?"

She frowned, not understanding. "I can tell them what happened, but I don't see how I could show them."

"There is a process by which we can see events as they unfolded through your eyes," he said. "Through your memories. We call it the Revelation. It is the surest way to be certain no detail is over-looked, and to ensure that all Elysians have access to the same information. It is the ultimate act of transparency."

Ultimate transparency… is this what Cameron warned me about?

Cameron's face flooded her thoughts. Her angel had laid him-self on the line to protect her for years, defying the laws of his people to keep her safe. The last thing she wanted to do was show his entire society the extent of that defiance — what he'd called his "disobedience."

If I say no, could they take my memories?

And what happens if I say yes?

She searched Enoch's face, looking for signs of hardness or tyr-anny but finding nothing but kindness and concern. Suddenly, she felt the strangest sensation, like a nudge within her heart, pushing her gently toward the right path.

Maybe if I agree, this will convince him that he doesn't need to tamper with my memories.

And besides. It's the next right thing.

She took a deep breath. "Yes. Yes, all right. If it will help."

A look of surprise overtook the king. "So quickly, you agree?"

She nodded. "It's important. It's bigger than me. And it's the right thing to do." She hesitated a moment before asking quietly, "Will it hurt?"

His expression softened. "No, child. We would never cause you harm."

Time seemed to suspend for a moment as a new understand-ing and a mutual respect settled between them. She was about to offer her arm to help him up when a figure materialized on the path and hurried toward them. It was Cameron, both of his eyes bruised blue-black.

"They told me you were out here," he said, visibly alarmed by the sight of them together. "What did I miss?"

"*Absolutely* not!" Cameron was pacing in very much the same way Brie had been just moments ago.

"It is the only way to convince everyone of her sincerity, son. Some divisions within the Court are against allowing this relic to remain in the hands of a human. There are those who believe she knows too much of our world, and we should—"

"I know what they would have you do!" Cameron sounded stricken, anguished. "But you can't! She's been through enough! We can't let Zadkiel rifle through her mind for all the realm to see! You cannot ask this of her!" He stopped his pacing directly in front of his father, his face the picture of devastation. "And you cannot do this to me. Not again."

Enoch moved compulsively toward his son for a fraction of a second as though he wanted nothing more than to gather him into his arms. He stopped himself short, clenching his hands together, white-knuckled, by his chest, struggling to maintain his composure. "There is nothing I can do, my son. If I could prevent this…" He swallowed hard, and his eyes shone. He finished in a husky voice. "If there was a way, I would find it."

Cameron looked for a moment like a twelve-year-old boy who had lost his only friend in the world before his face hardened. He shook his head and began to work himself up again, prepared to do anything to prevent this. "No. It's invasive. It's a violation of her privacy. It's—"

"It's what I want," she interjected quietly.

Cameron turned to her, shocked. "Brie, why?"

"Your father's right. This is the only way we can be sure that everyone knows everything I've seen. I'm new to this world. I don't know what's important. You're considered young here and compared to you?" She raised her hands in a lost gesture. "According to Ephriam, I'm a fetus. If I just tell them, I could overlook a detail that might be crucial and never know it. Not to mention, I'm sure my first impression didn't inspire much confidence within your court. You know, violating a bunch of time rules and fainting. Plus, the thing with Raphael."

Cameron opened his mouth to disagree.

She cut him off. "It's my choice, Cameron. This is what I choose."

Brie had no idea who won the sparring match.

Both Cameron and Tavi claimed victory and smeared the other's character to such a degree that Brie was inclined to believe them both. In fact, she didn't think the fight would have stopped at all if her conversation with Enoch hadn't caught Cameron's eye.

Tavi stayed with the guard and healed up a deep laceration on her arm with a golden glow. She cheerfully told Brie to please come back again soon and invited them to a bonfire with the troops that night down by the Elysian Sea.

Cameron took a moment to heal his injuries before walking her back to the villa, following a different path than they'd taken before. They only managed a few paces before he broached the subject. "How was your conversation with my father?" He tried to ask casually, but she saw telltale lines of tension in his forehead. "I mean, the rest of your conversation."

She smiled a little, resisting the urge to take his hand.

"We didn't talk about you much. Not that I don't intend to, mind you," she added with a mischievous look. "Give me some time, and I'll charm every embarrassing childhood story you've got out of your loved ones. Just give me time." She faltered.

He glanced at her face and took her hand just long enough to bring them to a stop, before dropping it to her side again with an anxious glance over his shoulder. "It really is going to be all right," he said. "The Revelation is perfectly safe. That isn't why I don't want you to do it. I just wish it didn't have to be you. You've already done so much."

She could see he was struggling to say more, so she remained quiet.

After a few moments, he raised anguished eyes to meet hers. "Is it any use at all to beg you not to do it?" He threw caution to the wind and brought her hand to his lips, tenderly kissing her fingers. She forgot how to breathe as he continued. "I've spent five years watching over you but an eternity waiting for you. We've only been together for a week, a week we've spent running from darkness." He held her hand to his chest. She felt his heart racing beneath her fingertips. "I don't think I can bear to lose you, Brie. When they see your memories, if they see *us*, if they see how I feel about you, I fear they will take you from me. And I cannot withstand such a loss. So, I have to ask. Is it any use, any use at all, to beg you not to perform the Revelation? Because I will. I will beg you not to do it."

Her throat tightened, and her stomach dropped. He'd never asked anything of her before, and it tore at her heart to refuse, but she swallowed and took a step closer. "I don't want to do it. And, of course, I don't want to lose you. But your father's right.

This is bigger than us. This affects your entire society — your *people,* Cameron. I couldn't live with myself if I didn't do everything in my power to keep them safe, the same way you've kept me safe. I know in my heart it's the right thing to do."

He hung his head, empty, like a swan who'd lost his mate. "I know... I know."

She looked imploringly into his face, desperate to give him some hope. "But you know what? I can't explain it, but I think that, somehow, it's going to be okay. I *believe* it is. I truly do."

He didn't respond, merely smiled joylessly. They continued down the path to the villa. "I suppose one thing's for sure. If you perform the Revelation, whatever memory issues you're having about the hospital are going to be a thing of the past." After a few more steps he added, "You really did save my life."

She kept her eyes forward. "I don't know what you're talking about."

He studied her face. "You really don't remember anything?"

Images swarmed unbidden through her brain: a screaming demon with half her face missing; a sound so huge, so terrifying, that nothing could withstand it; her own body hovering in the air, surrounded by pulsing spheres of lightning.

"Nope," she said. "Nothing at all."

It wasn't long before they reached the villa. It shone like a white shell under the strange, unchanging Elysian light, bigger than she remembered. From this vantage point, she could see another wing with adjoining gardens and an outdoor area with a round pit lined with purple stones and filled with wood.

THE PENDANT & THE PROPHECY 153

He led her through tall glass doors into a common room filled with bookshelves and a few pieces of Elysian art. There was also a small kitchen area she hadn't noticed the other day. He sat at a table and conjured a steaming mug, pushing it toward her as she sank heavily into the chair beside him.

"Jasmine?" she asked, inhaling the floral steam.

"It's a calming blend Raphael invented."

She looked at him with a slight grin. "It isn't going to get me high, is it?"

He shook his head. "I am never, ever going to let him live that down."

She took a sip. "Good Lord. Was that yesterday?"

"Technically, it was today. Everything for the past few days has been today."

Ignore that. In fact, ignore most of this. It isn't helpful.

They sat in silence for a while, letting their attention drift. Despite the mounting pressure, it felt like they'd found a bubble of calm.

He watched her sip for a moment before speaking. "So, to recap, I leave you alone for fifteen minutes, and you decide to open your mind and lay all your secrets bare in front of the whole of Elysium."

When you say it like that...

She sipped her tea. "Thoughts?"

He grabbed her hand and ran his thumb over her knuckles. "My girlfriend's insane."

Her heart fluttered, but she tried to keep her face casual. "Girlfriend, huh?"

He instantly froze and turned about a dozen shades of red. "Right. Well, we never really actually talked about it. Except when I was telling you why it couldn't happen. And then why I absolutely want it to happen. And obviously, everything is moving much, much too fast. I mean, technically, it isn't moving at all, because, time stream and what have you, but that really isn't the point, and — did it just get hot in here?" He grabbed vaguely at his collar, pulling it out of shape. The man could hold his own in Tavianne's arena, but a single word and he completely unraveled. "Of course, maybe *you* don't want to, and, of course, I respect that, and if you have a boundary there, what can I say except that it's probably wise? And then, I guess we—"

He stopped short as Brie eased onto his lap, sliding her fingers through his hair. She tugged gently, tipping his head back, and brought her lips just a whisper away from his. "Cameron?" Her breath feathered against his lips.

Every muscle in his body went taut. He held her waist, dumbstruck for a moment. His thumbs traced her hips, and he answered breathlessly, "Brie?"

"Stop talking and kiss your girlfriend."

The man did not need to be told twice.

Within moments, they were so tangled up in one another that they scarcely knew where one body ended and the other began. Her hair fell in perfumed cascades around his head, curtaining them in privacy as his hands explored gently upwards over her shirt. She inhaled and arched her back, feeling his breath soft and warm on the curve of her neck.

Someone coughed behind them.

Oh shit!

She flew back to her own chair, wild-eyed like a child whose hand had been caught in a cookie jar, while Cameron hastily adjusted himself, and they turned simultaneously toward the sound.

Mike was standing in the doorway. His cheeks were as red as his hair, and it was possible he'd never been this embarrassed before in his life. "Hey, guys. I'm awfully sorry to interrupt…"

Their tangled responses flew at him all at once.

"Not at all—"

"Really, what a thing to say—"

"What can we help you with?"

"What's up?"

He watched them floundering for a few seconds, framed by a cloud of what looked like pixies drifting past the window behind them. Then he straightened up. "I have a few questions if that's all right."

They exchanged a quick look, then pulled out a third chair at the table.

◆   ◆   ◆

Half an hour later, the policeman seemed to be taking it all rather well.

"So, when we woke up in the parking garage, we'd already been through the battle with you. With the demon woman. The goat lady."

Brie nodded, encouraged that he wasn't phrasing this as a question anymore.

"And when Sherry was acting all strange, it was because she was remembering the stuff she wasn't supposed to remember." Mike looked at Cameron. "Why can she remember things when your friend—"

"Ephriam," prompted Cameron.

"—When your friend Ephriam is supposed to be able to modify

our memories?" He looked back and forth between them, searching for answers. "And why can't I?"

"Honestly, I have no idea." Cameron took in Mike's worried face. "But if I had to guess, it would be for the same reason that Brie has always been able to see me, and she seems immune to most of my powers."

"And what reason is that?" asked Mike.

"This," she said, holding up her pendant.

Mike stared at it, then caught her eye. "May I?"

"Be my guest."

He leaned closer and took the strange stone in his fingers, turning it over and examining it in the kitchen lights. "It feels warm," he murmured. "And when Sherry touched it in the parking lot? That flash?"

Brie hesitated. "There's a lot about it I don't know. Honestly, I was hoping to find some answers here in Elysium, but I have more questions now than ever before. My best guess is the closer people are to this thing, the more it affects them." She looked down the hall. "For most of my life, Sherry has been closer to me than anyone." She looked back to Mike, who was studying her face. "I didn't know any of this until a week ago. Well, I knew something about it back when my mom died, but then I spent five years convinced I was crazy. Mike, I never would have exposed Sherry to this if I'd known what it was doing. If I knew there was any risk at all, I never would have involved her — never in a million years. Please, believe me. I love her more than anything in this world."

He leaned back and nodded slowly. "I know that, Brie. And not for nothing — she knows it, too."

Her eyes welled with unspilled tears as he placed a hand over hers.

"Give her some time to digest this," he continued. "The two of you are going to be fine. I can feel it." His voice turned thoughtful. "It seems to me like you've been trying to do the best you can in a crazy situation."

She turned her face away, determined to maintain composure in the face of his graciousness, and quickly changed the subject. "Do you have any other questions? I mean, it's a lot."

He hesitated, and suddenly looked very young.

That's a yes.

She grinned and prompted him again. "Don't be shy now."

"Is it okay if... Can I see?" he asked tentatively.

She tilted her head, puzzled. "See what?"

He looked at Cameron. "You know, like... can you do something?"

Cameron flashed a boyish smile. "Like a magic trick?"

Mike turned bright red right down to his neck. "I'm sorry. I completely understand. I don't want to make you feel like you need to perform your culture for me, if that is insensitive. You know what? It probably was, so never mind. I apologi— *Oh My God!*"

His face transformed into an expression of pure, childlike delight as Cameron levitated her mug of tea two feet off the table. His eyes shone as Cameron tipped the mug, which disappeared. The two drops of tea that spilled forth transformed into white peonies before they hit the table. Cameron picked these up and gave them to Brie.

"Thank you," she said, hiding a smile. She'd never seen him play magician before.

"Show me another!" Mike demanded.

And on it went.

When Brie finally left the boys to it, Cameron was creating piles of Mike's favorite peppermint candies and zooming them one by one through an obstacle course the policeman had built out of books and kitchen appliances.

She wandered down the hallway to Sherry's bathroom fortress. "Sher? Can I come in?"

No response.

She tried the door, but it was locked. She leaned back against it and slid all the way down to the floor with a sigh. "Sher, I know it's a lot, and I'm so, so sorry I didn't tell you what was going on. But please. Please, say something."

Met with nothing but silence, Brie closed her eyes and tapped the back of her head against the door — once, twice, and on the third time, the door suddenly opened, and she spilled backward inside.

Sherry towered above her, framed in the doorway like a giantess. She stood, looking down at her friend tangled up in her own hair. In a scratchy voice, she finally spoke:

"Enter at your own risk."

CHAPTER TWELVE

With Apologies to Julia Child

Sherry's wish-fulfilling bathroom did not seem to have even a fraction of the scruples that Brie's had displayed. After Brie scrambled to her feet and followed her best friend inside her fortress, she was visually accosted by a stunning array of...

Sherry's subconscious desires.

For one thing, it wasn't even a bathroom anymore. Wherever her giant teacup tub and facilities had relocated themselves to, Brie hadn't the faintest idea because she was standing in a luxurious, circular anteroom, surrounded on at least eight sides by doors.

It was beautifully appointed, furnished with elegant, modern chairs, plush fabrics, a harlequin pattern, white and black marble tiles underfoot, and overlaid with the softest carpets. Brie spied an ebony fainting couch adorned with tear-stained silk pillows. Beside it, a side table's drawers brimmed over with strings of pearls. Three mannequins stood in a floor-to-ceiling mirrored enclave, sporting the latest New York fashions. Countless boxes of shoes were strewn around, half-opened. A rare edition of *Pride and Prejudice* sat on a table nearby, along with what looked suspiciously like a Fabergé Egg.

A bunny hopped across the floor.

"You've certainly been busy," Brie began carefully.

"Not on purpose. This stuff just kept appearing. At first, it scared me, but it has its utility." An enormous cappuccino materialized on the counter, which Sherry took and started to drink like it was her job. Many identical, empty, white porcelain cups littered the scene.

Brie's eyes fixed on the tear-stained pillows.

It was trying to make her feel better, she realized. *The room was trying to get her to stop crying.*

And nothing worked.

"The one thing I can't get is a signal," Sherry continued, whipping out her phone and looking at Brie in cool accusation. "Though Siri seems to have discovered the joys of beat poetry."

That is actually surprising. I'll have to ask Cam.

"I'm surprised it gave you coffee," Brie said with a touch of jealousy. "Mine would only dole out herbal teas." She meandered to the nearest door, curious to see how many of them contained closets.

"Don't open that!" cried Sherry, too late.

Brie had already turned the handle and peeked inside, only to discover an entire spread of GQ cover models lounging around what appeared to be a hot tub, eating grapes in their underwear.

Is that a young Enrique Iglesias?

The Latin heartthrob caught her eye and started to sashay his way toward her. Brie slammed the door shut and whirled to face her friend. "*Sherry!*"

"I know."

"Mike is *right* outside! And you're in here collecting a harem!"

"Don't be crass, it wasn't my fault — they just kept appearing. I didn't know what to do with them, then that room just popped up out of nowhere, so I started stuffing them all inside."

There was a beat.

"I *bet* you started stuffing them all inside—"

"Brianna Weldon, don't you start."

Brie grinned and averted her eyes, only to let out a gasp. "Holy Moses, Sher — is that?" She was staring at a jacket embroidered all over with sunflowers. "That's the Saint Laurent jacket you're always going on about, isn't it?"

Sherry's voice was dry. "On any other day, I would be extremely proud you caught that."

There it is.

The cloud started to settle over them again, but this time, Brie wasn't going to allow it to drag them down into despair. "Screw that."

Sherry frowned. "I beg your pardon?"

"Sher, when was the last time we got to go on vacation together? As adults?"

"A vacation? That would be, never."

"Right. Our lives have been crazy."

Sherry shot her a look that could've melted steel.

Brie backtracked. "Okay, it's possible that isn't the most helpful phrasing right now, but you know what I mean. It isn't what we imagined, and I know you're mad as hell. But we're here, in this beautiful place, surrounded by angels, with the guys we like, in a magical room granting your every couture desire. And I want— no, I *demand* to show you around. There are things I want you to see. There are people I want you to meet."

Sherry stared at her, and for one of the first times in her life, Brie couldn't even begin to guess what she was thinking.

"I'll come with you," Sherry finally gave in. "But I'm not going to meet anyone. And this does *not* count as a vacation."

"Fair enough," said Brie, without the slightest intention of facilitating that request. "Can you get me a cappuccino before we go?"

Sherry gestured around the room. "It's a magical wish-granting closet, Brianna. Why can't you get it yourself?"

Brie decided that showing was easier than telling. "Hey, magical room? If it's not too much trouble, I'd love a double cappuccino with whip and a dusting of cinnamon. And a maple scone."

A fragrant herbal tea, a plate of apple slices, and stuffed dates appeared.

Sherry took this impassively. "That figures."

"Why does it figure?" Brie asked, poking at a date with a poorly disguised sulk.

Sherry shrugged into the priceless designer coat. "I've spent my whole life needing what I want. You've spent yours wanting what you need." She walked out of the room, calling for Mike and handing Brie the remains of her cappuccino.

Brie stood there dumbfounded, choking on that little truth bomb. She might have remained that way a long time, had the male models not started scratching at the door.

There are some sights you're simply never prepared for. Not even if your threshold of ridiculosity has been raised over the past few days to include such things as parallel realities and moon dates. One such sight, as the ladies discovered upon entering the hallway, was that of an Elysian warrior attempting to cheat at a potluck.

Ephriam was stepping his hulking form through a glowing portal, carrying an apple pie. This was out of place enough before Julia Child's unmistakable voice rang out behind him, saying, "Now remember to let it rest at least an hour before you cut it, or it'll ooze all over the place. Do come back anytime, you darling giant man! And thank you for the vanilla!"

Brie and Sherry merely stared.

Ephriam looked at them guiltily as the portal closed behind him.

Finally, he spoke. "If anyone asks? I made this."

"Was that Julia Child?" asked Sherry sharply. "The actual Julia Child?"

His face contorted furiously as he tried to shush her. "Not if anyone asks!"

Brie sighed and took Sherry's hand, leading her away. They walked in on their boyfriends, standing around the island of what was now a gourmet kitchen, with state-of-the-art appliances jetting from every cabinet and corner. Mike and Cameron appeared to be engaged in a culinary lesson of sorts. At least, that's what it looked like, judging from their matching, frilly floral aprons.

Mike immediately dropped what he was doing and came over to put his arms around Sherry. He lifted her chin and gave her a tender kiss. "Better?" he asked.

She nodded and rested her head against his chest.

Brie shifted her weight awkwardly. "It smells delicious," she said, peeking into a casserole dish. "What is it?"

"Gratîn dauphinois," Mike answered with no trace of correct pronunciation but an abundance of Southern charm. "It's one of Sherry's favorites. I thought she might appreciate some Earth food options for dinner tonight, given the nature of our arrival."

Ephriam stalked in behind them, placed the still-steaming apple pie on the counter, grabbed a stack of plates, and walked out to the patio without addressing them. Sherry skewered the back of his head with a glare, having far from forgiven *the nature of their arrival.*

"Ephriam has been helping. He's in charge of dessert," Mike explained.

"I didn't know you could cook," Brie said, bemused.

Mike was still holding Sherry and swaying gently, grateful that the fire-poker part of their adventure seemed to be behind them. He smelled her hair and smiled. "I'm already an Irish Catholic police officer with a taste for Guinness, Brie. I can't let all the stereotypes be true."

She couldn't resist. "So, you made potatoes?"

Sherry caught her eye, then glared daggers at Cameron while she said, "Hey, remember how that guy you hang out with sometimes turns into a golden ball and lurks in your purse?"

Cameron turned an unhealthy-looking shade of green.

Brie decided to stop teasing Mike.

"I'm going to take Sherry on a walk around the garden for a minute. How long until you're all done here?" she asked.

Mike and Cameron shot each other a look.

"We can come with you—" the angel started to offer when he was cut off by both women at the same time.

Brie's more reserved response, "That's all right, this is just for us," was slightly upstaged by Sherry's more emphatic, "*Absolutely not.*"

"Take all the time you need," Mike answered in the resulting awkward silence. "We can be ready whenever. Go, enjoy."

Sherry took Mike aside and whispered something in his ear. He nodded grimly. Cameron bit his lower lip, trying very hard not to laugh, and Brie pretended not to hear.

She wasn't sure, because she'd shouted a rather embarrassingly large number of things she'd half-forgotten while tripping on Raphael's magical elixir, so she couldn't remember if she'd quite gotten around to telling Sherry about her emerging superpowers yet.

Which very much included the gift of superhuman hearing.

This meant she heard perfectly when Sherry whispered, *"If he tries anything funny — I don't care how magical he is. He won't get far if you sever all his tendons and arteries. Remember, honey — vertical cuts up the limbs. Never horizontal."*

In less time than it took to whip up chicken piccata, the girls sat on a marble bench where Sherry had abruptly ended their garden tour and stared fixed at the sky.

Brie's enthusiastic description of her date on the moon died on her lips. She slid close to her friend. After a moment, she asked. "Was it the pixies?"

"It wasn't the pixies."

Brie nodded, thinking. "It was that vine that started reciting Chaucer, wasn't it?"

"Wasn't the literary vine."

There was a pause.

"It couldn't have been the—"

"Brie, what are we doing here?"

"Funny you should ask." She swallowed. "I need to present my testimony to the Elysian Court. Tomorrow."

Sherry gave her another metal-melting look. "I got kidnapped to an alien freaking dimension because *you have jury duty?*"

"Kind of," Brie replied hesitantly, biting her lip. "But it's more than that. I'm afraid it's more like I'm a witness. All the things that have been happening? This is bigger than me. There's more on the line than I probably even know exists. I need to show them what I've seen, Sher. This affects them. The things they're up against? They have a right to know what's going on."

Sherry nodded slowly. "Okay, that much I can get behind. Although I object *in the strongest possible terms* to their methodologies," she directed this part at the garden as though *it* was responsible for her forced relocation, "I understand the goal."

Brie breathed a premature sigh of relief.

"What I don't understand," Sherry continued, "is why are *we* here?"

"What do you mean, 'a *threat to dimensional security*?'" Sherry roared over a beautiful Waldorf salad.

Brie had explained that the secret of Elysian existence was taken very seriously. Although she wasn't privy to the specifics, they were probably all brought to Elysium not just for their own protection, but also to figure out why they were proving immune to Ephriam's memory-altering magic.

At the first mention that her memory had been tampered with, Sherry had shot to her feet and stormed back to the villa, where she proceeded to shout at the Elysian warrior while ravenously wolfing down the gorgeous meal that the men had prepared.

"If I have gotten myself landed on some terrorist watchlist, I have the right to be *informed*. I have the right to an *attorney*. I cannot simply be held against my will by a foreign government without charges or counsel. *This is America,*" she thundered.

Ephriam was grinding his teeth together so hard Brie could hear it from across the table. "It really isn't," he glowered.

"How could I possibly be a threat to an entire country I didn't even know existed?"

"This isn't a country. It's a plane of existence. And if anyone could find a way to threaten it without having a clue as to what they were doing, it would doubtless be you, Miss Walker."

She pointed a fork laden with perfectly sauced chicken at him and narrowed her eyes. "On that point, we agree. So just imagine what I can get done *when I know what I'm aiming at.*"

All parties found themselves in a strange predicament. Ephriam had never tasted human food before, as there had been no need. Sherry had consumed nothing but coffee since she was back on Earth yesterday. So, though neither particularly wanted to be in the other's company, both were completely unable to tear themselves away from the delicious feast laid before them.

And it was undeniably delicious.

At a stalemate with her adversary, Sherry finished her bite and took Mike's hand. In a completely different tone, she said, "The dinner is lovely, honey. Thank you."

Brie nudged Cameron. "It really is. You helped with these potatoes?"

Cameron tried to hide the fact that he was beaming with pride. "I cannot take any credit. Mike is a most excellent teacher."

"And you're a perfect student." Mike shot him a grin before turning to Sherry. "You should've seen it, babe — instead of folding in the butter, he did this thing where he folded space-time." He trailed off at the look on her face and went back to eating his meal with a mumbled, "Well, it was awesome."

"What are the options here?" Sherry was in multitasking mode. She swung her gaze back to Ephriam, demanding answers. "What could this 'court' potentially do to us?"

The Elysian sighed. "This is an unprecedented event, so I've no way of knowing. The standard procedure would be to wipe all the memories of these events from the participants, but this process doesn't seem to have an effect on you, likely because of some rare defect."

Careful, buddy.

Sherry growled. "So, you'd mess with our memories *again* if given half a chance?"

Mike whirled to look at Cameron. "Wait a minute — you've never messed with my memory, have you?"

Cameron froze, debated for a second, then opted for a half-truth delivered around a mouthful of piccata. "Ephriam did." He pointed at his surly friend.

Ephriam shot him a scathing look.

"The point is going to be totally moot after tomorrow, anyway. I'm doing this thing that'll clear everything up for everybody," Brie said quickly, trying to head off the impending rebuttal.

"Really? You think just by testifying about what you've seen, these 'angels will just let us go and leave us alone?" Sherry looked at her like she couldn't believe her naïveté.

"Sherry, it isn't like they've brought us here to harm us. They're angels. Or, okay, they're Elysians, but they are literally on the side of the angels. Angels can't be bad. And besides," she handed her plate to Ephriam, who had started collecting dishes. "I'm not just going to tell them. I'm going to show them."

There was a clatter of flatware, and Ephriam sucked in a breath next to her. "What do you mean?" he asked sharply.

She turned to him, startled. "I'm doing that thing King Enoch talked about. The Revelation."

Ephriam locked eyes with Cameron across the table.

Cameron started to shake his head.

"What?" Brie demanded. "That's what he said I should do. And it makes sense."

"And what exactly is the Revelation?" Sherry asked.

"It is exactly what its name implies," Ephriam answered bluntly. "It reveals all. Everything about a person. Every memory. Every thought. Every intention. It lays an individual bare for all the realm to see the very heart of them." Ephriam was still staring at Cameron with an expression that looked almost like pity. "To my knowledge, it has only been performed a handful of times since the creation of this realm. And only two other times, on a human. Brianna," the Elysian looked at her with an unfathomable expression, "you must reconsider."

Every head at the table swiveled to Brie.

She felt a sinking sensation in her stomach, but she felt something else, too. Certainty. She didn't know how, and she didn't know why, but she knew this was the right path. She stuck to her guns. "It's the only way to truly get everything out in the open. I've been living with secrets for five years, Ephriam. I've tried everything to convince myself that the lie was the truth. I've gone half-crazy trying to live with a fiction. We've tampered with the minds of people I love just to maintain a lie. I'm not going to do it anymore. I want to see. I want everyone to see."

A heavy silence fell over the room. So heavy, only one person could seem to break it.

"Well, that's a fine idea, Brianna," Sherry snapped. "Brilliant. You're going to do great. After all, when have you ever had an errant thought you might not want an entire alien host to see?" She aggressively speared and ate her last forkful of potatoes without breaking eye contact, then shoved her plate onto the stack in Ephriam's hands. He glared at her and took the dishes into the kitchen, muttering in an ancient language under his breath.

Sherry glared back and asked loudly, "Who wants pie? Fun fact about this pie…"

CHAPTER THIRTEEN

The Hero of the Dragon Hole

The skirmish that followed ensured that nobody got any pieces of pie, though several people got handfuls. The violence might have escalated further had a messenger from Tavi not shown up to remind them to come to the bonfire.

Mike and Cameron, who were rapidly becoming thick as thieves, had squirreled away packages of marshmallows, graham crackers, and giant blocks of chocolate. Cameron carried a fistful of sharp sticks. Brie didn't like the way Sherry was eyeing them at all. Mike promised this was going to revolutionize Elysian cuisine.

"Since Elysian cuisine doesn't really exist, I believe you," said Cameron with a laugh.

Brie reached over and carefully removed a glob of cinnamon sugar spiced apple from his cheek. "I think we may have overdone it on the pie," she said sheepishly. "I couldn't help it. Even after being subjected to a food fight, that thing was positively sinful."

"Overeating cake is the sin of gluttony," answered Cameron. "However, eating too much pie is all right because the sin of pi is always zero."

Brie stared at him blankly. Mike burst out laughing. Sherry shot him a look, but he raised his hands helplessly. "Honey, it's a math joke. You know I love a good math joke."

Sherry stalked forward to walk with Brie. "I hope you realize what you've done," she muttered darkly. "If those two run away together, I will hold you personally responsible."

Brie bit back a grin as they wound their way down to the wine-colored sea.

The Elysians had already started setting up the bonfire on a scale that kept with the fantastical surroundings. Piles of blue-flecked wood were stacked in large, stone-lined pits at intervals all over the beach. Around these, thick carpets, blankets, and mountains of pillows with tasseled corners were arranged. Bottles of amber liquid were already being passed around the legions of Elysians, loosening their tongues and encouraging laughter as they lit the fires — some red, some violet, some blue.

Tavi saw them and waved them over to a more familiar, orange-burning fire. She lit up when she saw Sherry. Quick as a flash, she raced over and started shaking her hand incorrectly. "Oh, it's you! Brilliant, I like you! I was wondering when you'd stop locking yourself in the bathroom. I have to say — though, I won't judge you for it, not much anyway. After all, interdimensional travel can be tricky your first time. We've all been there. But I *have to say* — a touch disappointing after your delicious threats back on Earth. I was rather hoping you'd roast Cameron to a cinder."

Sherry blinked, taken aback by the onslaught of friendliness. She cast a dark look at Cameron before shooting Tavi a smile. "The night is still young."

Tavi's musical laugh rang out. She released Sherry's hand and clapped her muscled arm around her shoulders. "Come on, let's get you something to drink."

Half an hour later, they'd settled into the pillows and each other's arms and were enjoying the warmth of the fire under that striking sky. The humans sat with Ephriam and Jequn, who Brie had met earlier in the ring. He apologized for dropping the lightning and kept shooting glances at her, looking quickly away when she caught him staring.

Brie sipped cocoa from a mug Cameron conjured with a flick of his fingers, much to Sherry's disapproval. Tavi buzzed from one campfire to the other, keeping an eye on her troops with her second in command, an eight-foot-tall woman with neon-orange hair named Arafel. At one point, Brie watched them clink their bottles together and share a private laugh.

She nudged Cameron. "They seem very close. Are they...?"

"Together?" Cameron looked surprised. "Nearly always. But it isn't like that. They've been best friends since," He looked lost for reference points for a second. "Before the moon controlled the tides."

Arafel went off to deal with a bonfire that had been fed a bit too enthusiastically and was now sporting flames that reached higher than her head. Tavi hopped over a log and settled gracefully onto their blanket, throwing her arms around them, hugging them close. Brie chuckled. The warrior woman's lack of personal boundaries would have felt invasive to anyone else, but paired with Tavi's complete lack of artifice, it was charming. Even Sherry thought so and seemed determined to dislike everyone and everything in Elysium.

"I heard about what happened with Cassius." Tavi shoved Brie playfully. "You really need to stop doing that."

"Doing what?" asked Cameron.

"Trying to curtsey."

He took a drink from his bottle to hide his grin.

"Who's Cassius? What happened with him?" Sherry asked with a weary sigh. She'd had to digest too many things outside the realm of the believable in far too short a period of time. The names, faces, impossible plant species, and situations all started to blur together.

Ephriam was about to answer, but Brie cut him off. "He seems like the second in command to King Enoch. He gave me a strange vibe. I don't think he likes me."

Ephriam kept quiet.

Because that's his boss. Cassius said that Ephriam reports to him.

Sherry narrowed her eyes. "Do we hate him?"

"No, of course not," Brie answered. "He's probably just not happy that I know about Elysium. And he probably doesn't like that I have this," she held up her pendant and sighed. "And he's probably right."

"He isn't right," Cameron said. "Yes, Sherry, we loathe him."

Sherry pursed her lips together. "I'll take it under advisement, but I only loathe people on principle if Brie tells me to."

Tavi looked fascinated. "Does she often tell you to?"

"Never," Sherry answered grumpily. "Even when she ought to. Haven't you noticed she's too good to hold a grudge? It's like she lacks the internal mechanism for malice or something. It's exhausting, holding back my glorious wrath." She scowled and poked at the fire with a stick.

Mike put his arms around her. "Don't worry, babe. With all the new enemies Brie's making, I'm sure there'll be plenty of opportunities to hold grudges and vent your magnificent rage."

Sherry brightened. "You really think so?"

Tavi let out another infectious, silvery laugh. Even Sherry cracked a smile. She'd been refusing all drinks, but when Tavi held out her bottle and raised an eyebrow in question, she surprised everyone by hesitating a moment, then taking a sip. Her eyes widened. "That's incredible. What is it?"

"It's ambrosia. Raphael makes it. It's one of the most medicinal things in his gardens. If there was anything wrong with you before? There isn't now."

Sherry was staring at her fingertips in fascination. "Why am I so shiny?"

"It also has a few side effects on humans," Tavi added, a bit too late.

Sherry looked at Brie in panic, but Brie patted her arm. "It's what I had earlier. You'll be fine. But a sip is probably enough."

Sherry nodded.

Arafel called out, and Tavi left to go see if she needed any help. After she was gone, Sherry whispered to Brie, "How did she get those scars?" Brie placed a hand on Sherry's knee and squeezed to shush her, but it was too late. Thanks to the Elysian's preternatural hearing, they'd all already heard. And to Brie's great surprise, one of them answered.

"She got them from one of the Seven," said Jequn from across the bonfire.

Their heads swiveled to him.

"Jequn, we do not need to frighten our guests—" Cameron started.

"On the contrary. I do not think they are nearly frightened enough." Ephriam nodded at the soldier and took a sip of ambrosia. "Tell them," he said.

Jequn continued. "Tavi was fighting with all the armies of Heaven, when Baal swallowed the sky and the sea itself. Humans still call the damage left in the seabed the Dragon Hole — The Blue Pit. A nearby Chinese dynasty had given over to such excess, such constant debauchery, that the spirit of Baal fed upon their gluttony and escaped his confines. He feasted on the world, devouring whole islands, whole species. He was supported by Azazel — Wrath. At the end of their battle, nearly the entire Elysian force had been wiped out. No, not wiped out. Devoured. Only three remained: Tavianne, Arafel, and Ephriam."

Brie looked over at Tavi, laughing and playing in the surf with Arafel. Her words from earlier in the arena came back with new meaning:

"It's a terrible gift to be less breakable than the ones you love."

Jequn continued. "Tavi used her body as a focusing lens against Azazel's own lightning and combined it with the light of heaven itself. She refracted all the energy in the heavens into the metal swarm, electrocuting Baal and Azazel and sending them back to their prison. She did not expect to survive. Ephriam is the one who pulled her back afterward and got her to Raphael, with Arafel cutting a path for them through the remaining wraiths. Even with his most potent curatives, Raphael could not restore her completely. He told me later — some scars are beyond healing because they are a part of you."

Brie touched her chest below her pendant, where the barest, the faintest trace of her own scar still remained.

Jequn had been staring into the fire the whole time he recounted the story, and now his gaze fixed on Brie. "I am staggered to be sharing a fire with not one, but two beings who have fought against the Seven and survived."

She turned bright red and tried to melt into the sand.

"So, some of the Seven have already been killed?" Sherry asked.

"Not killed. No. It's not known if they *can* be killed. They can be put out of commission for a few centuries, but they feed on the failings of humanity. And these days, there is more humanity than ever, and its failures grow more destructive by the hour. The population has exploded — everywhere, and every day, the Seven are nourished by millions of petty disputes and global atrocities. Killed? None but the Creator could do such a thing. Not when they are so well fed."

"Mammon isn't dead, then?" Brie's blood suddenly ran cold.
I thought she was gone.
I thought that part, at least, was over.

"It looked like you got pretty close," Tavi's voice unexpectedly rang out behind them. They all turned to look at her. She was standing with Arafel, leaning against one another. She raised her bottle in Brie's direction. "That's as well as I managed myself. Cheers."

Everyone took a solemn sip except for Brie. Arafel took note of this and asked, "You really don't remember what happened? You cannot tell us the tale?"

The unbidden images flashed across her mind again. Brie slammed her memories shut and shook her head. "I can't remember."

Arafel nodded thoughtfully. "I guess you will tomorrow."

"I do remember one thing," Brie said suddenly. "Mammon said I had no idea what sort of people were out looking for me. 'Dastardly fiends, with horrible plans,' she said. If that's true," she swallowed. "It begs the question. Who are they going to send after me next?"

Ephriam stared at her like he wanted to say something, but it was Cameron who answered. "The Council won't let anyone come after you. You have the full force of Elysium to protect you now. Whoever they send, they won't get far."

No sooner had the words left Cameron's lips than Mike pointed to the sky behind him with a troubled frown. "What's that?"

A strange orange glow had begun to gather and swirl. Every face on the beach turned to look as a lightning-white crack appeared. Small at first, it spiderwebbed out from its center, becoming huge within the space of a moment.

At a motion from Tavi, five warriors leapt to their feet and disappeared from the fireside without a word, flying toward the fissure, fast as thought.

"What's happening?" asked Sherry, bewildered.

Ephriam watched as Tavi's team worked together with seamless coordination to seal the crack in the sky shut once more. "Wraiths at the boundaries. Again."

"I have never seen them this active. Have you?" asked Jequn.

Ephriam did not answer but silently shook his head.

The friends shifted uneasily, and the Elysians stared at the fire in brooding silence until Mike changed the subject in a misguided effort to lighten the mood:

"Anyone up for s'mores?"

CHAPTER FOURTEEN

The Rogue's Gallery of Hell

For the longest time, Brie couldn't sleep. Her question from the bonfire kept ringing in her mind like a bell, vibrating everything it touched with a shudder.

Who are they going to send after me next?

Sherry and Mike were asleep in their bedroom, which had miraculously repaired itself from the damage caused by the fire poker. Cameron had fallen asleep on the couch with his arm around her. He was out so fast she wondered if the ambrosia might have gone to his head a bit. She closed her eyes and tried to take long, slow, steady breaths for what seemed like an eternity.

When she finally drifted off, she regretted it.

That's when the dream came.

She was in a storm, reaching for her mother. Closer and closer their fingers strained as the wind roared around them and rain whipped their faces.

"Hold on!" she heard herself scream. "I can almost—"

In a sudden surge of strength, her mother reached out and grabbed her wrist in a vice-like grip. It felt like nothing short of a miracle, but her relief quickly turned to fear when she was pulled closer and looked up into her mother's face.

Those were not her mother's eyes.

One was green. One was blue.

Brie woke with a start and took a second to orient herself and calm her breathing.

She was still on the couch with Cameron, who, for once, seemed unaffected by her nightmare. He didn't even stir when she eased out of his protective hold. She settled a pillow into his arms in her place and wandered down the hall.

She drifted to the large windows that stretched floor to ceiling across an entire wall. At a slight touch, a panel of the window slid open, and she stepped softly onto the patio, running her pendant along its chain absentmindedly.

I might find out tomorrow, she thought, looking down at the stone. It was familiar and mysterious, all at once, as it had always been. *Maybe tomorrow's the day I finally learn why you're in my life and why we seem so tied to each other's fates.*

She rested against the stone railing and looked up at the sky — those deep indigos blending into the ruby reds and pale violets.

She frowned.

Have those shadows always been there?

She could have sworn the sky hadn't been this dark during the bonfire.

It's late. I must be imagining it.

She'd nearly convinced herself, nearly decided that she should ignore the prickling dread in her stomach when the shifting shadows took on a deliberate, synchronized movement. What could have been dismissed as coincidence now revealed a chilling coordination. As she watched, the shadows coalesced above her into a looming mass, lurking behind the vibrant swirls of color like a predator closing in — like a shark, hulking toward her from deep water, growing more distinct as it honed in on the scent of blood.

Her heart raced. Her pendant warmed against her skin. Instinctively, she tightened her grip around its stone, retreating a step in fear.

The shadows arranged themselves into an enormous, monstrous face that twisted into a gruesome smile.

She had just started to scream when a crack appeared in the sky right between its eyes, first gold, then blinding white. Oil-black shadows started to wriggle through, twisting like a hundred tentacles, prying at the sides of the crack, trying to enlarge the opening.

Cameron was by her side in an instant. Mike and Sherry, a moment later.

Her pendant burned in her hand.

A battalion of Elysian warriors, led by Tavianne and Arafel, surged toward the rip in the sky. Bolts of energy and beams of fire shot from their hands into the writhing black mass, banishing it backward as a sea of Elysians knit the sky back together in powerful, precise, and tireless choreography.

Cameron turned to her, his urgency palpable, and addressed all three of the humans:

"Get inside. I'll send someone."

Before Brie could even respond, he flew fast as lightning to join the Elysians. Sherry and Mike pulled her back into the villa and shut the wall of windows behind them.

◆   ◆   ◆

An hour later, Cameron hadn't returned.

Five Elysian guards had reported to the villa on his orders and maintained a vigilant patrol outside, but none had any news about their prince. Brie didn't think they'd tell her if they did. Their suspicious looks and lack of eye contact left her wondering what secrets they were guarding.

Mike and Sherry had reluctantly returned to bed once Brie had promised to do the same. A promise she had no intention of keeping even as she made it. She was still pacing around when there was a knock on the door.

"Oh, thank goodness!" Brie cried, running over and flinging it wide.

It was the last person she'd expected to see.

She immediately reached for a robe and threw it around herself as her cheeks flamed. "Oh! I'm sorry, I thought you were Cameron."

Ephriam stood silent, staring at her.

"Is he all right?" she asked, tying her belt.

"Yes. He is in counsel with his father and Tavianne." Ephriam was studying her with an intensity she couldn't explain.

"What was that thing, Ephriam?"

"Those things," he corrected. "It was a wraith attack. An uncommonly coordinated one, but nothing our forces couldn't handle. They cannot even survive our Elysian energy field once they are inside. I cannot fathom why they continue to try to break in."

"But what about the face?"

He frowned. "What face?"

"The giant face in the sky! The crack opened up right in front of it!" Her voice had taken on a doubtful quality.

"We saw no face," Ephriam said.

"Are you kidding? It was as big as a mountain! I mean, it was only there for a second before the crack opened up. Nobody else saw that?" She wondered if her nightmare had spilled into her waking world.

"Perhaps you saw the shadow of the wraiths beyond our barrier." The way he kept staring at her was making her uneasy.

"Ephriam, why are you here? Can I help you with something?" she asked.

He seemed to make up his mind. "Come with me. There is something you need to see."

He led her past the guards, through the gardens, to a door she hadn't seen before, half-hidden by a giant flowering bush. He took a torch hanging near the entrance, lit it with a flick of his fingers, then led her deep into the palace, down a twisting staircase. Elysium was still bright at night — with the moon and the Earth both reflecting the sun's rays, it was like a full moon. Even in the darkest corners of the garden, a patch of shimmering gold and silver light was never more than a few steps away. But here, descending into the basement level of the palace, to a place lit only by whatever fire they brought with them?

What did Ephriam call that sculpture thing from the hospital?

Disquieting. Very that.

They wound down a hallway deep beneath the castle when Ephriam suddenly stopped. "You asked who they were going to send after you next," he said quietly. "I think you deserve to know the possibilities."

He stepped to one side. She looked behind him and gasped.

There, in the form of a painted mural, was Mammon. But not the Mammon she had seen, not a sneering cynic, callous and rageful, violent and cruel. This was a beautiful, golden woman with shining green eyes and laughter that almost seemed to spill out of the painting. She looked vibrant and lovely. And happy.

She was shocked. "Why are you showing me this?"

"I'm not here to show you what you have already seen, child. I'm here to show you what you haven't." With that, he stretched out his arm, and his torch illuminated the walls.

There were six more paintings. Three lined each wall of the hallway, leading to a dead end where the most enormous painting of them all towered, half-hidden in darkness. She walked toward it, past murals depicting beautiful, angelic beings. A short, golden-haired man with a clever, sharp-featured face, surrounded by every kind of technology and machine. Three sisters, or long-haired brothers, she couldn't tell, as glorious as a sunrise, rosy lips parted in laughter. Two more were depicted in the form of behemoth creatures, made entirely out of wings and eyes that looked very much like Raphael had when he'd frightened the daylights out of her in the throne room. One was a black-haired man who looked as though he was made entirely of muscles, smiling and flashing his eyes.

And there at the end, was the most beautiful of them all.

He shone like a star. His white hair rippled down to his waist. His eyes were the color of ice under a morning sky and shone diamond-bright, sharp with intelligence, sharper even than the blade by his side. He sparkled, glittered with beauty, with cleverness, with elegance. He was flawless.

"Who is that?" she breathed.

"That is Lucifer. The Morningstar."

She couldn't tear her face away for a moment, until it registered. "Lucifer?" Her eyes shot to Ephriam, then back up to the astonishing portrait. "Is that Satan?!"

Ephriam answered quietly. "Satan is another name for one of his cohorts, Azazel. I understand that much precious knowledge, once commonly known in the world, has now passed into ignorance and darkness. Much has been simplified that should have remained in its complexity. Satan, as you call him, is the cardinal sin of Wrath. This," he gestured at the glorious, white-haired being, "is the Devil himself."

Brie could think of nothing to say, but the angel wasn't finished. There was a book below the painting she had not noticed, too taken with the murals themselves to register any accompanying details. He opened it, and she cringed.

"This is the Mammon you saw, was it not?" He pointed at the picture.

Flashes of memory ripped through her — silver-tipped horns tearing their way out the forehead of a blonde-haired nightmare, legs elongating to animalistic lengths, stiletto-clad feet splitting into cloven hooves.

Brie nodded. She couldn't talk. He turned the page, and she let out a little cry, clapping her hands over her mouth.

It was the three beautiful siblings from the murals behind her, but they had been twisted into ugly, evil versions of themselves — red, skinless, with open, sucking mouths and sightless eyes. Unbridled hatred seemed to radiate from the page.

Ephriam turned to the next picture.

The black-haired man with the sword was now a skull-faced,

raging demon with a torso filled with fire, screaming at the sky like he would crack the world in half with his bare hands.

The next page was a snake the size of a city covered in oil-black scales.

The blonde man surrounded by machines was near-unrecognizable as a gigantic, morbidly obese man laughing grotesquely on top of a pile of bones.

Ephriam had barely shown her the next page, a sea of shimmering silver creatures when she slammed the book shut and backed away from him.

"Why are you showing me this?" she demanded again, suddenly angry. "Why would you do this? I'm already doing what Enoch wants."

He studied her, then answered carefully. "I admire you for agreeing to undertake the Revelation, but I do not want you to do it."

She wasn't expecting that. "What do you mean?"

He was quiet for a moment. "The only reason the King wishes this is because he cannot get the information without your consent. The only reason he needs your consent is because of your pendant." Her hand flew up to her necklace, and his eyes followed. "You should give them the pendant, submit yourself and your friends to a memory modification, and return to Earth. You should lead a happy life, free from pain and sorrow and the weight of more worlds than one hanging around your neck. You are but a child, Brianna Weldon. Such responsibility should never have fallen to you."

She looked at him, surprised that he seemed to care at all, let alone so deeply.

"We would protect you," Ephriam went on. "*I* would protect you. I would personally see to it that not a day of your life was troubled by the shadows that have hounded you for so long."

"Why would you do such a thing? Why would you *ask* such a thing?" she said.

"There are two reasons. First — I care for Cameron. Deeply. I have known him for thousands of years. I would not see him hurt by this. I know you care for one another." He trailed off for a moment, choosing his words carefully. "I think there are things you would not wish the Court to know — things you may want to keep between the two of you."

She absorbed this. "And the second reason?"

"You are in terrible, terrible danger." He gestured to the book that lay on its podium beside them now, bound in its black, worn leather like a sinister spellbook. "You are but a young girl who has fallen into the crosshairs of the most powerful evils the Universe has ever known. Even if you were to stand against them, even if you could somehow find a way to conquer the forces that seek to work against you — what would you have to become?" Her heart skipped a beat. "Would you wish to become such a thing?"

She looked up at the portrait of Lucifer, at its cold perfection.

He's right, you know.

How could someone like me ever hope to stand against anything like him?

Just then, she felt a warmth over her heart. She lowered her eyes to look, and her pendant emitted a faint, pearly glow. Ephriam took a step back, startled.

"No, no — it isn't me!" she said quickly, remembering the chasm in the parking garage.

The glow showed no signs of fading, and after a minute, he cautiously approached. "May I?" he asked. She nodded, and he carefully touched it, cupped it in his palm, and stared into its strange, colorful depths, raising it to his eyes. The moment he did, it flashed a bright white. Then, as suddenly as the glow had appeared, it vanished.

"What just happened?" she asked breathlessly.

The angel was frozen in shock.

"What is it? Are you all right?"

"Yes," he answered, though he was obviously shaken.

"Did you see something? What *was* that?"

But the Elysian was shaking his head and taking a step back, staring at her like he was trying to solve a great mystery.

"Ephriam, if you don't tell me what's going on right now——"

He tilted his head and held up his hand for silence. When he looked at her again, his expression had cleared. "I have misjudged the situation," he murmured. "'All things become visible when exposed by the light, for everything that becomes visible *is* light.'"

There was a beat of silence.

"Ephriam, let me tell you how much patience I *don't* have for poetic conceits right now."

"It is a quote from the Bible, Ms. Weldon. Ephesians."

"…I knew that."

He looked at her appraisingly. "If you say you must go forward with the Revelation, so be it."

That's a remarkable turnaround.

"Ephriam, what the hell just happened?"

"I will tell you when the time is right." It was as if a speech he'd spent all evening rehearsing was filled with arguments he suddenly, inexplicably, did not believe anymore. It was baffling and more than a little infuriating, especially considering this late-night tour through the rogue's gallery of Hell.

She was about to lay into him again when he placed an unexpected hand on her shoulder, seemingly intending some affection. "I see why he is so preoccupied with you. Frankly, that's why I can't believe he's letting you go through with it."

"Cameron?" she asked. "He doesn't want me to, but I told him I felt certain it's the right thing to do. And I don't know why I feel that way, Ephriam, but I do."

He simply nodded.

All at once, she remembered. "He asked if it would make a difference if he begged," she blurted out. "He didn't put me in that position. But he did ask if he could beg me not to go through with it. He's never done anything like that before."

"Can you really blame him after what happened the last time?" asked Ephriam sadly.

"What do you mean? What last time? What happened?"

"The last Revelation, Brianna. With his brother. Ethan."

◆   ◆   ◆

"How could you not tell me?" Brie burst into the villa with no preamble and planted herself before Cameron in accusation. It was lucky he'd gotten back, or she would have scoured the kingdom looking for him.

Sherry was right. What do I really know about this man? What else has he kept from me?

He was sitting on the sofa in the library, using Cong as a side table for a pile of books. He put down the one he was reading, *The Laws of Elysium: Volume One*, and looked at her, alarmed. "Tell you what?" he asked, bewildered.

"Ethan." Her eyes blazed at him in betrayal.

The blood drained from his face.

"Ephriam told me." Her voice was a tortured whisper. "Ethan, your *brother*, was the last person to perform the Revelation. And after he did it, he was never seen or heard from again." Her hands were balled into fists by her sides, and tears stood in her eyes. "How could you not tell me?"

He didn't answer. He didn't even breathe. He was staring at the floor, hands trembling. All at once, he looked up. "Let me show you."

He stood up abruptly and started walking down the hall. She followed him to the door marked with the letter 'E.' He took a deep breath and stood briefly, frozen with his hand on the door-knob, before opening it and stepping inside. She followed.

It was another magical bedroom, but the person who had occupied this room had other passions and interests. While Cameron's room was devoted primarily to science, history, and mathematics, Ethan's was devoted to art and culture. One entire wall was covered in paintings and sketches that ranged in skill level from early childhood beginnings to true mastery. There was a stage in one corner, and every imaginable instrument was stashed all over the room. Japanese comics vied for space on the bookshelves with volumes of Spanish love poetry. Hundreds, maybe thousands, of handwritten journals, were stacked so high they were being used as tables for more books. A black leather jacket hung on a peg behind the door, next to a slingshot and a kite.

But what caught her breath were the photographs.

Next to an antique Nikon camera were piles and piles of black and white photographs. Some were framed on the bookshelves and walls as well. A blonde-haired youth spray painting with Andy Warhol, a cigarette hanging from his lips. The same man, slightly older, sharing a beer with Che Guevara. Here, he was standing on a partially completed Eiffel Tower. Here, he was wearing full samurai battle armor, valiantly attacking a tree.

She stopped at a large, framed photograph, more faded than the others. In it were two boys playing in an apple tree. The one on top of the branch was unmistakably Cameron. His chestnut brown curls blew in the breeze over his perfect, laughing face. Below him, a blonde-haired boy hung from his feet, wedged into a crevice above the branch. He swung freely, arms crossed over his chest, his beautiful upside-down smile beaming from the photograph with near-palpable mischief.

"This is him," said Brie, softly.

She turned to Cameron when he didn't answer. He looked like he was in physical pain.

"I don't come in here," he said. "I haven't come here in a hundred years."

Comprehension dawned. "He's the reason you haven't been back to Elysium."

He nodded and walked stiffly over to her, taking the photograph from her hands.

"Ethan," He swallowed, as though even saying the name hurt. "Ethan is my adopted brother."

IS his brother. Present tense.

She was careful now, aware of the fact that there were factors at play here, wounds at play deeper than her own.

"Older or younger?" she asked.

"Older. I never knew life without him." Cameron traced his finger over his brother's upside-down face. "He practically raised me. Father was always busy with matters of the court, and when he spent time with us, it was always to talk about my mother. He seemed to think it was his duty to preserve her memory as vibrantly as possible inside me, since I was the reason I never got to meet her."

Her heart broke for him. "You weren't the reason—"

"It doesn't matter, now." He put the photograph down. "Ethan was never one for following the rules. You can see that he regularly revealed himself to humans. Involved himself in their affairs. Cultivated friendships. Relationships." His face darkened. "In the years leading up to his Revelation, he grew different with me. Distant. I tried to talk to him about it, tried to ask what was wrong. He never said. In the end, his disobedience grew to a point where it could not be ignored. Cassius presided over his Revelation before the court. Father did not... *would* not intervene. I didn't go. Ethan asked me not to. I waited for him in the garden. He never came back."

Brie could scarcely breathe. "What happened to him?"

"His wings were clipped," he answered.

"What does that mean?"

"His Elysian powers were restricted. Temporarily, my father said. Until he learned proper respect for our rules, our ways. Father thought living amongst the humans for a while would temper him, and he would come back to us — the prodigal son returned," he added bitterly.

"But he never came back," she finished.

He shook his head. "We never heard from him again. I looked everywhere, all his favorite spots. For years. Decades. I never thought he would..." He looked away.

"How old were you?"

"I was twelve." He looked back to her, his face the picture of sadness. "I wasn't trying to keep it from you, Brianna. I just don't talk about him. I can't."

She crossed the room to him in an instant and put her arms around him. "I'm sorry," she whispered. "Cameron, I'm so, so sorry."

He nodded and took in a shuddering breath. "Let's go back to the others. I'd like to keep his room as it was. Besides, it's almost time."

She followed him back to the living room.

Looking back on it later, it was amazing how close she'd come to learning the truth in that moment. If only she'd taken one last look, just a glance over her shoulder, she might have seen it.

One of the only colored photographs in the whole room; another shot of Cameron and Ethan together — a closeup of their faces, little boys laughing at some private joke.

Cameron holding out his chubby baby hand to hold his brother's finger.

Ethan's eyes glinting back at him with mischief — one green, one blue.

CHAPTER FIFTEEN

Zadkiel

The four companions took off early in the morning to meet with Tavi and offer Mike and Sherry a brief tour of the kingdom before Brie's date with destiny. The moment he saw the training arena, Mike's eyes flew wide as dinner plates. He soaked in the spectacle of the Elysian combat playground for a full silent minute before turning to Sherry and whispering with feverish excitement, "Honey, I have so many ideas." When Tavi suggested a hike to a vista she swore had the best view of the Elysian Sea, Brie and Cameron decided to go off on their own. They said they'd regroup in the throne room for the Revelation and left Mike scheming about an interdimensional task force.

Brie and Cameron spent the rest of the morning back at the villa, resting innocently in each other's arms, stealing some private moments for no other reason than to take comfort in each other's embrace. Both tried desperately to avoid the thought that this could be their last time together. Both failed. They sipped their tea, watching Cong take several hours to walk across the courtyard before starting off themselves, winding silently through the gardens toward the throne room.

The closer they got to the palace, the more Brie's resolve wavered. She dug her hands into her pockets and fiddled with the cinnamon sticks while her inner self yelled at her in blind fury.

What in the name of all that is good and holy are you doing?

Agreeing to some Vulcan mind-meld in front of a council full of eyeball monsters?

Maybe Cameron's right. And Ephriam. They wouldn't have asked you not to do this without a good reason. And you're going against them, why, exactly?

Because your magical necklace gave you a good feeling about it?

She found herself longing for a simple life on the run in a country with no extradition treaties and extra-dimensional planes.

Cameron broke the silence. "What are you thinking about?"

"Venezuela."

He looked at her, puzzled.

She sighed. "Nothing. Private joke."

He guessed her concern. "Please, don't worry. My father will arrange everything so you are as comfortable as possible."

"He said it wouldn't hurt," she said, alarmed.

"Of course not. I mean emotionally comfortable. The angels won't be in their true form."

"Ah." She stared resolutely at the path ahead, determined that he would not see her quake with fear at the memory of her last encounter in the Great Hall. "Fewer eyeballs, then?"

"Far fewer eyeballs," he assured.

"Thank Heaven for small favors, I guess." She went silent again and focused on the fantastical scenery.

As peaceful and unimposing as it had looked from the lovely vantage points in the garden, the closer they drew to the Great Hall, the more intimidating it all became. Her anxiety returned with a vengeance around the same time they passed beneath a gargantuan archway made of a solid piece of amethyst covered in row after row of glowing scriptures.

Remember when the sight of Daya Memorial Hospital threw you for a loop? Those were the days.

Cameron came to a stop and offered his best impression of a confident, reassuring look. "I'm just going to run ahead and make sure everyone has remembered to—" he caught himself, choosing his words carefully, "dress appropriately. Do you mind waiting in the courtyard for a moment?" She nodded, but her expression must have been telling a different story. He shot a quick glance over his shoulder, then stepped close, touched her face tenderly, and traced her cheek with the pad of his thumb. "I'll be right back. Will you be okay?"

She looked around. No matter where she went in Elysium, she always found herself in one of the most fascinating places she could imagine. "I think I can manage."

He pressed a kiss to her hand again and walked off quickly through the archway. She found a bench near a fountain and sat down before leaping right back up again and pacing back and forth.

It's all good. It's going to be fine.

She picked up a pebble and threw it into the fountain. The stones and water began to change colors. She backed away, thinking perhaps she'd done something wrong and tried to lean against a tree. One of its branches tried to give her a hug. She gasped and quickly disentangled herself from the boughs, backing away without looking, straight into something solid and alive.

"Oh, excuse me!" she said, turning around.

It wasn't until she lifted her gaze that she realized she was talking to a man with no head.

♦   ♦   ♦

Its body was normal enough. Too tall, too perfect, but recogniz-ably human — except for the magnificent wings, and of course, the missing head. In its place, an enormous, unblinking golden eye levitated, surrounded by a shining halo of light and four additional orbiting eyes.

It was as beautiful as it was terrifying, until it started to speak. Then, the terrifying aspect decidedly won out. The impossible being leaned toward her in a slight bow. "Greetings, child."

Brie took a quick step backwards and fell solidly on her behind.

It extended its hand to help her up. She stared at it and decided to stay put.

"Do not be afraid," a voice emanated from the staggering sight.

"I'm working on it," she swallowed, warily studying the float-ing eyes.

There was a beat of silence.

"I've forgotten my head again, haven't I?" the creature asked.

She managed a hesitant nod, wondering if she should offer to help look for it or simply sprint for the nearest exit.

It sighed, a sound like a dying star, and briefly shone blinding white. She blinked against the radiance. When she refocused, she was looking into two, and only two, great golden eyes in a human-looking face.

"My apologies," he said. "I'm dreadfully out of practice. I hav-en't taken on a humanoid form in ages. The skin is still a trial, though I must say, I like what your people have done with the clothes."

She stared appreciatively. She liked what *he'd* done with the clothes.

He'd paired a spotlessly white satin suit with a black silk shirt. It had a foreign cut to the collar and was trimmed with gold. One earring dropped elegantly from his right ear — a line of gold dripping down through a circle made of a light stone. The man himself was very much like Cameron — too perfect to exist on a normal physical plane — but there was something even more intimidating about him. His black hair shone in glossy curls down to the top of his shoulders, his skin glowed pale, and his face looked like a Renaissance painting, something a sculptor might go mad trying to imitate in stone.

And, of course, there were the wings — six of them, giant and covered in gossamer feathers.

"I am called Zadkiel," he introduced himself softly. "May I offer you a hand?"

With a nod, she allowed him to assist her.

"That's better." He flashed her a charming look. "It won't do to have you frightened of me, little one. Not when you're about to let me inside your head." He chuckled pleasantly as if it were a joke. She attempted to laugh as well but only managed to look rather sick. "So, you're the one all the fuss is about," he continued, bending down to get a closer look at her. She shrank away from him before she could stop herself, and he gave her a quizzical look. "Have I done something to frighten you?"

"No, not at all. It's just, the last person who said that to me? Our interaction went badly."

Zadkiel's face cleared in a look of understanding. "Ah, yes, I heard about Mammon."

Brie shuddered at her name.

"What are you doing in the gardens?" he asked, curious.

"Just pacing." Perhaps it was silly to keep her thoughts private with an archangel who was about to rifle through her memories, but she wasn't ready to let him in. Not just yet.

Fortunately, he didn't seem to require it. Instead of pressing further, he merely offered her his arm. "Shall we pace together?"

She froze where she stood, surprised by the offer. "I should probably wait for Cameron."

"We won't wander far. Cameron, as you call him, will be glad we've met before the Revelation. He will want you to feel as reassured as possible."

"You know him?"

Zadkiel flashed her a dazzling smile, and it felt as though the air itself warmed with joy. "I've known your Cameron since before he was born."

That settled it. She slipped her arm through his as he guided her through the palace gardens. While they walked, she noticed an increasing number of golden orbs following behind.

"Your arrival has caused quite the stir," he said as she finally whirled around, and all the glowing balls of light hid behind the branches of a giant tree. "You cannot blame the lost souls for wanting to take a look."

"Lost souls?" she questioned. "Cameron called them 'free spirits.'"

Zadkiel replied with a small smile. "Of course he did."

She waited for him to elaborate, but he merely walked on. As soon as she got up the courage, she managed to ask. "So, you're an angel?"

"Is that what your Cameron told you?"

"No, but I mean, the wings? The halo? Bit of a giveaway."

Zadkiel's eyes danced with amusement. "I am not an angel. I am an archangel."

When he again failed to elaborate, she asked. "What's the difference?"

"There are many kinds of angels. Some say Elysians are a kind of angel. Most are a different species altogether, created to praise the Creator and carry out Its will."

"And that isn't you?"

"We are completely unlike them. Some call us the archangels. Some, the Seraphim. To others, we are known as the djinn. All these names attempt to describe the same thing. Archangels are beings with free will, just like you." He looked down at her and winked. "How do you think some of us fell from Grace?"

She must have turned pale because he laughed and patted her arm reassuringly.

"Do not fear, child. You, among all mortals, have the least reason to fear. I heard a rumor that you dealt with one of our fallen sisters rather handily."

She slowed, startled. "Mammon, is your sister?"

His expression clouded for a moment. "She is."

Brie's mouth went dry, and she said defensively, "I don't remember what happened."

Zadkiel nodded and said nothing for a moment before replying. "It is good that your mind has shielded you from these events for now. The implications are too far-reaching for a mortal mind to comprehend." He placed a hand on her shoulder. "Such responsibility should not have fallen to you."

Gravel crunched under their feet as they stepped through an archway. The path opened up and curved into a circle surrounding a white, tiered fountain, surrounded on all sides by a bench.

She thought what a lovely place to curl up with a book when her attention drifted over her companion's shoulder.

"What is that?" she gasped, pointing in astonishment.

They were in a courtyard, surrounded on eight sides by eight enormous, towering mosaics made of shining tiles, each depicting a different, glorious creature. The one she was pointing to looked several stories tall and was made of hundreds of wings and thousands of eyes.

Zadkiel turned, amused. "Not what, but who. That is my brother Raphael. I believe you met him yesterday."

Her cheeks warmed. "Yes, I think I remember." She looked around at the other mosaics — the bright, sunlit counterpoint of the horrible murals Ephriam had shown her in the tunnels beneath the castle. "Are these all your brothers and sisters?"

"All those whom we did not lose in the Fall," he replied.

She unlinked their arms and walked to the walls, examining the works of art. She recognized Zadkiel, depicted holding a shield and a cross. Beside him was a beautiful, golden-haired being depicted in flight. She couldn't tell if it was a woman or a man. "Gabriel," read the caption. "What is the Fall?" she asked.

"It refers to the time when the archangels were divided in our opinion about whether to follow the will of the Creator or to rebel. Some, myself included, sided with the Divine. Seven chose to fight against the host of Heaven to carve out a new destiny for themselves, independent of God's will." Zadkiel stopped beside a mural of a beautiful, red-haired woman carrying a book. Below her was carved the name Jophial.

Brie traced the name with her fingers and asked, "Why didn't they like what God had willed?"

He smiled faintly. "Do you always like what God has willed, child?" As she silently contemplated this, he continued. "It was because the Creator willed that we could not intermingle with the humans and could not have children."

Brie was shocked. "You aren't allowed to have children? Why?"

Zadkiel answered in his mild, even tone. "It is not for us to comprehend the will of the Divine."

She bit her tongue, sorry she'd asked such a personal question. "So," she continued hesitantly, "what happened?"

"The Heavens prevailed." He indicated a mosaic of a particularly fearsome-looking man wielding a flaming sword. She recognized him from the poster and crayon drawings in Cameron's room. "Michael threw Leviathan into the desert prison and was sent to guard the Garden. The rest of the Seven were imprisoned on the mortal plane or cast into Hell. Sometimes, they were split into pieces so we could do both."

She came to a stop in front of the last mural. It was unlike the others. Rather than being suffused with light, this one was immersed in a thick, deep blackness. In the very center was a masked being with six wings in the same configuration as Zadkiel's, but covered all over with black eyes that seemed to blink and stare. The figure was beautiful but terrible. It was feminine, though it couldn't by any means be called a woman. It was closer to a dragon. Its rib cage was exposed bone. It had six arms, and in its six hands, its fleshless fingers carried a strange array of items: a golden scale, a small diamond dagger, a scroll, and a snake. Its very robes seemed to envelop the world in darkness.

"Who is that?" Brie breathed.

"Ah. That's Azrael." Zadkiel's wings shook themselves out and resettled as though he was uncomfortable. "We don't need to tell you everything all at once."

"I'd like to know," she pressed.

He remained silent for a moment as though debating whether to tell her. Then, as he explained, he pointed at all the murals in turn. "We all have our specialties. Raphael's is healing and life. He's also very good with… I suppose you'd call them 'spells,' though that is wildly inaccurate. He bound the Seven so they may never enter this realm or the Kingdom of Heaven."

He moved to the next mural. "Michael is a warrior. He commands Heaven's armies and protects what is most precious in the realms. Gabriel is God's favored messenger. Uriel specializes in light and knowledge and interprets visions. Jophial is a Watcher, full of wisdom, while Camael is associated with courage and strength. The dark one you see before you, Azrael, is the instrument of Divine Justice, but you probably know her as the Angel of Death."

Brie froze and stared at the mosaic. It seemed to stare back, with its obsidian eyes everywhere. "What does she look like when she takes on human form?"

"That is the closest I've ever seen her get to human form," he answered. "She was displeased at being called to pose for the portrait. She revealed herself to our artist for only a few moments. He required several decades of emotional leave time to recuperate upon completion of the piece."

Brie's eyes cut back to the mosaic. It glistened in the light, and she shuddered before curiosity got the best of her. "What's your specialty?"

"I am the Angel of freedom, mercy, and memory."

"Oh, that's lovely."

His face flashed with sadness so quickly she could have imagined it. "I suppose it is."

They walked on for a few moments before she got up the courage to ask. "What was it like when you were all together? What was Mammon like before she became how she is now?"

Zadkiel didn't stop. "She was magnificent. Ambitious. She loved beautiful things. When we were together, it was Paradise."

Brie struggled to process this, unwilling to accept that something as heavenly as Zadkiel could become something like Mammon, or that there was any relation between the horned creature who had tried to kill her and all of her friends, and the glorious, gentle being walking beside her.

Zadkiel turned to her curiously. "Do you truly not remember anything about your battle?" Her mouth went dry, and she shook her head. He nodded past her, and they saw Cameron approaching to bring them inside. "You are about to."

CHAPTER SIXTEEN

The Revelation

The throne room was as intimidating as Brie remembered, with one marked exception. This time, rather than alien-looking beings in the full glory of their natural forms, the seats were filled with...

Almost-humans.

It seemed every creature in attendance had received Cameron's memo to "dress appropriately" so as not to overwhelm their human guests again. Still, some were seemingly more experienced in the art of disguise than others. Amidst a group of Elysians who resembled Ephriam — all slightly too tall and perfect to be normal — one well-meaning soul had mixed up the position of its nose and mouth, one had a head covered all over with ears, and when another went to whisper to its neighbor, it covered its mouth with a hand that boasted at least fifteen fingers. Brie also saw something that looked uncannily like Cousin It.

It's the effort that counts.

She saw Tavi standing at Enoch's right hand with a company of guards who flanked the king on either side. Sherry and Mike were beside her. Mike's hand kept drifting to his side like he was reaching for his firearm. Sherry kept shooting looks at the assembled host like she wished she could call in an airstrike. When they caught Brie looking, they attempted to smile encouragingly without positive results.

They're here. It's enough.

Cameron came beside her and squeezed her hand reassuringly. Together, they walked up to the platform in front of the throne and were greeted by Enoch and two enormously tall individuals, one of whom Brie now recognized as Raphael, the dark-haired man who had inadvertently drugged her the day before. He offered her a contrite look, and in a show of bravado she did not actually feel, she winked at him, eliciting a grin.

Enoch lifted his voice, turning to the assembled host. "As you are all aware, strange events have begun to unfold on the mortal plane. Ms. Brianna Weldon has borne witness to these events, which for reasons as yet unknown, seem to be coalescing around her. She has consented of her own free will to undergo the Revelation, to inform our people about these events in full transparency, with nothing to hide."

A murmur ran through the stands. Her gesture was apparently more meaningful than she'd initially realized.

Enoch nodded at Zadkiel, who came up to join them on the dais. Two chairs facing one another had been prepared for them. They sat, she on the edge of her seat, him towering above her. The lights dimmed to dusky, twilight shades of grey and lavender. Zadkiel took her hand gently, bowed his head, and closed his golden eyes.

Nothing could have prepared her for what happened next.

It was as if she'd been shot backward through a tunnel at light-speed, whipping through her past further than she'd been prepared to go. Her eyes snapped open and shone brightly, like spotlights in the darkened hall, and her memories were projected like holograms for all to see. Back and back she went, further and further. Snippets of long-forgotten faces and conversations flashed by her before she could fully register anything, increasingly unfamiliar, until the last image she was expecting snapped into sudden focus.

It was her first memory.

She was a baby in her mother's arms, looking up at her parents' adoring faces. They were close to her but blurry. She felt supported by enormous arms and heard their voices cooing sweet nothings.

It's my photograph. I'm inside my favorite photograph.

As she watched, the focus shifted. Something shiny had distracted her newborn self. Her mother's locket. Brie watched as her own baby hand reached up as if to touch it. There was a flash of light. At first, she thought it was the flash of the photographer's camera until she saw the stone of her mother's pendant glowing softly as it touched her tiny finger.

Then, something went wrong. The picture shifted again, this time into a long, brightly-lit hallway lined on either side with doors of every shape, color, and size. Suddenly, she was floating in the darkness next to Zadkiel.

"Where are we? I don't remember this," she said, confused.

"This isn't a memory. It is an organizational structure so your mind is not overwhelmed by the sea of remembrance. We are still in the Great Hall," answered Zadkiel. She turned and saw herself still sitting on the marble chair, eyes bright like projectors, with Zadkiel before her, head bowed, his hand covering hers. A part of her balked at the sight, while another part was reluctantly fascinated.

My therapist would have a field day with this.

She looked past their seated figures into the rest of the court. She saw Cameron a step away from her, face painted in concern. Sherry looked as though she was about to jump out of her skin, grab Brie, and bulldoze their way out of there. They were the only ones looking at her, she realized. Cameron, Mike, and Sherry. All the rest were trained on the projected image of her as a baby.

"Won't this confuse the others?"

"They cannot see us here. They will see what is inside the doors you open. This way, you are not simply laid bare for all to ogle. Whatever you show them will be your choice."

She looked at him, both startled and touched. "I didn't realize I had any say at all. I was going to show them everything."

His wings rearranged themselves in what might have been a shrug. "I am the angel of memory, yes, but also of freedom and mercy. You should be able to choose to hold some things private, should you so desire."

I could choose to keep Cameron a secret — keep him to myself.

...And break my promise to Enoch and his people.

Her heart sank as she realized she couldn't do it. "Thank you, Zadkiel." She took a deep breath and looked down the hallway of her life. "But I promised Enoch I would show them everything, and come hell or high water, I mean to keep my word. I have to open all the doors."

He tilted his head slightly and gave her the strangest look. It was for such a brief moment that she almost thought she'd imagined it. He nodded and held out his hand. "Shall we?"

She began to open the doors, one after the other. As she did, memories came flooding out. The Brianna sitting in the Great

Hall projected all these memories from her eyes into brightly colored holograms for the Elysian court to see. She saw visions from her childhood in decades past. The time she and Sherry set off a bottle rocket at a construction site. The time her father taught her how to ride a bike. Her first day of preschool, trips to the waterfall, the time she saw a dead cat and cried for days. Images tumbled together into exactly what Zadkiel had described — a sea of memories. She was grateful to be removed from the chaos, to be seeing it from the outside instead of her own first-person perspective.

In her memories, she grew older. She had a crush on a boy who moved away. She argued with her mother about being allowed to wear high heels, and when her mother relented, she tripped and sprained her ankle. She and Sherry stayed up all night in her bedroom, giggling and sneaking snacks from the fridge. She practiced piano for hours, cried when the Backstreet Boys broke up and planted an apple tree that grew tall enough to climb. Sat in that tree and took a bite of its first fruit.

Then, things took a darker turn. As she approached a door that looked different from the others, framed in corroded steel instead of warm wood, she instinctively knew what was on the other side.

It was the day of the accident. The memory of her mother's death.

She glanced at Sherry.

It'll be okay, she thought. *I'll be right here. I'll just open the door and watch with the rest while they—*

But the memory seemed to have other ideas.

The others she'd watched like a movie.

This one pulled her inside.

♦   ♦   ♦

The scene shifted, dragging Brie into a memory she'd spent five years trying to bury. She braced herself, knowing what was to come. There was no way to escape it. She could only helplessly watch it unfold, trapped inside her past self on the precipice of the worst moment of her life, forced to relive it as if for the first time.

It began — their last conversation.

Her mother never once deviated from her school pickup routine. Always a dazzling smile, the same directive, and the same question. "Buckle up — precious cargo. And how was your day, beautiful?" Her mom reached over and squeezed her hand before pulling away from the pickup zone and merging onto the street.

"Sherry recruited the marching band to play me Happy Birthday, so I had to hide in the bathroom for a while. And she had me painted into a mural outside the art class."

"I wondered what grand gesture she had planned this year." Her mom shook her head with a grin. She was incredibly fond of her daughter's eccentric best friend, and over the years, she'd learned to take things in stride.

"What's that?" Brie nodded at the pink box in the backseat. She knew it was a cake from her favorite bakery. As the car began to wind toward the outskirts of town, she knew they were heading to their favorite family spot in the nearby woods, where the river tumbled over a short cliff into a pool. Still, half the fun was pretending she didn't know where they were going so as not to spoil the surprise.

"Oh, just a little something I picked up," her mother answered nonchalantly. She kept one hand on the wheel and pulled a smaller pink box from the middle console with the other. "To tide you over," she said with a smile.

Brie opened it to find a perfect chocolate cupcake inside. "Mmm, thanks, Mom!" As the car wound its way through the hills, Brie began licking off the chocolate frosting like a child with an ice cream cone.

Her mother's laughter chimed through the car. "I love that you still do that. It reminds me of when you were five." Her eyes misted at the corners as she shot Brie another glance. "But you're a young woman now. All grown up."

Brie decided to hedge her bets. "All grown up enough for my own car?"

Her mom grinned and reached over to tuck a flyaway curl behind her daughter's ear. "All grown up enough for me to be unendingly proud of you, Brianna."

It was a perfect moment — the kind that earns instant permanence in your mind.

That's when everything started to go terribly, irrevocably wrong.

It began with a soft, white glow that seemed to come from her mother's chest. Brie did a double take. "Mom? Is that your—?" Before she could finish the sentence, something careened from their periphery with shocking speed, taking up their entire field of vision in the space of a moment. It was an eighteen-wheeler, fire engine red, mercilessly huge, and on the wrong side of the road.

The impact sent their car flying like a ball of crumpled aluminum foil.

As they flew, Brie felt a pressure in her chest. The air swirled around them, and their hair floated with strange weightlessness as gravity briefly loosened its hold. Time slowed as the two women locked eyes — Brie's wide and uncomprehending, her mother's stricken with sheer, unadulterated terror.

They slammed to a screeching halt against the base of an oak tree.

Brie's head felt heavy and dull. She heard her name called twice, three times, faint as an echo, though her mother was still in the seat beside her. She couldn't answer, couldn't move, couldn't breathe. She felt nothing except the terrifying pressure in her chest.

She heard a seat belt unbuckle and sensed her mother's frantic scramble to her side of the car. She heard her gasp in horror and felt a fiery pain shoot through her chest at her mother's touch. Everything around her was turning dark red.

"No! No! God, NO!" Her mom's head whipped back and forth, but their phones had been crushed. There was no way to call for help.

It was getting harder to breathe.

It's my blood.

The sluggish realization was quickly followed by another.

That's too much blood.

There was no way she'd survive until someone found them. If her mom left to find help, she'd be dead by the time she got back. Her eyes welled up with tears, overwhelmed by a finality she'd never encountered before, by a thousand swirling questions she'd never considered.

Is there an afterlife?

Is my family going to be okay when I'm gone?

She wanted to tell her mom goodbye, that it wasn't her fault, that she loved her, but none of those things were possible any-more. All she could manage was a faint, "Mom?"

Her mother stared at her with an unfathomable expression. It seemed an eternity they had been sitting there, but only a few seconds had passed. Then, she set her jaw, pressed a kiss to her daughter's forehead, and said, "It's going to be okay. I love you, Brianna."

With that, she slipped her delicate teardrop pendant over her head and placed the chain around her daughter's blood-stained neck.

Every memory Brie had of her mother included that necklace. She'd worn it her entire life, never once taking it off. It was there in all Brie's baby pictures — she would be staring adoringly at her mother's face and playing with that pendant.

This is it.

I'm dying, and she wants to give me something meaningful to show her love.

Brie took a deep, shuddering breath — then realized she'd taken a deep, shuddering breath.

How is that possible?

She wanted to ask, but things were happening now — things she didn't understand.

She watched as her mother took off her cardigan. There was movement somewhere below her line of sight, an unsettling shifting inside her chest.

Her mother looked into her eyes and braced one hand against her sternum. "Honey, this is going to hurt." Then, she pulled as hard as she could and dislodged an enormous piece of glass from Brie's rib cage, tossing it immediately over her shoulder and focusing all her attention on her daughter.

"Brianna, take a breath for me. Brianna — *breathe!*"

Brie sucked in a deep gasp of air, still marveling that she was able to do so. First, one arm moved, then the other. She touched her shirt where it had torn and looked down to see the jagged, open gash in her skin mend itself slowly back together, fading from blood red to light pink in a matter of seconds.

She stared up into her mother's wide green eyes, mirrors of her own.

"Mom," she said tentatively. "How?"

Relief washed over her mother's features as she cupped her daughter's face in both hands, kissing her cheeks and checking her for further damage. Her lips parted to say something when the air around them grew suddenly cold. Unnaturally cold. Brie shivered in surprise, watching their breath puff white before their faces.

That's when her world fell apart for a second time.

That's when a beast made of shadows attacked her mother.

It threw her mom backward with the force of a comet, tackling her to the ground. Her arms flew up protectively but encountered no resistance — passing through the nightmare like it wasn't even there. She swung wildly as though she couldn't see her attacker. Before either of them could scream, another creature appeared out of nowhere to join the assault.

The creatures pushed her so hard that she cratered into the earth, still scrambling wildly to escape. There was a moment when nothing happened when Brie thought it couldn't possibly get any worse. Then, one of the creatures reached a shadowy hand into her mother's chest. A quiet gasp escaped her mother's lips — her eyes widened, then went blank. A kind of sheen glazed her features and abruptly dulled as if the light had drained out of her.

She went limp as a rag doll.

The first creature made a guttural noise and perched on her chest like a gargoyle — the second pawed at the ground around her face as though vying for a turn.

Brie struggled against her seat belt, screaming over and over. And then, she saw it.

At first, it was no more than a glint, as if the sun had flashed across the surface of a mirror. As she watched, it began to take shape, growing from a tiny sphere small enough to fit in the palm of her hand into something bigger and blinding. Her eyes burned, but she couldn't look away. It was as though someone had carved a knife into the surface of the sun, and a single drop had spilled forth, twisting and hardening into the shape of a man dressed all in white.

He took only a moment to orient himself before his piercing eyes fixed on the shadows. A burst of light shot from his fingertips into the monster, preying on Brie's mother. It let out an unholy shriek and dissolved into a writhing mass of oil-black ribbons before disappearing from sight. The second beast let out an ear-piercing screech of protest but didn't seem to like its chances. It turned and vanished.

The man stepped closer, all that blazing light gentling into something else. He knelt and touched a hand to the lovely face that had been so full of life only minutes ago. He didn't appear to be much older than Brie was herself, but there was something ageless about him all the same. Something in the knowing depth of his eyes that didn't seem like it could possibly belong to this world.

Brie stared, transfixed in disbelief, before saying the only thing she could manage:

"Help me!"

The man whirled to face her, eyes widening in shock, before looking around as though Brie couldn't possibly be talking to him.

It was bizarre. *Who else would I be talking to?*

The seat belt she'd been struggling against finally snapped open, and she fell out of the car, landing on her palms before scrambling to her mom. Brie held her protectively, rocking slightly, trying to pull her from the earth.

She's so cold. How can she already be so cold?

"Mom, wake up! Stay with me!" She lifted her eyes to the man, feeling like she'd strayed into a terrible dream. "Help me!"

But he remained frozen, staring down at her with a peculiar expression.

"Why are you just standing there?" she screamed. "Do something! Anything!"

He gazed at her, watching tears carve paths down her blood-stained cheeks.

"Please," she whispered. "Please. Help me."

In an instant, his eyes filled with resolve. He knelt by her mother's side and tenderly lifted her from the ground. With utmost care, he laid her down and placed two glowing palms by her temples, his expression one of unwavering concentration. He fixed his gaze just above the crown of her head, maintaining this focus for what felt like an eternity.

Brie's heart sank when he finally met her eyes and shook his head. "It is beyond me. I do not have the power to bring her back."

With a broken cry, Brie gathered her mother away from him into her arms. She heard her father's voice frantically screaming from a great distance. Both her name and her mother's echoed wildly off the trees.

"My dad's coming. He'll call for an ambulance—"

"Your father is too late," the man said simply.

"...She's not going to wake up," Brie said in a strange, calm voice. It wasn't a question. The crushing finality of the moment had taken hold.

The strange man glanced at her with a look of sorrow and kindness she would always remember. "I'll be taking her with me." He hesitated. "But, perhaps, there is something I can do. A way for you to say goodbye."

Brie could think of nothing to say. Her entire world had shrunk to that moment, to that corner of the woods, with the golden afternoon sun casting diagonal shafts of light through the tree canopy, bathing her mother in an ethereal glow.

She took her mother's hand, pressing it to her cheek.

The man closed his eyes and placed one hand on her shoulder and the other on the crown of her mother's head. As Brie watched, a glow rose from her mother's body like a mist. It hovered for a moment before surrounding Brie. She felt her mother's presence so strongly that she knew for certain she was touching her soul.

A pair of tears slid down her cheeks.

I love you, Mom.

As if in answer, her mother's voice rang inside her mind as clearly as if the words had been spoken aloud:

"You're my whole heart, Brianna."

With that, the glow shrank, concentrated, and passed into the palm of the man's hand. Brie stared at the place where it disappeared, weeping silently.

"She will be cared for," he said softly. "You may be sure of that." Brie's hands trembled, and he took them in his own. "I give you my word."

She lifted her head, her vision blurred with tears. "Your word," she echoed faintly. "I don't even know your name."

He hesitated a moment, almost like he was considering, before gently squeezing her fingers and replying, "It's Cameron." A lock of chestnut hair slipped into his face, humanizing him in a moment of imperfection. He looked at her like she was the most mysterious thing he'd ever seen. "And what is your name?" he asked.

She met his gaze for a moment. "Brianna. Brianna Weldon." She looked back down at her mother's face, feeling like she was in a trance. "Am I ever going to see her again? Am I ever going to see you?"

He looked lost for a moment before answering. "Such things aren't up to me, but I hope so." It looked like he wanted to say more when the pendant suddenly caught his eye. His face stilled for a split second, growing almost cold. He reached out as if to touch it with the tip of his finger before pulling his hand back. "That's a lovely pendant. It suits you." He pushed to his feet before hesitating and turning to the devastated girl. "Brianna?" She looked up. "Never take it off."

And just like that, he vanished in a burst of light, taking her mother's soul with him, leaving her with nothing but her body and a lifetime of memories.

She was still kneeling when her father raced to her side a few moments later, still staring at the place where the man had vanished, the taste of chocolate frosting still on her lips.

Then, in a flash, she was back in the Great Hall on her hands and knees, hyperventilating as Zadkiel held her and Cameron rushed to her side.

CHAPTER SEVENTEEN

Revelation Part II

In an act of supreme mercy, Enoch called for a temporary recess. His reason on paper was to give the court time to discuss what they'd already seen, but in reality, he'd made the decision after taking a single look at Brie's face. She was allowed time to collect herself — to catch her breath.

She decided to do this with the unicorns. Cameron had asked to come with her, but she couldn't even manage the words to refuse him. She felt exposed, vulnerable, lost. She shook her head frantically and bolted from the throne room like a bullet from a gun, racing all the way to the beautiful blossoming tree on the hill overlooking the pasture.

She stood there, chest heaving with the enormity of it all, when something soft touched her hand. She looked down and gasped. A colt was nuzzling her palm with its nose, careful to keep its horn away. Forgetting her troubles and her place for a moment, she reached out a gentle hand and stroked its velvety face and ears. It looked at her with the kindest expression before tossing its head and scampering back to its mother. She watched them, too mesmerized by the spectacular sight to hear someone approaching.

"Hey, you." Sherry walked up the hill and sat down on the grass, nestled beneath the shade of the solitary tree. She patted the grass next to her, and Brie took a seat.

The meadow stretched out before them. The whole herd frolicked in the sunlight, tossing their bright manes. There was something inherently soothing about it. Brie couldn't help but imagine all the times Cameron must have sat there himself. Overall, the centuries, over all the countless generations, he must have sat there, looking over the herd he had rescued because he couldn't bear the thought of a world without them.

"You weren't kidding," Sherry finally said. "There are unicorns."

Brie nodded. "So, there are."

There was so much to say. Neither one had any idea where to start. It was easier to be silent. It wasn't until their shadows grew long across the grass that Brie tried to speak.

"What I said earlier—"

"I should have believed you," Sherry interrupted, arms wrapped tightly around her waist. "The things you told me... I should have believed you. I never even considered it."

Brie turned, trying to read her expression. "I told you that monsters killed my mother, and I was rescued by a guardian angel who took her soul to heaven." She paused for emphasis, shaking her head. "You were supposed to believe all that?"

Sherry hugged her knees to her chest. "Your guardian angel is a conversation for another day, but to answer your question, *yes*. Yes, I was supposed to believe that. I'm your best friend. At the very least, I was supposed to..."

Their eyes met, and Brie finished her thought. "You were supposed to believe *me*."

Sherry nodded slowly.

"You held me together," Brie said softly. "You held me together, Sherry. When no one else could." Truer words had never been spoken, but her best friend had always held herself to impossibly high standards.

"I made you repeat a lie," Sherry replied flatly. Her voice was quiet, so unlike her usual tone. "For years and *years*, I wanted you to heal. You have no idea how many four a.m. internet searches I did, how many psychology journals I read, how many gallons of coffee I brewed, trying to find new ways to help you heal. And all the while, I was making you repeat a lie."

Brie's teeth sank into her lower lip as Sherry's eyes filled to a shine.

"I thought it was a nightmare," Sherry whispered, tears rolling down her cheeks. "I genuinely thought, this is something her mind conjured to protect itself. Not for a single moment did I even *think* it could be true." She turned her face, wiping at the tears.

Brie took her hand, fingers wrapping together in the grass. "One of us had to stay sane," she murmured, unable to resist adding, "I just never imagined it would be you."

There was a snort of laughter, followed by a gentle squeeze.

"You always expect too much of yourself," Brie continued, smiling faintly at the look of surprise on her friend's face. "I think you don't notice because you always just achieve it, but you ask the world of yourself, Sherry. You always have." There was a sudden clenching in her stomach, like the turn of a dull blade.

Just like I'm asking the world of you now.

"I'm so sorry I didn't tell you about the rest of it," Brie continued in a whisper, bowing her head. "I'd like to say it was completely for your benefit — that I was trying to protect you, and, of course, that's true, but it wasn't the only reason." A shiver swept across her shoulders. "The truth is, I was terrified to come running to you with another impossible story, fire and brimstone trailing in my wake. You have no idea how glad I was to put that phase behind us. Crazy Brie, with her crazy stories. I thought I'd seen the last of her. I thought I was finally going to be someone different — normal Brie, with her normal job and normal life and her home filled with thriving houseplants."

"All of which would die," said Sherry without condemnation.

"None of which would die," Brie continued as though she hadn't heard, gazing at the magical creatures grazing innocently in the pasture. "You have no idea how much I looked forward to being *that* girl."

Something stirred inside her chest, gone before it started.

I guess I'll never know her.

The unicorns tossed their bright manes, hooves flashing in the sun.

"But how are *you* doing?" Brie asked suddenly. Sherry turned to her with a questioning look. "Seriously. I know even the *idea* of the supernatural freaks you out. How are you dealing with all of this?"

Sherry frowned and plucked individual blades of grass from the hilltop as she tried to organize her thoughts. "I'm... furious, actually!" Brie couldn't help but grin as her best friend's attempt at graceful acceptance died before it truly began, leaving behind only honesty and pure, simmering rage. "Do I have to believe in *ghosts* now? Do I have to read my horoscope? Am I going to wind up in Purgatory if I don't confess all my sins and fiddle with a prayer-bead bracelet? Brie, do you know how long it's going to take me to make a confession that covers the past two decades of my life? Ugh!" She huffed and shook herself all over as if to shrug off the offensive parallel reality in which she found herself before pointing at the Earth, massive in the Elysian sky, and turning to Brie with a glare. "Somewhere on that big blue planet, there's a priest who has NO idea what he's in for."

Brie struggled for three whole valiant seconds not to laugh before dissolving into a fit of giggles. Sherry's determined pout lasted only a moment longer before she joined in.

She turned with sudden determination, offering Brie her pinkie like an olive branch of truce. Given the utopic backdrop, it must have looked utterly ridiculous, but the woman's face was as serious as a grave. "Still friends?" she asked solemnly.

Brie snorted with laughter. "What do you think?"

Sherry lifted a playful shoulder. "I think this is where we part ways, Weldon. In a pasture of mythological creatures that your neurotic boyfriend rescued in a fruitless attempt to fill that giant void where there should be a heart."

Brie cast a sideways glance, chewing on her lip. "You're going to like him again someday," she muttered under her breath.

"He kidnapped me from a parking garage with that hulking menace he calls a friend. I'll never like him again," Sherry glowered. "But seriously. Still friends?"

She turned in the grass, smacking furiously at Brie's legs until she did the same. They sat like children, with their knees touching.

"You tell me," Brie answered almost warily. She gestured to the dreamscape with a sweep of her arm. "One could argue this is entirely my fault."

The corner of Sherry's mouth curved with the hint of a smile. "You always apologize for things that aren't your fault," she answered teasingly. "I don't think you notice because you're so used to carrying the weight of the world on your shoulders."

Her eyes flicked to the pendant. "I guess now you're carrying it around your neck." She gave her a nudge. "Of course, we're still friends, you loon. You couldn't shake me."

They death-gripped each other's fingers, then came together in a sudden embrace.

It was hard to stay mad in a field full of unicorns.

It was even harder to stay mad at your best friend.

Brie and Sherry walked back into the Great Hall hand in hand. Together, they climbed the steps of the dais. Cameron shot her a worried, questioning look. Brie nodded to assure him she was all right.

This time, Sherry helped her settle into her chair. "I'm going to be right over there," she whispered loudly. "*Right* over there, Brianna." She added in a low undertone, "With a knife, Tavi gave me that no one else knows I have."

Brie sucked in a breath, praying for patience.

Heaven help us. Or maybe someone a little closer.

Enoch quieted the murmurs of the court with a wave of his hand.

Zadkiel came over and sat beside her on the chairs. "Are you ready?" he asked. When she nodded, he took her hand once more and, in a flash of light, returned them to the hallway of her memories.

She took a moment to orient herself before asking, "Zadkiel, can you help me this time?"

Until this point, she had opened the doors herself, peering at what was behind before flinging them open to let the memories play out. At her request, he joined her, opening all the doors on the left as she opened everything on the right.

She'd never seen her life from this vantage point before. Watching her story unfold like a movie, she saw details she would never otherwise have noticed. Her dad secretly checks on her every night. The way her friends went out of their way to look after her. The month after the accident, when Sherry had brought her breakfasts every morning and taken them away uneaten every afternoon.

I was so loved. So many people took care of me.

But even with all that, it wasn't enough to mend her broken heart. The year of memories after the accident seemed to be colored differently than the rest of her past — a descent into shades of grey.

Except for one thing.

It caught her attention almost by accident — there in the corner of the holographic images projected before the court — a golden glint of a thing, glowing brightly, keeping watch and staying out of sight. The more doors she opened, the more she realized it was always there. *He* was always there. It was Cameron, holding vigil — making sure she was never alone. Those nights, she heaved with dry sobs, thinking if only she could cry, just once, it might help to lift the crushing weight constantly holding her down. The days she spent insisting that what she saw was real until finally capitulating to her dad, Sherry, and her therapist's narrative that the angels and demons were something her brain had concocted to deal with the trauma of the accident. Those moments when she'd felt like the loneliest person in the world, Cameron made certain she was never actually alone.

The corners of her eyes pricked with unshed tears as she stared at the golden glow hiding in the corner of the last five years of her life. What must it have cost him to watch her like this? What must he have sacrificed?

All those years, I never realized. I never saw. He made sure of that.

She set her jaw and looked down Zadkiel's hall at the remaining doors.

Do the next right thing. For his people. No matter the cost.

She opened the rest of the doors.

Years of therapy, intensely personal conversations in which she doubted her own sanity, played out for everyone to see. One chapter after another, she allowed her story to be shown to an entire civilization, to show them what was coming — what had come for her.

The glowing, burning pendant. The attack on her way to Virginia. Cameron rescuing her. Lying to Sherry. Healthy people dying for no discernible reason. Stomping her foot, cracking her house. There was a murmur through the crowd of Elysians when a swarm of wraiths attacked her. There were shouts of fear when they saw Mammon for the first time. Before she knew it, Mammon was killing Dr. Matthews in the atrium, horns springing from her head as she nearly killed Cameron, too. A cheer rang through the court when the memory of Brie cutting off the demon's head with the strange sculpture was projected for all to see.

As Brie reached one of the last doors and turned the knob, from the corner of her eye, she glimpsed Zadkiel open a door, look inside, and abruptly close it again. As she opened her mouth to ask him what was wrong, the memory behind her door floated out and was projected, huge, horrible, and undeniable. She looked up and gasped. "That can't be. That isn't…"

It was her.

She was in the parking garage, floating like a human crucifix, Heaven's fire pouring from her eyes, her mouth, and her pendant. Her hair floated behind her, framing her like a vengeful spirit, as a dome of lightning cracked and pulsed around her. She was holding ropes made of light and was pulling a terrified Mammon toward her.

And the scream.

It sounded like it could crack the world and looked as though it was ripping Mammon apart. Brie watched in horrified disbelief as she told Mammon to go back to Hell in a voice that was not her own, and the demon collapsed in on herself like an imploding star.

There was utter silence in the Hall.

All she could hear was Ephriam's voice in her head. What he'd said to her last night, before the portrait of the Morningstar:

"Even if you could somehow find a way to conquer the forces that seek to work against you... what would you have to become? Would you wish to become such a thing?"

She didn't know how long she stood there before Zadkiel touched her shoulder and whispered, "We are almost done."

She felt utterly hollow. "Right," she muttered. "Let's get this over with."

She unceremoniously ripped open the door that held her resurrecting Rashida. Oblivious to the shocked gasps of the Elysians, she marched forward, tearing open the doors, not caring anymore what was on the other side.

More memories poured out. When Ephriam examined Kylie and later told Cameron she was a scion, there was a visible ripple through the crowd. Several Elysians stood up and shouted in a language Brie didn't understand.

On she went, opening door after door, until suddenly she came to one she could not open. She was used to the unencumbered give to the rest of them, so she nearly fell when it refused to budge. Frowning, she tried the knob again. It was strange, intricately carved from a red stone, and the doorway was circled in strange symbols. And it didn't budge an inch.

"Zadkiel, could you help me?" she asked, still struggling.

He came over and tried the door. It started to open, then immediately slammed itself shut, and the intricate carvings started to glow. The archangel frowned and used two hands to try to pry it open, but the door glowed brighter, and suddenly, with a burst of light, the pair of them were thrown violently from the hallway of her mind back into their seated bodies on the dais.

Brie's eyes stopped shining like projectors and went back to normal. Zadkiel dropped her hands, and they pulled away from each other, breathing heavily, staggered by what had just happened.

Cameron was kneeling by her chair. He placed his hands on her shoulder and searched her face. "Are you okay? What happened?"

She was still trying to catch her breath. "Yes, I'm... I don't know what—"

Enoch appeared beside them. "What is it?" he asked. "Why have you broken the Revelation?"

"She didn't," Zadkiel said, watching her intently. "The ritual is complete. You have seen all that you need to know. The rest of her memories were made here," he added, shooting Cameron a brief glance. He looked back at Enoch. "The Revelation is complete."

Enoch nodded and rose to address the growing noise in the court. Zadkiel continued to watch Brie's face until she noticed and nodded discreetly in thanks. With no trace of a smile, Zadkiel nodded back.

Cameron's face was anguished. "Are you really all right?"

"I'm fine." She tried her best to reassure him but was distracted by an Elysian who'd stood up and shouted at Enoch.

"How is this possible? She performed a resurrection without Divine consent. And she saved a *scion*. How can such a creature exist anymore?"

She was startled. The Elysian didn't just sound puzzled by this mysterious scion, he sounded angry — outraged, even.

Scandalized.

Enoch raised his hands in a placating gesture. "That scion is obviously a human child. Its genetic line must be so watered down that it evaded detection for centuries. And as for the resurrection, Ms. Weldon meant only to spare her friend a most unjust end. She did not realize the implications."

Brie turned to Cameron with a frightened look and asked, "What do they mean? What implications?"

Cameron opened his mouth to answer but was cut off before he could say a word.

"That just proves that this power is too much for any mortal to hold." This came from a familiar, black-haired, ivory-skinned Elysian seated close to the dais rather than in the stands with the rest of the Host.

Cassius.

CHAPTER EIGHTEEN

The Prophecy of Azrael

The black-haired Elysian glided toward them. He shot Brie a cold, impassive look before turning to face the court. "The girl cannot control her strength. She nearly shattered her own home apart. She summoned a dark horde by removing her necklace, forcing our Prince to fight for his life on the mortal plane — twice." Cassius spoke in a calm, methodical voice that smoothly belied the judgment and implied consequence that lay beneath.

"She also took down one of the Seven with no training whatsoever." This time, it was Tavi who spoke, stepping out from her place at the head of the Guard to address the court. "Surely, there is nothing more she needs to do to prove whose side she's on."

"The fact that she has inexplicable, unchecked, and untrained power does not bolster your argument the way you think it does, soldier," Cassius replied. "And as for whose side she's on? Though it's scarcely the point, it is reasonable to assume that she is on her own side, as are they all."

Brie frowned.

Is he talking about humans?

"The real point is, the child knows everything about our world," he continued, addressing those assembled in the Hall as much as he was responding to Tavi, like a politician playing to the crowd. "And the knowledge has spread. Now, her friends have seen evidence of worlds beyond their own. There is a reason we remain hidden from humans, Tavianne. Do you pretend to comprehend the chaos that would be unleashed if the secret of our existence became known?"

There was a murmur of assent from the crowd.

Cassius went on, "The warfare would be absolute. The death toll would be astonishing, even by modern standards. We are only a few tens of millions dealing with a population of billions. What do you think the Creator would say if we give them more cause to slaughter one another?"

Tavi narrowed her eyes. "Brie has proven herself to be brave in the darkest of circumstances. We all saw it — she overcame overwhelming personal grief to build a life for herself. She tried to keep our secret, even from those she loved the most. And she took down one of our most dangerous enemies." She came to stand beside Brie, who looked at her with gratitude. "What more could you possibly demand of her, Cassius?"

He folded his arms over his chest. "That she gives up the pendant, gives up the memories, and goes back to her life as though none of this ever happened. A mortal girl has no business fighting celestial battles. Let our own King Enoch take the pendant and Zadkiel the memory. Let our finest experts decide what they mean and what to do with them."

Cameron was on his feet in a heartbeat. "Over my dead body, Cassius," he growled.

The Elysian's face flashed with anger before he answered coolly back. "This court will get to you and your multitude of infractions in a minute. As the son of our ruler, you have been given far too much latitude, young sir. A lesson I rather thought you'd have learned more intimately than most. But it seems utter disregard for our most sacred rules — consorting with humans, meddling with resurrection — is a trait that runs in your family."

Cameron glared at him, his fists balled at his sides.

"Enough." Enoch's voice was calm, but laced with warning.

But Cassius was not finished. "Revealing our existence to even a normal mortal is itself a violation of protocol deserving of dire consequences, but to reveal our world to one so dangerous as she?" He looked at Brie like she was poison. "She should go back to her own kind."

"You can't take her memories away," Sherry shouted angrily, pushing to her feet. In a flash, Mike stood up beside her. "They're hers. How could you even dare to presume?" Mike took her hand and squeezed to warn her to be careful, shooting glances around the Hall at the innumerable powerful creatures watching this exchange play out.

"Her memories are inextricably tied to the most formative moments in her personal timeline, Cassius," said Cameron. "What would you have her do? Forget her own mother's death? Forget the years she spent trying to heal, trying to come to terms with it?"

"The aspects of those events that have no place in the mortal plane? Yes!" said Cassius. "Let Zadkiel modify all her memories. Let her believe it all happened in a normal way, in a human accident."

"And what about her father? Her friends?" pressed Tavi.

"It can be done for all those whom her story has touched. Let them all go back to their happy oblivion, to live out their brief, meaningless lives in peace," Cassius concluded.

The court began to rumble with whispers, then full arguments and shouts, as Cassius and Tavi both seemed to rally support to their side.

Cameron roared at him. "That is beyond the pale, Cassius. You should be thanking this woman, not planning to steal the truth of her story right out of her life!"

"If you lay a *finger* on her, I don't care who you are, I will turn you into an *ottoman*." Sherry looked prepared to make good on her threat on the spot.

Mike interjected too, in a strong, passionate voice. "Really, are you all going to stand here and pretend like you have a right to violate the sanctity of a human's mind when it sounds like non-interference is the cornerstone of your entire cultural identity?"

His argument made Cassius look around in surprise. "What would a human know about such things?"

Mike scowled. "There was a book of Elysian law in the living room. I read it."

Cassius' gaze flicked from Mike to Ephriam, who had come to stand by the humans. "Ephriam, I am surprised to see you so at ease in such company."

"This is not the time for petty prejudices, Cassius." Ephriam stood firmly by his friends. "There are forces at work here we need to understand. Our best chance to do so is by working with the humans, not by highlighting that which divides us and silencing them with our powers."

"Working with the humans?" Cassius abandoned all pretense of esteem and openly sneered. "Working with those sociopathic, genocidal viruses? They who destroy all that is

good in Creation? What have they ever been gifted that they
have yet to defile? The animals. The water. The earth. The air.
The seas and all that is in them. And now they are destroying
the very building blocks of life itself — they are destroying the
atom to destroy each other! The best thing that can be said
about humans is that they are short-lived. And you want us to,
what exactly? Let these ones go home, having seen our world?
To report to the rest of their kind that there are more species to
kill and more resources to plunder besides those on their own
evil, ruined rock?"

"Now, just a minute here, you insufferable, little—"

What Sherry said next would have made her mother faint.

In response, the entire Elysian host rose to its feet and started
arguing and shouting. A few were so upset that they couldn't
hold their human form anymore. Or maybe Cassius' speech
described how many of them felt, and they simply did not want
to. In the space of a minute, dozens of them burst into their
true form — four faces, wreathed in flame, ever-changing and
awe-inspiring. To Sherry's unending credit, this only gave her
pause for about two seconds before she yelled at them again,
going on about human rights and the Geneva Convention.

Brie was silent as she listened, too exhausted to speak up for
herself.

I've just shown my entire life to these people.

If that hasn't convinced them, their secret is safe with me...

I don't know what I could possibly say to change their minds.

That's when she saw her.

The little girl from the library, the one with floor-length black
hair, stood on the dais some ways away. Brie quickly walked over
to her as Tavi let out a particularly vehement-sounding oath in

a language she didn't recognize, but the little girl seemed to; she giggled and held her hand to her mouth.

"Hey, there," said Brie, kneeling down to her level. "What are you doing here, little one?"

The girl calmly looked at her.

Brie forced herself to smile. "Sweetheart, I'm not sure this is the nicest place for you to be right now. Some of the grownups are feeling angry." She looked around, trying to find the child's guardian. "Is there somewhere you're supposed to be? Is anyone here to watch you?"

The girl didn't answer. Instead, she gave Brie a knowing look, reached out her little index finger, and touched her pendant.

It immediately started to glow.

Cassius' voice suddenly roared into her consciousness again. "If King Enoch didn't summon her here for exactly this purpose, then what is she here for? What could she possibly be here for other than to give us the information we need and go back to her little life, nursing other mortals back to health, trying to stave off the inevitable?" He came striding up to the dais, addressing the increasingly unruly court and getting uncomfortably close. Brie stood, positioning herself between him and the little girl. "The best thing for this child is to forget that any of this ever happened and that any of us exist. No mortal should have access to such a powerful—"

Then, several things happened.

Cassius reached for her pendant.

Before he could touch it, it emitted a blast of energy that threw him across the entire length of the Hall to crash halfway up the wall on the other side. Silence fell as he slid all the way down to the floor, where he sat, blinking in astonishment.

Brie was horrified. "I'm sorry! I didn't... I didn't mean to—"

Shouts and chaos erupted once more. Enoch tried in vain to silence his court. Languages tangled together in anger, and several of the Elysian guards drew terrifying-looking weapons out of their sheaths.

The moment she saw the weapons, Brie whirled to the child again. She put her hands on her little arms and spoke to her in a calm but urgent voice. "Honey, I need you to get out of here. You need to go somewhere safe. Do you hear me? Somewhere sa— *Honey?!*" The little girl flashed Brie a smile and sank into the void.

The deafening noise of the assembled host faded into a dull hum in her ears as Brie stared, stunned, at the spot in the floor where the little girl had just disappeared. Shaking, she brought her hand to her pendant and held its stone up in front of her face. "What did you do?!" she asked in a horrified whisper.

They're right. I have to give it to them.

I cannot be trusted with something so powerful as—

Suddenly, someone screamed, and everything began to fall silent once more.

The lights in the Hall flickered. Brie turned around slowly.

A pool of black, ringed with purple and blue ripples of light, started as a small spot on the floor right in front of the dais and grew to be more than twenty feet around in a matter of seconds. The swirling vortex that had appeared beneath the girl returned, larger this time. Out of this blackest of voids, a terrifying figure rose slowly until it was fully revealed. It levitated a foot off the ground in swirling robes, black as midnight.

Azrael.

◆   ◆   ◆

You could have heard a pin drop. No one made a sound as the Angel of Death floated in silence. Brie forgot to breathe.

Enoch went ashen for a moment before remembering himself. "Azrael," he said, bringing his fingertips to his forehead in their Elysian gesture of respect. "Forgive us for starting without you. We were not expecting... It has been many years."

Brie couldn't believe it. "*Honey?*" she asked. Her voice was barely more than a whisper, but it echoed off the walls like someone had sounded a gong.

The terrifying archangel turned its head in her direction. Then, in a moment that would haunt Brie's nightmares for the rest of her days, the spectral figure tilted its head and spoke. Or rather, it did not speak, but a voice, as whispering and thin as a cold wind through tombstones, blared inside the minds of every being assembled in the Great Hall.

"I know you."

The entire host gasped. Brie thought she might swallow her tongue.

With her glittering, obsidian eyes, the skeletal figure, black as a starless sky, turned back to King Enoch. With one of her six arms, she pulled a palm-sized scroll from her robes. Brie recognized it from the mosaic in the garden. She levitated this to the king.

He plucked it from the air and stood silently for a moment before asking, "Are you certain?"

Azrael inclined her masked, skeletal head.

Enoch nodded in acknowledgment. No one made a sound as he broke the seal. A deep sound resonated through the Hall when the golden wax cracked, loud as a thunderclap.

The ancient king paused momentarily, unrolled it, and began to read aloud.

"One will come whose fate is tied to the Tears.
With six, she will stand, though Death will have its cull and Hell its prize.
Three worlds she will hold in the palm of her hand,
and the Divine Will shall shine through mortal eyes."

Not even a breeze would dare to rustle the air after Enoch read the scroll. Silence lay heavy for long minutes until a messenger raced in and flew to a stop, panting, in front of the dais. The poor Elysian took one look at Azrael and became immediately aware that he'd stumbled into something seriously over his pay grade, but he nonetheless delivered his message. "Please, excuse me, my King."

Enoch rolled up the scroll again and composed himself. "What is it, Aulus?"

"Forgive me, sire, I did not know you were in the middle of…." he hesitated.

Enoch grew visibly impatient for the first time since Brie had known him. "Speak, soldier."

Aulus swallowed. "It's about the device, sire."

The king's face stilled. He beckoned Aulus closer to him, who spoke in a faint whisper into his ear. All Brie caught was, "They think they can…" before his voice lowered to a range she couldn't discern.

Her head was still swimming with the message of the scroll. She couldn't take her eyes off Azrael. Sherry came over and took her hand, with Mike beside her, but still, she looked at the Angel of Death, who hovered silently. Waiting.

Brie broke away from the rest and approached her. "Miss Azrael. Your prophecy. Is it about me?"

The Hall fell silent.

The archangel nodded.

"And the Tears you spoke of. Do you mean this?" Brie held up her pendant.

"The Forbidden Tears," said Azrael. Her voice was like a planet moving.

"Why are they forbidden? Forbidden to me?" Brie asked.

Azrael shook her head. *"It must be you. The seven of you."*

"But why? Why must it be me?"

Azrael's fathomless, inhuman eyes stared into and past her own. *"In due time, you will tell me."* Then, she rose to her full height and spoke her last words to the court. *"Prepare for company, Children of Paradise. Pilgrims shall knock upon thy gates."*

She sank again into that black gravity pool and disappeared.

Brie looked around at the hundreds of silent, staring Elysian faces and felt compelled to speak. Before truly considering what she would say, she was addressing the court. "I'm sorry that I make you feel afraid. I know what it is to feel confused and afraid, and I wouldn't wish it on anyone. It's the last thing I'd ever want to do. Mister Cassius," She looked at the figure of the man who'd just moments ago rallied his people against her to fight for the removal of her pendant and her memories. She touched her fingertips to her necklace. "I'm so sorry. I didn't mean to do that. Please accept my apology."

Cassius nodded, rubbing the back of his head and casting a fearful glance at the place where Azrael had disappeared into the floor.

"I understand why you don't want humans to know you exist." she continued. "I wouldn't trust us, either." She looked at Mike and Sherry. "But there is good in humanity, too. There are admirable qualities: courage, loyalty, benevolence, respect." She looked at Cameron, who nodded in encouragement. "For whatever it's worth, I would never dream of telling anyone the secret of your existence. I am grateful for the protection you've given me and the great, compassionate service you perform for humanity, shepherding souls from one reality to the next. Whatever the decision of this court, I will abide by it, but I submit only for myself. On behalf of my friends, I ask that you consider their wishes. The sanctity of their minds should not be tied to anyone's decisions but their own."

There was a slight cough behind her, and she turned to see King Enoch.

"Oh, shoot. I'm so sorry. I should probably have... I didn't mean to just... I mean, it's your court, but you were busy, and it just felt like it needed to be said."

Her face flushed pink.

Way to stick the landing, Weldon.

She could swear she saw a flash of amusement on the king's face before he spoke. "This court will adjourn to review your Revelation, to examine the sculpture that beheaded the Fallen One Mammon, and to study the Scroll of Azrael, whose seal is now broken. The scroll's prophecy is a remarkable event, one we do not take lightly. We ask that you seek the archangel Jophial, the Watcher. We are in need of her wisdom and understanding during these confusing times." He locked eyes with Brie and continued. "My son will accompany you, as his fate seems tied to your own. I would like to know the reason why." He stared at her so intensely that she found herself fidgeting before he blinked and continued. "We thank you for your candor, and we thank you for your help. May you and your friends be met with good fortune. When we meet again, we hope to have the answers the other seeks."

He touched two fingers to his forehead, and she reciprocated the gesture. So did Sherry. Then Mike. Then Tavi, Ephriam, and Cameron. Soon, the entire court touched two fingers to their foreheads and bowed slightly.

"Be well, Brianna Weldon," the ancient king said. "May you ever go with God."

The general air of solemnity and gravitas lasted as everyone filed out and for the entire walk from the throne room back to the villa. Then, Sherry threw her purse onto the giant tortoise and asked the question that was on everyone's mind:

"What in the ever-loving hell was *that?*"

CHAPTER NINETEEN

Farewell Elysium

"I'm telling you, nobody else saw a little girl." Sherry was in her magical closet, ignoring Enrique Iglesias' husky pleas for attention through the locked annex door and fitting as much couture as she could carry into a series of vintage Louis Vuitton steamer trunks. Brie was there "helping," which mainly consisted of stealing Sherry's cappuccinos, as her own bathroom seemed quite set on its pro-herbal-tea agenda. Cameron had gone off with Tavi and Ephriam after dropping them at the villa, and Mike was pouring through a book, taking notes.

We bring the guy to a whole new world, and he's obsessed with the judiciary system.

"How could you not see her? She was right there!" Brie sighed and flung herself onto the fainting couch. "These things are handy," she said, running her hand over the velvet upholstery. "You should get one for your place while I'm away finding this Jophial."

Sherry smirked and kept packing. "Hand me that glove, will you?"

Brie reached behind her and picked up a single white, sparkly glove that looked strangely familiar. "Sher, is this what I think it is?"

Sherry snatched it out of her hand. "My niece loves *Billie Jean.*"
There was a brief silence.

"You cannot give a two-year-old Michael Jackson's glove," Brie
exclaimed. "It's worth like a million dollars. She'll drool on it."

Sherry gave her a devious grin and pocketed a pearl the size
of her fist. "Just planning ahead."

Brie wasn't sure what she meant, but she couldn't stop smiling.
As terrible, and traumatic, and indescribably weird as her day
had been, she couldn't consider it a bad one. She had her best
friend back.

There was a knock at the door. Mike cracked it open. "Hey,
ladies. Brie? There's somebody here to see you. Can I come in?"

"Sure thing, babe," called Sherry.

Mike stepped in and looked around with dubious awe. "Are you
sure you want to leave, Sher? Like, ever?" Sherry grinned at him,
but her face fell as Mike turned around with a puzzled expression
and asked, "Do you hear that? It sounds like Spanish music."

"Nope. And you don't hear it, either. Hand me those boots,
will you?"

Mike nodded obediently, refused to hear anything at all, and
handed her the boots.

Brie walked outside but stopped short when she saw who it was.
Her cheeks flamed instinctively as her stomach twisted with nerves.

"King Enoch," she said. "I'm so sorry. If I'd known you were
coming, I wouldn't have kept you waiting."

"That's quite all right, Ms. Weldon. I didn't send word on purpose. I didn't want to announce myself. May I...?" He drifted,
then started again. "May we speak for a moment?" He seemed
troubled, unsure of himself. She was once again struck by his
age and fragility. "There is something I must ask of you."

"Yes, of course," she said.

He nodded and walked past her down the hallway. She followed him until they stopped outside Ethan's room. She waited for him to go inside, but he absentmindedly traced his finger over the homemade "E," just as his son had assuredly done a thousand times before. When he turned to her again, it was not a king who addressed her.

It was a father.

"Please," he asked, his throat thick with emotion, "bring him back to me. Cameron is all I have left in this world." He drew in a trembling breath, trying to keep his composure. "I have not always been the father he deserves, but believe me when I tell you, my love for him knows no bounds."

Brie stared in surprise, then nodded swiftly. "I'll do everything I can, sire."

Still battling emotion, he let out a short, involuntary laugh. "Please, don't call me sire. Enoch will suffice."

She offered him a shy smile. "Only if you call me Brie."

He clasped his hand on her shoulder. "Brie, then." He gave her a look that bordered on fondness. "I think it's fair to assume you all have some questions. May I speak with the other members of your party?"

Members of my party?

"Um, sure. Sherry and Mike are just packing. Let me get them."

Five minutes later, Cameron returned with Ephriam and Tavi and joined them all in the courtyard. Enoch sat and addressed them with far less formality than had just been on display in the Great Hall. "I'm sending the Guard with you," he stated bluntly.

Cameron and Tavi exchanged a look.

"How much of the Guard?" asked Cameron.

"All of it."

"Father—"

"All of it, son. I cannot take risks with your life, not when the Seven are involved."

"I understand," Cam said respectfully. "But before you mobilize an army in a small Virginian neighborhood, Tavianne has an idea. I think it's worth hearing her out."

The king seemed in no mood to have his mind changed, but the man was built on patience. He turned to Tavi and folded his hands, waiting.

"My king," she began. "Of course, we need to establish a presence in their hometown, but we cannot do so in such numbers that our existence becomes known. The factions in court today have accepted that these three humans will be the first to roam the earth with knowledge of our people in over a thousand years, but they would not so readily accept it if we were further exposed."

Enoch considered this, frowning. "What do you propose?"

"Allow me to send a guard unit to observe and protect the scion. A *large* guard unit," she added when she saw Enoch's face. "Given what we saw in the Revelation, that's who the Seven were after. They were plotting to kill the child. We must ascertain why."

Oh my God. She's right.

"My team is already there," Tavi continued, "guarding her at the hospital, and I've twice now sent reinforcements to watch her and her family from every angle, at every moment, but there is more that must be done."

"What do you recommend?" asked Enoch.

"We must send surveillance teams up and down the eastern seaboard to investigate the strange deaths that the resurrected one described, plus additional teams to all last known points of angelic confinement."

"And what about my son?" Enoch pressed. "And the others?"

"Ephriam and I will personally accompany them and keep them from harm," answered Tavi.

This seemed to surprise him. "Tavianne, you have not been on a long-term mission to Earth since the Battle of the Dragon Hole."

"I know," she said. "It's time." She inclined her head to the old ruler. "We will return to their homes long enough to give the mortals a plausible excuse for their absence. Then, we will transport ourselves directly to the halls of Jophial. A legion of troops isn't necessary for such a mission. And Jophial would not appreciate an army showing up at her gates. As a small party, we can maneuver quickly and efficiently without drawing unwanted attention to ourselves. This is the best way to keep him safe," she added. "And our defensive force is needed here at home. The pattern of wraith attacks on the perimeter is cause for concern and constant diligence."

Enoch was quiet for a moment. "So be it," he said, nodding. "Make the necessary arrangements."

Tavi bowed slightly and was gone in a flash. Ephriam followed in her shadow. The rest of them continued to sit with the Elysian king, wondering what to say next and making awkward guesses about courtly protocol.

Luckily, Enoch saved them from any more excruciating attempts to display royal manners. "I have gifts for you all, to thank you for your assistance in these troubling times, and to help you on the journey ahead." He reached over to a table for a wooden box that appeared with a wave of his hand.

Sherry took the opportunity to guiltily scootch one of her new designer purses further under the couch with her foot.

Enoch lifted the engraved wooden lid and removed a translucent silver bag filled with what looked for all the world like marbles made of ice. He handed it to Sherry. "These serve two purposes. They can locate one another — give them to those whom you wish to track, and you will always know where they are."

Sherry took the bag, wide-eyed. "Ancient GPS. I love it. What's the second purpose?"

"They freeze time for approximately one Earth minute in a ten-foot radius when broken."

Sherry seemed to freeze herself and handled the bag far more carefully, though her eyes danced. "Your majesty, this opens up a world of possibilities. Thank you very much."

Enoch chuckled and moved on to Mike. "For you, Mr. Mitchell," he handed him a tiny, dried vine. "From what I've seen, I believe this is suited to your personality."

Mike took the little desiccated plant with a puzzled look.

"They are grapes that grow anywhere," the king explained. "Wherever you are, you will be able to survive and provide."

Comprehension dawned on Mike's face, and he warmed with a smile. "Thank you, sir."

Next, the ancient king pulled two bottles that looked to be made of the finest crystal from the box. "Miss Weldon," he caught himself, pressing them into her hands, "Brie. These are for you." One was filled with a familiar-looking amber liquid, and the other shone with its own light, radiant yellow-gold. "I believe you are familiar with our ambrosia draught already," he said with a faint twinkle in his eye. "And this," he touched the glowing bottle, "is the light of Elysium itself, distilled by our sharpest minds into liquid form. No matter where you are, as long as you have this, you are connected to this place."

Brie felt the significance of his words and bowed her head. "I'll do my best to be worthy of such gifts."

Enoch's face softened. "If I am not mistaken, young lady, you already are." He turned to Cameron. "And for you, my son." He took two things from the box again. One was a twisting horn from an animal Brie couldn't identify. Two holes had been carved near its small end and set with a large, bright yellow stone. "You know what this is," Enoch said softly.

He must have because he looked stricken and swallowed hard before answering. "Father, I will not have to use it."

The king nodded. "I pray that you are right."

Then, he handed him the second gift — an unassuming, golden key. Cameron's eyes shot up to meet his father in alarm, but Enoch smiled. "You think I didn't know all those years when you snuck out together? Now, go with my blessing. And son?" His voice grew husky. "Come back to me."

Brie looked between the two men. "King Enoch, thank you so much for your hospitality and generosity. If you'll excuse me for a minute, I need to say goodbye to Cong." She signaled discreetly for Mike and Sherry to follow her, and together, they retreated down the hall.

The two men sat awkwardly for a moment before the king broke the silence. "I think better when I'm moving. Let's take a walk."

♦   ♦   ♦

Enoch and Cameron left together, leaving the others to pack. The king's gifts were not the only ones they received before their departure.

Raphael soon appeared at Brie's window, still looking for all the world like a combination of Aquaman and Jesus, to give her an extra bottle of ambrosia and a pouch full of herbs with very specific dosing instructions.

As he turned to leave, Sherry nudged Brie, "I can see why you fainted," she said appreciatively. "He *is* gorgeous."

Raphael glanced back in surprise, looking rather delighted, and Brie flashed a grin.

"Show her, hot stuff," she prompted.

It took him a second to understand, and then, in a flash of light, he transformed into the towering colossus of wings and eyes that was his natural form. Sherry nearly fell over and gripped Brie's shoulder so tightly she almost regretted the stunt — almost. Then, with a bright white flash, Raphael returned to his gorgeous self, walking away through the garden, laughing and wishing them good fortune.

Zadkiel stopped by, too, appearing in the courtyard just a few minutes before Cameron and Enoch returned.

Brie went out to greet him but felt suddenly awkward.

How do you say hi to someone who just toured the entirety of your mind? Well, almost the entirety.

The archangel inclined his head. "What you did today was very brave indeed, youngling."

"Everyone keeps calling me that. I'm not sure you're taking into account how much this experience has aged me." She was only half-joking.

He was serious. "I think it will age you still further in the days ahead."

"That's…" she sighed. "Not particularly encouraging, but I think you're right." She hesitated, chewing over a question. "Zadkiel, what was that door? The red door? The one we couldn't open?" She paused again, nervous to add the rest. "And why didn't you tell anyone?"

About the door. And about Cameron's kiss.

It was something that hadn't occurred to her until later. Zadkiel had skipped over one single door — the door that held the evidence of their forbidden intimacy. It was a silent courtesy that had been extended before she even knew to ask for it and was over before she had a chance to show her thanks.

He shook his head. "I have never seen such a phenomenon before. I don't have the faintest idea what it is or what it means, but I intend to find out. I will consult with Raziel while you are away. In the meantime," he reached up and took his earring off. "Please, take this with you."

She took it and looked at him. "What does it do?"

"It carries no particular powers besides providing a certain clarity of thought when confusion threatens to overwhelm the mind. Call it a token of my esteem."

"Thank you, Zadkiel." Brie put the earring in her left ear. He helped her affix the back. "I appreciate what you did, too — offering me a choice."

"I'm the angel of free will," he said with a shrug. "It was my bound duty."

"Archangel," she corrected with a smile.

"Indeed." He lowered his face to hers, and she stared into those deep, golden irises. "Brianna Weldon, I wish you good fortune in your quest. May you and all your party stay safe and find the answers you seek." He nodded behind her at Sherry and Mike, then disappeared.

Not long after, Tavi and Ephriam flashed into sight again, decked out in gear reminiscent of their first encounter, flasks and weapons hanging off their sides. Cameron and Enoch reappeared as well and went to consult with the Elysians.

Brie frowned as Sherry, and Mike heaved another leather backpack onto the growing pile of luggage on the patio. "Everyone keeps talking about my party. What do they mean? It's just Cameron and me going to meet this Jophial person, along with Tavi and Ephriam, of course."

This was met with eye rolls and condescending titters of laughter.

"I said so, didn't I?" said Sherry, looking smug.

"Said what?" asked Brie, searching for clues in their faces and finding none.

"That you'd try to take this on all by your lonesome or leave with no one except your heavenly Ken-doll over there," Mike said with a grin. "That it wouldn't even occur to you that we're obviously coming too. There's no way we're letting you go anywhere without us, not after all the trouble you've managed to get yourself tangled up in."

Brie looked around in disbelief. "Sher. Mike. Look, I can't tell you how sorry I am that I've gotten you involved in whatever this is, but there is *no way* I will drag you in deeper."

"Right," Mike agreed cheerfully. "You're just going to leave us back home to carry on as though nothing's gone completely sideways while you trek off to God-knows-where with danger hot on your heels. Nevermind that we're definitely on the radar of some horrible, supervillain goat-woman who seems to be the sister of the devil himself. I'm sure it'll be fine."

His eyes twinkled as she floundered, grasping at straws.

"Ephriam and Tavi could take care of you instead of me," she insisted. "The Elysians will send other guards to protect me."

Ephriam folded his massive arms across his chest and looked utterly unamused. "I take my orders from no one but Tavi and my King."

"And I was ordered to stay with you," Tavi chimed in. "You might have an awfully special necklace, Brie, and I'm already quite fond of you, but I am the captain of the Elysian Guard. Unless my King commands me to listen to you, you'd have better luck trying to boss around the moon."

"That's... That's just..." Brie sputtered.

Sherry grinned wickedly and leaned over to stage-whisper to Mike. "I love this part when she tries to put her foot down. Her face turns all kinds of colors. Sometimes, she even stomps her foot, like she did when she was five."

Cameron, who had been holding back a chuckle, went a bit pale, perhaps remembering the time she'd stomped her foot and nearly broken her living room in half. His eyes flickered around the lovely villa, wondering just how much foot-stomping it could withstand.

Brie deliberately ignored this, turning stiffly to her angel. "Cam? A little help here?"

He chose his words carefully. "Brie, as much as I hate to disagree with you, they're already involved. Their faces are known to Mammon. It would be unwise to leave them in Virginia. They'll be much safer with us."

"Not to mention—" Tavi began but stopped short at the look on Brie's face.

Ephriam suffered no such compunction. "Azrael's scroll has prophesied that you are to be accompanied by six. There are six of us. Who our seventh will be, I cannot say."

Brie's blood ran cold.

Of course! Of course, that's what they've all been thinking!

"No," she whispered, then louder, "No!" A surge of panic swept through her as the image struck her again — Azrael's skeletal hand extending the scroll, that unearthly voice, heralding danger and doom. "She can't have meant you!" Brie cried. She jumped to her feet and gave a stricken look around the small circle. "Just... no!" She set her jaw, turned on her heel, and walked right out of the villa without knowing where she was going.

How can this be happening?

This isn't their fault. And it isn't their problem. Everything was supposed to go back to normal. They were supposed to go back to their lives.

Now, everything in my life, everyone I love, is in danger.

And it's all my fault.

Before she knew it, she found herself on the path to the sea where they'd had their bonfire only last night. She continued until she reached the shore and stood while the wine-colored waves lapped endlessly at her feet. She heard footsteps behind her and, without looking, knew exactly who it was.

"She can't have meant you, Sherry," she said, almost pleading. "It's too dangerous. Tavi and Cameron are just trying to make Enoch feel better — this is going to be *dangerous.* So much so, I can't even think about it. I have to keep distracting myself, coming at it diagonally in my head just to keep moving forward. You heard what the scroll said. *'Death will have its cull, and Hell its prize.'*" Her voice broke. "I couldn't handle it if anything were to happen to you, do you hear me? I'd break the whole world if something happened to you." Brie finished softly.

Sherry considered this for a moment, then nodded. "I get it." She waited almost a full minute before continuing. "Do you know why I get it?" She caught her best friend's eye. "Because I feel the exact same way." She offered a wry smile. "I guess it's a good thing we'll be able to keep an eye on each other then, isn't it?"

Brie let out an exasperated sound and bent down to pick up a handful of smooth pebbles. One by one, she started hurling them into the sea. Farther and farther, they sailed out toward the horizon. Sherry watched the uncanny distances with a disapproving frown.

"How would it even work?" Brie asked abruptly.

"Tavi warped back to the hospital," Sherry answered, "got me the same leave of absence that you have. And Mike's probably off with Ephriam right now, getting in touch with his supervisor, saying he's having a family emergency and needs some time off."

Brie stopped short, her arm drawn back to throw another stone. "You've already put your lives on hold? For this?"

"Not for 'this,' Brie. For *you*." Sherry shrugged to try to mitigate the gravity of the moment. "Like you wouldn't do the same for me." She picked up some rocks of her own and started tossing them into the waves.

Brie felt a lump in her throat as she watched the wind whip strands of hair around her friend's face. She blinked hard. "In a heartbeat," she said. She threw another, larger stone as hard as she could. It sailed farther than any of the others. "Am I the last person to put this together?" she asked suddenly. "Is that why Enoch is giving you gifts, and you're packing like you're immigrating to Europe?"

Sherry shot her the hands-on-hips exasperated look she'd been giving her since they were five. "Brie, what did you *think* was going on?"

Brie threw one last stone as far as she could, watching Sherry's accompanying grimace with a touch of satisfaction. "I thought they were trying to get back on your good side after you threatened to turn them all into furniture with your handy new knife."

Sherry scowled at the place where the rock had disappeared over the horizon. "Enough about our celestial misadventure. Can we please talk about these rocks? How long has this been going on? What are you now? Some kind of superhero?"

Brie sighed. "Yep. It's a whole thing."

They arrived back at the villa in a significantly calmer state than when they'd left. The others were waiting for them in the courtyard. Ephriam and Mike dragged two more steamer trunks to add to a frankly embarrassing mountain of designer luggage.

Enoch raised an eyebrow and asked dryly, "Is that everything?"

Sherry's face flushed. She knelt down and retrieved the purse she'd stashed under the couch earlier. "I'm sorry! I can't help it."

Cameron came over to Brie. He didn't need to say anything. She merely met his gaze and nodded. "I'm ready."

The humans and Elysians banded together and faced the king. On instinct, the entire group touched two fingers to their foreheads.

Enoch stepped forward and clasped Cameron's shoulder one more time. He looked like there was more he wanted to say — worlds more. But instead, he merely kissed his son's cheek before backing some paces away.

"May Heaven smile upon you all. Until we meet again," he managed in a gruff voice.

The world tilted and spun. In a flurry of golden light, they left Elysium to return to their world, their own Virginia shores.

CHAPTER TWENTY

The Tale of the Nephilim

They reappeared moments later in the same hospital room they'd occupied before Ephriam had whisked them away.

Before they could get their bearings, the door opened, and Denise walked in. Again. The charge nurse narrowed her eyes in irritation. "Walker. Weldon. It's been five minutes. What are you still doing here?" She didn't wait for a response. "You're on leave. Get out of here. I told you I need this room."

Five minutes? What the hell is happening to my life?

Before anyone could respond, Denise unceremoniously herded them out of the room. The party filed obediently into the hall seconds before a team of nurses rushed a patient into the room behind them.

It occurred to Brie that this could very well be the last time she ever saw her wonderful, intimidating charge nurse. She couldn't resist a last look back. "Thank you," she whispered. "Goodbye."

The rest of the day was equally fraught.

They checked on Kylie first. Under the pretense of saying goodbye before taking some time off, Brie and Sherry stopped to visit the little girl and wish her mother the best. The woman was still a bit of a basket case, which felt appropriate. She shook

Brie's hand for a long time, thanking her over and over with red-rimmed, brimming eyes, before Kylie giggled and said, "Mama, you don't have to do it that long."

Tavi shot Cameron a look of abject betrayal. "You *don't?!*" she hissed.

Once they were convinced the little girl and her mother were doing as well as could be expected, they said their goodbyes and left.

At first glance, the hospital appeared normal. It was only upon closer examination that they noticed the Elysian guards. They were trying — Brie had to give them that. Some posed as visitors, almost passably, except they were wearing sunglasses indoors and reading newspapers upside down while watching a news report about a freak hurricane brewing off the coast. An unnaturally tall orderly walked past and shot Ephriam a wink with gold-colored irises.

That much could pass as encouraging.

Kylie will certainly be well looked after.

What happened next made their hearts sink.

"I don't think you should," Cameron tried to tell Brie again as the elevator descended. "It's unlikely to be what you want it to be. She doesn't—"

"I know she doesn't," Brie said firmly, carrying a chai latte. "I still want to say goodbye."

A minute later, she knocked on the door to the morgue. A friendly-looking woman with skin the color of coffee and a beautiful headscarf answered.

Rashida.

"Hello. Can I help you?" she asked.

"Hi, there. Yes, I was wondering—" Brie started.

"You're Denise's new shadow!" Rashida exclaimed, opening the door a little more.

Brie swallowed, and Sherry ducked her head and looked away. "How can you tell?" asked Brie.

Rashida chuckled and nodded at Sherry. "I've never seen you before, but Walker over there has been talking up a storm about how her best friend from Georgia will come by any day now to show us all how it's done. Would you like to come in?" She stepped aside, allowing space.

"No, I can't stay. I just... I wanted to bring you this." She held out the latte.

"Aren't you sweet! Chai! My favorite. Thank you," the lovely pathologist said. "Are you sure I can't convince you to come in? I know it's the morgue, but it's also—"

"The coolest place in the whole joint," Brie finished.

"Exactly," Rashida's face was somewhere between a smile and a frown.

"We really have to get going. Thank you, Ida. And... see you around."

"Ida — that's what my friends call me. Thanks again." She shut the door as the party walked away.

Brie was devastated. It had only been a week, but the three women had grown close. Now, after Rashida's memory wipe, it was like none of it had ever happened. She looked over to Sherry, who seemed to be having an even worse time of it. As they waited for the elevator, she touched her arm. "Sher?"

Sherry looked up at the ceiling. Tears flowed from the outer corners of her eyes. She dashed them away before turning to Brie. "We are going to fix that as soon as we possibly can. And Brie? Don't *ever* let them do that to me. Ever. For any reason."

The elevator dinged, and Brie nodded slowly. "I promise."

♦   ♦   ♦

The plan had been simple enough.

They needed to go away for a while. They should get their lives in order and get ready to go. They'd split up, take care of what they needed to take care of and meet back at Brie's house.

When Mike had proposed this, they'd all nodded like this was the most elementary thing in the world, but what became apparent several hours later was that "getting ready to go" meant wildly different things to all parties involved.

Cameron and the Elysians already had everything they needed, so they were tasked with organizing Tavianne's guard units. Ephriam had ordered enough patrols to watch over not only Brie, Sherry, and Mike's homes but also their families and friends as well. When Sherry heard this, she shot him a look of gratitude. It was the first time she'd ever looked at the Elysian without trying to shoot lasers out of her eyes. Ephriam didn't know how to respond to this shift in their dynamic, so he glared at her and huffed off.

Mike said he was off to gather supplies and that he'd meet them in a few hours.

Sherry and Brie were a whole other kettle of fish.

Unpacking the sheer tonnage of luxury goods Sherry had looted from Elysium was a daunting task in and of itself. And now they had to pack for their journey as well. Sherry asked Brie to start transferring garment bags upstairs while she took a phone call. She disappeared outside, talking to somebody named Cory in hushed tones.

Brie was secretly thrilled.

This is all I wanted to do when I left Georgia — unpack with my best friend.

Brie opened her friend's closet cautiously, peeking between the rows of couture for any male models who might have stowed away when they left Elysium. Thankfully, she found none. She breathed a sigh of relief and turned her attention to the coats. The thick wooden pole supporting the hangers groaned ominously.

We need to talk about her obsession with outerwear. Or she'll need to build an addition.

That is, if we ever get back here.

It had been like that all day — moments of fun snatched away by the gravity of their situation. Brie let out a quiet sigh but composed herself quickly when Sherry walked in. "Who was that?" she asked.

Sherry ignored her. "Wanna go get coffee? And I need to stop at a toyshop for the twins."

Along with her baby niece Leah, Sherry's twin nephews, Taylor and Liam, had been her pride and joy for four years, and their birthday was coming up.

"What will you get them that could possibly beat Michael Jackson's glove?"

"I have a few ideas."

"By the way, Sher, what is *this*?" Brie held up the one garment that made absolutely no sense in the context of the glamorous, high-end closet. It looked for all the world like a pair of overall-style fishing waders, except for two minor details: it was hot pink and encrusted with about ten thousand rhinestones.

"Oh. It's for this thing I was going to take you to. Tomorrow, actually. It doesn't really matter, now." Sherry didn't meet her eyes.

Brie stopped short. She'd expected something frivolous, not emotional. "What thing? Why doesn't it matter?"

"It's called the Guinea Jubilee," Sherry said. "They do it here every year. Last year caught me by surprise. I mean, if I'd known you could run for queen of anything, obviously—" she raised her hand, palm side up, which meant nothing more needed to be said. "This year, Mike and I were running for king and queen. He has his own outfit here somewhere." She rummaged for a moment before pulling out another set of waders, this one custom-made and bedazzled to look like a tuxedo you could fish in.

I wonder if you can give a fish a heart attack.

Brie looked at the insane combination and then at Sherry's face, feeling that same pang in her heart that was becoming all too familiar.

"We would've won, too," Sherry continued, almost distractedly. Her hands continued moving, sorting through dozens of bags. "That other contestant, Karen from finance, has nothing on me."

Brie swallowed the lump in her throat. "Nobody does, Sher."

Her best friend shrugged and threw her the keys to her SUV. "Dunkin' D on the way?"

The shopping excursion had started out normally enough. They'd gone to a local toy shop and bought dinosaur puzzles, action figures, and a musical toy that was sure to drive Sherry's sister to the brink of insanity.

Then, the toys started going up in age.

A keyboard. A real one, not plastic and primary colors, but Yamaha, eighty-eight keys. A viola, "just in case they were into more of a string vibe." A pair of leather wallets. The entire classics section of the children's literature department. A pair of electric scooters with matching helmets. Every Pokémon card they could lay their hands on. Sherry swiftly filled up several shopping carts and kept piling on books and toys. They only stopped once they pushed past two women fighting over a Beanie Baby. The entire place was engulfed in shoppers and looked like a Black Friday mob scene. Brie had never seen a toy store so crowded.

"Sherry?" Brie asked, as her friend went through the birthday card display and chose two from every age option. "Who was that on the phone earlier?"

"That was Cory. He's going to run something over to your place in about an hour, so we'll need to hurry to get to the girl's stuff."

Brie watched as she started picking out cards for every year of her niece's life next. "Who's Cory?" she asked, though she suspected she already knew the answer.

"My mom's attorney. We're going to get some stuff sorted out."

"What sort of stuff?"

Sherry didn't answer and handed her the towering stack of birthday cards. "Just help me find Leah a prom dress, okay?"

When they all met up again at Brie's house, the wild disparity in their ideas of what it meant to "get ready" was on full display.

Brie had shoved a couple of practical outfits into her backpack, along with her passport, a bit of cash, her gifts from Elysium, and a refillable bottle of water. Cameron, Ephriam, and Tavi seemed to have wrangled the Elysian troops into a regimented schedule of rotating guard duty.

And Sherry had repacked Mount Louis Vuitton with about three seasons' worth of couture. "What?" she said when everyone looked at the photo Brie had taken with her phone. "It's being *teleported* everywhere. It's not like you're going to have to carry anything."

Mike grinned and hugged her from behind. His preparations were either the most sensible or the most unhinged of them all. Brie couldn't tell which.

What does he think we'll be doing?

Grappling hooks, lengths of tough, orange-colored synthetic rope, mylar tarps, and a water-purification system that fit into your thermos were sitting in a pile next to six identical black backpacks that looked like they'd survive an apocalypse.

I bet there are rations in there. Imperishable foodstuffs. Gloves.

Brie shot a look at the black satin opera gloves sticking out of Sherry's purse.

Sensible gloves.

"I think that's about everything," Mike said. "I included all the gifts King Enoch sent and a couple of books from Cam's library that seemed like they might be helpful, but I thought we might want to pack light."

Five pairs of eyes looked sideways at Sherry.

"To each their own," she said breezily.

Mike just grinned. "What did you two get up to?" he asked, eyeing Brie's sensible go-bag and Sherry's designer purse, complete with the opera gloves.

"We bridged the divide between the adorable and the morbid," Brie replied.

He frowned. "What do you mean?"

Sherry glared at her. "I picked out some birthday presents for Taylor and Liam."

Mike's face relaxed. "Oh! Well, that doesn't sound so—"

"And Leah. For the next eighteen years," Brie clarified.

His face froze. "Gotcha."

At that moment, the doorbell rang.

"I'll get it," said Sherry. She let in her attorney and another man who scuttled along behind him, carrying a grey briefcase. "I'll be back in a minute. I need to get something notarized." She disappeared into the kitchen, leaving the rest to stare at Mike's backpacks with a sinking feeling. Nobody spoke until she came back, saw the attorney and notary back out with a wave, and turned to the group. "Right, then. A good night's rest, and we take off in the morning?"

I guess. Except—

"Nope," said Brie, suddenly filled with determination. "Absolutely not." She looked around at her friends, old and new, who had all been through so much in the past few days. "We are *not* leaving first thing in the morning. We are taking one whole day to decompress and get you to that Guinea Jubilee. You're going to be the King and Queen of this little festival I've never heard of. You are going to wear that sparkly monstrosity, and you are going to have a wonderful time. In the meantime? Get these two dressed." She pointed at Tavi and Ephriam. It was a tall order to try to get those two to fit in with a human crowd, but if anyone could do it, Sherry could.

"Dressed for what?" Sherry asked, amused by the sudden change of energy.

"Dressed to go out. I know exactly what we need."

◆   ◆   ◆

Dave's Bar and Grill was no match for the celestial warriors.

Although the Elysians initially stared wide-eyed at the masses of humans packed inside, and the phrase *"They're more afraid of us than we are of them"* kept running through Brie's mind, they quickly acclimated to the vibe and started to loosen up.

The place was packed and already in a wild state before they arrived. Everyone was gearing up for the Guinea Festival, and a large number of "watermen" were at the bar, having spent the entire week fishing and crabbing in preparation for the festivities. Televisions blared, assuring the public that the freak storm brewing in the Atlantic wasn't supposed to make landfall and wouldn't interfere with the Jubilee.

Taking advantage of the chaos, Cameron marched them all into the kitchen uninvited and introduced his two seven-foot-tall friends to Frank, the chef, like he was the most famous celebrity on the globe. The bewildered and highly flattered man prepared them a feast fit for a king — if that king had a real affinity for traditional American bar fare. Frank prepared another round of food as the Elysians devoured their meal with matching looks of sheer ecstasy.

And another.

This is getting borderline absurd.

Ephriam was outpacing everyone, working on his fifth cheeseburger with a ravenous glint in his eye. Mike had long since given up trying to keep pace and was watching the spectacle unfold with open delight and fascination. Tavi refused to eat meat but inhaled onion rings and French fries like she'd just been rescued from a desert island.

Brie and Sherry were doing shots.

When Brie had casually mentioned Cameron's trick of vanishing alcohol from one's bloodstream, Sherry's eyes had gleamed, and she'd ordered a flight of top-shelf tequilas. With each shot, she was becoming less inhibited and more honest.

"Drink up, for tomorrow, we die!" she cried, throwing back another.

Cameron shot her a worried glance, but Brie shook her head. "She always says that." Sherry's ensuing laugh did, however, border on mania, so Brie leaned over to whisper, "But just to be on the safe side, maybe bring it down a notch." He nodded agreeing, and with a faint glow from his palms, brought Sherry's level of inebriation from about a nine to a more manageable four.

Sherry slammed her shot glass down on their table, wiped her mouth, and regarded everyone with a serious expression. "What's a scallion?"

The group looked at her, baffled.

"You know — the thing you called Kylie. An onion."

"Do you mean a scion?" Tavi stifled a grin.

"Yeah, that's it." She didn't display an iota of embarrassment. "So, what's a scion?"

Of all the questions she might have asked, the Elysians hadn't thought this would be most relevant to her, but Brie just smiled. Sherry had always been like this; if there was something she didn't know, she'd educate herself about every aspect of the subject. She always did this with her priorities firmly in order. Any unresolved questions about family, friends, children, animals, the environment, and now, apparently, onions needed to be addressed thoroughly and immediately, or she would lambast everyone within a ten-mile radius.

Of course, she's asking about Kylie first.

Ephriam lowered the remains of his cheeseburger as if the very mention of the subject had made him lose his appetite. "No one

THE PENDANT & THE PROPHECY 267

knows for certain, but it is widely accepted that a scion is a descendant of the Nephilim, or another celestial creature, and humans."

Sherry and Mike merely stared, then lifted their glasses to their mouths in unison. Interspecies offspring wasn't the kind of topic that immediately invited many appropriate responses. After she'd finished her shot, Sherry dryly said, "You understand, of course, that I don't know what that means, and it doesn't clear anything up at all, right?"

Brie frowned at Ephriam. "You and Cameron seemed shocked when you found out."

It was true. With all the crazy things that had happened over the course of the past week, there were only three times Brie had seen Ephriam's perpetually stoic expression give way to surprise. The first, understandably, was when he found out about Mammon's involvement with the scene in the parking garage. The second was just yesterday in front of Lucifer's portrait when he'd touched his finger to her pendant and been immersed in a flash of light. And the third was when he'd touched Kylie's forehead, then jerked away as if he'd seen a ghost.

Ephriam nodded gravely. "They were all meant to have died, Brianna," he said. "One of the primary reasons for the Great Flood was to wipe all traces of the Nephilim from the world, including their offspring. For millennia, we in Elysium believed none had survived the waters that washed the Earth clean."

For a long minute, the only sounds that could be heard were the waves of laughter and revelry from the other patrons of the bar.

"When you say offspring, you mean children — children like Kylie." Sherry finally said. "You're saying that you Elysians believed that they all drowned. *Drowned.* And you all just went along with it?"

"It wasn't our decision, Sherry," said Tavi gently. "The Divine Will doesn't consult with us."

Sherry looked at her levelly. "God told you not to save a bunch of drowning children?"

Tavi's face faltered. "No, not exactly."

"That seems like the kind of thing you should be able to speak about with exactitude, don't you think?" Sherry's face was stone.

Brie looked at her, shocked. "Sher, it isn't like they were the ones who sent the flood."

"Based on what I've seen, these two have more than enough powers to hold their own against an inclement weather event, Brie. And if ET here —"

"ET?" asked Mike.

"You know. ET. Ephriam and Tavi. Because they're aliens." Sherry waved away his grin. "If these two are supposed to be our allies against some kind of demonic evil? Call me crazy, but I'd like to know what sort of people my allies actually are."

Brie was silent at this. Sherry had a point.

I hate it when she has a point.

Brie looked between the Elysians. "Can you tell us exactly what happened during the Great Flood?"

Ephriam shared a look with the lightning-scarred warrior sitting in the booth beside him, then sighed, closed his eyes, and told them a story.

"Thousands of years ago, in the time of Noah, the world had fallen into sin. Lucifer, the Morning Star, had already fallen from grace with the Divine One and was locked away and guarded in the Pit. But though you can bury an adversary, you cannot so easily bury an idea. If you try, they only grow. Before his fall, Lucifer planted ideas like seeds of discontent in the hearts of many angels among the host. The chief principal among them was this: That any angel deserved to create as much as the Creator did, and the most wonderful thing anyone could create was a child."

"But that isn't an evil idea at all," said Sherry, her forehead furrowed. "Why would they be forbidden to have children in the first place?"

"We aren't," said Tavi. "But we are forbidden to have them in this world."

"I don't understand," said Brie.

"Think of it this way. This is the Creator's painting. No one else is forbidden to paint, but they'll need to get their own canvas," Tavi said while making motions with her hands that might have been mimicking the act of painting had the tequila not instead made her look like a manic puppeteer without a puppet.

Brie frowned. "Is that something that you can do? Create a canvas?"

"Not without help," said Ephriam. "And that is where Lucifer's deadly sin took hold of his followers' minds and strangled their reason. Rather than ask the Creator for help, they took it upon themselves to create their own world within the world of the Creator. Like rogue musicians playing a completely different song in the middle of a concert, in defiance of their conductor, Lucifer's ideas fomented a rebellion within the ranks of Heaven. It led to casualties on both sides and immeasurable loss amongst the people of Earth." He took a deep breath. "The pride of the Morningstar is a terrible thing."

Sherry gave a little shiver and leaned against Mike's chest. Cameron took Brie's hand under the table. A group of Guinea Watermen came in and sat themselves down in the booth nearby. The waitress was about to place a pitcher of Coke on their table when one of them stopped her and changed their order in a low voice. The waitress looked surprised but left and returned a moment later with a pitcher of beer and four glasses. She set these before the group with a brief nod. One of them started to pour. His hand was shaking.

"At first, the angels and the archangels kept their subterfuge quiet," Ephriam continued. "They seduced and married humans in secret, and their children were born and lived their lives in beauty and peace, sequestered from the rest of humanity, but it didn't take long for pride to rear its ugly head and give rise to ideas of superiority. The children of angels could be lovely and long-lived, and some possessed powers that far surpassed those of humans. What began as innocent questions about why they were not allowed to play with other children turned into adolescent resentment that they were forced to live apart from the rest of the world. By the time the children reached adulthood, they were convinced they were superior to the humans that populated the nearby villages. They began to call themselves the Nephilim, which in the ancient tongue means larger, stronger, or superior. Some translate it to mean 'giant.' They began to believe that humans were only fit for enslavement and that they, the sons and daughters of angels, should rule over the people of Earth."

Ephriam grew quiet for a moment, staring into space.

"That's when things took a dark turn," Tavi continued, moving the story along. "The Nephilim began to pair together not for love but to breed bigger, stronger, more terrifying offspring.

Angels who ought to have known better joined them, swept up in the frenzy of creation. Angels, unlike humans in form, entered into unions with villagers and even the Nephilim. Marriages were dishonored, and some angels even took Nephilim against their will for the sake of creating an army that none could oppose. We call them offspring, Sherry, because not everything born can be considered a child. Some weren't even recognizable as human. Some were born monsters." Tavi's expression grew dark, remembering. "The Greeks wrote stories about some. Their legends say a few survived beyond the flood."

"These were perilous days," Ephriam said. "The angels and Nephilim used their power not in the spirit of joyful creation but to make themselves even more powerful, time and again. Like a snake eating its own tail, these new creations revealed themselves to have an insatiable thirst to dominate and subdue. They began to involve themselves in the disputes of mortals, to build up armies of humans and pit them against each other under the thinnest of pretexts. A land dispute, a political disagreement — no excuse was too petty to justify a war. They'd set the human armies against one another and watch them fight like dogs in a ring, privately laughing, placing bets on the outcomes before swooping in to claim the lands left when all the people were dead. Those left alive began to follow the Nephilim, even worship them, instead of the Divine One."

"No one knows why the Creator waited so long to intervene," said Tavi. "Nor why the entire Earth was subjected to the flood. But when the waters came, when Noah and his family were the only ones spared, and when the waters receded, could the planet start anew? It was as if the Earth itself could breathe again. Believe me, Sherry," Tavi caught her eye. "There were those of us who wept bitter tears at the drowning of the world, but when it came down to it, who were any of us to believe we knew better than the Divine? Had we believed so, would we have been any better than the Nephilim?"

Sherry had no answer for her.

"The Nephilim were a blight upon the world," said Ephriam. "And they were not the only evil creatures wiped out in the Flood. The offending angels and archangels were rounded up and cast out of the light of the Creator into chains of darkness. The monsters that roamed the Earth were imprisoned or slain."

"What sort of monsters?" asked Mike, hanging on every word.

"Unholy creatures of which we no longer speak," said Tavi.

Brie interjected when Mike looked like he would press her for more information. "If all of the Nephilim were wiped out, and all the fallen angels were rounded up and imprisoned, why do you think that Kylie is a scion? And why did a fallen archangel ambush me and all my friends in a parking garage?"

The Elysians paused, throwing glances at each other before Tavi spoke. "There have been rumors for centuries—"

"Millennia," corrected Cameron.

"Millennia, even," she agreed, "That the Fallen Ones have found ways around their imprisonments. The Black Plague of the Dark Ages, the witch trials and hysteria that killed every open mind in New England, the unending greed of imperialism, the Zionist nightmare in the Holy Lands — it all amounts to pretty damning evidence that the Seven's evil influence has grown, become widespread."

Brie struggled to understand. "Do you mean to tell me that the Devil himself has escaped from Hell and is running around the Earth, causing havoc with all his friends? In *Virginia?*"

"Of course not," said Ephriam.

"Oh. Well, thank God." Sherry laughed nervously but stopped when Ephriam skewered her with a serious look.

"We mean that we see the hand of evil in the workings of humans in the world today. We certainly see them in the events of the past week. And while I'd like to believe we would know if 'the Devil,' as you call him, was loose upon the world, one cannot deny the obvious."

Brie's blood ran cold. "And what's the obvious?"

Ephriam looked at her. "Mammon is his sister, Brianna. And she told you to your face that she was the least of your problems. Some of the Devil's brothers and sisters have escaped. And they are hunting for you and your pendant."

Amidst the riotous atmosphere of Dave's Bar and Grill, the six companions fell abruptly quiet, suddenly feeling quite out of place. The waiter brought another round of shots to their table. Sherry grabbed hers and held it in front of her.

"Drink up," she said again, shakier than before. "For tomorrow, we die."

They left shortly after that.

If they'd stayed only a minute longer, they might have heard one of the Watermen in the adjoining booth say, in a trembling voice,

"It was like something swallowed the sea itself."

CHAPTER TWENTY-ONE

The Calm Before

The next morning, Brie awoke to a smell that had become foreign these past few weeks: breakfast — unburned, human breakfast.

She sat up on the couch, confused. It was definitely the unmistakable scent of coffee, scrambled eggs, and bacon frying. Under different circumstances, this might have been considered perfectly normal, but there was very little about the last few days that could have been considered normal. With a burst of panic, she leapt off the couch.

"Cameron?" she called anxiously, sniffing for smoke.

Her lovely angel had a dubious track record when it came to his kitchen experiments.

When she rounded the corner, Cameron and Mike were both sporting their lace-trimmed, frilly, floral aprons and wielding matching spatulas, engaged in another culinary lesson. Tavi was perched on top of the refrigerator, looking down at the spectacle with intense curiosity. At the same time, Ephriam was seated at the table, eating what appeared to be a metric ton of bacon.

Brie stopped short, relieved beyond measure not to see any flames. "Uh, hi," she stammered.

"Good morning!" Cameron exclaimed, dropping his spatula and sweeping her up in a hug. "I have finally done it. With the help of this brilliant man, I have achieved *breakfast*." His eyes sparkled as he looked for her approval.

She couldn't help but giggle. "It smells delicious."

"It is delicious," stated Ephriam in a voice that said this wasn't a matter of opinion. "I never understood his preoccupation with the human world before. I see now that it is because of bacon."

"It really isn't, E." Cameron rolled his eyes heavenward. Sherry's nickname was sticking.

"Then you are every inch the fool I believed you to be," Ephriam stated, around another mouthful.

Tavi pulled a fascinated, if slightly disgusted, look. "But you're eating an animal! How can you stand it?"

He waved a fork full of bacon in her direction. "Tavi, this is a pleasure beyond the scope of that which language can adequately convey. You simply must try it."

Tavi firmly shook her head.

"Any word from Sherry?" Brie asked, accepting a cup of coffee from Cameron.

"She's still in the room, but she isn't asleep," answered Mike, delivering a portion of eggs to Ephriam's plate. "She's busy signing all those birthday cards." He caught Brie's eye with a meaningful look.

Brie nodded. "I think I'll go check on her." She passed her untouched coffee up to Tavi. "Try this. It will change your life."

"What is it?" Tavi asked dubiously.

"Bean juice. No animals." Brie offered a reassuring wink.

Tavi nodded, poking curiously at the black liquid with a knife.

"Do you need any help?" asked Cameron as Brie walked out of the room.

"Nope. Just show Tavi how to add cream and sugar. And brace for impact. I have a feeling caffeine is going to have a real effect on that one."

♦   ♦   ♦

Five minutes later, Brie had fetched the ladder from the garage and was tapping against her own second-story window. She and Sherry had made a habit of sneaking into one another's bedrooms with their families' ladders since they were little. She didn't know what possessed her to do such a thing today.

I'm about to go on a quest to figure out what's been ripping my life apart. I deserve to have a little fun.

She smushed her cheek against the glass, making a horrible face, and laughed hysterically when Sherry yanked the curtains apart and jumped back, yelping in alarm.

Sherry flipped her off, pulled up the window, and snatched her inside. "What are you doing, you lunatic?!"

Brie tumbled to the carpet, still laughing, and threw her hands into the air. "It's our day of jubilee, Sherry! And by God, we've earned it."

Sherry couldn't help but giggle.

Brie got up and flopped onto her stomach on the bed, rifling through the pile of birthday cards. "What a morbid way to do such a joyful thing," she said.

"I don't see it that way," said Sherry.

"No?"

"Not at all. I think of it more like… Even in the worst-case scenario, my family will know I love them. Plus, they'll think I'm a powerful psychic who accurately predicted my own death and prepared accordingly. And best case scenario, I just saved myself a lot of time over the next couple decades."

Brie nodded sarcastically. "Good thing you did, too. I know how you hate shopping."

Sherry signed the last card with an unnecessarily rough flourish. "Could you just let me have this? Since we're tramping off into the world of angels and demons?"

Brie blew her a kiss. "You can have this."

"Thank you." Sherry looked at her archly as she licked an envelope. "You know, there's something we haven't talked about yet."

"Oh?" asked Brie.

Sherry sealed the last envelope and tossed it onto the pile. Then, she threw herself onto the bed next to Brie and turned to her conspiratorially. "You know how your boyfriend is a floating golden ball?"

Brie looked at her, surprised. "Boyfriend? Does this mean we… approve?"

Sherry propped herself up on her palm. "I wouldn't go *that* far, but I mean, it's pretty hard to hate the guy when I just watched him watch over *you* for five whole years, risking the wrath of his own dad plus an entire political body of nightmare creatures. He's obviously head over heels for you, which is the only proper response to knowing you, so… I'll provisionally allow it. Anyway, like I was saying. You know how he's a floating golden ball?"

Brie giggled. "Only sometimes."

Sherry fixed one of Brie's flyaway curls as she continued. "And not just any floating golden ball. His dad is the *king* of the realm of golden balls. Which means—"

Brie saw where this was going a moment too late to stop it. "Oh God, Sher—"

Sherry grinned and grabbed her hand. "He's a *prince*. The *prince* of the golden balls. And *that* means—"

"Sherry, this is me begging you to stop. I'm begging."

"*You could be a princess.*" Sherry shook her friend, reveling in both the bizarre truth of the situation and Brie's obvious mortification with mischievous delight.

Brie threw her arms over her head and groaned. "This isn't happening. This is not something that's happening to me."

Sherry's eyes had taken on a feverish shine. "You know that I've always wanted to go to a royal wedding."

A crash at the open window made them both sit up on their elbows in alarm.

It was Cameron. His face was ashen white. The ladder had somehow betrayed him by lifting away from the house wall, and was standing vertically in the air as he attempted to balance on top. His hair and the front of his shirt were covered in remnants of breakfast. Two shattered plates and two cups of coffee littered the ground below.

"I was… it was… I brought you eggs," he stammered.

Sherry stared at him impassively and didn't miss a beat. "On your face?"

With that, the ladder slowly tipped backward and crashed into the beech tree.

The girls stared at the window in shock as he weakly shouted, "I'm okay!" Then they turned back to each other.

"I mean," Sherry continued, "We'll need to get him trained first."

◆   ◆   ◆

They heard Ephriam before they saw him. Deep, satiated moans emanated from the couch. The Elysian lay in blissful repose, eyelids half-closed, finally subdued by the shocking quantity of bacon he'd had for breakfast.

Sherry and Brie descended the stairs, gingerly avoiding the couch on their way to the kitchen. There, as Brie had predicted, Tavi and her newly discovered affinity for caffeine proved to be a lethal combination. By the time the friends walked in, she had whittled nearly all the legs of Brie's table and chairs into eagle's claws. She was finishing the last talon as wood chips and sawdust flew around her.

Mike was watching her lightning-fast knife work with terrified fascination, but his face lit up when he saw Sherry. He crossed the kitchen and folded her into a deep embrace before pulling back. "All done up there?" he asked with a small smile.

Sherry nodded. "Finished. But someone had better get Cameron out of the beech tree."

Mike barely had time to flash a puzzled frown before Tavi yelled, "I'll get him!" and zoomed out of the house with all the manic energy of a blue cartoon hedgehog. Sherry's hair blew back away from her face, and she blinked, trying to reconcile what she'd just seen.

Brie touched her elbow sympathetically as she walked past. "I know."

"Are you just used to this now?" Sherry asked. "Does it get normal?"

Ephriam briefly stopped his moaning to emit a low growl and mutter something that sounded suspiciously like, "Presumptuous, egocentric younglings," before he was once again overcome by his bacon coma and lay still.

Brie ignored him and began preparing a fresh pot of coffee. "I certainly wouldn't go so far as to call any of this normal, but you do learn to roll with it." She raised her mug to Mike, and they shared a knowing look.

Cameron and Tavi returned to the kitchen at precisely this moment. His cheeks flamed red as he brushed leaves from his hair. Tavi was so jittery she appeared to be vibrating as she sprinted up to Brie, planted a kiss on her cheek, and lowered herself to eye-level with the coffee maker, watching hungrily as the dark liquid drizzled steadily into the carafe. Brie shot Cameron an inquisitive look. He flushed harder.

Oh, I'm going to have fun with this. Later.

For now?

Brie clapped twice to draw everyone's attention. "Now that we're all here, perhaps we should sit down and have a nice serious talk about everything."

Mike nodded, Sherry looked confused, Ephriam groaned, Tavi stared fixedly at the stream of coffee, and Cameron was still plucking twigs from his hair.

Brie let out a laugh. "Only joking! It's our Day of Jubilee!"

Mike and Sherry broke into laughter. Tavianne said, "But wait! What do we wear?"

Mike only laughed harder, and Brie bit her lip as Sherry said, "I can't *wait* to show you."

"If it's okay, there's something I'd like to do before we head to the festival this afternoon. I've had a craving for days." Brie looked at Ephriam's prone, hulking form, now sporting a distinct pooch from the bacon, and added, "And I suppose it falls to us humans to get these Elysians in order. Such children."

She'd already left the room and went to the hall closet when Ephriam opened one eye to fix her with a sullen glare. "Where are you going?" he called.

"Where are *we* going." She reappeared, wearing a soft grey cardigan over her ivory tank top. "I've been here over a week now, plus whatever time I spent but also didn't spend in Elysium. I've traveled to an alternate dimension, stolen a moon rock, raised the dead, and battled the demonic incarnation of a mortal sin. And I still haven't been to the beach."

This was met with amused chuckles before Mike asked, "You stole a moon rock? From where?"

"The moon." Brie removed a large basket from a kitchen cabinet and hit the refrigerator next. Upon opening it, she realized she had no food left. Undeterred, she closed it and turned to face the group, clapping Tavi on the shoulder. "Better take that coffee to go. We are going to have cinnamon rolls by the ocean. The *blue* ocean. The properly colored one."

Sherry opened her mouth as if to say something but decided against it and followed Brie into the hall to look for a picnic blanket. Mike heard her mutter, "Just roll with it," under her breath, but for once found himself unable to take his own advice.

"The moon?" he repeated. "Like the actual *moon*? Brie?" He hurried after them, shaking his head. "I'm gonna need us to circle back to this. *Brie?*"

Mike and Ephriam took turns skipping rocks into the ocean just off Gloucester beach. The policeman made a fair showing. The Elysian's flew clean out of sight.

Sherry laid back on the picnic blanket, covering her face with a sunhat. Ephriam joined her a few minutes later and covered his eyes with his braids.

"Just a quick catnap," Sherry said, "Before we head into town and I begin my reign. A little nap couldn't hurt, right? Just a little bit more sleep?"

"Couldn't possibly," answered Brie. "We need to wait for Tavi to get back anyway."

After the group had devoured the first batch, the warrior woman ran barefoot back into town, searching for more coffee and another tray of cinnamon rolls.

Sherry settled back into the blankets and closed her eyes.

"Walk with me?" Brie glanced up to see her angel standing over her, backlit with the morning sun.

She smiled and took his hand. "I would love to."

Together, they set off across the sand. The sun rose lazily above them. After a few minutes, they took off their shoes. He gave her a sideways glance. "I'd give anything to know what you're thinking."

Probably not.

"Actually," she began, "I have a kind of strange question." She hesitated before asking, "Is that really what he looks like? In the mural under your father's halls?"

"Who?" he asked, confused.

"Lucifer. The painting I saw was a far cry from all the red skin, horns, and forked tail like in the cartoons."

"I've never seen him," Cameron answered. "But it is said he's one of the loveliest creatures the Creator ever made."

"Fantastic." She picked up a rock and chucked it into the sea. It flew as far as Ephriam's skipping stones. She stared after it for a moment. "I keep forgetting about the whole—"

"Superpowers thing," finished Cameron lightly. "In your defense, you've had a lot going on."

"Maybe there's some utility in it after all," she said dryly. "If the devil comes to try to steal my necklace, I can throw rocks at him until he goes away." She held her pendant to the sun. Light glinted off the metal filigree in flashes, but where it touched the stone, it seemed to catch inside, glowing softly. "Why could Mammon see me even when I was wearing it?" she asked.

"I don't know, but I have a theory." He reached for the pendant. "May I?"

She stepped closer, allowing him to hold it. He turned it over in his hands. "It didn't occur to me until we watched your Revelation. That day in the woods, before the wraiths attacked your car on the way here, you told me it burned you out of the blue, but when you tried to take it off, it became heavy, like it was trying to stay around your neck."

"Yes," she affirmed, not at all sure where he was going with this.

"It healed your injuries from the accident, but not instantly — not before I carried you to the motel. It kept you healthy during your first week of work when you should have been exhausted and run down from the long hours. It enhanced your hearing so you could listen to Mammon's conversation with the doctor in the ER. It made you stronger the week before you faced her. It basically sent her back to Hell when she attacked you. And it started glowing in front of Sherry at the exact moment she needed to be told the truth." He paused before continuing. "We assumed that Mammon didn't see you in the conference room the first time you saw her because you were hidden under the table, but what if that isn't right? What if Mammon really *can't* see your soul's light when you're wearing the pendant? Unless..."

"Unless what?" Brie asked, hanging on his every word.

"Unless it knows that you need to be seen." Cameron took her hands in his. "Think about it. It's as though it's been guiding you, preparing you all along. It revealed me to you. It drew us together. It showed you danger when you needed to see it. And it only chose to reveal you to Mammon when Kylie's life was on the line. Maybe it's even the force behind your nightmares."

Brie swallowed and looked down at the stone. "You're talking about it like it's alive."

"Would that be the strangest thing that's happened lately?"

She sighed and chucked another rock into the sea, watching as it disappeared over the horizon. "It wouldn't even crack my top five."

They wandered longer than they meant to, walking in and out of the surf, holding hands in a silence neither felt the need to fill or break. By the time they returned to their picnic, the air had taken on a sharp, unseasonal chill. The others had repacked the SUV and were waiting for them. Tavi had yet to return from her snack run.

"Pleasant nap?" Brie asked Sherry.

"Delightful. I wasn't plagued by relentless visions of a watery genocide at all. What were you two talking about?" Sherry asked.

"You know, this and that. Cameron has a theory that the necklace is somehow alive."

Sherry's mouth opened and closed twice before her shoulders sank under the weight of such ridiculosity, and she merely responded, "Cool."

"That actually is pretty cool. Can I see it again?" Mike leaned forward with an outstretched hand, and that kid-in-a-comic-

book-store level of enthusiasm that Brie was coming to understand was his baseline emotional state.

Ephriam cut in. "I understand that at this festival, it is cus-
tomary to wrap bacon around other foods."

Brie looked at him in frank amusement. The Elysian warrior
got into the SUV and buckled his seatbelt. "Then, we should
leave at once."

Even Sherry cracked a smile. "We can find Tavi on the way."

◆　◆　◆

Five minutes later, they pulled up to Buck Rowe's Store, a lovely
local staple that felt like a place out of time. It had remained
unchanged since the 1920s — a quaint old country store with
original hard pine floors and a porch where locals sat on antique
rockers and had coffee and conversation in a thick Guinea dialect.
Every morning, the porch doubled as a local coffee shop. It was
always filled with patrons and radiated charm and authenticity.

As they pulled up, they were greeted with a delightfully strange
sight. The towering warrior woman sat on a wooden rocking chair
alongside two men whom Mike called "True Southern good ol'
boys." At least a dozen cantaloupe rinds surrounded her, and she
was eating the pulp from another while the gentlemen looked on
with steaming cups of coffee and matching looks of astonishment.

She leapt to her feet the moment they pulled into the parking
lot and threw her arms wide. "You made it!"

Brie, Cameron, Ephriam, and Sherry piled out of the SUV.

"We didn't know we were supposed to make it, Tavianne.
You were meant to come back with cinnamon rolls." Ephriam
scowled at her, but she merely laughed.

"I finished those ages ago. They were delicious," Tavi added appreciatively to one of the gentlemen, who tipped his hat in gracious acknowledgment. "Come here! Come here!" She ushered the friends onto the wooden porch. "Brie, this is Raymond, and that's Dickie. And inside are Hamilton, Robbie, and Bill." She grinned ear to ear, pleased she'd remembered. "They make the… oh, what did you call it, Dickie?"

"The meanest brew in town, darlin'!" he said, amused.

"Yes, that's it! Brie, his brew is *so* mean!" Tavi was delighted. "I love it. Oh, but I have to ask you something." She turned to the men in the rockers. "Would you excuse me for a moment?"

They nodded with a laugh as Tavi steered Brie some ways away by her elbow.

What happened next would haunt Brie for the rest of her days. Tavi obviously thought she was whispering privately, but the coffee had kicked in, and she was, in fact, stage whispering at a perfectly audible level and a shocking pace that scarcely allowed for any breathing. Everyone on the porch could hear.

"Listen, everything was going well, and these fine gentlemen were joined by a group of others just moments ago, people they called 'Guineamen,' and they were lovely, and they had the finest rubber boots I've ever seen, and they had these cantaloupes — Brie, do people know about cantaloupes? They're amazing! And they were selling them for something called 'fifty sense a piece,' but when I told them I didn't have any sense, Raymond just started laughing and said, 'Ain't that the God's honest truth, darlin', here take mine!' But he didn't give me any advice or extra sensory abilities. He just gave me shiny metal circles and told me to use those. So, I used those, and they gave me all the cantaloupes I could carry, and I was going to share, but they

were so sweet, and I ended up eating them all, but THEN—"
She sucked in a huge breath as Brie gaped, openmouthed, at the
speed of her tirade, "THEN, Brianna, the watermen asked if
they could shoot our horses! And frankly, I think that's an atro-
cious thing to do to such a magnificent animal, and I'm trying to
respect your culture, and I guess I understand that not everyone
can be a vegetarian, but Brianna, *do they shoot horses here?*"

Brie just blinked. Raymond and Dickie looked at each other
and broke into uproarious laughter. The friends looked on, baffled and uncomprehending.

"That isn't what they said, darlin'!" Dickie finally managed
to call out.

"It isn't?" Tavi whirled around, surprised.

"It's just their accent! They didn't ask to shoot your horses;
they asked if you wanted any shucked oysters!"

The human friends let out a breath they hadn't realized they'd
been holding and, with some difficulty, bid the men farewell and
wrestled Tavi back into the car.

CHAPTER TWENTY-TWO

The Guinea Jubilee

After a quick pit stop and costume change at Sherry's house, the friends headed to the Jubilee. They got caught behind a parade of fire trucks on the way and decided that with all the traffic, their best bet was to park in a secret spot Mike knew about behind the volunteer fire station. They walked the rest of the way.

Sherry and Mike caused quite a stir in their sparkling getup and soon branched off to walk in the parade themselves as though they'd been invited. Sherry was like a duck in water in her hot pink, rhinestone-encrusted Guinea waders. She attempted to speak in the Guinea dialect, something Brie had never heard her do and was failing miserably at. Nobody seemed to mind as she recanted a story about how a swimming horse from a neighboring island ended up at her friend's house and how the little animal was given passage home standing in a small row boat. Nothing seemed impossible for this little town.

Aside from the awful dialect attempt, Sherry fit in like she had been born there. She continued to wave at the crowds like Princess Di, signed a little girl's sticker book with an elaborate signature, and kept up a steady stream of campaign promises while beaming a Barbie-bright smile to the masses.

They screamed for her. They loved her.

She's great at this. I hope she runs for office someday.

Wait, what the heck am I saying? No, I don't!

She would give new and terribly literal meaning to the term "fashion police."

Sherry must have massively downplayed the festival's popularity because, by Brie's estimation, there were thousands of people every which way she looked. A nearby field had been transformed into a carnival that spilled out from the town. There were roller-coasters, spinning rides, and a giant Ferris wheel towering over everything. Children with painted faces shrieked with delight, burying their mouths in sky-high cotton candies. Booths of arts and crafts sported their wares, and a bevy of beautiful young women wearing evening gowns sang a song about America. People in uniform on horseback paraded one way while a classic car show dominated the other side of the street. Ephriam wouldn't have looked very out of place at all within the ranks of the anchor-hauling competition contestants. A couple blocks away, Brie could see the tail end of a footrace was being decided, and the podium for the medal ceremony had been set up. The sound of country music filled the air.

But the best part was the food.

She had never smelled anything so mouth-watering in all her life — and she'd recently visited a realm that was darn well close to Heaven. Barbequed pork ribs, piles of garlic-butter poached crab, deep-fried Oreos, popcorn and churros, candy, cakes, and bacon-wrapped everything was piled high, as far as the eye could see.

The friends froze in place. The crowds surged around them as they stood and looked for all the world like children in a candy store who had just been told they could have anything they wanted and as much of it as they liked.

Cameron cleared his throat. "What we have here is a classic case of target confusion."

Ephriam nodded. "Yes, I agree."

"I think the best way to handle this is going to be to—"

"—Try one of those things immediately." Ephriam was pointing to a bacon-wrapped hotdog and breathing heavily.

"And one of those," Tavi said, her eyes following a teenage girl's giant, whip-cream-covered Frappuccino as she walked past.

"And some of that," Cameron added, watching a vendor make cotton candy, transfixed.

"And definitely one of those," Brie looked at the gelato stand and started salivating.

The friends looked at each other, nodded determinedly, and attacked the smorgasbord.

◆   ◆   ◆

Hours later, it could safely be said that they'd overcome their target confusion.

"What a feast. A feast of nonsense," sighed Tavi happily, surrounded by a dozen empty plastic cups. Brie nodded in agreement, happily licking her ice cream cone. Ephriam was beyond words and merely grunted his assent. He'd just won a hotdog-eating competition.

No, that makes it sound too normal: Ephriam just annihilated a hotdog-eating competition.

The hotdog industry may never recover from this.

Cameron was sucking the butter off of a crab leg with a rapturous look. "Why don't we do this in Elysium?" he asked. "Human food is wonderful. Tavi, I think whatever I had when I was little must not have been made properly because everything I've had lately has been—"

"Shh! Shh, it's starting!" Brie interrupted.

Mike and Sherry were up on stage in front of them, next to their competition. Brie thought the other contestants looked lovely, but Mike and Sherry looked *fabulous*. It was like comparing a bottle of champagne to a six-pack of Sprites. A woman she assumed was "Karen from finance" looked at Sherry's hilarious and beautiful crystal-encrusted waders with such envy she was practically green. Brie had never had any doubts her friend would take home the tiara and scepter. Once Sherry decided to compete in something, the competition itself was merely a formality, but seeing it in person really hammered home the fact that it had never been a fair fight.

The contestants stood next to a hee-haw country band that seemed even drunker than their audience. And the audience *must* have been drunk because Brie had never seen such excess in all her life. People weren't just laughing — they were laughing until their sides hurt until they couldn't breathe, and their family and friends needed to pick them up off the floor, and then they'd laugh some more.

The band had been taking requests, but they never stayed with a song long enough to finish, always taking more and more requests until the music didn't even match itself anymore. Thankfully, a gentleman who must have been a festival official based on his suit, American flag top hat, and sash unplugged their sound equipment after their singer and guitarist tried to perform "Free Bird." At the same time, their drummer and keyboardist were locked in an operatic rendition of "Bohemian Rhapsody."

"I'm going to get one of those churro things," said Tavi, and ran away with superhuman speed. Ephriam and Cameron opened their mouths to protest this display of her powers, but nobody was looking, and besides, she was already gone.

Brie could barely hear the announcements of the third and second runners-up. "Shoot, I wish people would just—"

"CHILDREN," boomed a roaring voice to her left, making her jump out of her skin. She whipped around to see Ephriam towering proudly beside her. "Keep it down," he continued, in the same affected, hypnotizing tone she recognized from her first-ever car ride with Cameron. The noise around them faded to a low buzz.

"Ephriam! Are you allowed to do that?!" Brie hissed.

He offered her a lazy grin. "What they don't know won't hurt them."

She frowned a little. "Are you feeling okay?"

Just then, she heard some familiar names boom over the loud-speaker.

"MISTER MIKE MITCHELL AND MISS SHERRY WALKER!"

She leaped to her feet and screamed, "Wooooo!" The whole audience joined her, staggered to their feet, and clapped for her beautiful friend and her handsome beau as they accepted their crowns and sashes.

Sherry looks very natural holding a scepter. I wonder if the Elysians know anything about past lives. There's a lot I need to ask them the next time I'm there.

Mike and Sherry were beaming and getting their picture taken with the mayor for the local paper. Sherry was basking in the attention, soaking up the spotlight like she was born for it.

Tavi reappeared, holding churros between all of her fingers. "You have to try this," she said, waving a hand at Ephriam. Without questioning it, he dove in.

"Let's go talk to them!" Brie pulled Cameron through the crowd. He was reluctant to leave his tower of crab legs, but he followed as she pushed her way to the stage.

"Congratulations!" she beamed and waved at Sherry, who waved back with a big smile before pointing at the cameras and making a shrugging gesture. Brie captioned it in her head.

The newspapers want to take my picture, Brie.

What can you do? I must give the people what they want.

Brie grinned and shouted, "We're going to see the rest of the fair. Meet you at the Ferris wheel in an hour?"

Sherry gave her a thumbs up and made a phone sign next to her ear.

"Come on!" Brie pulled Cameron over to the saltwater taffy booth. "You have to try this stuff. Let's get pieces for Tavi and Ephriam, too. They're gonna love this."

Together, they strolled through the Jubilee with the Elysians, pulling pieces of taffy as long as they could before wrapping them around their fingers and popping them into their mouths. It was the way Brie had eaten them when she was little, and she was in fits of giggles watching Cameron try it now.

"It sounds *just* like my name!" Tavi kept saying excitedly, showing Ephriam all her taffy colors again. "Like we were *made* for each other! What other kinds of sweets do you have here?" She bounded ahead, checking out the booths and food stands.

"She seems very much in her element," Brie observed, laughing.

"Tavi is a joyful person," Ephriam replied. "This is a joyful event."

Just then, Brie saw something that made her not so sure. There was a man sitting by a garbage can, surrounded by an insane number of empty popcorn boxes. He looked sick; his stomach was distended, veins bulged in his neck, he was sweating, and his skin had taken on a greyish sheen. Her nurse instincts activated, and she was about to go over to ask if he was all right when he groaned, reached for another half-empty bucket of popcorn, and continued eating.

"Ephriam, how many of those food-eating competitions did you say were going on today?" she asked. "Do you think he's doing one of those? He must be doing one of those."

"What is that?" Ephriam asked in return, not listening.

"What?" she echoed, distracted.

"*That.*" He pointed at the barbeque pit, where a man had just opened a smoker, revealing a side of slow-roasted pork belly. It sizzled and glistened, deep reddish brown in the light. Brie felt Ephriam's entire body go taut beside her.

"I'm getting one." The hulking Elysian lumbered off.

He didn't hear Brie call out, "I don't think those are meant to be single portions!" She frowned, staring after him for a moment before turning to Cameron. "Should we be worried about him? He doesn't seem himself."

"It's the first day he's had off in a thousand years. Let's turn a blind eye, shall we?" Cameron was gawking at a snow cone in open fascination. "Brie, we have berries exactly that color in Elysium!"

She smiled. "You're right. Let's try one. Better get one for Tavi, too."

They passed jugglers, acrobats, and a full petting zoo, complete with a zebra from a nearby city's wildlife preserve. She nudged him. "I've seen better," she said with a wink, and he beamed with pride.

They walked past a high-striker machine, and he asked what it was. "Oh, it's a strongman game. Like a test of strength. You hit the base with a hammer and see how far you can make the weight go up."

He immediately got a little glint in his eye. "Shall I win something for you?"

She raised an eyebrow. "A little brother or sister for the bear from the claw machine?"

"Exactly."

"I don't know, Cameron. Do you think that Claw Machine Bear is ready for that kind of responsibility? What if he gets scared that we won't love him as much if he has a sibling?"

Her angel laughed and put his arms around her. "We'll just have to teach him that love isn't a finite resource."

She was smiling, too, and pressed her hips to his. "Isn't it?"

He shook his head and bowed it closer to hers. "It's infinite. It just goes on and on."

"*Step right up! Win a unicorn for the pretty lady. Sir! Do you have what it takes to make it all the way to the top?*"

The enthusiastic vendor was giving Cameron the hard sell, but it wasn't necessary. Her angel raked his hair out of his face and took the enormous hammer as casually as someone picking up a baseball bat. With a fluid, easy motion, he sent the weight flying straight to the top of the machine. The bell clanged in celebration, and Cameron handed over far too much money to the greedy-eyed attendant and took a giant, plush unicorn from a shelf. He handed it to Brie with a little bow.

"Claw Machine Bear is going to love this," she said happily.

"We should name that bear so we don't keep calling him that," he laughed.

"Claw-dius!" She proclaimed triumphantly.

"Brianna Weldon, have I told you lately that you are as brilliant as you are beautiful?" He gave her a hungry look, slipped his arm around her waist, and pulled her toward him.

"Look what these people have done to this cucumber!" cried Tavi, who appeared out of nowhere, holding a deep-fried pickle on a stick. "How is this even food? And why is it so delicious?"

Cameron made a soft grunting noise and let go of Brie's waist. She stepped away, flustered and blushing. "How much time do we have before we meet them at the Ferris wheel?" she asked.

He checked his bare wrist as though looking for a watch. "We could start heading that way about now."

They passed Ephriam, who was making his way with remarkable speed through the entire side of pork belly. At the same time, a small group of onlookers appeared torn between admiring the spectacle and stealing a bite for themselves.

As they walked on, they saw a person stagger off one of the spinning rides. She stumbled over to a garbage can, hurled, then turned and got right back in line for the same ride again.

"People are really into the spirit of this thing," Brie said with a nervous laugh.

It was true. The sounds, smells, and sights were all blurring together in a great, jangling clamor. People were pushing themselves well past their limits all over the place. Even now, Tavi was stopping at yet another frozen coffee stand, though Brie didn't know how much more caffeine even an Elysian heart could realistically withstand.

She turned to face Cameron. "You know what? It's all getting to be a bit much. Can we go on the Ferris wheel together?" She suddenly wanted fresh air and perspective.

He pulled her hand to his lips and kissed her fingers. "Only if we can bring the unicorn."

She broke into a smile. "You should get to name this one since I named Clawdius."

"Horny?" he suggested.

She stared at him, shocked. "Excuse me?"

He looked confused. "…Because of its horn?"

For a split second, all she could do was blink. She then made for the Ferris wheel. "On second thought, you are not allowed to name this unicorn. Or any unicorn. I am in charge of naming all unicorns for the rest of time."

He followed after her, bewildered. "What did I do?"

◆　◆　◆

The Ferris wheel was a beautiful call.

They'd managed to get on just as the sun was starting to sink toward the ocean, and everything in their line of sight was varying shades of pink and gold. The clouds in the distance only enhanced the beauty of the moment. The sunlight glinted off of them like metal and sparks.

"What a sight! This is gorgeous. I could stay up here forever," she sighed happily.

Cameron shot her a glance, and with a flick of his finger, the giant wheel stopped with them at the very top. She turned to him, delighted. With a cheeky smile, he scooted toward her, deliberately rocking the basket bench, laughing when she shrieked and threw her arms around him. "Mission accomplished," he whispered into her hair.

She nestled into his chest to watch the sunset. "Perfect." A minute passed as they rocked in bliss. "I'm so relieved I get to be here with you," she whispered. "After the Revelation, I thought... I was scared they would take you away from me."

His arms tightened. "I will never let that happen, Brie. No matter the consequences."

She nodded, then frowned. "Wait, what consequences?"

He was quiet for a moment and then said, "Brie? Let's just be on the ride for a minute."

"Yes, you're right," she said, tilting her face to his.

He shifted his body so she was halfway on his lap, causing the car they sat in to rock back and forth again. She laughed nervously and clung to him. He tipped her face up, and this time, he pressed his lips to hers. She sighed and melted into him, kissing him back, parting her lips, touching his tongue with the very tip of her own in tentative exploration. They tangled and touched, and she was worried they would tip the unicorn out of the car.

They might have gone on forever if she hadn't opened her eyes to the sunset while he was kissing her neck. If she hadn't seen that same formation of metallic-looking clouds again, much, much closer this time. If she hadn't realized that something about them, the way they moved, wasn't right. If she hadn't heard the frenzy of screams from the crowd below, watched   Ephriam throw up into a popcorn bucket, or seen Sherry and Mike feeding each other churros and laughing when the cinnamon sugar stuck to their noses. She might not have put it all together. That is until her vision suddenly zoomed into those clouds with super-natural insight to show her what they indeed were.

But it did.

She jerked back from Cameron, her blood turning to ice in her veins.

"Cameron, you need to start the wheel again. We need to get out of here now. Right now." She was tugging on his shirt without turning her face from the sunset.

He was still nuzzling her neck with the tip of his nose, trailing his fingertips up her sides. "We don't need to rush, Brie. Just a little more time…"

"Cameron!" her voice alarmed him, and he stopped to look at her. "The clouds!"

He threw a squinting glance into the sunset. "What's wrong? It's only a storm. The news said it wouldn't even make landfall."

"Cameron, start the wheel up *right now!*"

Another look at her face sobered him up. He flicked his fingers to start the wheel again, and the attendants began disembarking the passengers.

Her gaze was locked on the horizon, the sunset reflected in her eyes.

"Brie, what is it?" he asked.

She couldn't tear her eyes away when she answered him as the Ferris wheel lowered them far, far too slowly back to the ground.

"That isn't a storm," she answered. "It's a swarm."

CHAPTER TWENTY-THREE

The Oncoming Storm

"What do you mean it's a swarm?" Sherry panted as the group ran for their lives back to the SUV. "A swarm of what?"

Brie looked wildly at the others. "Ephriam? Tavi?"

"I see it," said Tavi.

The change in the group was instantaneous, and in the Elysians particularly, it was profound. The moment Tavi saw Brie and Cameron sprinting through the fair, all her sugared-up, bouncy energy and lanky, lounging grace transformed into the raw power of a coiled spring — every muscle drawn like a bow. Her pupils dilated as she stared at the horizon. As soon as they got away from the crowds, a knife appeared in her hand. With a small movement, it let out a loud pop and extended itself into a six-foot-long, double-headed golden spear laced with lightning. Ephriam closed his eyes in concentration for the briefest of moments. When he opened them again, he held a golden shield, and around his waist was a belt of horrifying-looking weapons. Cameron positioned himself between Brie and the horizon without seeming to think about it. His hands glowed at the ready in a protective stance. Mike stood beside him, armed only with the set-jawed certainty that whatever this threat was, it wouldn't get past him.

"What are they?" Brie asked, afraid of the answer.

"I cannot make them out at this distance," said Ephriam. "Tavianne, are they wraiths?"

"They're too fast, too organized." Tavi's tone was clipped and efficient. "And too densely packed. It's like a solid mass moving in perfect synchronicity. How it's managing to fly without crashing in on itself is... is..." Her entire body suddenly froze. Without turning, she spoke to them all. "It is Baal."

Cameron and Ephriam whipped around, faces shining with fear.

"It cannot be," said Ephriam.

"You see what I see, Ephriam. It is him, as he was long ago, in the Clash of the Three above the Dragon Hole." She stared unblinkingly at the horizon, remembering that unspeakable day. "He will blot out the sky," she said in a whisper.

"What is Baal?" shrieked Sherry. "What are you talking about? Those are clouds! Very dark... okay, in fact, improbably dark clouds! Moving towards us. Fast. Too fast. Oh God..." Reality broke over her like a wave. In a much quieter voice, she asked, "Tavi, what exactly is Baal?"

Tavi looked at her and spoke in a voice shot through with fear. "He who devours."

In a flash, everyone broke into action.

Mike, not knowing what else to do, checked their go-bags and swept Sherry back to the car. Cameron grabbed Brie's hand and started to run along with them. Tavi turned her spear back into a knife and slipped it into its sheath while streaking to their parking spot, fast as sunlight.

The minute they slammed the SUV doors, their flight's futility was made obvious. In the time it had taken them to get away from the Jubilee and reach the car, the swarm had halved the distance between them and doubled in size on the horizon.

"We need to get them away from here," Ephriam told Tavi before addressing the rest. "You must brace yourselves for the journey."

Mike, Sherry, Cameron, and Brie joined hands. Ephriam and Tavi made sure everyone was touching someone else before they bowed their heads. Their hands began to glow, but the world had only just begun to spin and shift when Brie suddenly yelled, "Wait!"

"What is it?" Cameron asked.

"How did it find us?" Brie asked, staring at the approaching threat.

"How is that relevant? We need to get out of here!" Tavi said. "You don't understand what it will do if we're caught."

"What will it do?" asked Brie stubbornly.

"We don't have time!" Tavi gave Ephriam a meaningful look, and they once again bowed their heads as their hands began to emit a faint glow, but this time, the world did not even begin to spin. The Elysians stopped, looked at one another with a frown, and tried again. Nothing.

Tavi slowly turned to Brie.

The pendant was shining on her chest like a bright star.

"Are you doing this?" she demanded. It was the first time Brie had seen her angry or afraid. "Brianna, if you are preventing us from leaving, you need to stop right now. You cannot know the danger we are in!"

"Then tell me," said Brie flatly.

Tavi took in a sharp breath and glared at her, then at the deepening black on the horizon. "Baal is the mortal sin of gluttony."

Sherry chimed in. "That doesn't seem so bad. I know we went a little overboard with the cinnamon rolls, and the festival sure isn't a model of restraint, and Ephriam's bacon breakfast almost certainly counts as a mortal sin—"

"It isn't a joke!" Tavi cried in an anguished voice. "Humans misunderstand the Seven all the time. You make them smaller to fit inside your mind. You turn them into bedtime stories to frighten children into good behavior, to keep them from overeating candy on holidays. This isn't like that at all." She took a deep breath before continuing. "There is nothing he doesn't devour. He is destruction, devastation, the annihilation of everything. Nothing sates his hunger. Nothing stands against him. In the battle above the Blue Pit, he reduced islands, the waves, and the sky itself to nothingness. The avarice of humans has only made him stronger over time. Whenever a species is hunted to extinction, whenever a human indulges themselves to death, whenever a company squeezes resources out of the ground until the Earth itself cracks and dies, you *worship* him. You empower him. And soaking up your worship in the deepest shadows, he has grown into this!" She flung her arm to gesture at the ancient demon, spreading like an ink stain over the ocean and sky. "More powerful than I have ever seen him before! So, for the love of all that is good and Holy, Brianna Weldon, *let us go!*"

Brie cringed under her words but managed to stop her hands from shaking. "But how did he find me?" she asked again.

Tavi let out a sound of pure exasperation, and her scars lit up from within for a moment before she visibly calmed herself down and answered. "I *don't know*. Why do you keep asking?"

Sherry, Mike, Cameron, and Ephriam were exasperated, too. Cameron tried to intervene, "Brie, we really don't have time for—"

"Because I don't think he did find me," Brie answered. "I don't think he knows where I am at all. I think Cam's right, and I don't think he can see me when I'm wearing this." She held up her pendant. "I think he came here because he's heading to the last place Mammon saw me — saw *us.*"

A spark of dawning realization shone in Sherry's eyes. She gasped. Confused, the others looked at her, so she clarified, her voice scarcely above a whisper. "It isn't coming for Brie. It's coming for the whole town."

Horror washed over the faces of everyone in the car as they turned to look at the Jubilee.

"Would it do that?" Mike asked loudly. "How could it do that? People would notice! People would—"

"People will believe whatever you tell them to believe," said Cameron. "Freak weather event. Gas main explosion. Terrorist attack. The forces of evil have been operating in plain sight under a thousand guises of 'normal' human atrocities for centuries."

Ephriam nodded in agreement. "Your species has allowed the abhorrent to become mundane. Why would any of you notice something unusual about yet another catastrophe?"

Brie ignored this and locked eyes with the warrior woman. "It's going to wipe Gloucester, and probably Yorktown, off the map, Tavi. Unless we defeat it, somehow."

Tavi shot a look at the horizon, then at Brie. "I am the most formidable warrior in the realm of Elysium. And I am telling you — we cannot defeat Baal."

Brie looked at her pendant.

Ephriam guessed what she was thinking in a heartbeat. "We cannot afford to hope that it will save us from so great an evil."

Brie straightened up with a look of resolve. "Then we'll just have to draw it away."

Mike nodded. Sherry jumped into triage mode, addressing the dangers in order of greatest urgency. "All right. So how do we draw it away from the town?"

Brie swallowed and touched her pendant. "I think I need to take this off."

"You're going to do *what?*" Cameron shouted.

Tavi stared at her. "If Baal sees your light, he will chase after you like a thousand hounds of Hell."

Brie nodded. "I'm counting on it."

Two minutes later, they were driving down the highway so fast they were practically flying back to the isolated beach cove where they'd spent that very morning. All the windows were rolled down this time despite the freezing winds suddenly descending on the coast. Brie was sitting in the front passenger's seat beside Sherry, who was driving like a maniac. Her pendant was sitting on her lap, and an ancient demon the size of a hurricane had taken the bait and was moving to intercept them.

They parked the car. Mike threw everyone a backpack, and they put them on as they ran together down to the beach.

Once they were all assembled in a row, the enormity of what they were about to do hit Brie like an asteroid. "This is a horrible idea!" she shouted into the gale-force, frigid wind as the blackness continued to spread through the sky, covering her field of vision.

"This is *your* idea!" Sherry shouted back, clutching onto her hand.

The six members of their little company shook in the wind but held together in their chain of resolve, allowing the swarm that was Baal to draw ever closer.

"Why did you listen to me?" Brie cried. "I don't know anything! By Ephriam's standards, I was basically born yesterday! Why would *any* of you listen to me?"

Five responses flew back at her all at once:

"Because Azrael broke the seal of her prophecy for you," yelled Ephriam.

"Because we couldn't teleport away from this suicide mission," growled Tavi.

"Because you're my best friend," shrieked Sherry.

"Because I'd follow you anywhere," said Cameron.

"Because you won't stop talking!" hollered Mike.

An awkward pause followed.

"All right, then," Brie said, a bit milder. "Nice to get a confidence boost before total annihilation, I guess. Thanks." All five of them gave her a scathing look. She decided to shut up.

"Does everyone remember what to do?" yelled Cameron for the fourth time.

"Wait until Brie's light draws it close enough that we're sure it sees us and the pendant. Do not under any circumstances allow it to touch us. Then, teleport immediately to Elysium because it won't be able to follow us there. Right?" Mike recited with a grin. The truth was, if the town where he lived, the woman he loved, and her incredibly strange friends weren't all in mortal danger, he'd be having the time of his life.

There was a chance Sherry sensed this because she shouted, "Michael Mitchell, you had better not be smiling right now!"

"Sorry, babe," he shouted back. "But I mean, *teleports!*"

"Damnit," Sherry cursed. "I'm in love with an idiot."

"Is he bigger than me?" asked Mike.

"Quiet, all of you!" shouted Tavi. "Hold on to each other as though your life depends on it because I assure you, it does." The wind carried her words away the moment they left her lips, but the others took her meaning and turned to face the sea.

The two-mile buoy disappeared from view.

Baal was nearly upon them.

Brie closed her eyes for a moment and, without even thinking about it, offered a silent plea to the Universe, God, or some far-flung benevolence she desperately hoped existed.

I don't know if anyone's listening, but if you are, I need your help.

I need you to protect my friends. I need you to protect this town.

Help us draw this monstrous thing far away. ...Please.

She opened her eyes and was nearly blinded by the light shining from her pendant. The others looked over to see where it was coming from. Sherry let out a soft whimper when she saw the white light pulsing like a heartbeat in her friend's hand.

Brie took this as a sign that it was time and placed the pendant back around her neck.

The wind immediately stopped. It didn't die down. It didn't slow to a stop after using up the force of its momentum. Every molecule of air stopped dead in its tracks like someone had hit pause in a movie. Without the wind, the waves settled down to nothing.

On a primal, instinctual cue, every hair on the friends' bodies stood straight up and crackled with a warning.

You are in danger.

Flee.

But the six companions stood their ground, uncertain what to do.

"Did it see us?" whispered Brie. "Tavi, why did it stop?"

"I don't know," Tavi answered in a low voice. "Either it saw us, or it's waiting for some instruction."

Sherry shuddered. "What could possibly give that thing instructions?"

Ephriam set his jaw. "Do not ask questions if you cannot handle the answers, child."

Brie felt Sherry's hand tremble, and she squeezed it gently. "We can't leave until we know for certain it's seen us." She was saying this as much for her own benefit as for anyone else's.

Tavi nodded grimly. It was plain from her face that she found this holding pattern to be torturous. "It is still far enough off that we can teleport safely."

The swarm was close enough now that they could hear it. Even over the sound of the dying waves, a horrifying buzzing noise polluted the motionless air. It was the sound of a million carrion birds on abandoned battlefields strewn with the dead — of a million flies devouring a banquet after all the guests had been murdered. It was the sound of death itself, and it chilled the company to their souls. Still, they unflinchingly held their ground. Right up to the point when the swarm of whatever nightmarish creatures comprised the ancient demon formed themselves into a face, which twisted itself into a smile.

At that point, it must be fairly said — they flinched.

No one was prepared when the face spoke in a voice like a billion hissing cockroaches that had, by some unholy hand, been gifted the power of language.

"DAUGHTER OF EVE," hissed the nightmare horde.

All six beings on the beach stood frozen for a few moments before Sherry whispered, "Brie... I think he means you."

"Yes, thank you, that's very helpful," Brie hissed back.

"GIVE ME THE PENDANT AND YOU MAY LEAVE WITH YOUR LIFE."

Brie stood in shocked silence. They hadn't prepared for this — for the oncoming swarm to stop at all, let alone speak. She looked at Cameron and, in his eyes, found nothing but protectiveness and terror. She looked at Sherry, who shrugged in the same "I don't know" gesture she'd used since early childhood. Finally, she looked at Tavi.

Am I expected to barter with this thing?

"Tavi? What should I do?" she asked.

The warrior's attention was fixed in pure concentration on the looming threat before them. "Keep him talking," she answered after a moment. "The more information he gives us, the more we'll have to report. The instant it moves, we'll disappear."

Brie swallowed, then spoke as loud as she could manage. "Um... respectfully, Mister Baal, I don't see how that's going to be possible."

The hideous, gargantuan grin opened and closed, and a sound that was possibly supposed to be laughter rent the air. It sounded like a car being put through a meat grinder — like a million knives sharpening themselves against one another. The six companions on the beach shuddered.

"HAVE THE BRIGHT ONES FAILED TO TELL YOU WHAT I AM?" asked the swarm.

Brie attempted to project confidence rather than be sucked down by the horror she felt. "Enlighten me."

"I AM HE WHO DEVOURS. NOTHING EXISTS THAT I CANNOT CONSUME."

"I did actually hear something about that," said Brie.

"THEN, WHY DO YOU STAND OPPOSED?" asked the face. "WHY DOOM YOUR FRIENDS TO A PAINFUL DEATH?" The metallic voice sliced through the air like papercuts. It hurt her ears as it continued. "GIVE ME THE PENDANT," it said again, "AND I SHALL LET YOU LIVE."

Brie didn't feel they were gaining anything from the exchange and didn't have any clue as to the right thing to say, so she asked the only question on any of their minds. "Right, I got that part. What confuses me, and perhaps you can clear this up, is this: if you're this all-powerful, all-consuming being I'm supposed to be afraid of, why have you stopped to negotiate?"

The swarm's face twisted itself back into a horrible grin.

"I HAVEN'T."

Time slowed to a crawl.

Brie heard her heartbeat in her chest — one beat.

Then, everything went wrong.

Ephriam doubled over, and out of his mighty chest burst something that looked like a metal lamprey — a scraping, silver eel with rings within rings of teeth where its face should be. It turned its horrible metal mouth back around and dove into his shoulder, eating as it burrowed. The Elysian roared in agony.

Another heartbeat.

Another silver monster seemed to sprout from Mike's thigh, surrounded by a fountain of gore — the ropes and ligaments of his muscles and veins bloomed a moment around the exit wound like a hideous flower. The silver beast turned on a dime and burrowed back in again.

Another heartbeat and the realization landed.

Baal hadn't stopped. He'd circled around and flanked them.

The creatures were coming from behind.

Sherry was screaming. Cameron pulled them into a circle, straining to keep everyone touching. Tavi was shouting instructions, encircling them all with her arms and pulsing electricity from her body to keep the horde at bay. She continued shouting, even as one of the metal animals evaded her lightning and burrowed itself into the back of her shoulder — strange, glowing blood shot from the wound.

Another heartbeat.

Tavi's electricity bought them a second, but at a significant cost. It was conducted through the swarm but also through the creatures already embedded in her friends. Tavi was saving them and electrocuting them at the same time. Her lightning formed itself into a sphere surrounding them. By Brie's next heartbeat, it was big enough to envelop them in a globe of light.

Cameron caught her hand, and they locked eyes as he transported them off the beach, leaving behind nothing but the echoes of their agonized screams.

CHAPTER TWENTY-FOUR

The Great Escape

They were moving through the dense membrane of time, but it wasn't like their previous journeys to Elysium — not at all. When it felt like they were about to break through to the other side of the border, she was shot through with paralyzing pain. Twice, three times, Brie sensed rather than felt them nearing the barrier of Enoch's realm, and three times, she cried out as her body was racked with shocks.

Something isn't letting us in.

Again, she felt Cameron strain to pull them through to the safety of his father's kingdom, and again, they were pushed painfully away. She didn't know how much more they could withstand when suddenly, they crashed onto something foreign, solid — something that felt like an island surrounded by rapids. Celestial forces swirled but couldn't seem to touch them here, wherever here was.

Tavianne's protective sphere of lightning flickered and went out.

Brie looked around, disoriented, at her friends. Mike was losing consciousness. Sherry clung to him, her hands clamped around his thigh, slick with blood. Tavi's eyes were closed, in pain or concentration, she couldn't tell. Ephriam was bleeding out.

"Cameron!" Brie screamed. "Cameron!"

But her angel wasn't looking at her. He was face to face with one of the metal lampreys from Baal's swarm. It hovered, suspended about a foot away from him.

Brie sucked in a horrified gasp.

It's going to kill him.

The metal monster darted closer, terrifyingly fast, but was stopped a centimeter away from his right eye by the most unlikely thing.

Energy from her pendant burst forth in a protective shield of light, blasting the creature away from her angel. It turned its gruesome metal body midair and shot back at them again when another bright beam of energy suddenly joined and strengthened the pendant's light. Brie looked around to see where it was coming from, only to discover through the lacework of lightning a familiar portal haloing a familiar face.

Her mother's pendant beamed out at her from the past, mirroring her own.

The light that now protected them formed a brilliant shield, and the moment the hellish creature zooming toward them touched its surface, an inhuman shriek pierced the air, and the beast sizzled into nothingness, leaving behind a plume of caustic, green smoke in its wake.

A metal monster burst from Mike's leg and shot away into the seas of time.

She turned to her mother, and they locked eyes for the briefest of moments. The light from their pendants connected the women like a lifeline through time. As their pendants went dark and the portal started to close, her mother's voice rang through the air, clear as a bell.

"You're my whole heart, Brianna."

With a burst of adrenaline, Cameron roared with effort, as though lifting something impossibly heavy, and transported them away. The six companions tumbled out of the ether. The last thing Brie saw before she hit her head on a rock and blacked out was a splash of glowing blood curling through the air, where it silhouetted black before a blinding sky.

◆   ◆   ◆

Brie had never seen a sun so bright. She squinted as it reflected off the endless dunes. The heat hit her so hard it felt like a physical weight — like someone had thrown them into an oven. She turned her head and tried to get her bearings. Mirages shimmered on the horizon. The only thing that punctuated the landscape for miles was the odd reddish boulder, mesquite bush, or cactus.

"Brie! Here, now!"

Her vision snapped back into focus, and she scrambled blindly toward Sherry's voice.

Her best friend was on her knees, ashen-faced. Brie watched as she ripped her belt out of her jeans and tied it around Mike's thigh. Mike made a series of soft, low moans as a red stain pooled around him in the sand.

"Brie!" Sherry yelled.

"I'm coming!" Brie cried.

As she fought through the sand and got closer, she could hear what Mike was saying. "I'm cold. Sherry, it's so cold."

"Brie! Your pendant!" Cameron shouted.

Her head snapped around to take in the rest of the scene. They were in a desert. Cameron was bent over Ephriam about fifteen feet away, hands glowing, trying to control the flow of blood. Tavi stood next to them, leaning heavily on her spear. Every few seconds, her scars would turn shock-white, then dim again.

"Brie!" Sherry screamed.

"I'm here," she panted. She pulled the pendant over her head and pressed it to Mike's exposed femoral artery.

Please. Please, let this work.

Suddenly, she heard Ephriam let out a groan. Cameron's unintelligible shout of joy was music to her ears. She allowed herself a half-second of relief that Cameron's oldest and dearest friend was still alive before returning to Mike.

The damage was catastrophic. If they'd been relying on human medicine to heal him, he'd never make it. A tunnel as wide as her forearm had been gouged through his leg. She saw veins, fragments of bone, and torn muscles. His femoral artery had been severed.

Sherry was beyond the ability to form words. She wrung her hands and stared at Mike as though willing him to heal. He had blessedly passed out. Brie held her pendant to the wound and prayed over and over that this would work for Mike the way it had worked for her all those years ago, after the car accident.

Please. Please.

She felt a strange shifting beneath her hands and lifted a finger to see what was happening. Sherry slowly knelt and watched with a mixture of relief, gratitude, and horrified fascination as Mike's thigh regrew and reknit itself together before their eyes. They stepped back as skin closed over the wound.

Sherry took a couple of heaving breaths, checked his vitals, and turned him over to check for further damage. She was in full nurse mode. Brie bowed her head, slipped her pendant back around her neck, and then blinked as something dripped into her eyes. She touched her hand to her forehead, brought it down, and saw that it was covered in blood.

I must have hit my head when we landed.

That explains... But I'm forgetting something.

Something important.

Ephriam was trying to stand up, as Cameron firmly tried to keep him down. "You need to take a minute. That thing ripped straight through you," he said gently. Ephriam grunted and obediently slumped back down.

I know that I'm forgetting something.

Brie racked her brain, trying to piece it together, but everything was still too fuzzy. Just turning her head from side to side unbalanced her, and she nearly fell over. She sank to one knee and placed her hands on the ground, hanging her head and panting.

That's when she saw it—every few seconds, flashes of a faint white glow reflected on the endless grains of sand.

Her head snapped up. There was Tavi, still motionless, slumped against her spear. Every few seconds, her skin lit up like lacework lightning. Her lashes fluttered, and as Brie watched, a trickle of shimmering blood leaked from the corner of her lips and fell to the ground.

Brie leapt up like a bullet from a gun.

"There were three!" she shouted. Cameron, Sherry, and Ephriam's heads snapped up to look at her. She swayed dizzily but ran as fast as she could toward Tavi, screaming all the while. "Cameron! There were three! Three of them!"

"Three of what?" he asked, disoriented.

"One died! One got away! *Where is the third one?*" Brie's scream tore her throat.

The other three followed her terrified gaze to Tavi, and it suddenly clicked.

She was shocking herself to keep the creature still.

The creature that was still inside her.

Eating.

"We have to get it out!" screamed Brie. "We have to help her! We have to—"

At that moment, several things happened in rapid succession.

Cameron tackled her out of the way and held her tight as Ephriam, drawing on some hidden store of strength, flew past them, carrying Brie's backpack. He ripped out the bottle of glowing Elysian energy and was beside Tavi faster than any of them could even track. He opened the bottle, poured some of the liquid over her wound, and pressed his hand to her shoulder, muttering in an ancient language. Her body glowed brightly all over; lightning pulsed through her scars and lit her from within. She was too weak to control it, and it shocked Ephriam repeatedly. Still, he stayed, pressing one glowing hand to her collarbone and drawing her to him with the other, closer and closer, though the lightning stabbed through him relentlessly. Brie smelled burning flesh.

She started to struggle against Cameron. "We have to help him!" she screamed.

"Just wait!" said Cameron.

Ephriam's mutterings increased in volume as the lightning increased in intensity. Coils of smoke began to wisp off his body, and just when Brie thought he couldn't stand anymore, he bellowed a final incantation at the heavens, and at last, the silver monster shot from Tavi's back. She vomited up a fountain of blood and fell limp in Ephriam's arms. Her scars went dark.

"To me!" Ephriam shouted, motioning to the others desperately. "To me! Before it—"

Cameron practically threw Brie into his beckoning arm and ran over to Sherry. Together, they dragged Mike over to join the rest of the group. Brie reached blindly forward to touch whomever she could to complete the chain as the sands beneath them started to tremble and slip from the dunes, and the earth started to quake.

The silver terror that had burst from Tavi's back had recovered from Ephriam's spells. It turned in mid-air and shot back towards the group. The Elysians concentrated all their firepower on the small monster, screaming with effort as the blaze that pulsed forth from their palms shone first orange, then red, then white hot.

With a sizzle, the metal shard blackened and fell to the ground.

The Elysians didn't drop their protective stance for even a second.

"We need to take it somewhere it can't hurt anyone," Cameron said, sweating with panic. "Baal can rematerialize anywhere, even if a splinter of him remains. If he escaped from the Pit, I can think of nowhere safe. Ephriam, where can we go?"

Ephriam just shook his head, shaking from head to toe, glistening with sweat and blood. "Anywhere we go, he can eat his way out. He can eat anything. He can eat air." He looked around wildly. "He will be here any minute, and we only have enough Elysian energy to transport once more. Twice, if we're lucky, but there's nowhere to go."

"There's one place," Brie said softly.

Every head turned to her.

"There's one place we can go that won't endanger anyone, surrounded by nothing but the vacuum of space." She locked eyes with Cameron as his face transformed with dawning comprehension.

He nodded and picked up the charred nightmare creature with one hand. "We'll have to do this fast. Ephriam, you keep your hands on Tavi. Sherry, Brie, hold onto Mike and hold onto each other. It's going to be very cold, and I can't take any air with us for him to eat. Do not break the chain, no matter what happens. Hold your breath. Are you ready?"

Brie and Sherry nodded, terrified.

"Hold your breath in three... two... one."

The celestial forces swirled around them for a moment. She heard Sherry whimper beside her and squeezed her hand to remind her to hold her breath.

Then, a shock of the coldest air Brie had ever felt hit them like a cement wall. They opened their eyes to the sight of the earth rising over the moon's horizon. Sherry gripped Brie's hand so hard it hurt. They looked frantically at Cameron and Ephriam, who held the bottle of the remaining Elysian energy in front of their group like a glowing torch. Cameron hurled the shard of Baal as hard as he could into the distance. The reduced gravity helped it travel even farther than it would have on Earth.

For five seconds, each of which seemed to last an eternity, the friends stood breathless, staring at the place where the shard had disappeared into the distance.

Then, as they watched in horror, Baal's face rose from the dust of the moon with an enormous, gruesome grin.

Tavi was right. It blotted out the sky.

It blotted out their view of the whole Earth.

Ten million silver monsters shot at them like arrows, glinting in the moonlight, as Ephriam and Cameron used the last of their strength and the last of the Elysian energy to transport them away.

♦   ♦   ♦

Sherry couldn't stop shivering. She was sitting beside Mike, arranging his unconscious body into the most comfortable position possible she could on the soft earth, checking him for damage. She appeared to be okay, except that her teeth rattled against each other so hard that, twenty feet away, Brie could hear their staccato chattering with perfect clarity.

They'd landed in the mountains this time. Somewhere in the American northwest, judging from the enormous redwoods. It wasn't cold. In fact, the sun was shining brightly, and there wasn't a cloud in the sky. The moss-covered rocks, dappled sunlight, and gracefully curving ferns belied an ancient, undisturbed forest on a perfect, idyllic day.

Idyllic except for the shivering.

And the blood.

Ephriam and Cameron were bent over Tavi, talking in their native tongue so fast that Brie didn't know how they could understand one another. She knelt with her pendant pressed against the gaping wound on Tavi's shoulder as the men held her on her side. She'd been there for five minutes, but the magical shifting she'd felt beneath her hands when Mike's wound sealed itself shut hadn't happened yet. The Elysian warrior's breathing was faint, and her pulse was thready. She was alive, but barely.

Which makes sense, Brie thought bitterly. *With all the time, I left her standing there.*

While it was eating her.

She hung her head.

Why didn't I see it sooner?

Every once in a while, she could understand a word of the Elysians' conversation. "Raphael." "Elysium." "Enoch."

She heard Sherry's teeth chatter again, closer this time. She looked up, to realize that her best friend had come over to kneel beside her.

"Sorry," Sherry said, her jaw still shaking. "I can't help it."

Brie shook her head. "I think you're entitled. Don't apologize."

"Right," Sherry said, staring helplessly down at Tavi. "You couldn't, either," she added. Brie looked at her, confused. "You couldn't help it, either. I can tell when you're beating yourself up, blaming yourself for something utterly beyond your control. I've had some practice recognizing the signs. You've been doing it for a while." Sherry watched Brie drop eye contact.

"She wanted to leave," Brie whispered. "She wanted to leave, and I wouldn't let her." She sucked in a breath that hurt her throat, still raw from screaming. "I wouldn't let us leave, and look what happened."

"You didn't let us leave because you wanted to save the town, Brie," Sherry said firmly. "Because you insisted that rather than just run away, we save an entire human town from being eaten alive by those *things*. Men, women, children. Babies. You saved God-knows-how-many babies from being eaten alive today, Brianna Weldon." Sherry sucked in another breath and gritted her teeth to stop them from chattering. "And just because I one-hundred-percent have PTSD from all of this and cannot stop shaking like a lunatic, does not mean that the fact that you are a hero is lost on me. So," she punched Brie in the arm, ignoring the ensuing "Ow!" of protest. "Stop criticizing yourself and act like a damn professional. What's the problem here? Why isn't it working like last time?"

The two of them scanned her body, analyzing.

"Mike's a human. She's Elysian," guessed Brie.

"Shouldn't matter," Sherry said matter-of-factly. "This magical nonsense wouldn't care about that — it's too powerful. What else is different? What do you think?"

Brie's face lit with comprehension. "Sherry, you're a genius."

"This is well-documented," Sherry agreed. "Why, this time?"

"That's what's different — what I'm thinking. With Mike, I was praying that this would work, that he'd be okay. Just now? You were right. I blamed myself for not seeing this sooner instead of focusing on healing Tavi."

"Do what you did before," Sherry commanded.

The men had fallen silent and were watching the women with rapt attention.

Brie bowed and repeated the silent prayer exactly as she had the last time.

Please, let this work. Help me heal, my friend.

Please, let her live.

For a minute, nothing happened. Then, Brie felt a warmth start to grow beneath her hands. She shut her eyes tighter and continued her silent chant.

Please. Please, let her live.

Tavi's scars suddenly glowed white-hot, and an electric pulse shot straight through Brie, who flew backward about five feet and landed on a bed of ferns.

"That's my girl," said Sherry. She went straight to Tavi's side and checked her over for injuries. She didn't turn around as she called, "You hanging in there, champ?"

Brie weakly held up one thumb.

"Is she giving me a thumbs-up?" asked Sherry. Ephriam nodded. She shook her head. "Always with the non-verbal when I'm not looking. Tavi? Tavianne. Wake up, lady. Can you hear me? How do you feel?"

Tavi's eyes fluttered but did not open.

Sherry turned to Cameron. "You," she barked. "Do the glowy-hand thing that you did on Ephriam. Focus on her heart. You," she pointed to Ephriam. "Her head. Do it now."

"We can't do it now, Sherry," said Cameron shakily.

"What do you mean?"

"We can't do it now."

Sherry glared at them but didn't have time to press further. She issued orders instead. "Ephriam, go through that bag over there. Give me that ambrosia stuff she likes to drink. I don't know much about Elysian anatomy, but starting there seems as good a bet as any." She leaned back on her heels as Brie staggered back to sit beside her, smoking faintly. "You smell like burnt hair," she added distractedly, wrinkling her nose.

"As problems go…" Brie trailed off.

Ephriam drew two crystal vials out of Brie's backpack. The first was nearly empty. The second was still filled with amber liquid. He threw it to Cameron, who held it to Tavi's lips momentarily. He waited a few seconds before giving her another sip, cradling her head in his lap.

"Right," said Sherry. "We'll give these two a few minutes to administer the ambrosia. Then, we'll check on Mike and figure out where we are, why we aren't in Elysium, and what we're going to do next. Right now, I need to throw up." She slapped her hands down on her thighs, rose to her feet, marched behind the nearest redwood, and hurled.

This was Sherry's trauma response — promoting herself to management and assuming responsibility for the situation. That, and shivering uncontrollably.

She was so right — we need her. I need her.

Thank God she's here.

Brie stayed where she was, watching Cameron and Ephriam as they tried to give their energy to their fallen friend. She wished desperately that there was something more she could do, but something told her it was out of her hands now. She let her mind drift away from the scene. Rather, she tried to. The moment she did, a high whine-like tinnitus filled her mind, and she was accosted with violent flashes of memory.

The face of Baal rising like death out of the moonscape, big as a city.

The glint of a thousand silver eels made of teeth shooting at her straight from Hell.

Her friends, screaming and dying in the desert sun.

Her eyes flew open with a gasp, and she struggled to control her breath.

On the other hand, let's absolutely not try to relax.

Just then, Tavi opened her eyes.

Ephriam gave a triumphant shout and wrapped his arms around her. Cameron sat back in the moss, so relieved he couldn't speak. Sherry marched back from behind the redwood, wiping her mouth with her hand. "How's she doing?" she asked in her caring nurse voice.

No one answered, so Brie offered, "I saw her eyes open."

"That sounds like progress in any species. Ephriam, let go so I can check her out," Sherry commanded.

Ephriam shook his head and continued to hug Tavi to his

chest, right up until she shocked him with another lightning bolt, which blasted him backward among the trees. Sherry followed his progress impassively as he slammed against a redwood and slid down to the forest floor. She walked over to Tavi. "You should probably take it easy on him. I think one of those silver things ate through his lung a few minutes ago."

"What?" Tavi tried to sit up, alarmed. "Is he all right?" She winced and held back a cry, holding a hand to her chest. She was unmistakably in a lot of pain.

Sherry nodded. "He'll be fine. He's the one who got that thing out of you. Tavi, I'm going to—" Another wave of lightning shot through Tavi's body, which convulsed with the force of it. Sherry barely paused before approaching anyway. "I'm going to try to examine you as quickly as I can. Do you think you can keep from blasting me into a tree?"

Tavi shook her head weakly. "I can't..."

"You can't control it. That's okay." Sherry palpated Tavi's stomach, turned her this way, and that tested her limbs, made her follow her finger with her eyes, took her pulse, and made a mental note every time she winced. She finished up with a worried look. "As I said, I don't know anything about Elysian anatomy, but if it's anything like humans, you should be—" There was another convulsion, followed by an electric flash. "—fine," finished Sherry with a frown. "Well, not fine. Pretty damn beat up. Weak, disoriented, and in pain, but on the mend. Except for that bit — the electrical part."

Cameron asked Tavi with a face full of concern. "Tavi, where does it hurt?"

Her breathing was still short and shallow. "Everywhere," she said honestly. "Everywhere."

Ephriam knelt beside her. "She isn't fine," he said in a fierce low voice. "She needs Elysian medicine. She needs Raphael."

"All right," said Brie. "Give me a minute to rouse Mike, and we can get going."

"We can't," Cameron's voice was dire.

"What do you mean? We'll just teleport to Elysium, and Raphael can take a look at her. I'm sure he'll have her fixed up in no time. His drugs are certainly strong enough." Brie looked back and forth between Cameron and Ephriam in rising confusion as her stomach filled with dread. "Cameron… why can't we go to Elysium?"

Her angel seemed at a loss for words, so Ephriam answered. "Because of what we brought to its borders. Because of the shards of Baal, we left behind in the Time Seas. We tried to cross into Elysium while the creature was still inside Tavi, Brianna."

Sherry cut in. "And so?"

"You saw in the desert that Baal can track even the smallest part of himself anywhere. He can eat his way through worlds, if need be, to make himself whole again. If even one shard of Baal entered Elysium, the rest of him could follow." Ephriam looked as though he was a thousand miles away. "The borders of Elysium have been sealed until the threat is eliminated."

Brie felt paralyzed and could hardly bring herself to ask. "What does that mean for us?"

Cameron forced himself to answer. "In the meantime, we have no powers, no way to contact anyone for help, and no way home."

CHAPTER TWENTY-FIVE

The End and the Beginning

"Okay. Okay. You're absolutely sure about this, then? There's no way through the... the...?" Sherry snapped her fingers, trying to remember the phrase.

"The Time Seas," offered Cameron.

"The Time Seas," she repeated, "without the possibility of being attacked by those silver things — without being attacked by Baal?"

"Yes," he replied. He rested his forehead in his hands. He was sitting on a large, moss-covered rock next to Brie. He took her hand compulsively, then let it go to massage his temples. "And by possibility, I mean likelihood. Right now, Baal has two options: either he stays on the moon with nothing to eat, or he's in the Time Seas. The answer is obvious — he will be patrolling the borders, hunting for the slightest crack, for anything coming in or out of the realm."

"Can you get a message through?" asked Brie, looking at Ephriam. "Or supplies out?"

The Elysian shook his head. "I have already tried. For now, the borders are completely sealed by the power of the archangels who happened to be in the realm at the time — Azrael, Raphael, and Zadkiel, at least, possibly more." Ephriam stared into space as though he couldn't quite believe this was happening. "Even our weapons are inaccessible to us, save the ones we have on us now."

Mike raised himself up onto his elbow. "Tavi, you know all the protocols. What will the Elysian guard be doing? And how long will the lockdown last?" He had woken up about ten minutes ago and was attempting to catch up on the events of the last half hour while stoically tolerating his girlfriend's relentless examinations. Sherry pushed him gently back to the ground, smoothing his forehead with one hand while checking his pupil response.

"The alarms will have sounded the moment any part of Baal touched the perimeter," Tavi answered, breathing painfully. "They'll check the border in teams, every inch of it, before they send squadrons out to hunt for the creature. Until they find it, he could materialize there at any moment." She broke off with a gasp, clutching her side.

Ephriam was next to her in a heartbeat. "She needs to be cared for by one of our kind," he murmured. "I am forever grateful for your help, but this is beyond your skills."

Sherry drew a shaky breath. "So, no way to get there, no way to get a message through, no way to get any supplies out. Anything else?"

"Yes," Cameron said in a low voice. "It isn't just Elysium that's sealed off to us now."

"How do you mean?" asked Brie sharply.

He turned to look at her. "It's everywhere. It's every *time*." He shook his head, at a loss. "We use the energy of Elysium to move. Without it, we can't go anywhere."

"So where exactly are we?" Brie was afraid of the answer.

Good news didn't seem to be on the menu this evening.

Cameron answered, staring at the ground. "In the final moment, Ephriam and I used the last of the bottled Elysian energy to get everyone back to Earth, but he didn't have the strength to aim anywhere in particular. I am the one who brought us here, and I don't even know where here is. All I specified when I was thinking of a destination was..."

"Was what?" Brie prompted softly.

"Was that we land somewhere very, very far away from any human settlement in case Baal followed us again." Cameron's face burned with shame. "We're probably hundreds of miles from civilization with no way to teleport anywhere. And it is entirely my fault."

Brie looked around at her five friends. They were some of the most competent people she'd ever known, and they were a mess. Baal's attack had shaken them to their core.

Sherry's consummate professionalism was starting to crack under the emotional strain of having just watched her boyfriend's leg get devoured by a silver hell beast and regrown by a magical pendant. She kept grabbing his hands and squeezing them to offer a reassurance she clearly did not feel herself — squeezing hard. Brie saw Mike flex his hand like it hurt, but he never once refused to hold hers.

Though it seemed insane, given what he'd just been through, Mike was probably faring the best out of them all. He kept his voice steady and calm and smiled at Sherry every time she looked at him, but he grabbed his thigh when he thought no one was looking to make sure it was still there. Brie saw his expression cloud with fear when he looked into the woods like he was searching through the trees for glints of silver.

Ephriam was a wreck. Pacing one minute, holding his hands to Tavi's side the next. He stared at his palms, desperately willing them to glow like he was used to, hoping to heal the wound he could not see. Twice, he threw a rock into the tree line because a bird had the audacity to take flight. Twice, the stones had embedded themselves into tree trunks.

Cameron oscillated between trying to keep watch over everyone and staring fixedly into the distance, fingers pressed to his temples like he was trying to will the right answer into his head — the right next step, the right course of action. Brie wondered if the same thing was happening to her and to him. Whenever things were quiet longer than ten seconds, her brain started screaming. Cameron had a haunted look in his eyes. She didn't need a mirror to know she had the same look herself.

And then there was Tavi. Brie couldn't imagine how much pain she must be in. If it was in any way manageable, she was sure Tavi would have managed to hide it. Watching the captain of the Elysian guard wracked with electric convulsions every few minutes and not being able to help was by far the worst part of what was happening. Everyone was desperate to ease her suffering, and nobody knew how.

But somebody has to know.

You're a triage nurse, Weldon. Or you will be if you ever finish your orientation.

Go. Triage.

She took a deep breath and started to break down the problem. "So, we're injured, alone, in a random forest, with no way to teleport anywhere. We've just been attacked by demonic forces, and the sun is going down." She looked around the other five, gave an exaggerated shrug, and smiled. "This exact same thing happened to me last week."

"I beg your pardon?" asked Sherry.

"Yeah, remember, with the—"

"The car accident in the woods. The boyfriend in your purse. Right." Sherry sighed. "That's never, ever going to sound normal, you know."

"Fair enough, but my point is, we're going to be just fine — all of us," Brie said firmly. She turned to the Elysians. "Ephriam. How about instead of attacking the local bird population, you build us a proper fire to keep us warm? Night will come quickly this time of year, so don't be stingy with the firewood." Ephriam immediately started off for the deeper woods, looking relieved to have something productive to do.

Brie stepped closer to Cameron and took his hand. "Listen, you. You did the right thing. The whole point was to get Baal away from people so he couldn't hurt anyone. You did exactly what you had to do and stuck to the plan perfectly." She squeezed his palm. "Now, can you rummage through these backpacks and see what Mike put in there for us? Maybe get a bit of a camp going to make Tavi more comfortable?"

Cameron looked at her gratefully and nodded.

Brie continued. "Mike, you have a good head for the tactical side of things. Would you mind talking with Tavi about what's going on to distract her while Sherry gives her another once-over to see if there's anything at all we can do? Sherry, do you think he's well enough to manage that?"

"Sure," they answered together. "Not a problem," Mike added a casual salute.

"What are you going to do?" asked Cameron.

"I thought I heard the sound of water earlier. I'm going to see if I can find us some. Anyway, I'd like to wash the blood out of my hair. I probably look like Carrie at the prom. Can't be great for morale."

Don't question it. Please, just go with it.

Seeming to sense her silent plea, he nodded once and turned to the backpacks. Sherry and Mike started looking after Tavi, Ephriam began stockpiling enough wood to last a family of five through a harsh winter, and Cameron started to inventory their supplies.

Brie turned and started walking through the woods.

It hadn't been a lie, per se. She had heard the sound of rushing water, doubtless courtesy of her newly enhanced senses, but she wasn't in search of just water — she needed to be alone.

We were at the beach. It was a lovely day. What the hell happened?

No. No, stop that. Don't look behind you.

What the hell do we do next?

She kept putting one foot in front of the other, willing the high-pitched ringing in her ears to stop as she drew closer to the stream. She focused on the sound of her footsteps on the forest floor. The soft crunching of leaves intermingled with the babbling of the stream reminded her of the hike to the waterfall back home in Georgia when she'd visited her mom.

It was fast-moving water, well on its way to becoming a river. She followed it until she found a spot where it widened, and the banks weren't steep or rocky anymore. A nearby meadow sloped gently to the shoreline and gradually smoothed into pebbles and sand.

She knelt down to look at her reflection.

Carrie indeed.

The left side of her head was covered in blood — hair stuck to her skull in matted tangles. She took off her shoes and dipped her toes in the water. It was arrestingly cold, but the relief she felt was exquisite. Without really thinking, she flung herself forward and plunged all the way in, sinking purposefully to the bottom.

She closed her eyes and realized that everything was quiet. She couldn't hear the ring of tinnitus, and she wasn't being subjected to the hellish onslaught of images that followed, or, at least, she wasn't until she thought about them. Once she did, for a brief moment, it was there in her mind again — that face, the face of death, hovering over the desert sand, Ephriam and Mike being ripped apart, and Tavi bravely protecting them all even as she was being eaten from within.

There, where none of her friends could hear, Brie let out a single scream of frustration. Her hair floated around her, and the current carried away the bubbles of breath and rust-colored bloodstains. She pushed to the surface again. It was the craziest thing when she pulled her head from the water; she could have sworn she saw a fox on the opposite shore. She blinked, and it was gone.

She stood, sopping wet, walked back to the tree line, and wrung out her hair as best she could. She took ten deep breaths in through her nose and out through her mouth, just as Dr. Rogers had taught her many years ago.

Before she headed back to the others, she turned her face upward.

"I don't know if there's something out there watching over us," she directed to the sky. "But if you're there? Thank you. Thank you for getting us out of that." She paused for a second. "Or, curse you for getting us into that. I'm not sure at this point if the Universe is trying to kill me or is desperately trying to keep me alive." She searched the darkening blue for answers and found none. "Either way — I think it'll succeed."

She shoved her hands into her jacket, and all of a sudden, the image of Azrael, the little girl in the library, flashed into her mind.

"What have you got in your pockets?"

◆   ◆   ◆

As Brie returned to the others, the sun dipped below the horizon, painting the sky a beautiful fire-orange and outlining the magnificent redwoods in gold. As she walked to the camp, she was pleased to see a fire going. Her friends were draped in mylar blankets and sharing a bottle of water. Ephriam was adding to a growing pile of firewood.

Cameron set aside the map he and Mike were pouring over. "Did you find what you were looking for?" he called out.

She kept walking toward them. "Even better," she called back. "I found what I didn't know I was looking for."

Sherry shot her a worried look as she drew closer. "Brie, if ever there *wasn't* a time for poetic conceits—" But she stopped short when Brie pulled something gold and shiny from her pocket. "What's that?"

"This," said Brie. "Is our way out of this forest." She pressed her fingertip to the small gold clasp and unfolded the lens, clicking it into place and holding it up. "See?"

Five blank faces stared back at her.

Sherry stood up and moved closer. "She's hit her head," she said. "We were all so worried about Tavi, we didn't see how hard she hit her—"

"Sherry," said Brie. "Look."

She pressed the magnifying glass into Sherry's palm. She took it dubiously and held it up to her eye. Then, she gasped.

"What?" asked Mike, sitting up higher on his elbow. "What is it?"

Sherry lowered the magnifying glass with a grin. "It's our way out of here."

She handed it to Mike, who looked through it and then passed it around to the others. When they each looked through the strange glass, a beam of blue-white light pointed in a direction that didn't change no matter which way you aimed the lens. You only had to follow the light and you were going in the right direction.

And they knew it was the right direction because the lens revealed something else as well: roads, structures, and people. Miles away, perhaps hundreds of miles, but they were there.

Brie turned to Cameron. "Is there any of the Elysian liquid left?"

"Only a few drops. Not enough to go anywhere."

"Is that enough to get a message to your father?"

He and Ephriam exchanged a frown. "With a little ingenuity, it might be."

"Good. Tell him we're all right, and where we're going."

The rest of them looked at her in amazement.

"Where *are* we going?" asked Ephriam.

Brie couldn't resist. "To the Garden."

That night, the six friends fell asleep under a sky filled with stars, dreaming of the impossible quest they'd start in the morning.

They didn't know they were being watched over by a fox.

A fox with one green eye and one blue.

♦   ♦   ♦

"You would have known what to do." The ancient monarch sat on a marble bench in his private atrium. "You always did," he continued. "You were always the one who knew how to get through to the children — how to show them the path without forcing them, how to guide them while leaving room for their dissent." He touched a wrinkled hand to the wall and looked through the strange, transparent stone at the scene frozen within. A beautiful woman in white linen robes knelt by a sapphire pool filled with water lilies. Her black hair rippled down to the water's edge as she reached for a stone. Forever reaching, frozen for eternity in a perfect moment.

His wife. Cameron's mother.

Tears filled the king's eyes as he pressed his hand to the wall. "He sent word. He's all right. They got away, and they're heading for Eden." A tear spilled down his cheek. "I do not know how to protect them anymore. We have one son gallivanting around Earth, on the run from the Seven, with a human girl, and the other—"

A knock at the atrium's gate interrupted him.

With a wave of his hand, the transparent stone became opaque once again. He dashed the tear away and called out in a hard voice. "Come."

A soldier approached and bowed.

"What is it?" Enoch asked. "You know I am not to be disturbed in this place."

"I know it, my lord." The Elysian kept his eyes on the ground, with a look on his face like the chill of death itself. "But… the sculpture they brought from the battle with Mammon. The team has succeeded; it has been opened."

"Well? Get to it, soldier. What's inside?"

The poor boy looked like he was going to be sick. "It isn't what, sire. It's who."

EPILOGUE

The white-haired man approached the swirling, furious silver swarm with an air of elegant unconcern. He stopped mere inches from its grinding teeth and smiled comfortingly.

"There, there. Is somebody feeling upset? That's understandable. I'd be upset, too, if I'd allowed myself to be trapped off-world by a handful of insignificant, mortal toddlers." He drew back his hand and slapped the horde across its gigantic, hideous face.

A flash of blinding silver-white light cracked through the space between them. When it faded, there wasn't a horde opposite him but a morbidly obese, sobbing man. He cradled his cheek in his hand and blubbered. "It wasn't my fault! I was only trying to—"

"It's all right." Lucifer inclined his head toward Baal and extended his hand to help him up. Together, the two walked some steps away, one a vision of beauty, glimmering in the moonlight, the other a horror, lumbering precariously along behind, like a beast being led to slaughter, nearly collapsing under his own weight.

Lucifer continued, "It's better this way. You were drawing attention, eating through all those villages. This way, you'll be out of sight and out of mind until the moment comes to strike."

"But couldn't I just—?" Baal began.

"No," Lucifer interrupted sharply. "You cannot rejoin the remaining shards, not until we've breached the gates."

Baal reared back and wailed, "There's nothing here! I shall starve!"

Lucifer smirked. "Come now, brother. What must you think of me? I'd never let anyone so valuable as you wither away. In fact, I've brought you a present."

With a wave of his hand, a shimmer appeared — a shimmer which solidified into a deer. The poor creature had only a moment to tremble with cold and confusion before Baal leapt at it, with a ferocious agility that was terrifyingly out of place with his massive body, and tore out its throat with his teeth. He set upon the thing immediately, devouring it, bones and all.

Lucifer looked on with mild disgust before turning his eyes to the Earth, hanging in the sky.

"Soon," he murmured. "They will bring us inside the gates. They will give us the Tears. They are turning within the lock even as we speak. They do not even know they are the key."

Behind him, Baal finished his rapacious meal, licking the last drops of blood from his long, unkempt fingernails. With a chilling howl, he raked his hands through the moonscape, tearing claw marks through a pair of initials that had been carefully drawn into the dust.

B.W.

ABOUT THE AUTHORS

Shirley "Sam" Withrow grew up in Gloucester, Virginia. She spent eighteen years as an emergency room RN until a bizarre dream shifted her timeline, and she set out to write her debut novel, now a series. She watched her wild imagination come to life, and her humor with the world shine through. She currently lives in Cape Coral, Florida, with her husband and bearded dragon, Iggy.

Amelia Rose Pinkis was born in California. After her time at the University of California Santa Barbara, she married her college sweetheart, began writing and editing professionally, and now lives near Lake Geneva with her husband and their four beautiful children.

COMING SPRING 2025

THE 3RD INSTALLMENT OF
THE FORBIDDEN TEARS SERIES

PARADISE
BREACHED